TRAPPED

Anna Smith has been a journalist for over twenty years and is a former chief reporter for the *Daily Record* in Glasgow. She has covered wars across the world as well as major investigations and news stories from Dunblane to Kosovo to 9/11. Anna spends her time between Lanarkshire and Dingle in the west of Ireland, as well as in Spain to escape the British weather.

Also by Anna Smith

TRAPPED
ANNA SMITH

Quercus

First published in Great Britain in 2021 by Quercus
This paperback edition published in 2021 by

Quercus Editions Ltd
Carmelite House
50 Victoria Embankment
London EC4Y 0DZ

An Hachette UK company

A CIP catalogue record for this book is available
from the British Library

PB 978 1 52940 713 6
EB 978 1 52940 711 2

10 9 8 7 6 5 4 3 2 1

Typeset by Jouve (UK), Milton Keynes

Printed and bound in Great Britain by Clays Ltd, Elcograf S.p.A.

Papers used by Quercus are from well-managed forests and
other responsible sources.

For Eilidh, our beautiful little angel,
whose light shines forever in our hearts.

We hope when we have nowhere else to go.
Hope gives us real power – the power never to give up.

PROLOGUE

Billy Dobson would do anything if the price was right. He didn't ask questions, he didn't need to know the background or why he was being asked to do a particular job. It was purely business. He had murdered and robbed; he had planted bombs almost as often as he'd planted drugs to smear whoever he was ordered to smear. In the Ulster Volunteer Force you did what you were told and you kept your trap shut. That was the reason he'd been chosen for this one. He would pick up fifteen grand when it was done, and a flight out of the country to wherever he wanted. Because once the shit hit the fan, it was crucial that neither he nor the UVF were on anyone's radar during the investigation. All he had to do once it was over, was to put the call in to his commander and say 'job done'. Then he had to get off his mark.

The first part of the task was easy. Executions were part of his life, and he'd carried out at least a dozen of them during the Troubles – usually a traitor who'd turned grass to the cops, or some guy who'd been blagging UVF money.

This one was no different, in terms of what he had to do. Earlier in the evening, as planned, he had executed the two men. He didn't know their story, only that they'd got greedy. It was swift and clinical, a bullet in the back of each head. Then he'd driven their car, the bodies slumped in the back seat, to the country road on the outskirts of Milngavie. He parked it well out of the way in a lay-by close to a dirt track road, and waited. The next part was going to be trickier, he'd been told. It involved some bird who'd be driving down the same road within twenty minutes. He'd assumed he had to put a bullet in her too, but that wasn't the deal here. This was different.

He waited at the roadside. He'd been told she'd left the place and was on her way down. But that she wasn't alone. His mobile pinged. They were only three minutes away. He got ready. He got out of the car and onto the roadside, when he saw the lights from the approaching car at the turn of the bend. He staggered and waved his hands urgently, as though he was injured and in need of help. The car slowed down and pulled in to the side of the road, hazards flashing. In seconds, as planned, his men came from the bushes, three of them, guns blazing. Then the car doors opened. An older guy climbed out, hands raised.

From where he stood, the full moon lighting up the dark, he could see the shock and rage on the old guy's face. Then he saw the woman get out of the back seat, hands in the air. She was tall, slim, youngish. And pregnant, by the looks of it.

'Don't move!' he shouted. 'Stay where you are or you'll all die right fucking here.'

He wondered if the old guy, standing silently fuming, was her father. He looked like he knew they were well and truly fucked.

Dobson watched, appreciating how swiftly his men worked. Rab Downey and Davey McKay had been hand-picked for this. The pair of them pulled the bodies out of the black BMW and dragged them over to the woman's car, wedging them into the back seat. Then they went back to the BMW and lugged over two holdalls – which he knew contained cocaine and sub-machine guns. Then as the woman stood horrified, they planted them in the boot of her car. Billy prowled around her, keeping his gun on her. She looked as though she was about to buckle. Maybe she was thinking about the baby she was carrying.

Dobson made his phone call.

'Job done,' he said.

He climbed into the BMW, and from his rear-view mirror, as he roared off, he could see the old guy peering into the back of their car where the dead men lay. Dobson put his boot down, almost going into a ditch on the bend. By the time the lights of the motorway came into view, he could hear the wail of the police siren. He smiled to himself. He was good at this shit.

CHAPTER ONE

Kerry Casey felt sick, a mixture of nerves, exhaustion and dread, as she was escorted in handcuffs by two female guards to the reception area of the prison entrance. From the corner of her eye, she could see the male officers looking at her from behind the glass reception. She tried to keep her eyes straight ahead, the tangle in her gut tightening, as she stood waiting for a few seconds. Then she heard a loud clunk and a low buzz as the door of the prison opened and she saw daylight, the rain coming down in sheets, bouncing off the steps and the ground beyond. She shivered, the icy blast slicing through the polo-neck sweater and jacket she was wearing. She felt grubby and unwashed, in the same clothes she'd slept in, her skin dry and irritated after splashing some water on it from the sink in the cell where she'd spent a sleepless night at Cornton Vale Women's Prison.

When they'd brought her here last night in the dark she

had almost been on the point of collapse, still in shock from what had happened just a couple of hours earlier. It was like being in the grip of some terrifying nightmare where you kept flailing around in the bed, trying to wake yourself to consciousness, but the hellish dream kept pulling you back in. At one point, as she was being registered at the reception area, Kerry's legs had buckled, and the two female police officers, who'd accompanied her from Stewart Street police station in Glasgow, helped her to a chair. A doctor was summoned, and she was taken to a side room. The middle-aged Asian woman GP sat next to her in the chair and spoke softly, asking her how far along she was in her pregnancy, and whether she had any history of fainting episodes or blood pressure issues. Kerry had struggled to speak. She was on the verge of tears and her throat was so tight with emotion that she kept halting and tightening her lips to stop herself from breaking down. She was aware of the two police officers glancing at each other and then at her. They'd have seen this before. She wouldn't be the first pregnant woman they'd brought in to face a night in the cells before appearing in court the following morning. Kerry might have looked and dressed better than some of the suspects brought in here, but right now she was no different, just another custody case awaiting her first appearance in court. The doctor had told her to lie on the narrow iron bed. And as she gently pressed the stethoscope onto her swelling stomach, again, Kerry filled up, her chest aching, thinking of the heartbeat inside her, ashamed and terrified that she had brought her unborn baby to this. Even though she was completely innocent of what she was being accused, she wouldn't have been targeted if she wasn't who she was. The doctor had smiled at her and told her the baby's heartbeat was strong and that she had to try as far as she could to relax and get some sleep overnight. Once the doctor had left, the officers helped her to her feet, then the door opened and a female prison guard came in and relieved the cops of their charge.

Kerry was told to follow her, and she walked behind her, handcuffs off as they went through the automatic door and through to an open area, with a staircase going up to a long row of cells above. The place was dimly lit and she assumed all the prisoners were sleeping as there wasn't a single sound.

'You're on the ground floor,' the officer said to her, pointing vaguely to a row of blue-painted cell doors. 'You'll be sharing with Natalie tonight, but you might be moved tomorrow.'

'Sharing?' The word was out before Kerry could stop it.

The officer glared at her and simpered a little.

'Did you think you were getting the presidential suite?'

Kerry cursed herself for being so naive, and despite her rage that she shouldn't be here, she knew it wouldn't be smart to argue. Self-preservation, she told herself.

'Of course not. I ... I just wasn't sure if it was single cells.' She looked at the officer, then at the floor.

The officer walked on towards the last door on the corridor.

'As you're pregnant, you'll probably get moved to a different cell tomorrow, though you'll still be sharing. But tonight this is the only one free.' She was about to put the key in the door when she glanced over her shoulder at Kerry. 'Natalie is a bit of a handful, but just ignore her. Try to get some sleep.'

Kerry stood behind the officer, filled with dread as she eased open the door. Then, as soon as the light from the hall shone into the darkened room, there was an almighty roar from inside.

'Fuck is this! I haven't done anything. Fuck off!'

The officer opened the door wide and walked in, turning to beckon Kerry. She followed, her eyes adjusting to the dark. Jesus! There was a ghostly, skinny figure upright on the top bunk bed, clutching a bed sheet to her as though her life depended on it.

'It's okay, Natalie. Just calm down, now,' the officer said, firm but reassuring. 'This is Kerry. She'll be your cellmate for tonight. Just arrived. So just relax and go back to sleep.'

Natalie sat wide-eyed and scowling.

'She'd better no' touch my fucking stuff! Fucking tea leaves everywhere in here!'

'She's not interested in your stuff, Nat, now play nice and

get back to sleep while I get Kerry settled.' She turned to Kerry. 'Right. You're in the bottom bunk. There's a night-dress on the chair and some juice and a snack if you want.'

'That's my fucking snack! My nightdress!' Nat snapped.

'No, it's not, Natalie. You know that. You were told earlier you'd have a guest tonight. So button your lip and go to sleep. Be nice to Kerry. She's pregnant.'

Nat's eyes flicked Kerry up and down and rested briefly on her bump. She said nothing, then lay back down and turned to face the wall.

'Doors will click open at seven,' the officer said. 'If you need the toilet during the night just bang on the door and someone will come and take you.'

Then the officer turned and left, closing the door softly behind her, plunging Kerry into darkness, and leaving her standing in the middle of the stuffy, dingy room that smelled of sweat and something like very stale, cheap per-fume. Kerry glanced around her, and from the window she could see nothing but the blackness outside. Her eyes tuned to the dark and now she could make out a chest of drawers across the room and on it were a couple of photos – one a framed picture of a little baby. Kerry softly picked her way across to the bottom bunk and sat down. She didn't even want to take her clothes off, to strip in this grim hole of a place and lie down. But she couldn't sleep in the clothes she had on as she'd been told she was going to have to appear in the custody court in the morning. Silently, she took off her sweater and folded it on the chair, then her bra, and her trousers. In the dark she could make out the silhouette of her swelling tummy and she touched it gently. She pulled on the nightdress which smelled clean and fresh, and then lay down on the bed, staring at the mattress on the bunk above. She was frozen with fear, barely breathing, listening to her heartbeat in her chest. Then the silence was broken by an anguished voice from the top bunk.

'I've got a wean, you know. They took him off me. The social work. Cunts!'

Kerry lay still, not sure whether to engage or stay quiet. She said nothing and the silence seemed to go on for ever, until from above she heard sniffing and heaving.

'Cunts took my wee laddie!' Nat sobbed.

Kerry held her breath, then she spoke. 'I'm so sorry,' she said softly.

For a long moment there was nothing, no sound from above, then soon there was the sound of her cellmate breathing deeply in slumber. Kerry turned on her side, curled up into a ball and wept.

Now, she was being nudged forward by the guards and they stepped outside into the rain. There was a large, dark blue van, like the ones Kerry had seen countless times on TV or when she had been a young lawyer, arriving or pulling away from court, transporting prisoners to and from jail. The windows were high and tiny with bars on them; a man in the passenger seat jumped out and dragged open the heavy door.

'On you go, Kerry.' The prison guard gave her a look and jerked her head towards the van.

The prison officer walked ahead and Kerry followed alongside the officer she was handcuffed to.

'You all right?' The guard turned to look at her, from dark brown, tired eyes.

Kerry nodded, swallowing hard again at the briefest touch of kindness. She took a breath as she stepped forward and into the van. *You can do this*, she told herself. *You have to.* Inside, she was plonked onto the thin plastic seats and the guard put her seatbelt on. Kerry expected the door to be slammed shut by the man who stood outside, the rain soaking his face, but it wasn't. She sat for a couple of minutes, shivering, then the prison doors opened again, and another two officers came out with a woman, handcuffed just as she had been. Kerry watched the scrawny dishevelled woman. She looked to be in her early thirties, and her dyed hair was matted and hanging like rats' tails. Her short denim skirt barely covered the tops of her thighs, and her black tights were laddered right down to her red sling-back shoes. She trembled in her tiny bomber jacket and plunging black T-shirt. She looked like a prostitute and teetered as she walked, jerking her arm away from the guard who was holding her. She stopped in her tracks as though she was refusing to go any further.

'Just fucking get your hands off,' the woman spat.

'Come on, Ash,' the guard said. 'Don't start with your crap now. You know how it ended the last time.'

The woman turned to her, defiant.

'Aye. But I shouldn't even be here,' she protested. 'This is all a fucking fit-up. That cunt of a cop.'

'Come on,' the guard said as she nudged her forward. 'Save it for your lawyer.'

The woman said nothing and walked on, climbing into the van. She stood for a moment as the door slammed shut, and gave Kerry a long hard look.

'Did they give you your glass of prosecco, hen?'

She might have been trying to smile but it was more of a snarl. Despite herself, in spite of the terror and anguish tearing at her insides, Kerry made eye contact with the woman and gave her a sympathetic smile, which she seemed to acknowledge, blinking smudged mascara eye-lashes to reveal bright blue eyes full of rage and hurt.

They drove from Cornton Vale to the motorway in silence. From where she was sitting, Kerry could see through a small space to the windscreen. They went past fields and cows and farmhouses, then onto the M8 motorway, rain lashing all the way towards the city centre. She thought of last night and of Natalie, and how this morning when the doors buzzed open, she had climbed down the ladder quietly, then had turned to her and said nothing, just stared blankly from eyes that seemed dead. Nat had been dressed in a T-shirt and jeans, and Kerry had glimpsed the slash marks on both wrists and forearms – some old, some recent – that made her look as though she was a self-harmer. When she'd left, Kerry had got dressed quickly but sat on her bunk as the corridor filled with the noisy chatter of women. From the vague smell of food coming from somewhere downstairs she'd assumed they were going to break-fast. Kerry hadn't followed Nat out of the cell, and when a prison guard stuck her head around a few minutes later, ask-ing if she wanted breakfast, she'd declined, saying she would just wait and eat the snack. The guard had shrugged and left her, the cell door open, so she could later peek outside and see prisoners moving around the communal area. In the weirdest way, it looked like business as usual.

The van weaved its way down to Clyde Street then across the Jamaica Bridge and on towards Glasgow Sheriff Court. She'd been told that her lawyer would meet her inside the court and she'd be taken downstairs. The officer who had been slightly pleasant turned to her.

'I don't know if you'll have been here before, Kerry, but you'll be taken to a holding cell, and your lawyer will come and talk to you. Then you'll go up for your appearance in front of the sheriff. Your brief will give you all the details.'

Kerry nodded as the van turned off the road and into what appeared to be the back of the Sheriff Court. It crossed her mind that there might be photographers out-side, if the news of the arrest of the head of a notorious

Glasgow crime family had leaked out through the police. It didn't take her long to find out. The van pulled up, and they sat for a few moments. Then she heard the sound of locks sliding and door opening.

'Okay, ladies,' the other guard said. 'Showtime!' She ushered Ash to her feet and marched her out of the van.

Kerry stood up, the nausea rising in her. She tried to breathe slowly as she was helped down the stairs out of the van. Then, in the drizzle, she heard the whirr of cameras and blinked as the flashes went off. Instinctively, she put her head down, as she'd seen prisoners do on news footage of them arriving in court. She was one of them now, whether she was guilty or not. The papers would be full of it in the morning. Christ! This was really happening.

'Fuck me, man!' Ash turned to her. 'Are you some kind of fucking celeb?'

'No,' Kerry said. 'I shouldn't even be here. I've done nothing.'

'Aye. Join the fucking club, mate. We all say that.'

'No. But really. I'm innocent.'

'Sure. But why are all these cameras here? Taking pictures of you? You famous or what?'

'No,' Kerry said. 'I'm a businesswoman.'

'Oh, right,' Ash said. 'A gangster?'

Kerry glanced at her but didn't answer. She went past the throng quickly and in through the back entrance, onto the charcoal-grey tiled floors and downstairs into the cells. Her senses were shocked and prickled by the noise, the smells of unwashed bodies and dirty clothes, the stench of fear and anger and shouts. Cloaked lawyers in smart suits walked briskly, clutching folders, rushing between clients who waited in cells. Kerry looked along the row of cells, some with two or three prisoners inside them, each cell guarded by a prison officer. Then she saw Marty Kane striding towards her like a vision of hope in all the gloom. It was all she could do to keep herself from bursting into tears.

'Kerry!' Marty said, as he reached her.

She wanted him to embrace her, this stalwart family friend, this uncle figure who had been her rock and her shoulder, especially in recent months. But he didn't. Here, Marty was her brief – no more. He shook her hand and held it for a long moment, but his eyes looked anguished behind his rimless glasses.

'Don't worry,' he whispered. 'Come on. Let's have a chat before you go upstairs.'

He led her and the officers to a cell and Kerry was ushered in and sat on a tubular plastic chair, the officer behind her.

'Do you mind taking the cuffs off?' Marty asked.

The guard stood for a moment, glanced around.

'I'm not supposed to.'

'Look. She's not going anywhere. You can see that.' He gave her a pleading look.

The guard said nothing, came across and unlocked the

cuffs. Kerry rubbed her wrists and put her hands on the table. Marty put his briefcase to one side and reached across and held her hand.

'Are you bearing up, Kerry?'

She swallowed.

'I'm trying to, Marty.' She felt her lip trembling. 'But Christ! What the hell happened? Where's Danny?'

Marty jerked his head.

'He's down the line a bit. I've already seen him. A good friend of mine will appear for Danny, as I'll be representing you. But we are working together. Danny is fine, but he's worried sick about you. Did the doctor come last night? I told them they had to get someone to see you.'

Kerry nodded. 'Yes. She examined me. Everything's fine.' She bit her lip. 'Well, I mean, as fine as it can be. I shared a cell last night with some girl who scared the living shit out of me. You've got to get me out of here, Marty.'

'Okay. I'll do everything in my power. Right. You'll know the sketch here, from your early days as a lawyer. You'll be taken up for a first appearance, they'll read the charges. We'll move for bail, obviously.'

Kerry watched as he looked away from her to his briefcase.

'Will you get bail, Marty?'

She'd been read the charges last night: murder, cocaine and possession of arms. Bail was at best a remote possibility.

'I hope so. It'll be difficult, given the charges, but it depends on who the custody sheriff is. The procurator fiscal who's taking custodies this morning is a bit of tough nut, making a name for himself. So it'll be a struggle.'

'Christ!' Kerry said. 'What if I don't get bail? I can't do a long wait in jail for a trial. I . . . I can't.'

Marty said nothing for a few beats. She knew he wouldn't lie to her, that he would have to lay it on the line.

'As I said, I'm hopeful. But if you don't get bail today, then we'll keep at it over the next few days. I'll move for it on health grounds, you being pregnant. You'll be back in Cornton Vale while I fight it, and while I move for an early pleading diet. But the most important thing is that I want to get these charges dropped. They're utterly ridiculous.'

Kerry was hearing it, but as if it was coming from a distance. A pleading diet. She knew what it was all right. She'd have to make a plea at some stage and then await trial. It could be anything up to one hundred and ten days that they could hold her. More than three months. Her mind raced and she felt nausea again. Her baby might even be born in jail.

'Jesus, Marty!'

'Let's keep it in perspective at the moment, Kerry,' Marty said. 'I'm not expecting this case even to go to trial. It will get ditched once they take a long hard look at the evidence and forensics. Even if you do get sent back to Cornton Vale, I don't expect you to be there long, before the charges are dropped.'

Kerry nodded. She had to stop herself being frustrated at Marty's calmness. This was his job. He was practical and pragmatic, while she was on the verge of hysteria.

'I have to believe that, Marty. But you make it sound as though it's easy.'

'I know it's not, sweetheart,' he said softly. 'Right.' He stood up. 'I'm going upstairs now to the court to see how far away your place is. When you go up, I'll be there. Just take it easy, try and stay calm. I know it's difficult.'

'Will Danny be there?'

'Yes,' Marty said. 'You'll be in the dock together.'

'Jesus.' Kerry shook her head. 'It's unreal.'

Marty pulled his lips to a sympathetic smile. Then he left.

CHAPTER TWO

The shriek of the flutes and thunder of the Lambeg drum at band practice upstairs was loud enough to hear at the far end of the White Horse pub. They were playing 'Derry's Walls', the anthem that celebrates the siege of Derry when the Irish rebels were defeated. The customers tapping their feet to the sounds of sectarian hate were happy enough though, and that's all that mattered. This pub was their spiritual home as much as Ibrox Stadium was on a Saturday afternoon. And it wasn't as if many tourists ventured down to Bridgeton looking for a bit of real Glasgow. If they did happen to wander in here, the death stares of the customers hugging the bar would make them swiftly turn on their heels.

Gimpy McGarvie was polishing tumblers behind the bar. He watched the swing doors as Gordy Thomson and a couple of his sidekicks walked in. One of the doors was held open and Dick Lambie entered, standing for a moment to soak up the atmosphere, like a general surveying his troops. Gimpy stared at this so-called band of brothers, a ruthless bunch of thugs who would pull out the lungs of anyone who dared cross them. Not that many did. It was unspoken in the White Horse that the UVF Glasgow section met here as they'd done all through the years of the Troubles. It was here in the back room that the flute bands practised, and later trained in weapons, assembling guns and taking instructions from uniformed UVF officers who led silent, double lives. The customers who were simply Rangers fans with no Loyalist connections may have known all of this, but if they did, they never spoke of it, because walls have ears, and if they were heard whispering in corners about the UVF or criticising them, then they would be history. Gimpy McGarvie hated the whole fucking lot of them. He hated football and everything that it meant in Glasgow, where you were on one side or the other. But he was trapped. He had nowhere to go, and he was paying off a hefty debt that right now felt like it would never come to an end.

'Awright, Gimpy?' Thomson said as he got to the bar. 'Cheer up, for fuck's sake. It might never happen.'

Gimpy snorted and managed as close to a smile as he could get with this wanker. His name was Steven, but they called him Gimpy on account of his right leg being shorter than his left, after having polio as a child.

'An' then again it might.' Gimpy shrugged.

He wasn't afraid of Thomson or the two pricks at his side now leaning on the bar hoping for a floor show. Lambie scared him though.

'You know what you need, Gimpy,' Thomson said, stabbing a finger at him. 'A right good ride. That would sort you out, big time.'

'Aye,' Billy Black chimed in, his skinny face and tongue darting out like a reptile. 'You'd need to get somebody to help you get your dodgy leg over though.'

'Fuck off!' Gimpy spat at Black. 'Enough of your shite. Drinks. What you want?' He glared at each of them, his expression flat, hoping the flush of rage he felt rising in his chest wouldn't reach his face.

Dick Lambie was already sitting in the corner where he could see who was coming through the doors and who was leaving. That kind of thing was important in any bar if you were Dick Lambie, drug dealer, loan shark, UVF Loyalist commander and feared killer.

Thomson sneered. He'd had his fun for the moment.

'Two vodkas with soda and lime for this pair of pussies, and Jack Daniel's and a dash of Coke for me and Dick.'

Gimpy didn't answer and was glad to turn away from them and face the gantry. As he picked up glasses and pushed them under the optics, he caught a glimpse of himself in the mirror and was raging that his face was red. He stood for a moment, chipping lumps out of the ice in the bucket, imagining it was the face of Gordy Thomson or any of these useless fuckers. But he knew he had to compose himself, and he did. He turned, added the mixers to the drinks and placed them on the bar. Thomson handed him a twenty pound note. He turned to the till and keyed in the order and took out six pounds change. He went to hand it to Thomson who had a Jack Daniel's in each hand.

'Keep it, son. You'll be able to get a hand job down at Glasgow Green for a fiver.' Thomson grinned.

The two picked up their drinks and sniggered as they turned their backs and headed across to where Lambie was sitting with his arms folded, his face serious, as though he hadn't heard any of the bullying.

Gimpy wiped the top of the bar and served another couple of customers, then sat down on a bar stool and looked up at the big-screen television mounted on the wall. He turned up the volume a little as the nine o'clock news came on, recognising the lead item showing images of Glasgow Sheriff Court. The strap headline at the bottom of the screen read, 'TWO IN COURT ON MURDER AND DRUGS CHARGES'.

Gimpy watched as the report followed.

'A Glasgow businesswoman and her uncle appeared in court today charged with the murders of two men who died yesterday. Thomas Lumsden and Peter Hawkins were found last night near the switchback road on the outskirts of the city. Both had sustained gunshot wounds to the head and were pronounced dead at the scene. Kerry Casey and Daniel McGowan were arrested later

by police and have been accused of the murders. They face additional charges relating to the possession of drugs and firearms. Both appeared in Glasgow Sheriff Court today and made no plea or declaration. They were remanded in custody.'

Gimpy turned down the volume as the news moved on to another story. He glanced down the length of the bar to where a group of customers had been watching the news in silence. The flutes upstairs struck up 'The Billy Boys', breaking the eerie quietness that had suddenly filled the bar. He knew that nobody would be talking about these murders – at least not in here. Most people in the bar would know the dead men, both customers, who worked for Dick Lambie. Gimpy knew them by name and reputation. They had shifted Lambie's drugs on the Manchester run and worked together on drops and picking up money. If they'd been murdered, no doubt it would have been a hit. The pair of them had been in here two days ago. If they'd stiffed Lambie for money he wasn't surprised that they'd ended up with bullets in their heads. But what he couldn't work out was why this Kerry Casey bird and her uncle were in the frame for it. The Casey family were big-time gangsters. Everybody knew that. They didn't get involved in small-time drug deals, so why would they be bumping off two of Lambie's thugs? He rinsed the cloth under the tap, wrung it out and wiped the length of the bar, making a furtive glance in the direction of Lambie and the boys who sat in silence, their faces like flint.

*

It was after midnight by the time Steven got back to the council flat on High Street in Glasgow's East End, where he lived with his mother. By the time he had climbed the tenement stairs to the second floor, his leg was aching from being mostly on his feet since his shift started at five. He pushed his key into the lock and went inside, careful to walk softly down the hall, as his mother would be asleep by this time. Or so he hoped. Then as he got to the kitchen, he heard her coughing. Her twenty fags a day lifetime habit was now taking its toll and rendered her more or less bedridden. It broke his heart. He knew she wouldn't be long for this world the way she coughed and was so breathless. But even though he knew her quality of life was getting worse every month, he couldn't bear the thought of her not being there. She'd been the rock of his life, her and only her. His father had pissed off when he was a toddler and it was his mum who'd taken on two jobs to keep the house and put food on the table. He'd watched her grow weaker over the years, the emphysema taking its toll, and the feisty bright woman, who in another life might have actually been somebody, was now breaking away in front of him. He stopped for a moment in the hallway and held his breath. He looked up at the fading pattern on the old wallpaper that had been there since he was a kid, and the damp patch spreading like varicose veins towards the ceiling. Like everything else in the flat, from the old fridge to the cooker, it needed fixing, but there was never enough money.

'That you, Steven?'

She was the only one who called him by his name.

'Aye, Ma. It's just me. You all right?'

He went to the slightly ajar bedroom door and stuck his head in. In the darkness he could see her head on the pillow, the duvet cover pulled up high under her chin. Her wispy grey hair was thinning and in the light from the street her cheekbones were emphasised and her face looked hollow. She had the grey, papery complexion of a lifelong smoker. She coughed again and he went forward, sat on the edge of the bed.

'Christ!' she managed to utter between coughs. 'This is a bastard, this cough.'

'You want me to get you something, Ma? I'm going to make a cup of tea. Did you eat your dinner?' Steven watched as she eased herself up a little on the pillow, wheezing.

'Aye, son,' she replied. 'A wee cup of tea would be lovely.'

'You want a bit of toast an' all?' Steven stood up.

'Only if you're making it,' she wheezed and lay back.

Steven smiled to himself as he left the room. Nearly every night it was the same routine. He tiptoed down the hall when he got in, hoping he wouldn't wake his ma. But nine times out of ten she'd call out for him, and nearly every night he made toast and they sat in her bedroom, him on the chair, her propped up on pillows, enjoying the toast and talking until he could see her eyes get heavy and she slipped off to sleep. She just wanted the company. He went into the kitchen and pushed two slices of bread into the toaster. Then he looked at the worktop and could see her dinner plate was already washed and on the rack. He went across to the bin and lifted the lid. Inside was half of his mum's mince and potatoes he'd left for her. That happened a lot these days; she seemed to be losing her appetite. He'd taken her down to the doctor and the GP told them it was part of her weakness, that she would eat smaller meals, but to do his best and make them nutritious. Steven often cooked ham soup, which at least got some vegetables inside her. But he knew this couldn't go on for ever.

'This is lovely, Steven,' his ma said, munching on the toast and sipping her tea. 'I was a wee bit peckish, and maybe that's why I couldn't get over to sleep.'

Steven sat on the old wicker chair by the window a few feet from her bed. He wanted to say to her that she was peckish because she hadn't eaten much of her dinner, but he knew it was pointless. There was nothing to be gained from giving her a row. He'd come to that way of thinking in the last year, when he'd seen how rapidly she was declining. At first he was angry, even with her, for her inability to do things for herself – like cooking sometimes, going outside, meeting people at the café nearby, all the things she used to love but had given up on. Then he realised that he was angry because the child in him knew he was losing her and raged against it, not wanting to consider a life without her. She was all he had, and he was annoyed with himself for that too. At thirty-seven he should have settled down by now, but it hadn't happened. Probably because the limp made him self-conscious and people had made fun of him since he was a little boy, so he lacked confidence. He didn't think anyone would be interested in a half-crippled man, and that was just how it had been. It was safer to be with his mum in the house away from all the crap that went on outside. Here he was loved and cared for, and there was always a warm smile for him any time he came in. Working in the pub, he'd listened to all sorts of stories from guys talking about their shitty marriages, their wives cheating, or themselves playing away, their kids driving them crazy. It struck him that there was a lot to be said for being on your own. He'd only had one girlfriend, when he'd been around seventeen, and it had lasted a while, but she'd got offered a job with her sister in Jersey and she'd taken the opportunity to get out of Glasgow. He couldn't blame her. But she'd broken his heart.

'So was it busy down in the pub tonight?'

'Not bad. Usual crowd,' he said. 'There was band practice so the racket from upstairs would burst your head.'

His mum shook her head. 'See all that stuff, Steven, all that hate? It makes me pig sick. I don't know how you can stand working in the place.'

He shrugged, ate his toast and took a swig of his tea.

'It's a job, Ma.'

Steven turned his head away and looked down at the

steady drizzle falling on the pavements and the roads shiny black from car head lights and the hazy glare of street lamps. He couldn't tell her it was more than a job. It would kill her if she knew that he was trapped in that bar because Dick Lambie and his mob had told him this was a job he would want. He had borrowed money from Lambie two years ago after his car had packed in and he wanted to take his mum on a holiday to the seaside. It had only been fifteen hundred pounds, and he took his mum to Ayr for a week and they'd had a fantastic time, but by the time he'd started paying the debt it'd quickly become two grand, because even the £50 a week he was paying barely touched the extortionate interest rates they were charging. Basically, all Lambie had wanted was someone he could manipulate. Steven had then been used to drive his men on a robbery. They'd broken into the home of an antique dealer and battered him almost to death and stolen some jewellery. He had only been the driver, but once he'd done that, there had been no way back. He'd told Lambie he wanted out and that he'd find a way to pay back his debt, which was now sitting at three and a half grand, but Lambie had said to do what he was told and get on with his job and then implied that worse would happen if he did not. So he had to listen, and hope to Christ he didn't get asked to do another job for them. But he knew it was only a matter of time. He looked across at his ma and could see her eyes heavy as she lay on the pillow. She'd eaten her toast but her half-empty mug was tilting from her hand.

'You looked tired, Ma. Why don't you try and get over to sleep?' He went across to her. 'Let me take this cup away.'

She didn't protest and he eased her back on the pillow, not too far as her chest got worse if she lay flat. He glanced at the oxygen canister in the corner.

'You want the oxygen on to help your breathing?'

'Aye, okay, son.'

Steven took the mask off the top of the canister and eased it onto his mother's head, making sure it was comfortable and covered her nose and mouth. Then he switched it on.

'How does that feel?'

'That's nice, son.' Her thin lips pulled back into a smile. 'You go and get to your bed now.'

Steven nodded. 'I will,' he said, as he turned towards the door. 'You want the light on or off?'

'Switch it off. There's enough light from the street lamps. That'll do me.'

He watched as she closed her eyes.

'Goodnight, Ma. See you in the morning.'

But she was already asleep.

Steven went into the living room and clicked the laptop on, going onto the news to see if there was any more information about the murders. He remembered Lumsden and Hawkins being in the pub and that Thomson had been talking to them. The boys had looked worried. There had to be something to that, but what puzzled him was why the Caseys were involved in it.

CHAPTER THREE

Kerry was being led up the stone stairs by a policeman. Her stomach was in knots, but she was glad to be out of the cell and the pit below, because a few minutes earlier all hell had broken loose. Police officers had been attempting to take a prisoner from his cell when he'd started lashing out, kicking and screaming abuse at them. Two more officers had waded in as they'd bundled the man out of the cell and into the main foyer. One of them had had him in a head-lock, but then from nowhere, the man had stabbed a policeman in the stomach. Kerry had heard the shouted 'He's stabbed me!' and she'd strained her neck to see the policeman, blood seeping out of his shirt. By this time, the man had been disarmed and pushed face down on the floor, his face bloodied from the force with which he'd hit the deck. There had been angry shouts from officers of 'Where did he get the fucking knife?' Then he'd been cuffed and dragged to his feet. Kerry had heard the officers being told to relay back upstairs to the court that there would be a delay in getting this prisoner up to the dock. Other prisoners in cells had egged him on, screaming of police brutality. The cop with the bloodied shirt had been ushered away along the hall to be treated.

Now at the top of the stairs, the door was opened and Kerry got her first glimpse of a courtroom in years.

It was the silence that hit her first, as she took in her surroundings. The sheriff up on the high bench, dressed in wig and gown, looked over the top of his half moon glasses then back to the papers in front of him. Marty Kane, in his black cloak, was seated at the huge square table below the sheriff's bench. He turned fully around to see her and gave her a sympathetic nod. The officer behind her nudged her forward. Then as she took a step, she saw Danny in the dock. He looked up at her, his face pale and tired, and for the first time since her mother had been killed she saw him look vulnerable. He tightened his lips as though to say to her it was okay. The policeman ushered her forward and as she stepped into the dock, she saw a flurry of activity in what was probably the packed press benches. This was a big story for the papers today – *Gangland crime boss in the dock for double murder.* She swallowed hard and shuffled into the dock, taking her seat next to Danny. Their knees touched and she turned her head to look at him as he whispered, 'You all right, sweetheart?' Kerry nodded but said nothing. She was far from all right. She was sitting in the dock next to her uncle, accused of crimes she had nothing to do with, surrounded by the public and a press bench who would be all over the story. The baby inside her was making a visit to the court, and it wasn't even born. There had to be some horrible irony in that. She thought of Vinny, of how mortified he would be if he had to see this, but how he would instinctively know she was innocent. For a fleeting moment she wondered if she would ever see him again, and with that thought she had to bite back tears.

A clerk from the front of the bench below the sheriff got to his feet and read out the charges. How do you plead? The cops urged both her and Danny to her feet.

'M'lud, I appear for Miss Casey on these charges. She pleads not guilty.' Marty sat down and Danny's solicitor stated that his client would also be pleading not guilty.

Opposite Marty, the depute fiscal got to his feet.

'M'lud, in view of the severity of the charges I move for no bail for either of the accused.'

'Objection, your honour!' Marty was on his feet.

The sheriff peered down at him.

'Go ahead, Mr Kane.'

'M'lud, my client, Miss Kerry Casey, is four months pregnant – and although in good health, the events of the last twenty-four hours have taken their toll on her. I move for the sake of her health that she be allowed bail, and if need be tagged. But I don't see that incarcerating her while we await proceedings would do any good; in fact it would be detrimental to her health and the health of her unborn child. She is of no absconding risk and could be monitored by daily visits to the police station and is willing to surrender her passport. I move that bail be granted.'

The sheriff said nothing.

'Mr Prentice?'

The depute fiscal was already standing up, hands in one pocket, a sheaf of papers in the other outstretched hand.

'M'lud, I have moved no bail for a reason. Miss Casey and her business empire have connections and residential property and businesses across Spain, and even if her passport has been surrendered I think there is still a risk of absconding. These are grave charges, the gravest of charges. Two men have been murdered, and a large quantity of cocaine and arms have been found in the boot of a car belonging to the Casey organisation. I believe there is a serious risk by allowing bail and I would move against it '

The same for Danny.

The court was silent as the sheriff sat back. In the stillness he could be heard taking a long breath through his nose and letting it out slowly as he studied the charges, glancing up from time to time to look at Kerry and at Danny. Eventually he spoke.

'Bail refused.'

No explanation. Not that it was required, given what the fiscal had just said. And no words indicating that he had given much consideration to Marty's plea for bail. It was over. Kerry could feel a choking in her throat as Marty turned to face her then got up and came across. He put an arm out to touch her shoulder.

'Kerry, don't worry. We're working on this really hard, around the clock. These charges won't stick. I'm sure of that. Just try your hardest to bear up. I'll come down and see you before you go.'

He nodded to Danny.

'You bearing up, Danny?'

'I'm all right, Marty. This isn't my first rodeo.'

His voice was flat, with a hint of black humour. Danny obviously had learned how to remove himself from this by keeping focused. Kerry stood up but her legs felt shaky. The officer held her arm and guided her out of the box and down the stairs again to the cells.

'You all right?' the officer said to her once they were in the cell.

'Not really,' Kerry said, feeling tears in her eyes at the kindness. 'But I'm trying.'

The officer nodded. 'I'll get you a cup of tea for the journey.' She looked at her watch. 'They'll be leaving in about fifteen minutes. Just waiting for Ash.'

Kerry looked at her, wondering who Ash was, then the officer said, 'Ash, the woman who was with us on the journey in. She's up for shoplifting and police assault. She's broken her bail terms, so she'll be getting locked up until her trial.'

Kerry said nothing, remembering now, and the officer

went out of the cell and along the corridor and disappeared. For a few minutes Kerry sat alone, listening to the shouts and arguments along the row of cells. It seemed they were all fighting with police, blaming them for everything that had led to them being here, protesting every time they were being moved. Only a couple of prisoners went silently, and Kerry sat watching them being led along towards the stairs, wondering what their stories were, how different they would be from hers, and yet how close they were at this moment.

'Fuck this shit! This is fucking pish, man!'

Even before the doors to the prison van opened, Kerry just knew it was Ash. She watched as the door slid open, and Ash stood, refusing to go any further, her hands in cuffs, an officer on either side.

'Just get in the bus, Ash.' One of the officers forced her forward. 'You're not going anywhere standing here.'

Ash stood for another moment, and Kerry watched as her legs seemed to lose their stiffness and a defeated look spread across her face. Ash glanced inside and her eyes met Kerry's, and for a moment they locked, both in recognition that whoever they were, whatever they'd done, they were in the same boat – at least for the journey.

'Come on!' The officer pushed her again.

'Aye right, ya bitch. I'm going.' Ash gave up the protest and climbed inside.

The officer gently eased her around so she was two seats behind Kerry on the opposite side. Kerry glanced back and their eyes met again, and she thought that somewhere in Ash's hooded, bloodshot, hopeless eyes, there was a glint of defiance. The engine revved as the minibus moved off. Kerry fixed her eyes on the gap she could see through the screen. They travelled through the town, towards High Street and then onto the motorway. She could see the turn-off that would have taken her up to her own house, her own bed, to the comforts of the life she had been living and taking for granted for the past few months. God knows when she'd ever see that again, the voice inside her nagged. But she ignored it. She couldn't think that way. She was a lawyer. She had studied criminal law as part of her degree, even though she hadn't practised it any more than was necessary to get her final qualification. But she knew enough to know that these charges surely wouldn't stick. Marty had assured her, and yet here she was, heading back to Cornton Vale to await her next court appearance and trial. As the minibus turned onto the M8, Kerry's mind drifted to the previous night, and she tried to go over every moment of it, before her life went into freefall.

Nothing had been any different from normal. She had been in Milngavie with Danny to see an old family connection, to look at buying some prime property that had suddenly come up and had to be acted upon swiftly.

Then they had been heading back towards her home, driving along a country road, when suddenly this guy had staggered around the road, waving them down. Danny had been immediately suspicious, even if she hadn't. He hadn't liked the look of it. But the man had been staggering, and Kerry had said we can't just drive past. What if it's a trap, Danny had said, and Kerry had argued that the guy was in trouble, blood on his face. They had to stop. Looking back now, at how quickly it happened, she knew she should have listened to Danny. But there was no point in thinking like that now. The question that was nagging her was *why*? Who would frame them like this in a clearly planned, professional operation? There was nobody in the city of Glasgow who would even think about doing that. Even the one or two shady characters who fancied their chances would be incapable of pulling this off. Sure, she'd made enemies of the Colombians, but as far as she knew that was over. Her mind was full of several scenarios, none of them making any sense. It occurred to her that Quentin Fairhurst could be behind it. Was that even possible? It had to be someone with a deep-seated grudge, so maybe even the Colombians were still in the frame after what she did to them.

In a way she was grateful to have these thoughts flooding through her mind, because it was keeping her from thinking about her situation right at this moment, as they turned off the main road and into the Cornton Vale entrance where she had no idea what lay in wait for her.

CHAPTER FOUR

Dick Lambie never shirked from a job, no matter what it was. He was a proud Loyalist, the son of a proud Loyalist, a soldier who would defend Queen and country no matter what it took. His UVF commanders had been able to see that he would take orders and ask no questions by the time he was a teenager. And by the time he was in his twenties, he had carried out a number of robberies, hits and beatings at the behest of the UVF. They had given him stripes for that and he was now Commander of the UVF Glasgow platoon. That was only part of his life though. On top of that he was allowed a free hand in drug dealing, and as long as he kept within his own turf and gave the UVF a slice of his profit, he could pretty much run his own show. He'd built up a reputation for getting things done swiftly and clinically. If Belfast accepted a job and it needed a foot soldier to make it happen, often the job would go to Lambie. He would be handsomely paid for his efforts, and over the years his business had built up. He had two bookies, a taxi firm which was handy in shifting drugs, and a haulage firm which was even better when transferring money and weapons back and forth to Belfast. He also had a substantial book in moneylending across the east side of the city where his henchmen ran a tight ship, with massive interest rates that doubled and tripled, trapping people for ever in their debt. He'd made a small fortune because people who couldn't pay would end up signing cars, houses and sometimes even businesses over to them. And lately, people-trafficking had become his new enterprise, where he was making a good skin out of supplying foreign women to brothels and escort agencies. Lambie knew nobody would think about taking him on or they'd face the UVF thugs.

When the job came up to frame the Caseys it had been something he'd had to take a second look at. He knew he couldn't, and wouldn't, refuse. But this was dangerous shit. This needed thinking through. If he fucked this up, the Caseys would be all over him like a raging inferno. The top UVF man, Wattie Townsley, had travelled from Belfast to meet him and give him the details of the job. They'd met in the White Horse and what was required had been laid out for him. Frame Kerry Casey had been the main goal. He'd known who she was – the bird that had taken over from Mickey Casey, that cocky Taig, who'd swaggered across the city with his sidekick Frankie Martin, taking scalps on every turf. They hadn't come for him though, and he'd been well puffed up with that, because it had made him feel too big for them.

But framing Kerry Casey in such a way that she wouldn't see the outside of a prison cell for a long time had been a big ask. Over two hours and several drinks, he and the Mid Ulster Brigade commander had gone over the possibilities and between them they had come up with murder, drugs and firearms. A triple whammy that would ruin the Caseys, and who knew, might just open the door for him to take over. But that was for another day. By the end of the night, he'd been told he had to make it happen, and if it involved sacrificing two of his bodies, then so be it. But you couldn't just wade in and take two random people off the street. They had to be dealers to make it look right. And the Caseys had to be seen to have been attacking them because of who they were and who they worked for. That was when Lambie had suggested going for the two pricks Lumsden and Hawkins, who he'd known were skimming off a bit too much of their share. On top of that, Lumsden had been riding his young cousin and had got her pregnant, and that was just not on. He was too thick to be bringing up a wean, and the wee cunt denying it made matters worse. So his days had been numbered anyway. It was all about planning the operation carefully and making sure they got Kerry Casey bang to rights. It had been a bonus to get her uncle Danny too, an old-fashioned hoodlum who'd lived to tell many tales. Lambie's gut had done a little anxious twist when he'd realised that there was no going back, after he'd seen her on the television going into court, the look on her face . . . Tough shit. He'd done his job. And if you're caught with two stiffs in your car, a haul of coke in the boot and a couple of machine guns, you're going to need a very good lawyer to get you out of the hole.

Lambie could see that Billy Dobson was edgy and keen to get paid and out of Glasgow. They were sitting at a table in the White Horse in the early afternoon, a few feet away from where Thomson and his two sidekicks sat. There was no need to involve them in this part. Thomson's job had been to be on hand along with his boys to make sure Dobson got away from the murder scene before the cops arrived to catch Kerry Casey red-handed. It was them who had moved the stiffs into the back of her car and planted the guns and coke. They'd been well paid, and they were well paid anyway for the steady work they did for Lambie, enforcing, collecting and dealing out any slaps that had to be dealt. But Dobson was about to get handed a good wedge here, and it had to be just between the two of them. Lambie was glad the pub was quiet, but even if it had been busy, punters knew better than to barge into his company if he looked like he was having a meeting. He looked up at the bar, where Gimpy McGarvie was working away, stocking shelves. He'd clocked Gimpy stealing a couple of furtive glances across at them, and he made a mental note to get Thomson to keep an eye on the wee shite to make sure he wasn't getting curious or anything stupid. Lambie had had Gimpy on a tight rein anyway, ever since he'd driven the getaway van on a robbery, and even though Gimpy'd told him afterwards that he wanted out, Lambie had persuaded him otherwise; once you were in with Lambie's mob, you didn't get out. Well, not alive, anyway.

Lambie put his hand in the inside pocket of his jacket and brought out a brown padded envelope. He put it on the table and slid it across to Dobson.

'Your wages, mate. It's all there. As agreed.'

'Cheers, mate.' Dobson picked it up and stuffed it into his jacket and zipped the pocket. He gave Lambie a look. 'I know I don't need to count it.'

'Aye, not in here anyway,' Lambie said. He lifted his mug to his lips. 'Anyway. Good job, Billy. Not that I expected anything less. The boys across the water are well pleased.' He paused, looked up at the television. 'Did you see it in the news? The Caseys will be going fucking apeshit trying to figure this out.'

'I know,' Dobson said. 'That's why I'm fucking off to Barbados tonight.'

'You got a place there?'

'No. But I have friends.'

'Well, keep your head down.'

'No problems, Dick. I've been here before. Though this was a bit different.'

'Aye,' Lambie said. 'For me too. But I don't ask questions.'

'Yep.' Dobson stood up and zipped up his jacket. 'Right. I'm off. Good to see you, Dick. We'll talk again, I'm sure.'

'We will, brother. You look after yourself now.'

'I will.'

Dobson turned and walked towards the swing doors, and Lambie watched him as he left. He got up from the table and went across and sat beside Thomson and the boys.

'Listen, I know I don't need to tell you this, but you can guarantee the shit will be flying over this Casey bird and her uncle being in jail. They'll have top lawyers and investigators trying to prove they're innocent. So now, more than ever, it's important to keep your traps firmly shut. Understand?'

'Of course, boss.' Thomson said, and the other two nodded their heads vigorously.

'Now, are there any loose ends you've not told me about?' He looked from one to the other. 'Anything at all we need to mop up?'

There was an awkward silence which made Lambie suspicious. Thomson shifted in his seat.

'What?' Lambie leaned on the table, glaring at all three of them. 'Tell me.'

'Well.' Thomson picked at his fingernails, trying to avoid eye contact with his boss. 'There was a bit of a problem with the car – the one we used for getting us all away from the scene.'

'Aye. You were supposed to burn it.'

'I know. But it's not burned yet. It was all a bit mental, all happening that fast and the cops were all over the shop by the time we were two hundred yards down the road. We had to get off the road as quick as possible, and the last thing we wanted to do was torch a motor anywhere near it in case it attracted attention. In fact, torching any motor that night or the day after just seemed too risky.'

Lambie listened to Thomson and processed what he was saying. He had a point, even if he hadn't done what he was told.

'So where's the motor now?'

'We took it to the scrapyard, but even that's risky.'

Lambie thought for a moment before he answered.

'Well it needs to be dealt with quickly. You need to get the car torched, or drive it somewhere into a quarry or something. But it needs to be done.'

'I know.' Thomson jerked his head towards the bar. 'I was thinking about getting Bo and Gimpy to go today and take it out to the quarry. Just drive the fucking thing in and it will disappear.'

Lambie waited for a long moment. Gimpy wasn't a hard man, by any stretch of the imagination. But he would be handy enough to do something like this, and he knew he'd be too shit scared to open his mouth or ask questions.

'Aye, that's fine. Give him a couple of hundred quid.' He eyed Bo. 'And make sure you don't go opening your mouth about anything on the journey.'

He glanced at Thomson. They both knew that Bo had a coke problem, which he claimed he was keeping in check, but it was dodgy and Lambie didn't like it. Once this had all settled down, he might tell Thomson to take Bo for a long walk somewhere and make him disappear.

CHAPTER FIVE

Kerry hadn't slept much in her cell and had lain tossing and turning. She had heard the shouting and laughing, and sometimes crying, from other cells after lights out; and in some perverse way it had been like a sleepover on steroids. As she lay in bed waiting for the doors to buzz open, dreading what fresh hell she faced, she reflected on last night.

When she'd got back to jail after the court appearance, a senior guard had taken her to one side and told her she would still be sharing with Natalie until another cell became available, possibly the following day. The guard by now was well versed on who Kerry Casey was, and she'd fixed her eyes on her with a stern warning.

'You'll be a bit of a celebrity in here, Kerry, as your court appearance has already been on the lunchtime news. So be careful. I'd love to tell you there is a great bunch of girls in here but that's not the situation. There are one or two hard cases who will want to take you on.'

Kerry had put her hand up to stop her.

'Look,' she said. 'None of this is the way it's being pre-
sented. I've done nothing. I've been framed. I'm not some
gangster looking to swagger around jail. Please believe me.
That's not who I am. Christ, I'm pregnant and I'm sitting
here, stuck in jail for something I absolutely didn't do.'

The guard hadn't looked convinced. She'd probably
heard it all before.

'Fair enough. I hear you. But the best thing for you to do
is just keep a low profile and get on with things until your
lawyer can get you out – if that happens.'

Kerry nodded but didn't say anything.

'Now,' the guard said, 'here's the drill. As a remand prisoner, you don't have to work, because you've not been
convicted of anything. So you're free to hang around your
cell all day, but I wouldn't advise it. You'll go native. The
best thing for you to do is be like the others, have a job and
get on with it.'

A job, Kerry had thought. *In here*. She said nothing and
waited.

'There are three areas you can work in to fill your
time. There's the hairdressing salon, where you could
help and learn a few things; there's the bicycle repair
shop – that's one of the main jobs we do here, repair
bikes for charity for them to sell on – or you can make
greetings cards for charity. So that's something you
might want to consider. We also grow our own vegetables

and flowers so we have a good garden out there if you're into that. Up to you.'

Kerry had sat for a moment, trying to let this sink in. It was surreal. The guard had described it as though it was her first day at a holiday camp and these were the various activities that were available. But there was no mention of lights out, lock-up, the fact that there was no toilet in the cell, or that she was surrounded by broken women, some angry, some pathetically sad, some of them killers. There was nothing to do here but buckle down and hope Marty could get her out soon. Eventually, she spoke.

'I understand. And thanks. I suppose working with the greetings cards might be interesting.' Kerry could scarcely believe what she was saying, wondering who she was right now. 'But can I ask you a question? What about the girl Natalie I'm sharing with? Is she dangerous? She told me she has a baby the social work took off her, and she is very angry.'

The prison officer had sighed and sat back, stretching out her legs and studying her polished sensible shoes.

'Natalie,' she said. 'She's a bit of a poor soul, and like a lot of the people in here should probably be under psychiatric care. But she committed a crime and they sent her here. It's not the first time. She's in and out like a yo-yo. Drugs, mostly, shoplifting. But she stabbed someone in the street two months ago, and that's why she's here. She suffers paranoid episodes. She self-harms. It's a sad case, but we have to just do what we can for her.'

Kerry was worried that she might be angry with her for being pregnant, but didn't want to appear stupid by asking, so she just nodded.

'She was crying in the night.'

The guard shrugged. 'That happens. A lot of them do that. For most of them, there's been a shitload of misery before they ever got in here.' She looked beyond Kerry. 'But hey. It is what it is. And you're here now. So if you're wise, you'll just keep on people's good side and won't get involved in any of the shit that goes on – drugs, pills, the kind of stuff that seems to get smuggled in here no matter what we do.'

After what Kerry had felt was akin to a pep talk, she'd been given some clothes and showered and dressed before the evening meal.

When she'd walked into the big dining hall she had felt all eyes on her and the chatter had fallen silent.

'There's the Godmother in now!'

Kerry had heard the sarcastic cat-call and a few giggles and cackles, and glanced around to see where it was coming from, but blank faces had stared back at her. She'd picked up a tray and gone up to the canteen hatch where they'd been serving hot food. She'd filled her plate with stew and mashed potato and vegetables, and found that she was hungry despite the nausea she'd been feeling most of the day. She'd told herself that no matter what they served she'd have to eat because of the baby, even if she had to force herself, but this stuff hadn't looked too bad. She walked away from the counter with her tray, not quite sure where to sit as some of the girls were in groups and almost everyone was looking in her direction. She hadn't wanted to barge in to anyone's company so she'd sat at an empty table, and the murmuring had continued. She'd wondered if someone would approach her and had been trying to work out what to say. She hadn't had to wait long, because into the place walked Ash, who'd spotted her immediately and waved. Then she'd collected her food on a tray and came over and sat down, as though they were two old friends in a café who hadn't seen each other in a while.

The weirdness of it all had taken Kerry's mind off the hellishness of her plight. Because here in front of her were women with *real* problems, women whose lives had been very different from hers, and many of whom had ended up here because of drugs or mental health issues. They hadn't looked too dangerous, but this was prison so she'd had to assume that some of them at least were in for serious offences. She knew she was privileged compared to them, but she was in prison and pregnant, and somewhere she felt hurt and angry that it was all a bit of a lark to them to make fun of her. She hadn't been sure what to expect from other prisoners but she hadn't expected that.

'You all right, Kerry?' Ash had said as she plonked herself down.

'Yeah,' Kerry said. 'Kind of shellshocked, I suppose. Looks like people are enjoying me being in here – pregnant and all as I am.'

'I don't suppose you've been inside before?' Ash said, devouring a mouthful of mash which she'd smothered in gravy.

'No.' Kerry glanced at her, then back at her plate.

'I heard who you are, by the way,' Ash whispered. 'You're famous! Notorious!' Her eyes had widened as though she was in the company of a celebrity.

Kerry hadn't answered, and sipped from a glass of milk.

'They're all talking about the gangster boss.'

Kerry had given her a look and sighed. She hadn't wanted to have this conversation. But Ash had persisted.

'I knew as soon as I looked at you that you were different. Know what I mean?' she went on. 'You look well-heeled. That's why the other women will see you as different. Some of them will be fascinated by you, but I'm not going to lie to you, Kerry. There's one or two hard-faced bastards in here who might take a pop at you.'

'Christ! I don't want to fight or argue with anyone,' she said, putting down her knife and fork. 'Look, Ash, I run a business organisation.' As she'd said it she'd known it sounded ridiculous, even to her. She'd dabbed the corner of her mouth with a paper napkin. 'We have business interests in Glasgow and also abroad.' She'd paused, looking into Ash's eyes. 'But I have nothing to do with these charges against me. I have no clue why this happened. I swear to God.' She'd put her hand on her stomach. 'I swear on my baby's life. I have no idea. I'm completely innocent, and so is my uncle Danny. We were just driving home when we got flagged down by this guy who looked as though he was in trouble.'

Ash had nodded sagely. 'Fitted up then,' she said. 'Cops, probably. They fit people up as a matter of routine. Drugs mostly. If they want to do you, then they'll do you. If you're a gangster and they can't get you the right way, they'll set you up. That's the polis for you.'

Kerry had looked at her, perplexed. She hadn't suspected it was police, as she was sure there would have been some indication that they were looking at her beforehand, maybe some kind of gypsy warning. Danny still had some good friends in the police who had remained loyal to the Caseys.

'I don't know,' she'd said. 'But somebody fitted me and Danny up. Now I'm stuck in here, and anyone with any sense would know that I wouldn't get involved in the kind of crap that I'm charged with. It's ridiculous.'

She hadn't wanted to give the girl her life story, because Ash was too eager to talk and ask questions, and she would probably broadcast their conversation around the jail. 'Somebody did this to me. But I don't know who or why. My lawyers have a team working on it. And one way or another I will find out who is behind it.'

Ash had been silent for a moment, eating a few mouthfuls of food, then she'd sniffed and looked at her.

'Lucky you,' she said. 'A team working for you. People like me, we just get fucked in here and the duty lawyer gets handed a case that he'll have seen a million of, then he does his best to get you out. But this time I'm not so sure.'

'So what happened?' Kerry wanted to divert the attention from herself. 'I heard that you broke bail conditions.'

Ash had looked at her, a little surprised.

'Oh, I suppose the screw told you that,' she said. 'Yeah. That's right. I was picking up a bit of stuff from the shops' – she winked – 'you know, as you do, for the resetters, and I got caught. The store detective was a rough bastard and manhandled me so I knocked him on his arse. Then they held me till the cops came. It all ended up a bit messy.' She paused and held out her hands, shaking and bruised. 'I'm on methadone, trying to get off heroin, and doing not bad. But in here, they won't give me it as I'm on remand. So they gave me diazepam just to take the edge off it. But bottom line is by the time the cops came I was a bit wired, so I stuck the head in the officer. Blood everywhere. I think I broke his nose.'

'Oh,' Kerry said. 'You charged with police assault?'

Ash had shrugged. 'Aye. Not for the first time. But I was provoked.'

Kerry hadn't wanted to argue. She wondered where Ash came from, what her story was, how she ended up routinely being in and out of jail. No doubt it would be the same story she'd heard as a young lawyer, or reading the newspapers or watching the news. A different world.

'Where are you from?' Kerry ventured. 'If you don't mind me asking.'

Ash looked at her flatly. 'Ask away.' She shrugged. 'I'm from the East End – down by Glasgow Green. I grew up there – well if that's what you can call it. Dragged up, more like.'

'You got family?'

'Not any more.' Ash looked dark. 'My ma was dead by the time I was sixteen. It was her who put me on the game. So it's not as though I have a lot to thank her for.'

Kerry had sat in stunned silence. There was no answer to this.

'Your mum?' She couldn't help herself.

'Aye. She was a heroin addict. I grew up watching her inject. By the time I was thirteen I was smoking hash with my mates, dodging school and stuff. Then my ma decides that I'm old enough to earn my keep. She took me down to the Green and pimped me out. Well, not actually her, her pimp did that – cunt that he was. But she went along with it. Punters like the young ones, so I made good money. And now there were two of us earning, and she could afford more heroin.'

This was too much to take in and Kerry was chilled to the bone by her revelations, but suddenly felt as though she was intruding in Ash's life by letting her pour all this shocking information out. She found herself looking at Ash, almost in disbelief. How do you come back from your mum pimping you out to paedophiles at the age of thirteen? She didn't know what to do or ask or say, but she knew she was expected to say something.

'Christ, Ash,' she said. 'I'm shocked. How did you cope?' She'd shaken her head. 'So young.'

'Heroin,' she said. 'It takes all the pain away. Nothing can touch you when you get a wee smoke of that stuff. See the moment that shit kicks in, it's like being under a warm blanket and everything looks easy and all the things you've been crying about and were scared of just melt away.' She sniffed. 'And once you find that place, you're in. Your life has already gone.' She looked away, and for a long moment, Kerry could see that the memory was hurting.

'I can imagine,' Kerry said. Wanting to feel empathy she added, 'I have a good friend whose daughter was a drug addict. It was a terrible time for the family, but she's out of it now. She got into rehab.'

'Lucky her. There's no rehab for most of us though. Just a methadone script, and that keeps you going, unless you find money and can get smack to top it up. But I'm trying not to do that.'

They'd sat finishing their food, both of them silent, Kerry stealing glances at Ash, wondering at how a spirited girl like this, in other circumstances, could probably have been anything she chose to be. People would say that if you make the wrong choices you can end up hitting rock bottom. From where Kerry was sitting right now, she was as close to rock bottom as anyone else in here.

After dinner, there had been a couple of hours of free time for the prisoners, where some made phone calls to family and friends, lay around in their cells, or watched television in the communal area. Most of them had sat around on sofas or chairs that reminded Kerry of the big common room for sixth formers at school, though it was a world away. She had been on a couch with Ash, both of them drinking tea, a little further away from a group of women who sat together around a table.

'Don't look now,' Ash said, 'but see that big table, that's where two of the hardest cases in the jail sit. One of them, Big Aggie – the heavy one with the cropped hair – she's a lifer. In here for battering an old man to death when she was off her tits on drugs one night. Mind you, I don't know if it was just the drugs. She's out of her fucking tree anyway. Flies into fits of rage sometimes, and once she punched a prison warden so hard she nearly lost her eye. She got an extra four years for that. But I don't think she'll see daylight on the outside for the rest of her puff.'

Kerry risked a glimpse up from the magazine she was thumbing through. Big Aggie seemed to be holding court with the other girls, telling some story that had them in fits of laughter.

'That's her girlfriend,' Ash said. 'The wee fat one next to her with the black curly hair. Nicola. They're together.'

'I see,' Kerry said, not really knowing what to say.

'You get a lot of that in here,' Ash went on. 'You know, lassies being together. Sometimes they're not really lesbians, but just gay in the jail, if you get my drift. Gets a bit lonely in here, and some of the girls just hook up with each other while they're inside.'

Kerry hadn't been sure what was coming next so she'd said nothing, then Ash had said, 'It's no' really my bag though. I like men. I had a boyfriend for a while, but we split up about six months ago. Drugs. He's just wasted. What about you?' She glanced at Kerry's bump. 'Is the da in the picture?'

Kerry had let out a sigh. She really hadn't wanted to go into it.

'Yes,' she said. 'But it's a long story, and he's away working at the moment.'

Ash nodded, as though she'd made her own mind up that the father had done a runner.

It had been getting close to lock-up and some of the girls had already drifted back to their cells. Kerry had been dreading going back into the cell with Natalie, wondering what was in store for her. She hadn't seen her around since the dinner hall, but now she spotted her coming along the corridor from their cell, striding towards where Kerry and Ash sat.

'Oh fuck!' Ash said. 'Here comes trouble.'

Kerry looked up to see Natalie standing over her, glowering, her face flushed and angry.

'You stole my fucking stuff,' she said, jabbing a finger.

Kerry, bewildered, looked up at her.

'I . . . I didn't take anything, Natalie. I don't know what you mean.'

'You took my perfume,' she spat. 'And my jumper. And that wee toy I keep for my boy. Where the fuck is the toy?'

The room had fallen silent, and all eyes had turned on Kerry. She'd glanced from Ash to her accuser.

'Nat. I didn't take anything,' she said. 'I didn't even see anything. I don't know what you're talking about.'

She could see Nat was shifting from one foot to the other, agitated. Kerry hadn't known what to do, and glanced around hoping to see a prison guard or anyone who could step in to help before this got out of hand.

'My toy!' she'd shrieked. 'You took my toy! Probably for that wean you've got in there. Well give it fucking back! It's for my wean not yours!'

'Nat—'

But before she could say anything else, Nat, as quick as lightning, had grabbed her by the hair, almost yanking her off the couch. Kerry yelped with the pain, feeling her hair being torn out by the roots. And in a few seconds all hell had broken loose. Ash had jumped to her feet and was all over Nat, trying to prise her hands off Kerry's hair, then two girls had jumped up from their chairs and seized Nat around the waist, one of them trying to gently coax her to let go. As she finally did, with a handful of hair, Nat had burst into tears and fled off down the corridor towards her cell. Kerry sat clutching her head, a searing pain at the temple where the hair had been wrenched.

'You all right?' Ash said, sitting down close to her. 'Let

me see.' She examined her head. 'Aye, she got a clump of your hair, all right.'

Kerry had swallowed her tears, sensing everyone's eyes on her. And then Big Aggie and a couple of the other women had come towards her. She had been terrified, but she'd got to her feet on shaky legs.

'Not a big hard woman then, eh? Not a gangster then?' Big Aggie said, smirking.

Kerry didn't answer.

'You better no' have taken her stuff.'

'I didn't take anything,' Kerry said. Her head had been pounding but she'd stood her ground. 'I would never do that.'

Aggie had stood legs apart and glared at her. 'Well, just so you know. Big-time gangster or no, Kerry Casey – we're watching you. You're nothing in here. You might be all rich and fancy outside, but in here you're just a fucking number like the rest of us.'

Kerry didn't reply, but she stood and stared Aggie down long enough for her to turn and walk away. When she did, Kerry sat back down, biting her lip.

'Well done, Kerry. That fat cunt knows you stood up to her there. But you need to watch your back now.'

She'd looked at Ash but said nothing, wondering what the hell was going to happen when she went to her cell later.

CHAPTER SIX

It had led to another night with not much sleep, Kerry lying terrified in case Nat was going to attack her again, her scalp aching from the hair having been torn out. When she'd come into the cell about an hour after the incident, Nat had lain in bed, silent, her face turned to the wall. Kerry had got dressed quietly and slipped into bed, barely breathing. Then the lights had gone out and the doors had clicked shut for the night, and Kerry had lain there, dreading what might happen. But then, out of the blue, Nat's voice had come from above.

'I'm sorry,' she said. 'I didn't mean to hurt you. I . . . I just can't cope sometimes.' Then the sobs.

'It's okay, Nat,' Kerry said. 'I understand. It's okay.'

It wasn't okay though, not by any stretch of Kerry's fevered imagination was anything okay, and she wondered if anything was ever going to get any better. She had lain thinking about Vinny. Remembering their last days together, his smile, their shared laughter and experiences, filling her head with any thoughts that would take her out of the hell she was in at the moment.

After breakfast, where Ash and Kerry sat together, Kerry was aware everyone was still looking at her, nobody speaking to her or nodding in her direction.

'That was some stooshie last night,' Ash said. 'Are you all right? Did you sleep?'

'Not much. But I'm fine. Nat said she was sorry. And she was crying. She's a poor soul, Ash.'

'Aye. But a dangerous one too. She shouldn't be in here.'

A prison guard approached their table, and looked towards Kerry.

'You'll be moving cells later,' she said, then turning to Ash. 'You too. The pair of you will be in together. On the first floor.'

They looked at each other, and Kerry could see Ash's eyes light up, and she wondered if hers had too. She didn't care how much Ash talked her head off, at least she wasn't going to turn on her.

The guard looked at her. 'And when you're finished here, I'll take you across to the mother and baby unit.'

Kerry smiled. 'Thanks.'

Later, as they left the main building and walked across the grounds to the mother and baby unit, the guard turned to her.

'They have everything there – cots, all sorts of baby clothes, bottles and breast pumps. It's lovely. We make sure a young mum and her baby are well looked after. It's not the baby's fault it's in here.'

Kerry looked at her, stung by the words. The mother and baby unit in prison? Had it really come to this? Not in any of her nightmares, in everything that had happened over the past few months and years, could she have ever imagined that she would be pregnant and in jail and being shown around the mother and baby unit in case she gave birth inside. The thought terrified her. She walked around the unit, which was bright and colourful, and in truth as welcoming as any baby nursery most young mums might create themselves. There were cupboards full of utensils, baby food, sterilisers, and packs full of nappies from newborn to a year old. And piles of baby clothes, pink and blue and white. Kerry gazed at them, thinking that if she'd been at home she would have been out shopping for all of these things, building her little nest for her baby. If the worst came to the worst and she had to give birth and come back here while awaiting trial, it wouldn't be the end of the world, even if it might seem that way at the time. At least it was safe and clean, and her baby wouldn't know, maybe would never know, the start it had in life. In a room off the main area, there was a young woman sitting on a chair bottle-feeding a baby that looked no more than a few weeks old. The girl looked up with tired eyes and a grey complexion, and she smiled at them.

As they left the building, Kerry looked at her watch again, as she had done from the moment she had woken up that morning. As she'd left her cell on the way to breakfast, she'd been met by a guard who'd told her she would have a visitor today, by the name of Sullivan. She had been thrilled. John Sullivan, the undercover detective she had arranged to meet at Bridgeton Cross yesterday, was coming to see her to talk about Vinny. Marty had called late last night to inform the reception. When Kerry had called Marty back this morning, he'd reported that Jack had gone to meet Sullivan, and told him what had happened: that Kerry had been set up and was in jail. Sullivan had been reluctant to identify himself even to Jack, so he had said very little. Jack had asked him to relay the information to him, but he'd refused, saying he would only speak to Kerry. He'd agreed to see her in jail, which he'd told Jack was a risk, but it was one, it seemed, he was prepared to take. Kerry wasn't even sure what the set-up was in terms of visiting, whether it would be in an open room with lots of other prisoners, or whether there would there be an opportunity for a private chat. She hoped so.

When they got back to the main building, Kerry joined the line of prisoners gathered in the communal area where she'd been told to wait to be taken to the prison visitors' café. She listened to the excited chatter of prisoners looking forward to seeing relatives and loved ones, still in a bit of shock that she was part of this. She'd barely had time to get her head around it. As she stood on her own, the other prisoners in groups, she was taken to the side by an officer and told she would be seeing her visitor in the family centre. Other prisoners looked at her and some glared, as she appeared to be getting preferential treatment. She didn't know if this was for remand prisoners, but hadn't presumed that anyone would be able to give her preferential treatment. But she followed the woman and the three other prisoners anyway. They were taken outside and across a courtyard, to the family unit. Inside, there were tables and chairs and pictures on the wall, giving it a pleasant bright look, like a café or a small community centre. She could see four people sitting at tables, two men and two women, one with a child. The women in front of her joined the men at the tables. Then at another table a man sat alone. She had no idea who she was looking for, but assumed it must be Sullivan. He had close-cropped hair, was unshaven and tired-looking. She saw him look at her as though he recognised her, and he half stood up. She walked towards where he sat.

'John?' she said softly as she got to the table.

He nodded, gesturing for her to sit opposite him. She slipped into plastic chair and they both looked at each other. His face was tanned and lean, with several days' stubble, and his eyes were bloodshot with dark shadows under them. She wondered what kind of role he had in the undercover operation. If he was undercover, moving among junkies, he looked like he would fit in no problem.

'Thanks for coming, John.'

'Christ, Kerry. I'm so sorry for what's happened here – I mean this.' He gestured the surroundings. 'It must be a nightmare for you.'

She nodded. 'I've done nothing. Nothing. I hope you know that. We were framed by someone and I have no idea who or why.' She shook her head. 'I was even more distraught that it happened because I couldn't come and see you as planned. Thanks for talking to Jack and coming here.'

He sat forward. 'I didn't want to say anything to him, I mean, no details. Obviously I don't know him from Adam and the only person I wanted to talk to is you. It's a huge risk for me coming here. If my bosses knew I'd be in serious trouble.'

'Thanks. I appreciate that.'

He sighed, frustrated, shook his head and rubbed his chin.

'It's a mess, Kerry. I'm not going to lie to you.'

Kerry blinked her acknowledgement. She wanted information, as fast as possible. She was so grateful to be next to someone who had actually been close to Vinny that it was all she could do to stop herself reaching out and touching him.

'I understand,' she said. 'We only have an hour, so if you can just tell me everything. I need to know what we can do about this.'

He swallowed. 'I just want to say I'm so sorry about

everything. I'm shattered and worried sick, and I'll be honest, I agonised about coming to you with this, but I didn't know what else to do.'

Sullivan looked edgy and watchful.

'So, tell me.' Kerry leaned across the table. 'I'm glad you got in touch. I've talked to my people. Anything we can do to find Vinny we will. He . . . I . . .'

He reached across but stopped short of touching her hand.

'I know,' he whispered. 'I know about the baby. Vinny told me. It was the first thing he said when he got back to Spain after he'd seen you in the hospital that time.' John smiled. 'He was so made up.' Then he shook his head.

They sat for a moment in silence, then Kerry spoke. 'So, what can you tell me? I mean, about the operation? I'm going to need places, locations and stuff like that, maybe some names, so I can get my people on the ground in Spain to make discreet enquiries.'

Kerry listened, making sure she took it all in, remembering all the details. He told it as though he was reliving it.

The two of them, he said, had been on their second stint working undercover together. He and Vinny had first worked together in Colombia three years ago – in Medellín and in Bogotá – infiltrating the cartels, and over time helping to snare a couple of mid-range hoodlums involved in transporting cocaine to Europe and Miami. The American Drugs Enforcement Agency officers had also worked with them over the years, but that had been three years ago, and in recent times they had been back in the UK, with Vinny working out of the Met in London most of the time. The operation they'd been sent on in the south of Spain was to infiltrate and gather intelligence on a Colombian gang that was looking to grow their set-up and take over a smaller gang of Albanian operators that had gained a foothold in Spain and was growing in Europe. Both he and Vinny lived in separate apartments and it was John's job to get himself in with the Albanian gang, while Vinny was winning over the Colombians and the Spanish hard men. It had been beginning to come together, he said.

'We both felt we were getting closer to being able to organise a move on these gangs. My cover with the Albanians was that I had connections in the UK and across Europe, so I was able to come up with some people who could help their smuggling operation. The Colombians always want to be top dog in any drug-smuggling operations, but they can't really ignore the Albanians, because they are a growing force, and just as brutal and ruthless as the Colombians when it comes to protecting what they have. So, it was working, and the people I was in with were meeting the guys Vinny had got himself in with.' He paused. 'You with me, Kerry?'

'Sure,' she said. Kerry knew he had to paint the picture, but she was anxious to hear what happened to Vinny. 'So, did it all fall apart? Is that what happened?'

John nodded, leaned in a little.

'I'm coming to that,' he said, taking a sip of tea. 'When Vinny and me would meet on our own, we were always totally meticulous in terms of where we went, and obviously made sure nobody knew we were working together. We know how to do this stuff.'

Kerry looked at him and thought he sounded as though he was trying to convince himself, and could see from the drawn look on his face that he must have asked himself a dozen times whether there was anything he had done wrong that could have led to Vinny being snatched. She didn't say anything. She just gave a slight nod in support.

'Mostly we talked on the phone, but every couple of days we would meet – always in a different café or restaurant, and always far enough away,' he said. 'We were both relaying our intelligence back to the bosses in the UK, and we knew that when the time was right we would be able to deliver the main players. We were working on intelligence about a shipment of cocaine coming in on a yacht to Cadiz in the coming weeks.'

He sat back, took a long breath and pushed out a sigh, eyes cast down at the table as though reliving the moment.

'Then, two months ago, I got a call from Vinny to say he was about to leave his apartment and would meet me in our usual place up in the hills behind Marbella. He said he had some hot stuff that was going to mean things would start to move quickly, and we'd have to talk about getting the bosses involved and how we were going to manage our own escape from this.' He stopped, swallowed. 'And then. Nothing. Fucking nothing.'

He fell silent, staring down at his hands as though looking for answers, and picking at his chewed fingernails. Kerry watched him, and for a while they sat there, as she tried to visualise Vinny leaving his apartment on the morning he disappeared, and how the scene might have unfolded. She blinked away images that were flooding her mind of him being grabbed, bundled into a car, hooded, and probably beaten. *Two months ago*, she thought. And who knew, maybe all this time he was being held somewhere on the Costa del Sol, perhaps even close to where her base was with Sharon and Vic and all her business interests. She tortured herself with the thought that he could have been so close. It was a long time to have been snatched with no move made by the kidnappers, not even to make any ransom demands. But maybe they didn't even want a ransom, she thought. Perhaps all they were required to do was find the mole in their outfit and eliminate him. These Colombian bastards were smart enough to know that if they'd discovered that Vinny was an undercover cop, then making him disappear would completely destabilise the authorities. They would enjoy that before they started posting parts of his body to his bosses. Kerry rubbed her face to try and blot out the terrifying thoughts in her head.

She took a deep breath, and stretched her hand across so that her fingers touched John's.

'John,' she said. 'We have to believe that Vinny is still alive.' She could see by his expression that he wasn't anywhere near convinced that Vinny was alive, but she had to make him believe it. 'I know, given your work and the stuff you get involved in, it's all pointing to the Colombians disposing of him. But maybe that's not happened. Maybe they're holding him, biding their time. What do you think?'

He sat back and for a moment said nothing, then he spoke.

'It's possible, Kerry,' he said. 'I want to believe that, and that's why I came to you.' He paused. 'Our bosses aren't doing much. I don't think there's a lot they can do. Once I found out from my own sources that Vinny was seen leaving the apartment and being bundled into the back of a car, I knew the game was up.'

'When did you pull out?' Kerry asked. 'How did that come about?'

'I just carried on as normal in my own undercover, meeting with my usual people, and keeping my ear to the ground. Then I was beginning to get some vibes that the Albanians and the Colombians were suspicious that there was more than one spy in the camp. The Colombians, I heard, were suspicious that it was the Albanians who were not being careful enough, and the Albanians were coming back to them saying that they were watertight. I was beginning to feel that the next person they looked at would be me. So the decision was made for me to pull out.' He paused. 'I didn't want to, but I knew I had to.'

Kerry kept her eyes on him and she could see from his expression that John was feeling guilty, he felt he'd abandoned his friend and colleague to save his own arse. Much as she didn't want to blame him, she couldn't help being angry that he was here and Vinny wasn't. She didn't know what to say, so she said nothing.

'I feel like shit, Kerry, and that's the truth,' he said, shaking his head. 'Why Vinny and not me? You know what I mean? That will haunt me every day until I know what happened to him. And if Vinny is out there, I need to find him. I need to bring him home. I'll do anything it takes.' He looked into Kerry's eyes. 'I'll take leave of absence from my job and pitch in with your guys. Anything.'

He looked as though he was struggling with emotion, and she could see how difficult this was for him. She nodded slowly.

'You might have to do that, John,' she said. 'If we're going to work on this together, you can't be a cop.'

He gave her a long hard look. 'I'm in,' he said. 'Whatever it takes.'

The guards checked their watches and glanced at each other, a sign that visiting was over. Couples hugged each other and the mother kissed her daughter. Kerry stood up and wasn't sure whether to shake John's hand in case it looked too formal. She leaned across and hugged him a little awkwardly. Then they stood apart.

'From now on, Jack will be in touch with you, once he knows what we're doing. I know he has plans in mind.' She leaned a little closer. 'It might involve you going there.'

'Whatever it involves,' he said. 'I'm ready.'

The doors were open and the visitors made their way out. As they left, the people stood there, some sniffing back tears, others with faces set in empty, determined silence. By the time Kerry got back to her cell, her mind was racing. She had to find out what had happened to Vinny. She had to find him and bring him home.

CHAPTER SEVEN

As soon as Steven arrived at the scrapyard to meet Bo Black, he could see from his eyes that he was coked up.

'Gimpy, ma man!' Bo greeted him like a long-lost friend, even though he'd only seen him yesterday when they'd been making arrangements.

Steven looked back at him, deadpan. He hadn't even been told what exactly he was going to be doing, only that he'd to come down to the scrapyard to go on a special job. He'd been suspicious as soon as the job had been given to him yesterday by Gordy Thomson. Lambie had plenty of foot soldiers. If they were having to ask him to be involved, it had to be something extra dodgy, something they didn't want to get their hands dirty with. Steven had reluctantly agreed, because he knew he had to, but also because he was told he would get three hundred quid upfront, even before the job was done. The money would come in handy to get the fridge-freezer fixed at his ma's house, and there would be some left over, so he could take her out shopping and maybe buy her a new coat. That would cheer her up. But right now, he didn't like what he was seeing. He stood in the yard, strewn with car wrecks, rusty engines, old wheels and burnt-out motors. Thomson's mate owned it and Steven knew it was the place where ringed cars were taken and rebuilt then sold on to one of his second-hand car dealers.

'So what's the job, Bo?' Steven asked, digging his hands into his trouser pockets, trying to look as though he wasn't worried.

Bo swaggered towards him and stood so close to him that Steven could smell his rancid breath. He could see his eyes were wild and bright from a recent line.

'You're not supposed to ask questions, Gimpy. You're job is to do what you're told, ya prick.'

Steven said nothing, but he could feel his face burning. He was sick of the ritual humiliation of this wanker and his mate who treated him like an imbecile. Steven stepped away from him and turned his back.

'Hey! Where you going, Gimpy? I'm talking to you, ya cunt.'

For a moment, Steven thought about turning around and decking him, but he knew the consequences would not be good. He was saved by a voice coming from the Portakabin behind him.

'Hey, Bo! What the fuck you doing, man? Behave your fucking self!'

Steven turned to see big Gordy coming down the steps

and striding towards them. He caught hold of Bo and turned him around.

'Look at you! Fucking idiot!' he spat, grabbing a handful of Bo's polo-neck jumper. 'What were you fucking told? Lay off that fucking charlie till we get the job done. Honest to Christ, man, you're a fucking liability, you are.' He let go.

Steven watched, uneasy, as Bo's eyes blazed. The cocaine had made him think he was a hard man.

'A fucking liability?' he snapped back. 'You weren't saying that the other night when I was dragging Lumsden and wee Hawkins into that bird's motor. I wasn't a liability when I put a bullet into Tam Gillespie's head because Dick wanted him out. Liability?'

The silence was deafening, the air crackling with rage and tension as it seemed to dawn on Gordy just what Bo had said out loud. Steven looked at the ground, trying his best to pretend he somehow hadn't heard Bo's mouthing off. But his head was buzzing with what he'd just witnessed. Did Bo really say it was him who dragged Lumsden and Hawkins out of that bird's car? That bird? What bird? It had to be Kerry Casey. Jesus Christ almighty! It must have been a set-up. They must have framed Kerry Casey and her uncle, so that they were now in jail charged with murder and possession of drugs and guns. Fucking hell! That was off the scale. And he also remembered Tam Gillespie's murder – he'd worked for Lambie but had been found in a shallow grave six months ago. Bo did that too? Steven wished the ground would open up and swallow him. Then the silence was broken by another voice on the steps of the hut.

'Gordy!'

Steven looked up. It was Lambie, standing with his arms folded. He had heard everything.

'Gordy!' he barked again. 'In here! Now!'

Gordy turned and walked towards the cabin, and Bo followed. Then Lambie called out again.

'You stay where you are, Bo.'

Bo stopped in his tracks. He sniffed, wiping his nose with the back of his hands. Steven heard him mumble.

'Ungrateful bastards.'

Steven wished he hadn't heard Bo's outburst, because he'd clocked Lambie glancing at him as Gordy walked towards the Portakabin. He stood around for a few minutes, nervous, wondering if Bo's rantings were that of a man coked out of his nut, or, even more worryingly, if he was actually telling the truth. After what seemed like an age, Gordy came back out of the hut and strode towards them.

'You've to go inside, Gimpy,' he said. 'Boss wants a word.'

Steven's gut dropped. He said nothing and limped across the yard and up the stairs.

Inside, Lambie was sitting behind a desk, and he got up and came around so that they were facing each other, a couple of feet apart. Lambie's six foot frame towered above him, and his jowly face had a pinkish, piggy complexion. Steven stood, barely breathing.

'See that shite out there, Gimpy?' he said. 'That pish that Bo was shouting?'

Steven blinked but kept quiet.

'Well, that's all it is. Pure pish. Bo's out of his tits on coke, and raving like a fucking lunatic as if he doesn't know the difference between something that he saw on the TV news and something that actually happened. You understand me, Gimpy?'

Steven nodded. 'Aye.'

'So,' Lambie went on, 'as far as you're concerned you never heard any of that shite. You pay no attention to it. Okay? I've told Gordy he'll need to deal with Bo. He's been at this coke too much now, and it's clouding his judgement, his ability to do the job. Can't tell reality from fantasy. Daft cunt. Know what I mean?'

'Aye.'

'So. You just ignore it. You've a job to go on with the pair of them. You'll be told what you've to do when you get there. You can drive one of the motors and Gordy will take the other – with Bo in it, so you don't need to listen to any more of his shite. Just follow Gordy's car. All right?'

'Aye.'

Lambie went into his pocket and took out a wedge of notes. He peeled off several fifty pound notes and handed them to Steven.

'Your wages,' he said. 'And remember.' He put his finger to his lips and looked at Steven, his eyes narrowed.

'Thanks,' Steven said, because he didn't know what else he could say. He just wanted to get out of here and far away. He felt he was suffocating.

During the drive out towards Stirling, Steven thought about nothing else but what he'd heard Bo shouting back at the scrapyard. What if it hadn't just been the rantings of a coked-out nutjob? What if Lambie, or whoever, had really set the Caseys up for murder? He couldn't understand why anyone would do that. All he knew about the Caseys was that they ran most of the show in Glasgow, and apparently a lot more on the Costa del Sol. They were gangsters, all right, but not in the way Lambie and his mob were, robbing and moneylending and running their protection racket on the east side of the city. Lambie was grubby. What he did was grubby, especially the loan-sharking. Over the past couple of years working in the pub, Steven had heard of some of the lowlife shit Lambie's boys had pulled to get money out of people whose debts had spiralled because of their extortionate interest rates. He was one of them, and he knew how trapped they felt, but Steven had to convince himself that he was working his way through it, that better days were coming. Otherwise he'd have given up and plunged into a depression. But the Caseys were different. He remembered the funeral of Mickey Casey and the carnage when some mobsters from Manchester came up and riddled the whole pub with bullets, like something out of a

Hollywood gangster movie. And he'd seen the funeral of Kerry Casey's mother on the television, and remembered feeling a bit sorry for what the woman was having to go through. If someone had done that to his mother, they'd be paying for it for the rest of their lives. But none of this led him to thinking why Lambie's boys would set them up. There had to be a reason for that. Whatever it was, he wasn't about to go and investigate. This was his day off from the pub, and he just wanted to get this job done and get back home in time to make his ma's dinner. He followed Gordy's car as it turned off the main road and onto a farm track that took them a couple of miles into the country. He saw a sign for Bannockburn, and they drove on, then Gordy took the cut-off to Cowiehill quarry.

The rain was coming down in sheets by the time the two cars trundled along the track that led to the quarry. It looked eerie under the leaden sky, the choppy water stretching for ever over a ridge that led up to the edge. Gordy's car stopped and Steven drew up alongside him. He pulled on his jacket and climbed out of the car, the rain lashing his face, the wind cutting through him. He watched as Gordy and Bo got out of their car. Gordy looked pale and edgy. He lit up a cigarette and handed one to Bo, who pushed it between his lips.

'Fucking freezing, man, isn't it!' Bo said, gazing out across the water.

'Aye,' Gordy said. 'Let's get this done and get the fuck out of here.'

Steven shuffled around from one foot to the other, not sure what he was supposed to do next. He didn't want to ask. Eventually, Gordy drew deep on his cigarette and tossed the rest of it away.

'Right, Gimpy,' he said. 'That motor you're driving. It's to go in the quarry.'

Steven glanced at him. He had gathered something like this was going to happen. They were getting rid of a car that they'd probably used in a robbery. Might even have been the car from the other night. He wasn't about to ask any questions. He said nothing.

'You're going to drive it to the edge, and then jump out, then we'll get behind it and shove it over. It's about fifty feet down from here so the impact as it hits the water and the weight of it will make sure it goes under quick and stays there.'

Steven nodded but said nothing. Bo stood looking at him, his face pale and his eyes a little heavy. Gordy must have told him again to lay off the coke till the job was done, because he'd lost the crazed look he'd had earlier.

'Right,' Gordy said. 'On you go, Gimpy. And go slow, for fuck's sake.'

Steven shivered with nerves and the cold. Right now, with these two thugs, he wasn't sure if he was actually going to be made to go into the quarry as well. Whatever they'd done with this car, they had to get rid of it, and he was a witness. He calmed himself down. They knew he wouldn't breathe a word of this. He took the steps to the car and got in, switching on the engine. It was only about fifteen feet from the front of the car to the edge of the quarry, so he had to concentrate as he edged slowly ahead, conscious that he was riding the clutch to make sure the car inched at a snail's pace. He kept it going until he could see the lip of the cliff, then he stopped, and switched the engine off. He got out and looked at Gordy and Bo, but they said nothing.

'That's fine, Gimpy,' Gordy said. 'Right. Get to the back of the car and get ready to push.'

Steven went to the back of the car, and for a second wondered why Gordy and Bo weren't following him. He stood behind the car, waiting for them, then, as he looked across the roof of the car, he froze.

'Right, Bo,' he heard Gordy say. 'In the motor. This is the end of the road for you.'

He saw the startled look on Bo's face. 'Wh . . . What the fuck, Gordy! Don't even joke, man.'

He watched as Gordy put his hand inside his jacket and pulled out a handgun. He pointed it at Bo.

'In the fucking motor, Bo.'

Steven felt his mouth drop open. His legs suddenly started shaking and he had to steady himself against the car.

'Gordy!' he heard himself shout, his voice shaky. 'What the fuck, man?'

Gordy turned quickly and pointed the gun at him.

'Shut your fucking mouth, Gimpy. Just do as you're told.'

Bo burst into tears. 'Aw, come on, man!' he pleaded. 'Fucking stop it, Gordy. We're mates. Like brothers, man.'

'In. The. Fucking. Car.'

'But what for? I've no' done anything,' Bo whimpered.

'You've become a fucking liability. You can't be trusted. Shovin' that shit up your nose all the time.'

'I'll stop. I promise. I'll never take it again.'

'Shut it, Bo. I've got my orders. Now get in the car. It's nothing personal.'

Bo glanced around and for a moment Steven thought he was going to make a run for it, but he knew he had nowhere to go.

'Don't even think about it,' Gordy said. 'Get in.'

He moved closer to him, keeping the gun pointed, and with his free hand opened the door. He grabbed Bo by the back of the neck and pushed him, then put the gun to the back of his head. Bo put his hands up and got into the passenger seat. Steven could hear him screaming and crying and pleading. But it was only for a couple of seconds, because the next sound was the bang of a gunshot that echoed in the air and across the grey murky black water. Steven flinched, his legs like jelly. Gordy slammed the door shut, then turned to Steven. He waited for him to point the gun. He thought of his ma. How would she find out? He saw her sobbing, bewildered, going to pieces. He swallowed the lump in his throat.

'Right. Start pushing.' Gordy shoved his gun back in his jacket and walked to the back of the car.

Steven felt relieved that he'd been spared and terrified by what he'd just witnessed.

'Come on,' Gordy said. 'Don't just stand there like a pussy. Get your back into this.'

He bent down, put his shoulder to the metal and started to push, aware that his legs were weak and shaking.

'Come on to fuck, Gimpy!' Gordy strained. 'Push harder.'

Steven forced his legs to stop shaking and pushed with everything he had. He felt the car move forward a little. They kept pushing. He turned his face away from Gordy and gave it a huge heave until the car teetered on the edge of the quarry. Then they both gave one final push and over it went. Steven straightened up and tried to compose himself, his whole body trembling as though he was in shock.

'Right,' Gordy said. 'Let's go. You're driving.' He strode to the other car, got into the passenger seat.

For a couple of beats, Steven stood there, frozen, as his eyes scanned the landscape, the rain soaking his face and sweeping across the quarry. Nothing would ever be the same again. He went across to the car, got into the driver's seat, and with trembling hands turned on the ignition. He reversed away from the quarry and, in stunned silence, turned and headed back down the road they'd come.

CHAPTER EIGHT

In the weeks after Kerry and Danny's arrest, Jake Cahill worked quietly in the background, trying to dig up any intelligence on Vinny's disappearance. As a rule, he preferred to work alone, so whatever he did he was answerable only to himself. But he'd agreed to pitch in with this John Sullivan undercover cop, who had come to Spain to find out what had happened to his mate Vinny who'd gone missing.

It wouldn't be the first time. Jake had worked covertly with the police in several countries across the world. But you would never have seen it recorded in any documents, and nobody in any official capacity would ever admit that they had hired a hitman to do their dirty work. You would never hear it from Jake either. Nobody really knew for sure what he did or where he was, and that's how he preferred it. He lived in the shadows. It had to be that way if he wanted to stay alive. But he had always been particular about working with cops. He wouldn't simply just take on a hit for money if his conscience told him not to. He had never bumped anyone off who didn't tick the right boxes for him – a genuine threat to national security, a twisted psycho who had murdered innocent people, or a terrorist. He had never killed for cops so they could cover up their own shitty mess. He'd been asked to do that more than once, but he always refused. Not that he saw himself as any kind of crusader, for he had also taken people out of the game for gangsters like the Caseys, for the IRA, and one time for a politician whose child had been murdered and the killer had got off on a technicality. He'd done that one for free. Jake worked alone almost all the time. And he'd told big Jack when he called him that he wasn't keen to work with someone he didn't even know. But he'd agreed, because Jack had filled him in on what had happened to Kerry and that her and Danny were banged up on charges that they'd clearly been framed for. On top of that, Vinny was the father of Kerry's child, and he knew she'd be torn apart, so there was no question of him refusing. Like everyone else, Jake thought Vinny was probably dead by now. But he'd agreed. And now, as he sat and listened to this Sullivan cop giving him all the low-down of their operation, his mind had not changed.

They were having dinner in a restaurant in the Marbella hills that Jake knew was quiet and far enough away from the tourist haunts along the coast. There was a half-empty bottle of red wine on the table which they had drunk over the steak dinner while Sullivan updated him. None of the Albanian mobsters who Sullivan had infiltrated, he told him, knew that he was back in Spain, so he'd been keeping a low profile, talking only to the one trusted contact that he had. From what he'd told him it was not looking good. He talked, Jake listened.

'My man told me that he'd heard from a reliable inside source that it was the Colombians who took Vinny. He said his contact is Albanian and that they know nothing about the kidnapping, but they were well pissed off that the Colombians were accusing them. It caused a rift, but it's all died down a bit now and they're working as normal. He's going to be working with the Colombians in the next few days as they are cutting up and moving a batch of cocaine. The Albanians are transporting it to northern Spain and then to UK. So I'm told.'

Jake was glad to see that the couple of drinks before dinner, and the wine, had made Sullivan less agitated. He'd been edgy, obviously not happy to be back in Spain as he was probably a target by now. But he'd been impressed by his determination to come back and try to find his mate. That took balls. But Jake didn't want to tell him everything he'd been doing from his end, because the fewer people who knew, the better, so he simply listened and nodded in all the right places. He would tell him when the time was right.

It hadn't taken Jake long to discover for sure that it was the Colombians who took Vinny, so Sullivan's contact was spot on about that. Over the years in Spain, Jake had known a lot of people who moved in all sorts of high and low places. Some of them were lowlifes who got used by gangsters to put their names to bogus property deals for laundered money, or to open false bank accounts with fake ID to move dirty cash. Others were players. Some of them Colombians. Not all of them he would trust with this kind of enquiry. But yesterday one of his contacts had come back with what might turn out to be be solid information. A Brit, he said, was being held in a house down the coast in Tarifa while the Colombian cartel decided what to do with him. He'd been there for nearly two months, apparently, so the time frame would be right for the date Vinny disappeared. Of course, this could be any Brit the Colombians had picked up for various reasons. But if it was someone who had betrayed them he would be dead by now, unless they were planning to use him for some other purpose – ransom demands or whatever. If it was Vinny who was being held, and the Colombians knew he was an undercover cop, they might make a ransom demand. But in the unlikely event of the British authorities agreeing to meet it, Vinny would still get the chop. That much Jake was sure of. The Colombian kidnapping recently of Marty Kane's little grandson in Glasgow was different. He'd been an innocent child, and even though the Colombians were vicious, ruthless bastards, most of them would think twice about murdering a child. Plus, they'd thought they'd be getting a whole lot out of the Caseys by keeping him alive. But an undercover cop? No matter what the ransom, he would be murdered. Definitely. So, whatever was going on, Jake had to get closer to it. He had to find out where in Tarifa this Brit was being held. That was the first step, and he wasn't ready to tell Sullivan about it yet.

'So what do you think went wrong that blew Vinny's cover?' Jake looked at Sullivan. 'Or, both your covers? Because from what I hear, it makes me think that both your covers have been blown. How do you think that happened?'

Sullivan shook his head and pushed out a sigh.

'I don't know, Jake,' he replied. He lifted his glass to his lips and sipped. 'I mean, I have my thoughts, but I don't even know if I can go there.'

Jake gave him a long look.

'Well, you're going to have to if we're ever going to find out what's happening here. No point in holding out on me.'

Sullivan looked surprised, and a little hurt, a bit like a teenager who'd done something stupid and dangerous. He put a hand up.

'I'm not holding out on you, I promise you that.' He bit his lip. 'But I don't want to give you information that might not be accurate.'

'Listen.' Jake sat forward. He didn't want to say, listen,

mate, because he hated the way everyone was everyone else's mate these days – even strangers. 'Only when I have all the information in front of me – in front of us – can we decide what direction we're going in. So get it out there, for fuck's sake.' Jake waved the waiter across,.

Brandy?' Jake asked, and Sullivan nodded. He spoke to the waiter. '*Dos, por favor.*'

Jake watched the waiter go back to the bar, then turned to Sullivan and waited for him to talk. Finally, he did. The chatter in the restaurant had died down as a few of the other diners started to leave, so Sullivan pulled his chair a little closer and sat with his elbows on the table.

'Okay,' he said. 'I've got this niggle that someone we were dealing with from time to time has stuck us in it. Problem is, it's another cop.'

Jake raised his eyebrows. 'Seriously?'

'Not sure, but I've got my suspicions.'

'What kind of cop? Brit?'

'No. Spanish. Part of the DEA over here. We didn't deal with them every day or anything like that, but now and again we would give them some information, and the same with them – if they had any intel to give us, they'd pass it on.' He paused. 'It was a woman officer.'

Jake's face was impassive as he watched Sullivan stare into his brandy glass. A woman. That might explain a lot. It might explain his edginess and need to come back and see if he could dig Vinny out. Sullivan looked guilty as he made eye contact. Now they were beginning to get to the heart of the matter.

'A woman,' Jake said flatly, holding his gaze. 'Go on.' He had a feeling he knew what was coming next.

Sullivan took a gulp of the brandy, and Jake could see that he needed it.

'She was with the DEA – has been for about five years, and has been on the ground here most of that time. When Vinny and me first arrived, she was one of about three officers we met, and we agreed we would keep in contact, but Vinny and me were very much left to our own devices. We didn't get in touch with them much, until one time she called me and passed on some good inside stuff on the Albanians. I met with her, and after that we had dinner a couple of times.' He paused then corrected himself. 'More than a couple of times. And, well ... we kind of got involved.'

'You mean you had sex with her,' Jake said, matter-of-fact. 'Look, Sullivan, I'm not here to listen to your confession. You getting shacked up with some cop bird is down to you. I'm sure you've told yourself a million times that you should have known better. But hey, these things happen. Don't beat yourself up about it. Is that what you're doing? Is that why you're here? Do you think she double-crossed you?'

Sullivan looked defeated. He'd told none of this to Kerry, or she would have relayed it to Jake, but he was clearly depressed about it and feeling guilty. Jake didn't need someone working with him who was not a hundred per cent focused on the job at hand. So he had to hear the rest of the story, then put it to bed.

'I don't know for sure,' Sullivan said. 'We hadn't seen each other for about ten days, when she suddenly called me and we met up. In all the times me and Vinny met with DEA contacts we played it close to our chests, because we know how stuff gets out, and it was the same with Luisa – I never divulged anything to her that we were currently doing. But she knew the basics – that Vinny and me had infiltrated the Albanian and Colombian gangs and were working on the plans for a bust. That was all, though.' He paused for a long moment. 'That night, we slept together, but during the night I was a bit restless, and was aware that she had left the bed. I don't know why I was suspicious; I mean, she could have been in the bathroom for all I knew. But something told me to get up, and so I did. I quietly went into the hallway, and from where I stood, I could see that she had my phone in her hand, and although I couldn't be completely sure, it looked like she was reading my text messages.' He sighed, put his head back and looked forlorn. 'That's all I saw. I can't say if she was reading the texts, and anyway, Vinny and me were always careful what we texted to each other, so there would be nothing that crucial on it. But the fact that she was reading my texts . . . I mean, what the fuck! Why would she do that?' He shook his head. 'It was a couple of days later that Vinny disappeared. She hasn't been in touch since, and I haven't called her. Not even to tell her about Vinny.'

Jake had had a feeling from the moment he'd met Sullivan that he was deeply troubled, and not just about his missing cop mate. He could see now why finding Vinny was more important to him than any undercover job. They sat in heavy silence for a while, then Jake spoke.

'So, if this woman did betray you, who do you think she was working for? The Albanians? The Colombians?'

Sullivan shrugged. 'The Colombians would possibly make more sense – she spoke the language and has been here for a few years, so she would have seen how they've grown, known the main players.'

Again, they said nothing for a few moments.

'So how do you feel about getting in touch with her now?' Jake asked, then seeing the surprised look on his face he added, 'Maybe you could get some information out of her – see what she knows. If she's involved with these people, she might even know where Vinny is, if he's still alive. Or what has happened to him.'

Sullivan looked at him and blew out his cheeks.

'If I thought it would help, I've no problem with seeing her. But if she's set Vinny up, she's hardly going to tell me anything.'

Jake nodded slowly. 'Yeah,' he said. 'Might not be wise if she set him up. But if we could find a way to keep an eye on her, see who she's involved with. You never know where it might lead us.'

Sullivan said nothing, but from the look on his face, he was beginning to wonder what he'd got himself into by asking the Caseys for help.

CHAPTER NINE

Steven had slept very badly as he'd constantly replayed the scenes from the quarry. Every time he closed his eyes, he could see himself at the back of the car, heaving it to the edge and into the inky blackness. There was no way back from this. Whatever he felt, however repulsed he was about what had happened, the fact was that he was an accessory to murder. Actual murder. Christ! This was what people like Thomson and Lambie and scum like them did – and he'd heard tales of punishment beatings and whisperings about hits on individuals – but this wasn't who *he* was. Cold sweat prickled his body. What if the cops came calling? Even if he wanted to, he could hardly come clean and tell them what had happened. Because it was *his* shoulder pushing and shoving behind the car until it went over the edge. He was trapped. His chest felt like there was a belt tightening across it as he tried to breathe. He sat up, calming himself down until he managed a deep, slow breath. In the quietness, he could hear his mother, her phlegmy, rasping cough, and he sat until he could hear the coughing ease and the stillness return. From the crack in the curtains, he could see the rain heavy on the windows. He lay back down on the bed, praying for the morning to come. At least, then, he would be busy. He'd be making his mother breakfast, preparing a snack for her lunch, then heading to work in the pub. Much as he was dreading going to work, he knew he had to do it, get it over with. When they'd come back to Glasgow yesterday and Thomson had dropped him off outside his flat, he hadn't spoken. He'd simply said to him, 'See you tomorrow, Gimpy,' and turned away.

Steven was almost finished his shift at the bar, and he was counting down the minutes. All day, he'd been shattered, edgy, his head feeling like it was about to explode under the pressure. He wasn't even thinking straight, giving people the wrong change, the wrong drinks, or smashing a glass. He was like a zombie, barely getting through the day, all the time watching the door, expecting Lambie or Thomson to walk in. But they didn't, until fifteen minutes before he was due to clock off. When the door opened, it was Lambie he saw first and his stomach dropped as their eyes met. Lambie stood for a few beats staring straight at him, unblinking, until it was Steven who turned away. Thomson strolled up to the bar as Lambie took a seat in the corner.

'All right, Gimpy?' he said as he leaned on the bar.

Steven nodded.

'What can I get you, Gordy?'

Thomson leaned in a little, fixed him with a look, his mouth tight. 'I said you all right, Gimpy?'

Steven swallowed. 'Aye.' His mouth felt dry. He had no idea how to respond.

'Fine. Then keep it that way,' Thomson said. 'Two pints. Bring them over. Boss wants a word.'

Steven didn't answer. He was glad Thomson had turned to cross the bar, as his hands trembled a little when he lifted the pint tumblers and placed one under the font. *You have to calm down,* he told himself. *If these cunts get wind that you're shitting yourself, you'll be next.* Slowly, he pulled the pints, watched as his hands stopped shaking. He glanced around the bar; only four or five regulars were in, two of them playing pool and the others sitting with newspapers open in front of them, studying the horse racing. He picked up the pints of lager and came out from behind the bar, then crossed the room towards Lambie and Thomson. He placed the pints on the table, and stood awkwardly.

'Sit down, Gimpy,' Lambie said, his eyes flicking to the chair opposite him.

Steven sat down. He looked from Lambie to Thomson. He could hear his heart beat. He clasped his hands in front of his stomach in case they started shaking again.

Eventually, Lambie spoke. 'You all right, Gimpy?'

Steven managed a shallow breath and nodded.

'Aye.' Then he felt his face redden, and he couldn't stop himself. He leaned across the table. 'Well, er, I mean, fuck's sake, boss. I don't know what to say.'

Lambie lifted the pint to his lips and took a long drink. Thomson did the same. Steven felt light-headed. What the fuck was he supposed to say here?

'You don't know what to say?' Lambie said, his brows knitting as though he was confused or about to get angry. 'What do you mean?'

Steven looked from one to the other, frustration and fear and anger almost spilling over. But he knew he had to keep it in check.

'I mean, about yesterday, Dick.' He glanced at Thomson who was staring straight ahead. 'About Bo. About what happened.' He shook his head. 'Fuck me, man! I had no idea I was getting dragged into that.' He shifted uncomfortably in his seat. 'Fuck me!'

Again the silence. Then Lambie sighed and looked a little perplexed.

'Listen, son,' he said, in an almost fatherly tone. 'It was a bit of business that had to be dealt with. Bo was a fucking liability. You could see that yourself. Too much charlie and too big in the fucking mouth. There's no room for that in this business.'

A liability. He remembered Thomson saying that to him before he shot him.

'I mean, what if the cops find out?' As soon as he said it, Steven knew it was the wrong thing.

Thomson rolled his eyes in a Jesus-Fucking-Christ look. Lambie's face grew dark. He leaned across the table.

'Fuck the cops!' He lowered his voice. 'Get that out of your fucking head. Nobody is going to find out anything if you keep your mouth fucking zipped. Got that?'

'Of course. Christ! What the fuck would I want to tell anybody for? I was fucking there, for fuck's sake.'

'Aye. You were. And just remember that,' Lambie said, something close to a smirk on his lips. Then he said, 'Look, you did well enough yesterday, and you'll get a few extra quid on top of what I gave you. Okay?'

Steven said nothing. There was no point. Anything else he said here would be digging a hole for himself. The bar door opened and Geordie came in ready to start his shift.

'Time you were out of here,' Lambie said. 'On you go now.'

Steven stood up. Lambie gripped his wrist. 'And remember what I said. Keep it fucking shut.'

Steven looked down at him, then turned away towards the bar. He went into the back room, collected his jacket and went straight out of the door, without a glance in their direction.

On the way home, Steven took a detour and walked down to the Clydeside and along the Broomielaw, just to try and take his mind off where he was at this point. Once or twice he stopped, stood by the railing and looked down as the river flowed past, and he remembered one day years ago when he'd seen the cops and the riverboat picking up a bloated corpse from the river. Probably a suicide. Again, Steven was plunged into the image of the darkness of the quarry as the car went over. If he threw himself in here now, it would be over in a few minutes. All the fear, the hurt, the pain would be gone. But what about his ma? It would kill her. He walked on for another twenty minutes, the soft rain on his face and the physical exercise making him feel a little better. But he would never really feel better ever again, because everything had changed now. Everything. The lights on the hotels and bars along the Clyde and the traffic were all familiar, as if nothing had changed, but it had. And there was nothing he could do. He was a prisoner now. He looked at his watch. His mum would be expecting him home soon. He stopped at the supermarket on the way back and picked up some groceries that would do him and his mum for a couple of days. He had to put this shit out of his mind completely. He didn't know if he could do it, but he had no alternative but to try. Once into his street he turned into the tenement flat and went up to the second floor, pushing his key into the lock, surprised to find it open. Then as he went down the hallway, he stopped in his tracks. He could hear a man's voice. He froze. Then he heard his mother's voice. What the fuck! He took a couple of steps down the hall, his heart pounding.

'That you, son?'

'Aye, ma,' Steven said through a tight throat.

He walked towards the bedroom door and pushed it open, terrified of what would be on the other side. To his horror, it was big Gordy. Sitting there on the bedside chair next to his ma lying propped up on her pillows.

'I've got a visitor, Steven.' His mother smiled, but he could see it was more of a grimace. 'Your mate Gordy, from the pub.'

A cold calm came over Steven. Whatever he did here, he had to show nothing to his mother. This fucker was in his house for one reason only, to monster him. To let him know that he could get to him, to torment him with the thought that if he didn't keep his mouth shut, then Lambie and his mobsters could get to his mother. He suppressed the urge to scream, to cross the room and fucking throttle this cunt and throw him out of the window.

'Gordy!' he said. 'This is a surprise.' He glared at him. 'How did you get in?' He glanced at his mum. 'Ma, I told you not to open the door to anyone.'

'I didn't,' she said. 'Gordy said you must have left the lock off.'

Gordy smirked. Steven said nothing. No, he fucking didn't leave the lock off. He never did that. Even in the stupor he had been in that morning he would never leave without locking the front door. Gordy stood up.

'Anyway,' he said. 'I best be going now, Steven. I just popped round as I was in the area. But I'll away now and let you make your ma's dinner. She says you're a great cook, by the way.' He gave Steven a hefty squeeze that hurt his arm as he passed. 'You're full of surprises, you are.'

Steven said nothing. Rage and fear burning a hole in his gut.

'I'll let myself out,' Thomson said.

Then he left. Steven stood there, afraid to look at his ma for a moment, then he turned and rushed to the bathroom and promptly threw up. When he'd composed himself and came back into the bedroom, his ma was sitting on the side of the bed, trying to get up.

'Right, Steven,' she said, in a voice that used to reprimand him when he was young. 'You're in trouble, son, aren't you.'

Steven shook his head. 'No, Ma.' He knew she would see through him.

'Listen, son. I'm not going to hear any of your shit. Do you think I'm buttoned up the back? That bastard who came in here, was here for one reason. I know he broke in. But I'm a better liar than you and I played along with it. But I know why he was here. It was to threaten you. I'm right, am I not?'

Steven stood, tears in his eyes. He shook his head.

'Ma,' he said. 'I don't know what to do.'

'Tell me,' she said, motioning to the chair, wheezing, stretching her arms out for him to help her to her feet. 'Get me into the living room, and sit your arse down there and tell your ma what's going on. Because nothing and no bastard alive is going to threaten me or my boy.'

CHAPTER TEN

As the weeks went on, Kerry had buckled into prison life because there was nothing else for it. She'd taken a job in the workshop where the prisoners made greetings cards. The job was menial but hours went faster and the routine stopped her obsessing about her plight. She knew Marty would be working on all the legal aspects of the case to get her released, but it wasn't coming fast enough for her, and always there was the niggle that it might not even happen. The prospect of being stuck in here long term didn't even bear thinking about. She also knew that Jack and the troops would be all over Glasgow trying to find out who was behind the set-up, and retribution would be swift and deadly when they did. Kerry was even sleeping a little better since moving into a cell with Ash on the first floor. Despite Ash talking non-stop when they went to bed, at least she didn't feel under threat. She listened as Ash described her upbringing in the East End of Glasgow and how she had become resigned from an early age that there was no way out. In the darkness after lights out, Kerry had also found herself telling Ash some of her own story, about her father and of growing up in Maryhill, then being sent to Spain as a young teenager, away from any trouble in Glasgow. Ash was fascinated, and a good listener, and Kerry even told her about her brother Mickey's murder and her mum's shooting at the funeral, and that was how she reluctantly became head of the Casey empire, and how she was going to take them on to better things. Somehow, off-loading all of this to a complete stranger had been liberating, and as the days went on, Kerry wondered if she was naive to hope that in Ash she might have forged a loyal friendship that could continue after they were both out of this place.

In the communal area after dinner, Kerry watched as the bickering between two women became more heated. The pair of them – girls in their early twenties – were already celebrities in the jail since their recent arrival. Their stories had been plastered all over the media after they had been caught red-handed with suitcases of cocaine smuggled from Spain. It was clear from early on that despite the prospect of lengthy jail sentences, the women were enjoying the notoriety that the high profile case had brought them. Kerry had kept well away from them – as she had with almost everyone else in the prison apart from Ash and one or two other women – as well as making sure she gave Big Aggie and her cronies a wide berth. The arrival of the two drug-smuggler girls – Tracy and Libby – had shifted the emphasis away from Kerry, and she was glad they were now getting all the attention. Every time an update of their case appeared on the news, a good-natured roar went up in the community room, and Kerry couldn't quite understand why they were celebrating when their lives were being squandered. But it wasn't lost on her that when everything was stripped back, she was no better than them. The Caseys had made a pile of cash from the huge haul of cocaine they'd stolen from the Colombians. While the Caseys had cleaned the drugs money and invested it in their hotel and property business on the Costa del Sol, drugs mules like these two girls were lower down the food chain and used as fodder. Kerry had plenty of time to reflect on this in the long hours in jail, and sometimes she felt ashamed at who the Caseys were, who she was. But there was nothing she could do to change that except stiffen her resolve to make things different for her and her organisation.

She sat, flicking through a magazine, as the women tried to keep their voices down while they quarrelled.

'It was your fucking fault anyway,' Tracy, the tall, skinny girl with the long dark hair spat at her friend. 'You were the one who said it was all going to be so fucking easy.'

Libby, petite, blonde, with angry narrow eyes, turned to her. 'My fault? My fucking fault?' She leaned across to her mate. 'If you hadn't got into so much fucking debt and done your job right, they wouldn't have forced you into it.' She shook her head. 'You were told to just sell the fucking pills in the clubs, but that wasn't enough for you. You had to get fucking hooked on it yourself. Like a fucking zombie you were.'

Her friend sat in silent, simmering rage. She glanced around, where everyone who had been listening and watching quickly turned away and pretended to be uninterested. The prison officer at the tea area flicked a glance to her mate on the other side of the hall. Kerry felt uncomfortable. Ash pulled her chair a little closer to her and whispered, 'I think this is about to kick off.'

Kerry didn't answer. She checked the clock on the wall and wished the twenty minutes to lock-up would move faster so she could get away from this. Suddenly it was mayhem. The tall, skinny girl picked up her cup of hot tea and threw it over her pal. The scalded girl shrieked.

'You've fucking roasted me, you skinny cunt!'

Tracy's hands went over her face but she lashed out with her feet, and then everyone was on the pair of them, the wardens dragged them away from each other kicking and screaming. An alarm wailed and two other wardens came rushing in to break it up. Big Aggie and her crew waded into the mayhem, booting a couple of the wardens and punching and kicking anyone who came near them. Then from the corridor Natalie came shrieking towards them and started banging her head against the wall until two wardens grabbed her and held her down to save her from herself. More wardens arrived to break up the mêlée and shout to everyone to calm down or nobody was getting out of their cells at all tomorrow. Kerry sat, horrified. She could see that Tracy's face was scalded but it didn't look blistered yet. The tea they served was never boiling hot the way you would make it yourself – probably in case this kind of thing happened – but it was hot enough to hurt and burn. When things calmed a little, Tracy was taken away, presumably to the hospital wing. Her co-drug mule was escorted out without protest, no doubt headed for the governor's office. Free time was over, one of the senior wardens shouted, and everyone was ordered to their cells. Kerry lay on the bottom bunk, wishing she'd wake up from this nightmare, terrified that this might be the life her child would be born into, guilty that she was only in here because of who she was. She wouldn't have been framed if she wasn't Kerry Casey. She lay on her side, touching her stomach. She suddenly felt a little flutter of life, and she promised that no matter what happened, her baby would never have a life like the people around her. She would make sure of that.

In the morning, Kerry awoke with the same sinking feeling she did every day. She thought of Vinny, wondered where he was and if she would ever see him again. But right now this was where she was, and that little life pushing against her was all she needed to get through these days. Ash was already up and dressed, sitting on the top bunk, her legs dangling. When the doors clicked open, they went down to the breakfast room, ready for the morning ritual. The room was buzzing with the chatter about scenes from last night. Tracy and Libby were nowhere to be seen.

'Awright, Kerry?' Ash said, spooning cereal into her mouth.

'Yeah,' Kerry said, sitting down. 'That was some carry-on last night.'

'Aye,' Ash said. 'As I was telling you last night, it's not the first time I've seen it all kicking off in here. One of the lassies got stabbed by another prisoner the last time I was in. It was all over the papers.'

Kerry sighed and went and got herself some breakfast at the hatch where the women were dishing up eggs, bacon and sausages or yoghurt. When she came back, Ash was buttering toast and sipping from a mug of tea.

'It's all quietened down now. I think that Tracy is in the hospital. She's not bad though.'

'What will happen now?' Kerry asked. 'Will her mate get charged with assault?'

Ash shrugged. 'Dunno. The guv might see if she can sort it out. I mean these lassies were best mates, and what happened last night was all the frustration – blaming each other and stuff.'

'Do you know much about the girls?' Kerry asked.

'Only what I hear from the other lassies. They were mates out in Ibiza and working the clubs. Selling drugs is normal out there. I think one of them got into it and was taking more than she was giving back to the dealers, so they put her under pressure to bring stuff in.'

'Christ!'

'Probably what's happened is the dealers offered to clear Tracy's debt and give them four grand each.' She paused, looked at Kerry. 'It's not as if they could refuse, know what I mean?'

'Yeah.' Kerry nodded.

She saw one of the wardens coming towards their table and looking at her.

'Kerry,' the warden said, 'you've got a visitor later today. Only got word last night, but we were in the middle of all the scene here, or you would have been told.'

Kerry looked up, surprised. 'Who is it? My lawyer?'

The warden looked at the clipboard and checked.

'Someone called Sharon.'

Kerry waited in the visiting room, a routine that she'd become used to now with visits from Marty, or Jack or Maria in the past days. Much as she longed for and was delighted to see people, when the actual visiting moment came, she was always anxious over what news they might bring. Every time Marty visited, and that was at least twice in the past week, she prayed that it would be news that things were moving forward. Poor Marty. He always tried to stay positive, urging Kerry to be the same, that soon this would all be over. But each time he came, not much had changed. They were working on it day and night, his team scanning every scrap of evidence the police had. And Jack too told her that they would get to the bottom of this. He was his usual determined self, confident that the Caseys would find out who framed them and make them pay. He already had top hands out there, picking up any word on the street. Someone had to be behind this, but so far nothing was coming up. Maria had mostly just cried when she came, and that had set Kerry off as well. Both of them sitting there in tears, holding hands across the table, both of them wondering where those carefree girls they'd been as children in the streets of Maryhill had gone. Kerry was looking forward to seeing Sharon, and was glad Jack had suggested bringing her over from Spain to pitch in while Kerry was inside. He'd brought Vic over too. Not that the Caseys were short on numbers or muscle, but Jack felt that Vic had proven to be a class act, between his role in the smuggling of the Colombian cocaine, and then escaping jail in Spain. He told Kerry it would be good to have a man like that at his side while Danny was being held in remand in Barlinnie prison.

As she waited, Kerry noticed Tracy was being brought in by one of the wardens. Her face was scarlet and angry from the scalding on one side, but not blistered, and she looked as though she'd been crying. Kerry sat a few places away from her, and made a sympathetic face when the girl sat down.

'Fuck are you looking at?' Tracy spat.

Kerry didn't answer, but looked away. There was no point in trying to make any conversation with Tracy, and the last thing she needed was to make any more enemies. Then the doors opened and the visitors filed in. When Sharon appeared, Kerry saw her stop in her tracks for a moment and look across at her. She flashed her perfect five grand smile and sashayed towards her. Then when she got within hugging distance, Sharon held out her hands in a gesture of how-the-hell-did-it come-to-this. Strangely, just seeing her, and the brassy confident way she strode into a place like this, gave Kerry a boost. If the tables were turned, Sharon would no doubt be running the show in here in a week. Kerry stood up and Sharon took her in her arms and hugged her hard. Kerry bit her lip to hold back the tears that were never far away these days. When they parted, Sharon gave the place a cursory glance around.

'Not the worst gaff I've been in.' She shrugged, planking herself on a chair.

'You've been in jail?'

'No. Not as a guest. But visited plenty,' she said. 'Obviously when Knuckles was inside. But also a couple of women I've known over the years ended up inside. Long time ago, but I can tell you it was nothing like this.'

'It's not exactly cushy,' Kerry said. 'I'm sharing a cell and there's not even a toilet or shower. Once you're locked up that's you in for the night!' She shook her head and smiled 'I'm so glad to see you, Sharon.'

'How are you, girl?' Sharon searched her face. 'Are they looking after you all right? How you bearing up? I would have come sooner but I've been up to my eyes.'

In this kind of backs-to-the-wall mood, Kerry could see that the last thing Sharon would expect from Kerry was tears. She'd have to man up, and Sharon was just the woman to tell her that, if she started blubbing. She swallowed the lump in her throat and pulled herself up straight. She told her about the first couple of nights, sharing with Natalie, and then of the unprovoked verbal attack by Big Aggie which terrified her. But she didn't want to make a big deal of it in front of Sharon, who'd seen much more hardship in life than she had.

'It's not bad, actually. I mean, for a prison, it's not bad. You get fed all right, and your time is taken up. And to be honest, most of the girls are all right.' She shook her head. 'Some of them are poor souls. Girls who didn't even get a chance in life.'

Sharon nodded. 'Yeah. I'd say half of them are like that. Poor bastards.'

'I'm so glad you came, Sharon. Thanks. What about your Tommy? Did you bring him with you from Spain?'

'No. Little bugger wanted to come with me – bunk off

school for a bit and come here – but I wouldn't let him. He's staying with a good friend of the Caseys. Irish family, and he's mates with their son, so it's all good. And he's well protected with them.'

'So how are things over on the Costa? I feel as though I've been here for ages, not being on the phone every day being briefed by you and everyone else.'

Sharon sat forward, clasped her hands.

'Well, it's all going just about as well as it can over there. Fingers crossed, we're only a few months away from the grand opening of the best hotel complex on the Costa del Sol. So far there's been no trouble, security is tight as a duck's arse, and the place is looking fantastic.' She smiled. 'But don't worry, pet, you'll be out of here in no time and over there putting your own mark on it. I promise you that.'

For a long moment they sat there, Kerry appreciating her enthusiasm, but still her heart sinking a little.

'I hope so,' she said. 'But every time I see Marty or Jack – I know they are working their butts off – nothing's happening yet.'

'It will, pet. It will,' Sharon said. 'Sometimes, if you shake the trees at the right moment, something good falls out, and that's what will happen here. Trust me.'

Kerry nodded, more to please Sharon than to convince herself.

'So how are things since you came back? Is Jack doing all right?'

'Yes,' she replied. 'Vic and Jack are working away behind the scenes. Someone obviously set you and Danny up, so it's just a question of finding out who. Once that happens, the rest will be easy. Whoever did this will fall apart. So just give it a bit of time.'

Kerry managed a smile.. 'I felt the baby move a little last night. It happens mostly when I'm in bed.' As soon as she said it, Kerry regretted it, because she could feel her eyes filling up. She touched her mouth and tightened her lips. 'Sorry. I'm not going to cry, but it's always a great moment, and sometimes it gets to me that I'm feeling my baby move in a place like this.'

Sharon reached across and touched her hand. 'Never mind that, girl. Your little baby will know nothing of this, and by the time it's born, you'll be relaxing at home.'

Kerry smiled in appreciation. Then changed the subject.

'Still no news of Vinny,' she sighed. 'It's so hard to come to terms with it on top of everything else that's going on. Was there just nothing on the grapevine in Spain over the recent weeks?'

Sharon gave a perplexed sigh, shaking her head.

'No, love. Nothing at all. I'm not sure I would have heard anything anyway, given how these guys work undercover. But I know plenty of villains over there who hear things, and nobody's cracked a light, not even anything about a cop going missing.' She paused. 'But you've got Jake Cahill on the case, I hear, and that copper guy who was working with Vinny. So something will happen. I'd trust Jake with my life - more than that, he saved my life. If anyone can track down Vinny, then it's Jake. You just have to keep yourself up, make sure you eat properly and keep your spirits up. This will be over soon, Kerry. It will.'

Kerry nodded. Then she listened as Sharon told her about Vic and how it had been lovely to have him back in her life. She noted that Sharon was careful not to paint too rosy a picture because of Kerry's own situation, but she could see from her demeanour that she wasn't just being tough and determined, but that she was the happiest she'd ever seen her. And Kerry was happy for her. If anyone deserved a break it was her. Eventually the bell went, signalling visiting over, and Sharon stood up. She opened her arms.

'Come on then. Big hugs. Not tears, pet. That's not how big girls are.'

Kerry couldn't help but smile at the grittiness of her friend, and she resolved there and then to be brave and more like her.

CHAPTER ELEVEN

Once Steven had settled his ma in bed and put a movie on for her to watch, he sat in the living room staring blankly at the screen on his laptop. He felt ashamed and guilty that he'd buckled under the shock of Thomson's menacing visit, and had spilled everything out to her earlier. He'd had no option really, because she'd insisted he tell her what the hell was going on, and promised that no matter what he told her it wouldn't shock her. Steven had sat there, fighting back tears, and told her what had happened at the quarry, and that he was now a part of a murder. His ma had sat quietly listening, her mouth set in anger that he had been compromised by the hoodlums he worked for, but she'd said he should have told her before it got this far. He'd told her about what he'd overheard in the scrapyard from spaced-out Bo, that Kerry Casey and her uncle had been framed by Lambie and his mob for murder. He said he didn't know why they'd done it, but it was clear that they had. It was as though some steely rage had taken over his ma, as she'd listened, shaking her head occasionally in disbelief. They'd sat in silence for a while once he'd finished the story.

'So what do you know about this Kerry Casey and her mob then?' his ma had asked, finally breaking the silence.

Steven shrugged. 'Only what I've read in the papers, and stuff a while ago when her ma got killed at her brother's funeral. I'd heard of that Mickey – the brother who got killed by some mobsters from Manchester. But I don't know too much about them.' He paused. 'They're big stuff though. Bigger than Lambie and his crowd. But at the end of the day, they're all the same. Gangsters.'

His ma nodded. 'I suppose so. But that girl is in jail for something she didn't do, so right now she needs all the help she can get.'

Steven had looked at her, but said nothing. It had crossed his mind at one point that he should get in touch with them. But that would be like signing his own death warrant. Wouldn't it? His ma had said nothing more, just looked at him with a determination that he hadn't seen in her face for a very long time.

'Take me into my bed, son,' she'd said. 'Tomorrow's another day.'

Now alone, Steven typed in 'Kerry Casey murder charges' on his laptop on Google search, and several newspaper headlines with the story appeared. He called up the latest one, her court appearance, and saw that her lawyer was Marty Kane. He knew, from trials over the years, that Kane was the famous defence lawyer who always seemed to get criminals off serious charges. Then he searched for his legal firm in Glasgow and found the phone number. But at eight thirty in the evening, there would be nobody there. He looked and found an out-of-hours phone number, and before he could stop himself he pushed the call key on his mobile. A woman's voice answered.

'Kane Associates, can I help you?'

Steven found himself suddenly struck dumb. He hadn't even thought through his opening line. He wanted to hang up, call back when he'd worked out what he was going to say, then the voice again.

'Hello? Kane Associates? How may I help you?'

He swallowed and eventually spoke. 'Hello. Sorry. I was looking to speak to Mr Kane. Marty Kane? Is he there?' Steven cursed himself. As if a top lawyer would be sitting by the phone at this time of night.

'No. Mr Kane is not here, I'm afraid. This is the out-of-hours number for Kane Associates, but perhaps I can help? Are you a client of Mr Kane's? Have you been arrested by police?'

'No, no,' Steven blurted. 'Not a client. I . . . I've not been arrested. But I wanted to speak to Mr Kane. It's a . . . It's ab . . . about Kerry Casey.'

Silence from the other side for what seemed like a long time.

'Kerry Casey,' the woman finally said. 'Do you want to give me an idea what you want to talk about regarding Miss Casey?'

Steven was flustered. He did not want to go blurting anything out over the phone. He should hang up before it was too late. But he couldn't. He had to make some kind of move here.

'Actually I'd rather not say at the moment. But I'd like to speak to Mr Kane if that was possible?' He paused. 'I . . . I have some information that may help Kerry Casey.'

Another brief silence, then the woman spoke. 'Okay, do you want to give me a name, a number, and I can let Mr Kane know?'

Steven hesitated a few seconds. 'Yes.' He reeled off his name and mobile.

'Thank you,' the woman said. 'I'll get Mr Kane to call you. It may not be tonight though, possibly in the morning. But I'll pass your number on to him.'

'Thanks.' Steven hung up, and sat back on the chair. What the Christ was he doing? he asked himself.

He went into the kitchen and shoved the kettle under the tap and put it on to boil. He stood, looking out of the kitchen window at the drizzle. When his mobile rang at the same time as the kettle pinged, Steven jumped. He dashed into the living room and picked up his phone. It was a mobile, no name on the screen. He didn't say anything when he slid the accept key.

'Steven? Marty Kane here.' The voice was sharp, clear. 'You called my office? The out-of-hours lawyer passed your number.'

'Y-Yes. I called you, Mr Kane.'

'Good. I'm glad you did. You have some information regarding Kerry Casey, my assistant tells me?'

Steven took a breath and swallowed the dry ball in his mouth. The man sounded firm but friendly.

'Yes. I have,' Steven said. 'I know something. I . . . I know she didn't do that murder . . . I mean, kill them guys.'

A brief silence, then Kane spoke. 'Okay. And can I ask you, Steven, how you know this?'

'I . . . I don't know if I want to say anything over the phone. To be honest . . .' He paused, could feel the tension building up. 'I'm scared, Mr Kane. Because of what I know.'

Two beats, then Kane again. 'Okay, Steven. I understand that you may not want to speak on the phone, but if you have information, then as Kerry Casey's lawyer, I'd love to hear it. So how about we have a meeting? We could talk face to face?'

The lawyer seemed friendly, understanding. Steven stood for a moment, the phone pressed so hard to his ear it was beginning to hurt.

'Yes,' he finally said. 'We could meet. I'm okay with that.

But I don't want to go to any office. I . . . I can't be seen. You know what I mean?'

'I do, Steven. And don't worry. We will meet away from the office.' The lawyer paused. 'How about tonight? Can we meet tonight?'

'Tonight?' Surprised, Steven heard his voice go up an octave. 'You mean like now?'

'Sure. As soon as you can.'

'Oh. Well. Yes. Okay, I suppose.'

'Good stuff. Tell you what, Steven. Let me give one of my people a ring, and I'll call you back in five minutes. You okay with that?'

'Yes,' Steven said, not really knowing if he was okay or not, his mind almost paralysed with panic.

'Let me call you right back,' Kane said, and the phone went dead.

Steven stood for a moment, staring at the phone, catching his breath. He'd done it now. He'd made the call. He wasn't even sure he was doing the right thing, but right now he didn't have a lot of options. He went back into the kitchen and finished making his tea as though he was on automatic pilot, and somehow making a cup of tea normalised everything he was engulfed in. By the time he poured it into a mug, his mobile rang in his pocket.

'Steven.' The voice of Marty Kane.

'Hello, Mr Kane.'

'Are you in Glasgow?'

'Yes. I am.'

'Great. How about we meet in twenty minutes at Waxy O'Connor's? You know it? It's just off Queen Street Station. It's a quiet enough place.'

'Aye. Yes. I can go there. It's not that far from me.'

'Perfect. I'll see you there in twenty minutes and we can have a chat then. You okay with that?'

'Yes. I'll be there, Mr Kane.'

'Good. How will I recognise you?'

'I have a limp.'

'Okay. Twenty minutes then.'

The line went dead.

CHAPTER TWELVE

Jake had been tailing the Spanish undercover cop, Luisa, and it was looking more and more like she was a dirty cop. He'd enlisted the help of Sergio, one of his oldest contacts on the Costa del Sol, an ex-Guardia Civil cop, who'd been bumped out of the force for shooting a people-trafficker he was supposed to be arresting. Sergio knew who every player was among the various cartels who ran the show – from English to Dutch to Colombians, as well as the Spanish hard men who ran their own gangs and worked with all of them. As soon as Jake had mentioned Luisa's name to him, he'd known who she was. Sergio knew she was undercover, so it was no surprise when she'd been seen in the company of major drug dealers. But the people they'd observed her with over the last few days were not the kind of criminals she would be getting that close to if she was a cop. It was good to have Sergio's insight, but for now Jake was on his own.

He had watched from a safe distance as Luisa left her apartment in Mijas Costa, then followed her car all the way along the coast to Tarifa. The small town was as far south as you could go in Spain, and the next stop was the ferry to Tangier. Jake had trusted Sergio enough to tell him that he was trying to find a missing British under-cover cop. But the Spanish ex-cop had been surprised that Jake's information indicated that Vinny may be being held in Tarifa. As far as Sergio knew, and he knew a lot, the car-tels had no base of any note in Tarifa. The town was too small, and there were too many authorities swarming around because of the ferry traffic to Tangier to make it a viable base. But he supposed it just might be the kind of place they would keep someone they'd kidnapped holed up in an apartment. And now, Jake followed Luisa's car, keep-ing three vehicles behind as she drove into the warren of tight streets that made up the old town. She parked her car, and he ditched his close by, then he watched from a doorway as she disappeared into a building at the corner of a side street that led into the heart of the town. There were a few tourists wandering around some of the little gift shops, so he didn't look out of place as went into a small bar close by and sat at the counter so that he could still see onto the street. He ordered a coffee and some tapas as he scanned the building opposite. It looked more like local residential accommodation than the holiday rental apartments you saw dotted along the seafront. There were four floors, with one main security entrance, steel bars on all of the windows. Only the top floor had the steel shutters pulled down, which usually meant the residents were out for the day, or it was unoccupied. Jake sipped his coffee, nibbled at the tapas and waited. So much of what he did involved waiting and watching, and he was a patient man. Nearly an hour later, Jake was still waiting, on his second coffee and reading the newspaper for a third time. Then he noticed the main door of the apartment open and two men come out. They stood for a moment, glancing around them as one of them lit a cigarette and offered one to the other. They looked in their thirties or early forties, dark stubble and grubbily dressed. Jake kept his head in the newspaper but from behind his dark glasses, his eagle eyes homed in on the unmistakable bulge in the waistband of both the men. They were armed. For a few moments they stood there, not even talking or looking at each other. Then the door opened again, and Luisa came out. Jake kept his eyes on them as all three walked towards the bar where he was sitting.

They stood in the doorway, glancing around the empty place, one of them looking straight at him. Jake ordered another coffee from the barman and turned away from them to face the gantry. He was glad when two couples who looked like British tourists walked into the bar from the street. In the mirrored gantry, Jake watched as the Spaniards sat at a table in the corner, before one of them came up to the bar and ordered three beers, then ambled back, pulled out a chair and plonked himself down with the others. The Brits at the bar were ordering tapas and beers. They were just off the ferry from a trip to Tangier and were raving about the atmosphere and the industrial-scale hard selling of the Moroccans from the moment they'd stepped off the boat. As they opened their plastic bags and compared trinkets they'd bought, they were laughing. Jake was glad they were a distraction from his lone figure at the bar. He sipped his coffee, and in the pauses of the Brits' chatter, he listened hard, trying to pick up any thread of the Spaniards' conversation. It was difficult as they spoke quickly and in lowered voices, but his Spanish was good enough to make out some of what they said. One of the men seemed to be frustrated, looking at Luisa as he spoke. Jake was sure he said something about being pig sick of staying in the apartment, and it was only supposed to be for a few days. Luisa seemed to be trying to placate him, and he heard her whisper the words 'Soon it will be over'. *What will be over?* Jake wondered. Of course, they could be talking about a drug deal or anything in their personal lives, if it hadn't been for the fact that Luisa might be a bent cop, and her two amigos were armed. They might even have been undercover cops, but Jake suspected not. If they were talking about someone they were holding in the apartment, then the words, 'soon it will be over', were not good. If it *was* Vinny, and they had kidnapped him, then those sorts of people didn't just let their captives go free. Jake decided to sit tight. He read the newspaper again for a few minutes then watched as they drank up and left. When they did, they stood outside for a moment as Luisa spoke to them. Then one of the men went along the street towards a small supermarket, and the other went back into the house. Luisa went back to where she'd parked her car, and Jake wandered around the street behind the building to see if there was a fire escape outside. There wasn't. Only one way in. He allowed enough time for Luisa to be back in her car and on her way out of the village before he went back to his car, and followed.

Jake watched the look on Sullivan's face as he walked through the doors into Party Pam's lap-dancing bar tucked away in the backstreets of Fuengirola. The cop stood for a moment, scanning the dimly lit room. A stag party was in full, tacky swing, as a topless girl gyrated her hips over one of the lads who sat grinning, his hands firmly by his sides. The big black bouncer stood nearby, leaning on a fake stone pillar, poised in case any of the stags reached out to the girl. Sullivan eventually found Jake sitting at the circular bar, close to the edge of the stage where a half-naked waif wrapped herself around a metal pole. Jake, his arms leaning on the bar, swirled his glass of whisky and turned his head as Sullivan came up beside him.

'Party Pam's?' Sullivan rolled his eyes.

Jake shrugged. 'It's far enough away, and I'm friends with the owner.'

He jerked his head towards the bar where a brassy blonde in a leather miniskirt and thigh-high leather boots stood watching the pair of them.

'Is that Party Pam?' Sullivan asked, his face breaking into a smile.

'It is,' Jake said. 'But I've known her since she was just Pam.'

Sullivan snorted, bewildered, as the barmaid came over and leaned towards them, all cleavage and whiffs of perfume.

'What can I get you, sir?' She looked at him, then at Jake.

Sullivan pointed to Jake's glass. 'One of them, please,' he said.

'Jack Daniel's,' Pam said. 'You want another, Jake?'

Jake nodded, threw back the last of his drink and pushed the glass towards her. Pam poured two hefty measures of Jack Daniel's over ice and placed them on the bar. She caught Jake's eye and smiled, then retreated to the other side of the bar where two punters sat taking in the floor show.

'Surprised I didn't know about this place all the time I've been out here with Vinny,' Sullivan said, sitting up on a stool beside Jake. 'I mean, lap-dancing bars are not really my thing, but it might be the kind of place some of the low-ranking dealers would come to.'

'It's only been a lap-dancing bar for a year,' Jake said. 'It used to be just called Pam's. She ran it with her husband for years, but he died. Unknown to her, all the time she'd been running the place, her man was up to his arse in debt with the thugs who run the protection rackets along here. So suddenly, she's told that she either changes the bar to suit what they think will make money, or she fucks off with nothing. She's a good woman and a good friend. And one of these days those bastards will get their comeuppance.' He turned away from Sullivan, and flicked a glance at Pam. 'She knows a lot of people. Not much moves along the coast here that Pam doesn't hear about.'

Sullivan nodded but said nothing.

For a moment they didn't speak, then Jake asked, 'So, you heard anything on the ground since the other night?'

Sullivan sighed. 'A bit,' he said. 'I spoke to one of my Spanish contacts yesterday and he told me that he heard the Colombians did take an undercover cop. That was all he knew. But he said they killed him.' Sullivan shook his head, depressed. 'Shit. I hope he's got that wrong.'

After a long moment, Jake leaned a little closer.

'Listen, Sullivan. The word I'm getting is that an undercover cop who got snatched might be in Tarifa. The guy told me he didn't know his name, but I don't suppose they're kidnapping undercover cops every day. So if it's true, it has to be Vinny.'

'Any more details? We should go there, should we not?' Sullivan suddenly brightened.

Jake looked at him for a few beats.

'I already did,' he said. 'I was there today.'

Sullivan's face fell. 'Oh.'

Jake could see the frustration and disappointment.

'Look, Sullivan,' Jake said, 'it wasn't the time to be going together. Trust me on that. And anyway, I was following your bird Luisa.'

'She's not my bird, Jake. Come on.'

'Fair enough. I'm not trying to put you down, but some things I am better doing alone. That's how I do business. You need to understand that. You're not in the cops now, with a team briefing every day. I do things my own way. Okay?' He paused, looking at Sullivan who swallowed the put-down. 'Anyway. I was tailing Luisa, and she went right into Tarifa.'

'Really?'

'More than that,' Jake said. 'I'd got a tip about Tarifa a couple of days ago, but was waiting for the right time. I wanted to do a recce first, to see if anything stood out. It's a funny little place – a lot of Moroccans live there, but lots of Spanish too, and there are also tourists around. And plenty of security around the harbour where the ferry goes to Tangier. It wouldn't be an ideal place to hide someone – plus it's well down the road from here. But if they had an apartment or something, they could blend in like locals.'

'So what happened?' Sullivan asked.

Jake told him about the bar and the building with the

shutters, and how two guys had come out of the building followed by Luisa. He told him about the snatches of conversation he'd overheard, and how the guys had stayed on but Luisa had gone back to her car.

'I followed her all the way back and she went into Marbella to a bar on the seafront. The place was busy, but she must have been meeting somebody. I managed to get a good vantage point and I watched as she met with these two guys.'

Jake picked up his phone from the bar and showed Sullivan a picture of Luisa sitting in the bar with a well-dressed middle-aged man and a younger, burly-looking guy who could be the older man's minder. He watched the shocked look on Sullivan's face as he took the phone from his hands and looked closely at the pictures.

'Christ, Jake.' He shook his head. 'That's Diego Lopez. The older guy. He's the top man, for fuck's sake! The Colombians sent him over here after Pepe Rodriguez got shot during the shitstorm with Kerry Casey's gang.'

He looked at Jake, who kept his face impassive. An image flashed into his mind of him firing his sniper rifle from high up in the hills right into Rodriguez's chest. One of his best hits.

'I heard on the grapevine,' Jake said, 'that the Colombians had sent someone to take over. But I've never seen him. From what I hear, he keeps in the background. Not flashy and strutting around the way Rodriguez did. And he doesn't do business with anyone from the UK or Dublin any more. Only deals with the Spanish and other crews . . . And, of course, perhaps the Albanians these days, as you discovered.'

'Do you think they took Vinny as some kind of revenge because of the Casey war? To get back at Kerry?'

Jake shrugged. 'I don't know. How would they even know who Vinny was? He was just an undercover cop, and even if they'd worked out that he was actually a cop, they wouldn't know there was any connection to Kerry Casey. How would they know that?'

Jake watched as Sullivan suddenly looked like he was going to fall off his stool. His head sank to his chest and he stayed that way for a few beats. Then he looked up at Jake, fear in his eyes. Jake knew the answer before Sullivan even spoke. He closed his eyes and let out a long sigh.

'Fuck me, Sullivan!' He glared at him and lowered his voice. 'You fucking told Luisa? What kind of fucking pillow talk was that, for Christ's sake?'

Jake controlled his rising anger. Rage never got people anywhere. But he couldn't believe how naive this guy was.

Sullivan put his head in his hands.

'What the fuck did you tell her? Did she ever meet Vinny?'

Sullivan nodded. 'Only once. We were all undercover cops. All in this together. Or so we believed.'

Jake shook his head in disbelief. 'Yeah. Until you're not

fucking in it together,' he said. 'What did you tell her? *When* did you tell her?'

Sullivan sat saying nothing as the music thumped out and the dancers swirled and twirled their routine. Pam was at the edge of the bar, watchful. Then he spoke.

'It was one night after a long dinner. When I was getting to know Luisa a bit more and finding out about her life, her family and background. We both talked about life and stuff. There was a lot of wine drunk, and we were talking about the Colombians and the way they operate. I mean, we were on the same side, Jake. We were working for the same thing. Then I told her about Vinny and the Caseys and that he was involved with Kerry Casey.'

'Did you tell her that she was pregnant with Vinny's baby?'

Sullivan dropped his head to his chest.

'Fuck's sake!' Jake muttered.

CHAPTER THIRTEEN

Waxy O'Connor's pub was big, shadowy and spread out, with dark corners and secret nooks that you could hide in if you wanted to keep your company private. Steven was glad of that, and also that the Irish bar was the kind of place customers of the White Horse would not be seen dead in. In the White Horse, anything Irish or Catholic was considered a no-go area, so at least he wouldn't bump into any punters who might mention that they'd seen him here. He was soaked through by the time he got to the pub, having been caught in a downpour as he left his flat and headed up to the place. Once inside, he shook the rain off his hair and stood just at the doorway, his eyes flicking around the main bar area. The place was quiet – only a handful of people were at a couple of tables. None of them looked in his direction as he came in, and from the images of Marty Kane he'd seen on his laptop, he definitely wasn't there. He looked at his watch, and he was bang on time.

The barman eyed him as he walked across the room and nodded to him, but he didn't order a drink. He went around a corner and into a dark wood-panelled area where there was another, smaller, bar. Two men were at a table and they both looked up. One of them was definitely Marty Kane. Steven acknowledged them and walked across. He was conscious of the other guy glancing at him as he limped towards them.

'Steven.' Marty Kane stood up, stretching his hand out. 'Thanks for coming.'

'Mr Kane,' he said, quietly. The lawyer's handshake was firm and warm.

Steven raised his eyebrows at the other man next to him who stood up.

'This is Jack,' Kane said. 'He's one of the main men in the Casey organisation, and a close friend of Kerry and Danny.'

Steven shook the outstretched hand of the big man, but his expression had none of the softness of Kane's. It made him feel a little uneasy, and the lawyer seemed to notice it.

'I asked Jack to accompany me, Steven,' he said, motioning them to sit down. 'He's helping run things for the organisation at the moment while Kerry and her uncle are being held.' He paused, lowered his voice. 'Jack is also very interested to hear any information or help you might be able to give us.' He put his hands out in a placating gesture. 'Now, just relax. You're not in any danger here, so don't worry. And listen: if you're concerned that you have something to tell us that might put you in danger, then don't worry. We will look after you.'

Steven didn't answer, because he didn't know what to say. But he guessed that Jack was one of the main henchmen in the Casey gang, and if Steven was going to throw any light on who might have framed Kerry, then this guy would be desperate to get his hands on them.

'What you drinking, Steven?' Jack asked, standing up.

'Just a pint of lager, please.'

Jack said nothing and went to the bar. Steven could see both their glasses were full. Kane's looked like a whisky and ice, and Jack's was a pint of Guinness.

They sat for a moment not speaking while Jack went to the bar. Steven wiped away a drip of rain that was trickling down his face, conscious that Kane was watching him.

'You all right?'

'Aye.' Steven nodded. 'Bit nervous though. I thought you'd be on your own.'

Kane glanced up at the bar.

'Don't concern yourself about Jack,' he said. 'He's one of the most decent men I know. Like family to the Caseys. As I said, we'll look after you. Okay?'

Steven nodded again. He got the message. Jack came back from the bar and placed the pint in front of Steven.

'There you go, mate,' he said, sitting down.

'Cheers.'

Steven didn't think he wanted to call this big guy 'mate',

not yet, anyway. He lifted his glass and took a long drink, then placed it back down. After a long moment, Kane leaned a little closer.

'So, Steven. You said on the phone that you knew that Kerry Casey was innocent.' He raised his eyebrows. 'How do you know that?'

Steven swallowed and nervously ran a hand across his face.

'Well . . . Because I know, or I think I know . . . actually I'm sure I know, who did it,' he said. 'It was a set-up.'

He saw Jack, his arms folded as he sat back, glance at Kane, but nobody spoke. He knew they were waiting for him to elaborate. He took a swig of his drink and sniffed.

'Look,' he said. 'It's best if I start at the beginning, fill you in on where I work and who I work for. And how I know who did it. Is that okay?'

'Of course,' Kane said. 'Take your time. Nobody is in a hurry here. Just tell whatever you want, however you want.'

Steven took a breath and puffed out as he tried to relax. The only thing to do now was to let it all go.

'I'm a barman in the White Horse,' he said. 'You know it?'

Jack nodded slowly but said nothing.

'I know it,' Kane said. 'Big Rangers pub down the road.'

'More than just Rangers, Mr Kane. It's a UVF shop. You know, Ulster Loyalists?' He leaned in and spoke in a whisper. 'Ulster Volunteer Force.' He glanced at Jack who was nodding silently and fixing him with dark eyes.

'I'm aware of that too,' Kane said. 'Oh, and please, not Mr Kane. Call me Marty, Steven.'

'Okay, er . . . Marty,' Steven said, a little awkwardly. 'You might know that the pub is owned by Dick Lambie?' He turned to Jack, whose eyes blinked a yes and looked at Kane.

Then Jack spoke. 'Yep. I know that too. I don't know Lambie, but I know of him. He's a bitter Orange bastard; more than that, a big UVF man. He does what he's told. Takes his orders from Belfast.'

Steven nodded. 'That's seems right. The bands practise in the back room of the pub on a Monday night, but it's all a front for UVF training. I've seen them in there – weapons and stuff.'

'Aye. Not at all surprised.'

Steven took a drink, and sat for a long moment. Whatever he said now, there was no going back. He would be a marked man for the rest of his life. He could feel the nerves in his stomach travel up to his chest and neck and his mouth was dry. He could see Jack and Marty looking at him, waiting. He had to say something.

'Look, guys,' he said. 'I'm honestly shitting myself here. If it ever gets back that I'm doing this there will be a bullet in my head. No doubt about it. I . . . I . . .' He covered his face with his hands for a second. Then he felt a hand on his. It was Jack, pulling his hands away and looking straight at him.

'Listen, son,' he said, his hand holding his wrist tight. 'You have nothing to fear, because once you tell us what you know, we will take over. You will be safe. You understand that?'

Steven almost buckled at the sincerity in the big man's face. He meant it. But could he really trust him? What if they just used him and disposed of him the way Lambie did with Bo? But he'd come this far, so it was too late to cut and run. If he didn't tell them now, they'd come looking for him and make him talk. Yet his gut told him there was something decent about this big guy, and he glanced at Marty who was waiting patiently for his next move.

'I . . . I've got my ma though,' Steven said. 'I live with my ma, and she's old and stuff and she's got emphysema. She's not well. So it's not just me I have to worry about, it's her an' all. I mean, for fuck's sake, I came into the house the other day and this fucker was sitting at her bedside. He'd just done that to frighten the shit out of me – broke in, to let me know that he could get to my ma if I opened my mouth.'

Steven stopped and bit his lip as tears sprang to his eyes. His head dropped to his chest. *These guys must think I'm a right tit*, he thought, trying to compose himself.

'I'm sorry,' he sniffed. 'It's just that she's the most important thing to me. And I've put her in danger.'

Marty reached across. 'Okay, listen, Steven. Just take your time. I know you're scared, but just take it easy.'

'Aye,' Jack said. 'Don't you worry about your ma. We'll look after her too.' He grabbed his arm again. 'Listen to me, son. We can get you and your ma away from here. If that's what you want.'

Steven looked at him, surprised. He hadn't expected this. Christ, he didn't know what he was expecting. He hadn't even thought this through. He just knew that he had nowhere to turn, and going to the Caseys had seemed his only option.

'You can? You'll make sure she's all right?'

'Of course.' Jack nodded slowly. 'Now, go on. Tell us from the start. Everything you know. In your own time.'

'Okay,' Steven said.

Then he began his story. He told them everything. He started with how long he'd worked at the bar, the insults and bullying of the hard men who drank in the place, who had slagged him about his limp. How they called him Gimpy – the name that had stuck with him all through childhood after he'd had polio. He could see they were hanging on his every word, glancing at each other from time to time, as he told them about how he'd been roped into the loan-sharking, had borrowed a small amount of money, and had had to work for Lambie as a result and would never be able to pay his debt because of the extortionate interest. And then he told them about Gordy Thomson, of Bo and the quarry, and how he'd been a part of it, forced to help in the execution, because that was what it had been. He said how he'd been shocked when Bo had said earlier that day that he was part of the set-up of Kerry Casey. And that he'd also executed another guy months earlier for Lambie's mob. And he told them how Lambie had told him to keep his mouth shut. He'd thought about going to the police there and then, because he knew that Kerry Casey was innocent, but it was too dangerous. Eventually, when he finished, he sat forward with his head in his hands. He had no idea what was going to happen from here, but the life that he'd been living was about to change and he would have no control over it. They sat for a long time in silence. Finally, Jack spoke.

'So it was Lambie and his men who did the hit. They executed these two guys and made it look like it was Kerry and Danny.' He spoke as though he was narrating the story, his eyes burning with rage. He shook his head, then whispered, 'Cunts. They won't know what hit them.'

Steven glanced at Marty whose face showed nothing. He wondered how much this guy was really involved in all the things they said the Caseys had done over the years. But right now it didn't matter. He was in their hands.

'So,' Steven eventually said. 'What now? I mean, what do I do now?'

Silence. Jack looked at Marty then to Steven.

'Here's what you do, Steven,' Jack said. 'You go to your work tomorrow as normal. Can you handle that?'

Steven puffed. 'I think so. I'll have to.'

'Right. You have to be able to pull that off. You go as if everything is normal, and you finish your shift, then you go home. And that's it. You'll be out of it for ever.'

'What? What do you mean?'

'You've told your ma everything, right?'

'Yeah, I have.'

'Okay. So how ill is she? I mean, can she move? Can she be moved out of the house to another place?'

Steven ran a hand through his hair.

'Aye. She can walk. But not far. She gets oxygen and medication. But she could be moved.'

'Okay. Then you go home from here. Get some stuff together you need – clothes or things you need to pack. Not everything you own. Just enough to keep you going. Get everything together, and we will take care of the rest.'

'What do you mean?'

'We'll find a place for you and your ma – away from here. A safe place. A safe flat somewhere on the outskirts of the city and you can stay there till we get this mess cleaned up.'

'You mean live somewhere else?'

'Yeah.' Jack looked at Steven. 'You can't stay in Glasgow once we start looking at this. You know that, don't you?'

'Aye. Yeah. I know. But my ma's lived there all her life, in that flat.'

'In High Street?' he said, something like a half smile breaking in his face. 'Well it's maybe time she went somewhere else. You said she doesn't even go out, didn't you?'

'Aye.'

'Well, we'll take her somewhere far enough away. Some place these fuckers won't get close to you.'

'Christ, man! I don't know how far I'd have to go once they start looking for me.'

Jack nodded slowly. 'You can let me worry about that. I won't let anything happen to you. I promise you that. And I know one thing, son. Kerry Casey won't let anything happen to you.'

Steven looked at Marty for confirmation. He nodded but said nothing. He was a lawyer, for fuck's sake. He wasn't about to say anything sitting here that would incriminate him, place him on the same page as serious criminals. But it was clear that he was leaving the heavy stuff to Jack. Kane would not be going to the police with this information, that's for sure. But one way or another, the guilty men would get their day.

When Steven pushed the door open to his flat, the blaring of the television from his ma's bedroom told him she'd probably fallen asleep while watching. But there was a sudden grip in his stomach that maybe someone had followed him and who knew, maybe they were already in here. He stood for a moment, feeling the nerves go straight to his legs. Then he heard the shout.

'That you, Steven? You all right, son?'

The sigh of relief he let out almost brought him to tears, and he quickly composed himself.

'Aye, Ma. I'm fine. Pissing down out there.'

He took off his jacket, shook the rain off it and hung it on a hook in a recess in the hall. Then he walked down to the bedroom. His ma was propped up watching some US crime show she followed about gangsters and hitmen and gangland executions. Something inside him almost smiled, and he wasn't sure if it was the irony of the moment or just the fact that he'd unburdened himself to some guys who had made him feel that they wouldn't abandon him. He went across to the bedside chair and sat down, leaning closer to the bed, and his ma pushed the remote to pause her television.

'Ma,' Steven said, 'how do you feel about going away from here for a while? Out of this flat. Maybe even out of Glasgow.'

His ma said nothing for a long moment, her eyes searching his face.

'You went to the Caseys, son?'

'I did.'

She was silent as she looked at him, then beyond him towards the open door into the hall. Then she took his hand.

'You did the right thing. Let the Caseys sort this out their way. I'm ready to go when you are.' Then she pushed the play button on the remote and started her show again, her eyes going from Steven to the television. 'Now go and get the kettle on and we'll have a cup of tea. Then we can pack.'

Steven stood up, the scene on the television a dark wood with some guy on his knees blindfolded and a gunman behind him aiming at his head. He left the room and went to the kitchen.

CHAPTER FOURTEEN

Jake was at the quiet end of the bar in Party Pam's, far enough away from the pole dancer and the blaring music. Pam had called his mobile to tell him she thought there was someone in the bar he might want to check out. Jake hadn't told her any details of what he was doing – only that he was looking for someone who may be being held in Tarifa. Even though he trusted her implicitly – and shared her bed on occasion – Jake always kept his own strict lines of secrecy when he was working. Pam knew what he was, though, how he made a living, and she never questioned, never judged. That was what made her so special to him, and why she was one of the few people in his life who ever got as close as she did. He was at the bar within ten minutes from his frontline beach apartment in Los Boliches, where he lived a completely anonymous life. Now he sipped the JD over ice and listened to Pam as she leaned across and spoke softly to him.

'Third guy down the bar,' she said. 'Just beyond the group of blokes with the champagne. Colombian, I'd say, given his accent. He's on his own now, but he was with two others, also Colombians I think – they left just before you came in.'

Jake took his time to sneak a discreet glance along the bar and into the mirrored gantry so he could see the guy sitting on the bar stool. From what he could make out, he was around forty, his lean face was unshaven and he wore a black shirt with sleeves turned up to his elbows. He was sipping whisky over ice and had a bottle of Sol beer on the side which he swigged from alternately.

'I see him,' Jake said. 'How many of them has he had?' He lifted his glass indicating to Pam.

'Four shorts,' Pam said. 'And as you know, my shorts are not short. And that's his second beer. The others who were with him were buying him drinks, and they'd had a fair skinful before they left him.'

'I wonder why he didn't go with them,' Jake said.

'Maybe he wants a dance.' Pam rolled her eyes. 'Who knows. The others left anyway, the usual back-slapping and man-hugging before they went. But the reason I called you is because of some stuff I overheard them saying. Might be nothing, but you never know.'

'Sure,' Jake said. 'I'm glad you did.'

He waited for her to speak. But before she did, she had to walk down the bar to serve a customer, and Jake watched as the Colombian eyed her as she bent down in her tight jeans to get some beers from the fridge. She came back to Jake and stood polishing glasses, leaning closer to talk.

'So. It was hard to make out exactly what they were saying – you know what it's like with the music and how fast they speak. But I distinctly heard one of the guys mentioning Tarifa, and that's when my ears pricked up. I had to busy myself behind the bar so they wouldn't think I was clocking their conversation. But I heard your man down there saying he didn't want to go back there, that he was bored shitless looking after the *coño*.'

'He actually said that?'

Pam nodded. 'Yes. Well, in Colombian. But that's what I heard. I'm sure.'

Jake took a second glance at the figure down the bar, but he didn't think he was any of the two men he'd seen when he'd been down in Tarifa for the recce. Maybe they rotated them, and he'd been there a couple of days before he arrived. Or it might even be nothing. But he had to find out.

'Anything else you could make out from their conversation?' Jake asked.

'Yes. Something about a boat. And a long swim. There was more than that, but I couldn't hear exactly what they were saying, and I didn't want to hang around too close.'

'Sure,' Jake said. He was already working out his next move. He looked her in the eye. 'I need to get him in a situation where I can ask him some questions, Pam. You get my drift?'

'Leave it to me,' she said softly as she turned away from him.

For the next twenty minutes, Jake watched as Pam paid more attention to the Colombian who had been sitting gazing at the pole dancer. Pam had slid a drink across to him and leaned on the bar so she was almost whispering in the guy's ear that this was on the house. The Colombian was swallowing the bait, suddenly sitting himself upright and leaning in on Pam, brushing his fingers on her arm as she got close to him. He couldn't take his eyes off her, and whenever she moved away to serve a customer, the Colombian eyed her and smiled at her each time she passed. Pam was good at this, and it wasn't the first time Jake had asked her to help him out like this, luring some lowlife into a trap.

Almost half an hour later, the shift change came into the bar, and that was Pam's cue to give the Colombian the nod. She owned an apartment upstairs from the bar, which she occasionally used if she didn't feel like driving to her villa down the coast in Elviria. She'd invited the Colombian upstairs for a drink, and the guy knocked back the dregs of his drink, his eager eyes waiting for the signal from Pam that it was time. Jake slipped off the bar stool and left through what looked like a cupboard door. From the other side, he went along the corridor behind the bar and pushed open the fire exit door that opened into the deserted backstreet. To the left was the tight steel staircase fire escape that led to the terrace of Pam's apartment. Jake stood in the shadows, waiting. The exit door was pushed open, and Pam came outside into the street, the Colombian close behind her, his hands reaching out to touch her as she turned towards the entrance of her apartment. He pushed himself close up behind her as she put her key into the lock. His arms went around her waist and he nuzzled her hair. Then just as Pam slowly unlocked the door, Jake was there. Before the Colombian had the chance to even turn around, Jake was on him, hustling him through, hurling him against the wall, then punching his face so hard he buckled. Jake knew he would be easy to overpower as the Colombian was half drunk. But whether he would talk, if he even knew anything, was another matter. He squeezed the Colombian's throat and held it as he gasped for breath. He saw his bulging eyes glance at Pam as she slipped past Jake and disappeared, the Colombian realising the set-up too late. He pulled the door closed behind him, and pushed the Colombian until he was lying on the stairs. Then Jake pulled out his gun and shoved it between his eyes, using his other hand to reach below the man's shirt and yank the pistol from the waistband of his jeans.

'Please, *señor*,' the Colombian pleaded. 'I sorry. She is your woman. I not know.'

Jake said nothing and cocked his gun. The Colombian looked like he was about to cry.

'Talk to me,' Jake said, bearing down on him, 'about Tarifa.'

The Colombian tried to feign confusion.

'Tarifa? *Que*? Please, *señor*. What you mean?'

Jake removed the gun from his forehead and quickly fired a shot that grazed the side of the Colombian's knee. He screamed in agony and blood pumped out.

'Next shot goes in your head. Talk,' Jake spat. 'You have the cop in Tarifa. You have five seconds to live or die. Five . . . four . . . three . . .' He cocked the gun again, pushed it into his head.

'Please. I am a dead man. They will kill me.'

'Fuck them! You have two seconds . . . Two . . .'

'Stop! Please! I not know. They tell me to sit. Guard the English boy. That's all.'

'His name?'

The Colombian shook his head. 'Vinn . . . I not know. We don't talk to him.'

'Is he hurt?'

The Colombian closed his eyes, bit his lip, shook his head vigorously.

'Not me! I not hurt him!'

'What happened?'

'I don't know. I promise you. They cut the finger off. Much blood. He is sick with infection. I not know. Please. I only there one day and one night.'

'Those men you were with at the bar. They your bosses?'

'*Si, mis jefes*. They tell me to go back tomorrow to Tarifa. They take the boy away the next day.'

'Where? Where are they taking him?'

The Colombian shook his head, snivelling as Jake forced the gun into his temple.

'I don't know. The boat, they said.'

Jake took the gun away from his forehead and stood over him.

'Okay. You have two choices here, *entiendes*? *Dos opciones*. You die now, or you do as I say and live.'

The Colombian was silent for a moment, swallowed, his Adam's apple moving in the redness of his neck.

'You police?'

'No.'

'My bosses. They will kill me.'

'Your choice. You help me, and you live. I'll make sure of it.'

'No. Please, *señor*. You cannot kill all these people. They will find me. They will find you.'

'They won't. Trust me. You work with me, or I kill you now.'

After a long moment the Colombian sat up and nodded his head. Jake grabbed him by the shirt and pulled him to his feet, holding the gun at his back as he walked on shaky legs out of the door. Jake pushed him towards his car and opened the boot.

'Get in.'

'Please no, *señor*! You are going to kill me.'

'No. I'm not. Get in.'

The Colombian climbed into the boot and curled up. He looked up at Jake, his face contorted as though waiting for the shot to be fired. Jake slammed the boot closed. Then, as he went around the car and opened the driver's door, he took his phone out and pressed the key for Sullivan's number.

'It's me. I've got someone we need to look after tonight. Meet me in Los Boliches – in Bar Sol. It's two streets back from the beach.' He hung up.

CHAPTER FIFTEEN

In her dream, Kerry was laughing and walking in the city centre with Vinny, his arm around her shoulder as they talked. The street lights lit up the pavements that were shiny from the rain, and they walked slowly, not clear where they were going. They were suddenly struck by how silent the town was: not a sound, no traffic, no people, just the two of them. Then in the dream she looked at Vinny as his face became concerned and he started to take a step backwards, touching her hand as he went. He wasn't speaking, just moving backwards, and all the time she was reaching out to him, but gradually he vanished into the darkness, and she tried to run after him, to catch him, but her legs were heavy and she couldn't move from the spot where she stood as she watched him disappear. When she woke up her face was wet from crying. It was then that she heard the commotion, an alarm sounding, urgent shouting, doors banging. Prison wardens were yelling at everyone to stay in their cells.

'What the fuck!' Ash said, as Kerry heard her stirring in the top bunk.

Kerry sat upright, the ceiling light blaring. She swung her legs out and stood closer to the door, her ear pressed against it, but all she could hear was the shouting, and wardens telling prisoners to calm down, that there had been an incident.

'Something's kicked off,' Ash said, getting out of bed.

'I heard the guards say there's been an incident.'

'Shit. That's bad,' Ash replied.

An incident. Kerry stood, trying to think what it could be. Perhaps another fight with the two girls from the other night. But it couldn't be because it was only seven and the doors were just about due to be opened and she was sure Tracy and Libby wouldn't be sharing a cell after what happened. She sat down, anxious, the noise outside getting quieter, but the low murmured voices of what she assumed were wardens could be heard around the area. It was only about fifteen minutes, but it seemed longer, as Kerry and Ash stood, clutching towels, ready for the communal shower area. Suddenly the doors clicked open, and the prisoners emerged from their cells. The wardens were walking up and down, ushering them to go for showers and then for breakfast, turning away whenever someone asked what was going on. As they made their way along the corridor, everyone was talking in hushed tones. Someone's topped themselves, one of the girls said – what else can it be? Kerry glanced around the line of people going downstairs, some of them filing off to the shower area, and others to breakfast. She and Kerry went straight in for breakfast and sat down.

'What's going on?' Kerry asked.

'Dunno for sure,' Ash replied. 'But I heard someone saying a lassie hanged herself during the night.'

'Christ! No way.'

'Dunno. That's what Miranda who works in the hairdresser's said, and the others are saying too. But the wardens are saying nothing.'

'That's awful,' Kerry said.

'Aye. I knew there was something up when they kept our cells locked. It's either some lassie has attacked a warden or someone's done themselves in. Fucking terrible, if that's what's happened.'

Kerry and Ash joined the queue at the breakfast hatch, but she had no appetite after all this. The very idea that a girl would hang herself and die alone. How desperate did you have to be to do that? She hoped it wasn't true. But she had to eat, for the sake of the baby, so she took some toast and cereal along with a tangerine and went across to the table. The room was filled with the low murmur between the women, as opposed to the usual chatter and arguing or banter that usually went on around the tables. It grew quiet when the doors opened and the governor walked in. Kerry looked up, and from the greyness of her face she could see that she was shocked. The governor, a big strapping woman in her forties, looked pale and drawn, and Kerry noted that the doctor who had examined her when she'd arrived stood beside her. Again, low whispers could be heard across the room. One of the wardens banged a table for quiet, and the place fell silent.

'Ladies,' the governor began. 'I know you're anxious to know what kept you in your cells this morning. I'm afraid I have some very bad news to impart to you.'

Kerry watched as the governor wrung her hands, glancing at the doctor as though looking for support. She paused to clear her throat, then went on.

'I'm afraid I have to report that there has been a death in the cells overnight. Linda Martin has died. Her death is under investigation, therefore there will be no further discussion about it. I ask you to remain calm and please have your thoughts and respect for Linda and for her family at this time.'

'Did she top herself, ma'am?' The brash voice came from Jenna, a thickset girl at the back who was in for stabbing a Glasgow Pakistani newsagent in the eye during an attempted robbery at his shop. 'Where were all you cunts when it happened?'

The atmosphere shifted from shock to anger.

'Aye. What happened? Wee Linda was just left on her own, was she? Left to fucking die?' Brenda, a lifer, shouted.

The words hung in the air, and the governor and the

prison wardens glared at her. Nobody spoke. The rest of the girls glanced at Jenna and then the chatter grew louder. A warden shushed at the girls to be quiet.

'Now everyone needs to calm down, please. The incident is under investigation. Just go back to your breakfast and if there is any more information available as the day goes on, then we will let you know.' The governor looked around the room, perhaps hoping to see a friendly face, but there were none. 'But please, ladies, think of Linda and her family at this time. And if anyone has any concerns then speak to a member of staff.'

With that, she turned and left. The low chatter became louder and the atmosphere heavy and edgy.

'Must be true,' Ash whispered to Kerry.

'Christ! That's just terrible.' She shook her head. 'What was Linda in for? I only saw her around, but she seemed to be all right, well as all right as you can be in here. Did you know her?'

'Aye. A bit,' Ash said. 'I met her the last time I was in, and she was okay. Just a bit mental and doing stupid things. She self-harmed. She had a lot of marks on her arms and neck from suicide attempts. But to be honest, she wouldn't be the only lassie in here with that.'

'Do you know what she was in for?'

'I know she was out, but then ended up back in just last week. So she must have done something to break her parole, as she got out early the last time.'

'Did you speak much to her in the last week since she came in?'

She shook her head. 'Only once. She remembered me from before, but she knew a few people here too. She told me she was raging that she was back in and this was all wrong. But she said nobody was listening to her.' She stopped, bit her lip. 'Fuck. I wish I'd listened more to her, or tried to get to the bottom of what she was feeling. Fucking place, this. I mean, some people are in here and they just shouldn't be here. They've got mental health issues and it's a psychiatric unit they should be in, not a jail. Wee Linda. She'd been through the children's home system stuff, so Christ knows what happened to her. She told me that ages ago, but she didn't know why she behaved that way. Sometimes she was up and high as a kite, then she could be in the depths of depression. I mean, you'd think someone might look at that before they pap her in here.'

'Do you think it's true? That she killed herself last night?'

'Oh aye. Bang on true, all right. Did you see the look on the governor's face, and the rest of them? They're shocked. A lassie has killed herself on their watch, and that's going to fuck them up big time. Know what I mean? You heard the reaction of the other girls here, because the fact is that it could be any one of us, and they managed to miss that something bad was happening. This could end up in a riot.'

'I hope not,' Kerry said, dreading scenes of fighting and wrecking. 'I don't know what good it would do, Ash. But there will be an investigation into it, and once the press get a hold of it and things like that, it will mean trouble. But what a tragedy for Linda. So young.'

'Aye. She was nineteen. Fucking ridiculous!'

For the rest of the morning, on the surface, it was business as usual, with prisoners going to their jobs and workshops. But Linda's death was everywhere. Prisoners spoke in whispered tones, angry, sad and anxious, many of them already mentally fragile. Kerry noticed that the wardens seemed more attentive, talking to girls and trying to allay their fears. During the lunchtime break in the canteen, the television news had Linda's death as the number one story, and everyone sat in silence as the newsreader said an investigation was under way into how the prisoner had been able to commit suicide. The blame game had already started and the media would whip it up, once any of Linda's relatives were tracked down and talking to the press. The atmosphere in the canteen was uneasy and heavy, and when the bell went for lock-up, nobody moved. It was as though everyone felt safer, less vulnerable, united if they had each other around them. Eventually, the wardens rounded people up firmly and ushered them to their cells. Before they went, they announced that there would be a service later in the prison chapel for anyone who wanted to attend and reflect on what had happened today. Nobody spoke and they shuffled in silence to their cells.

In the late afternoon, before dinner, the women who were around went to the chapel. Kerry made her way down the corridor and others also came from wherever they were. The chapel was non-denominational, just a wooden cross, and a solitary candle burning at the front. It smelled of polished wood. There was no music, nothing, just the gloominess of the place and all the girls sitting on pews in some kind of stunned silence. Then, from the back of the room, the minister came in alongside the Catholic priest. They stood at either side of the cross, and the girls looked at them expectantly.

The minister spoke first.

'I'm so glad so many of you have come along this afternoon to reflect on the tragic death of Linda, who was taken from us too soon.'

Everyone sat listening as he talked of the difficulties of life away from family and how hard it was to adjust to being in prison, and he appealed to anyone who had any worries or problems to share them with staff, or with himself or the Catholic priest. The women sat with glazed expressions on their faces.

Then the priest spoke. 'It's in moments like this that we feel bereft,' he said, looking around the chapel at the women. 'We feel abandoned and desperately sad that one of our own was so overwhelmed with the difficulties bearing down on her that she felt her life was worth nothing. That is what it must seem like to some of you, perhaps a lot of you here, not just today but in some of your darker moments. But you must understand that *your* life *is* important. From the day you are born, your life is important. Now I know that it may not seem that way in a place like this, and what brought you to this. But you must never feel that this is all there is, because there are people on your side. You are important, and one day, perhaps when you are out of here and you look back on the difficulties that this period of your life brought, you will understand that.

'So I appeal to you, please do not give up. Think of what your life can mean to so many people, even if you feel family and friends are not always on your side. You can make it different with the help available here, and with the help of God. He is always listening and watching, and he loves you no matter what you have done. His love is unconditional.

'Linda's childhood was tragic and she faced issues that overwhelmed her. That is the great sadness we feel today for her and for what has been lost. But for all of your sakes, don't let Linda's death be something that sets you back. Of course we feel sad. But we must try to live the life that Linda could not, wasn't able to, because of her state of mind. Is that not something worth thinking about? Perhaps as we sit here in the quietness of this chapel where all of us are equal, we could think of our own lives, what we can bring to them, and how we can turn around our futures. For ourselves and for Linda, who wasn't able to do that.'

As he stopped and stood back, Kerry glanced along the pews and could see some women in tears. Big Aggie and her partner sat holding hands, their faces tight more with anger than sorrow. Then the warden came forward and spoke.

'Most of you here only knew Linda from the time you met her inside, and it's the same for us staff. So we wanted to ask Linda's friend Josie, who probably knew her best, to come up and say a few words so that we can think of her today.'

The skinny girl in her early twenties, dyed blonde hair, the skin on her hollow cheeks dry and grey, came forward. Her eyes were red from crying and she was sniffing as she stood in front of the chapel clutching a piece of paper. She looked awkward, shifting from foot to foot. Then she took a breath, put her hand to her mouth to compose herself, and finally spoke. From where Kerry was sitting, some of the girls were already in tears and Josie hadn't even started.

'I knew Linda when we were both fifteen and cutting about Easterhouse together,' she began. 'I just wanted to say that she was more than what people thought about her – I mean by being in here. She was more than just . . . this.' She spread her hands. 'Aye, we did some stupid things, got into trouble, and Linda got into some big trouble. It was all the drugs, I think – for me, anyway. But with Linda it was more than that, and she was up and down all the time, and it was like nobody really knew what to do with her.

She lost a lot of mates with her mood swings and some of the violent things she did. But her heart was big, man.' She broke down. 'Her heart was as big as the moon, man. And people just couldn't see that.' She stopped for a moment, swallowed, and around the chapel sniffs could be heard. Kerry could feel her throat tighten, stung by the courage and hurt in her voice. Then Josie unfolded the piece of paper she'd been holding, and wiped her nose with the back of her hand. She held up the paper.

'Linda wrote this for me when she first came in here last year. I wasn't in jail yet, but I'd been charged. I hadn't been to see her, well, because, well, I was just up to my neck in my own shit, drugs and stuff. But I kept it. And here it is. It's, well, it's not a poem, but it felt like a poem, or as close to a poem as I ever saw.' She wiped her nose again and read from the page. 'This is what she wrote.

' "One time on a bus trip to the beach with my ma – I was seven, I think – I saw a sunset, of orange and red and gold. It was awesome. It's where the miracles happen, my ma told me. I asked her do people live there, and she said she didn't know, and that was the secret of the sunset. But she said every day the sun comes up it's a miracle. I asked her can I go there, and stay in a place that's bright and gold and makes everything look beautiful, because it's dark here and grey all the time. And she said to me, one day, you'll be part of the sunrise and the sunset, and nobody will be able to touch you or hurt you and you will never

ever feel sad. When we went home that night, she put me to bed and I fell asleep thinking of the place where the miracles happen. In the morning when I woke up, my ma was gone. I never saw her again."'

Josie looked at everyone, sniffing back her tears.

'I don't really know why she sent me it when she was in jail, but maybe she was trying to encourage me or something. Who knows. But I used to read it sometimes, and every time I saw the sunset or the sunrise I thought of Linda. Maybe that's where she is now, in this place where the miracles happen. Maybe we can think of her that way, that she's not hurting or sad and the place she's in is beautiful, like the sunset, just the way she wanted it.'

Music floated out of the wall-mounted speakers, and Kerry recognised it from the film, *The Mission*. Soulful, moving. Kerry sat, tears streaming down her cheeks, the grief and the pain of the girls palpable. In the time she'd been in here, she'd spoken to only a few of them but knew very little of their lives, what brought them to this, what pain, suffering. Most of them she just saw in the corridor or in the workshop and the canteen. You never knew what shit they carried around on their shoulders. She wondered what their lives were, vastly different from hers, one of privilege and travel and opportunity. These girls, most of them never had any of that. The strains of the music faded and the women sat for a couple of minutes, then slowly they filed out and into the corridor in silence.

CHAPTER SIXTEEN

Dick Lambie sipped his coffee and gazed out of the small, grimy window from his office in the back of the body repair shop. He'd be glad to get out of this fucking place for a couple of weeks. Even though the office was along a corridor and at the very back of the building, the stink of the fumes from the paint shop caught the back of his throat. It was one of the reasons he didn't like coming into his office, and did most of his business on the phone or in a quiet area of the White Horse. But the moneylending had to be done somewhere quiet and well out of the way. The body shop he owned was a perfect front for most of the business Lambie did, from shifting drugs to loan sharking. And every Friday morning he had to be here to make sure the punters he'd loaned money to were up to date and paying back on his lucrative terms. He left a lot of the basic stuff, like roughing up anyone who needed it, to Thomson and a couple of the lads, but on a Friday he liked to be there in person to collect the money and make sure other things were running smoothly. He looked at his watch. In a couple of days' time, he'd be sipping cocktails on the deck of a cruise ship around the Canary Islands with his wife Nora. It would be the first proper holiday they'd had in four years, as mostly it had been a week here and there in Alicante or Torrevieja, where he had money in a bar with two of his UVF mates. But it was his silver wedding anniversary next month, and Nora had insisted they go on a cruise. Truth was, he was actually looking forward to it, even if he was wary of the kind of pricks you met on a cruise ship and being stuck with them for ten days. He'd resolved to keep to himself. But all that aside, he would be out of here and away from the fumes and the shitty weather, and relaxing. He could hear footsteps in the corridor, and then a knock on the door.

'It's me, boss.'

'Come in.'

It was Thomson. He walked in and pulled a chair over to sit opposite his boss.

'There's a few punters out there already, boss,' he said. 'It's pissin' down. So they must be desperate.'

'Good,' Lambie said. 'That way I don't have to listen to their moaning about my terms. Are they new punters?'

'Two of them I haven't seen before, but one is wee Davey Johnson – he'll just be making his payment.'

'Fine. We'll bring them in shortly,' Lambie said. 'But

first, I want to go over a few things I need you to look at while I'm away.'

'Sure. No problem.'

Lambie was about to speak, when Thomson's mobile rang. He gave his boss a perplexed look as he took it from his pocket and pressed it to his ear.

'Jean, I'm in a meeting. What is it?'

Lambie assumed from the way he spoke to her that it was Jean, their cleaner at the White Horse. He watched the puzzled look on Thomson's face as he listened to what she was saying.

'Did you phone his mobile? Right. Okay. Give me a minute to sort it.'

Thomson hung up and Lambie could tell from the look on his face that something was wrong.

'Gimpy's not turned up for work. Jean's been in cleaning the bar.' He looked at his watch. 'It's twenty past eleven and the wee cunt's not there yet. He's not answering his phone. Seems to be switched off.'

Lambie did not like the sound of this at all. He knew Gimpy had been reluctant and scared of what they'd forced him to do over the last few days. But he knew he had no way out. He was into them for a lot of money and he had nowhere to go. Thomson had paid his sick ma a visit, just to let him know that they had him well stitched up.

'Try his number again,' Lambie said.

He watched as Thomson scrolled through his phone and

then pushed a key. After a few seconds he held the phone away from him on loudspeaker. An automated voice told them, 'This person's phone is switched off.'

'Fucking switched off,' Thomson said. 'I'll switch the wee cunt right off.'

'What do you think?' Lambie said. 'I mean Gimpy's not daft enough to do a runner. Maybe he's sick or something. Or his ma's taken a turn for the worse – especially after seeing your ugly mug at her bedside.'

Thomson didn't flinch at the sarcasm.

'Don't think so, boss. Something stinks. I feel it.'

'Send someone round to his flat. See if he's there.'

Thomson scrolled on his phone again and spoke to someone.

'Bobby. I need you go round to Gimpy's flat. You know where it is? High Street, above that newsagent shop. Go round there and see if he's in, or if anyone's in. Wee bastard hasn't turned up at the bar this morning. I need to know where he is so I can punch the fuck out of him.'

He hung up. Then keyed in another number.

'Terry. It's me. Listen, mate. Wee problem at the bar this morning. That fucker Gimpy's not turned up and the punters will be outside waiting for it to open. I know you're not due on until five, but can you go in and open up? Extra shift. Double time?' He glanced at Lambie and shrugged at his raised eyebrows. 'Fine. Thanks, mate.'

'Double fucking time? It's not a bastard charity I'm running.'

'I know, I know. But we just need the bar covered and smartish, until I find out where Gimpy is. I just don't like this.'

Lambie sat back and clasped his fingers across his stomach as he processed the possibilities. There was no way in the world Gimpy would just disappear. Even though he might be scared and worried about his part in Bo's death, it's not as if he could go to the cops. And he wouldn't run out on his ma. *He'll turn up*, he assured himself. *Just get on with the next couple of days, then it'll be sunshine and relaxation all the way.*

'We'll worry about Gimpy when we need to,' he said. 'Go and bring the punters in. Make sure you know who the new ones are first though, before I see them.'

Twenty minutes later, after tying up three new punters in loans with exorbitant interest rates they would never be able to repay, Lambie watched as Thomson wrote all the transactions down in the black book. Then he looked at his boss as his mobile rang. He pushed it onto loudspeaker.

'It's me, Gordy. He's not at his house. Door was locked, so I let myself in. But no sign of Gimpy. And guess what. His ma's not there either.'

'Fuck me, fucking gently,' Lambie muttered as Thomson finished the call.

*

Cal Ahern walked briskly, but made sure he didn't break into a run as he went towards Jack's car.

'How much did you get?' Jack asked when Cal climbed into the back seat.

Cal leaned through the space between the driver's and passenger seat and held out the wedge of cash.

'Three hundred quid,' he said. 'I asked for four, but they said they would up it in a couple of weeks, that they wanted to make sure I made my first payments on time.'

Cal glanced at Steven in the back seat. He'd only met him yesterday in Jack's office where they'd told him what the set-up was and what the job entailed. He didn't know much about the guy, but he seemed sound enough, and the fact that he'd been bullied by loan sharks meant that Cal took to him straight away. He still had nightmares about his mum and the scumbag sharks who'd had her in their grip. If there was a chance to do any moneylender over, he was up for it. Jack had told him the Caseys were going to be looking after Steven and his mum for the foreseeable future, because he had given them crucial information that could prove Kerry and Danny's innocence.

'Well done, son,' Jack said. 'So who did you deal with?'

'Thomson did the deal, setting up the terms and stuff. Lambie just sat there, didn't say too much until the end, till they gave me the money.'

'What did he say?'

'He asked why I didn't have a job. And I told him, I did

have a job at the supermarket but I got sacked four weeks ago for punching the duty night manager. He seemed to like that.' Cal smiled, hoping he'd said the right thing. 'Then he said to me that he would see how I got on with the repayments and that he might have some work for me.'

'Good,' Jack said. 'Let's hope it doesn't come to that.'

'Aye,' Cal said. 'You bet. Lambie said he was going on holiday in two days, and that when he comes back in a couple of weeks I should come and see him at the White Horse.'

'What? Lambie says he's going on holiday in two days?' Jack looked from Cal to big Gary, the driver.

'So he says.'

They were silent for a long moment, then Jack turned to Steven in the back seat.

'We'll need to move quick on this.'

In the White Horse, Lambie sat listening as Bobby told him how he'd been all over Gimpy's house looking for clues that he'd done a runner. He said there was nothing to suggest that he'd packed up and gone, because a lot of his clothes and his ma's clothes were still there. Bobby had searched through drawers and piles of papers and couldn't find any passports, but he suggested that maybe someone like Gimpy didn't even have a passport, as nobody could remember him ever going abroad. He hadn't found any stash of money, but that wasn't surprising, as Gimpy had none. Lambie nodded as Bobby spoke. It did occur to him that perhaps his ma was in hospital, or maybe they'd gone away for a couple of days, but he wouldn't have done that without letting them know, especially after what had happened with Bo. But the big problem was that Gimpy's phone was switched off. That meant he didn't want anyone to get in touch with him, and that could only be a bad sign. Lambie checked his mobile again. He still hadn't heard from Thomson, who'd gone out with Billy over an hour ago to move a package from a dealer and make sure it was put to the right guy to take it to Belfast. It was two kilos of cocaine that had been paid for, so it needed to be done. He rang his number again, but it went to messages, and the same for Billy. Where the fuck were they? He finished off his whisky and stood up. There was no point in sitting here getting paranoid. Thomson would probably phone him by the time he got to his house. He pulled on his coat and nodded to the barman.

'If Gordy comes in get him to phone me pronto.' He turned and left the bar.

Outside, the wind was whipping up and he buttoned his coat, even though his silver Mercedes was parked close to the door. The street was deserted and for a fleeting moment Lambie considered going back into the bar and getting one of the boys to drive him home. Christ. What the hell was happening to him? He was never usually spooked by anything, but something about Gimpy's disappearance made him deeply uneasy. He took a breath, cleared his throat and hawked onto the pavement, then unlocked his car.

It pinged and lit up as he went towards it. He got inside, sinking into the comfort of the leather seats like a cocoon, protected from everything. He pushed the button to start the engine and it purred to life, then he drove off. He headed out of the East End and towards the south side of Glasgow over the Jamaica Bridge. He turned on the radio as he got up past Shawlands Cross, and out towards Kilmarnock Road. Then suddenly he froze. The cold metal of a gun was pushed into the soft flesh just below his right ear.

'Take the next on the right, cunt. One word and your brains will be all over the windscreen.'

Lambie felt his bowels churn and for an awful moment he really thought he was going to shit his trousers. He said nothing. The gun pushed further. He turned right at the junction, his heart pounding, as he knew he was going down a darker, more deserted street that led to units and Portakabins. He slowed down.

'Did I tell you to slow down?'

The gun was pushed harder into his neck. He glanced quickly in the rear-view mirror and could see a figure in a black ski mask. He picked up speed again. 'Turn down here,' the voice said. 'Keep going till I tell you to stop.'

Lambie said nothing. Sweat trickled down his back and his face was flushed. He felt physically sick. He drove his car over potholes and puddles and kept going, past Portakabins, until he saw a light on in the very last one at the end of the deserted pitch-black road.

'Pull up right there,' the voice said.

He eased his car over the last few potholes and pulled over. He knew there was a gun in his glove compartment, but it was useless because he couldn't move a muscle. When the car stopped, a big shaven-headed guy built like a wrestler came out of the Portakabin and towards the car. He opened the door and shot him a maniacal grin. Then he popped open the glove compartment and took out his gun, grinning again as he stuck it in the waistband of his jeans.

'Listen,' Lambie said, aware that his voice was shaking. 'What is this, guys? Am I getting fucking robbed here? If it's money you're after, just say and I'll give you whatever you want.'

'Shut the fuck up!' The voice from behind him opened the back door, as the big guy kept a gun on him.

'Right! Out!' The masked man opened the driver's door and pushed the gun to the side of his head.

Lambie instinctively raised his hands as though he was being arrested and kept his head down as he got out of the car. His legs nearly gave way as he stood up.

'Move!'

The masked man got behind him and pushed him towards the Portakabin. The bald knuckle-trailer went ahead and opened the door. He walked up the wooden steps on shaky legs and was pushed inside, the harsh strip light making him strain his eyes, and the smell ... the smell of fear and sweat. Then he saw Gordy. But he had to blink to make sure it was him, because his face was a mass of blood and his left eye was swollen up like a balloon. Standing at the desk with his arms folded was a big guy he knew only by sight. Jack Reilly. He'd never met him, but knew who he was. He worked for Kerry Casey. At that moment, Lambie knew he was well and truly fucked.

CHAPTER SEVENTEEN

The bar was three streets back from the front line beach cafés and restaurants in Los Boliches, and was mostly used by the Spanish locals. Jake Cahill liked it because when he was in there, he was never likely to encounter any nosy tourists and have to engage in conversation with them. He rarely spoke to the locals either, and that's what appealed to him about the Spanish. They were private people, didn't ask questions, didn't talk much about themselves – probably something that hung over from the Spanish Civil War, and the secrets and betrayal of each other that still lingered. That suited Jake perfectly. Especially tonight, with a terrified Colombian in the boot of his car. He looked up from his drink to see Sullivan coming through the doorway towards where he sat at a table close to the window.

'What's up?' Sullivan said as he drew back a metal chair and sat down. He looked around him. 'Thought you said you had someone.'

'I do,' Jake said.

'Who is it?' Sullivan said, then nodded to the hovering waiter to have the same as Jake.

'He's Colombian. He was in Party Pam's with a couple of his buddies earlier, and she overheard a conversation about Tarifa. She phoned me to come down.'

'Yeah?' Sullivan pulled his chair closer.

Jake nodded. 'She didn't pick up much of what they said, but enough to know that it was about watching someone in Tarifa. When I got to the bar he was on his own, and pretty pissed. He had the hots for Pam, so she lured him outside where I could have a chat with him.'

Sullivan's mouth curled to a wry smile.

'A chat?' He spread his hands. 'So where is he now?'

Jake jerked his head in the direction of the street, and watched as Sullivan looked out of the window. 'In the boot of my car.'

'Oh fuck! Did he say much?'

'After a bit of coaxing, he admitted he'd been in Tarifa looking after some English boy. Vinn.'

'Fuck me! He said that? He actually said Vinn?'

'He did. He's scared shitless, so I think he might work with us.'

'Christ, Jake. The Colombians will hunt him down.'

'That's *his* problem.'

'So what do we do now?' Sullivan took a swig of his Jack Daniel's, wincing at the strength of it.

'We have to take him somewhere we can talk to him properly. Your place, I think. My apartment is too exposed on the seafront. Someone might see us.'

Sullivan shrugged.

'Is he walking? I mean, can he walk?'

Jake's face was deadpan as he shrugged.

'He's got a bit of a knee situation, but he'll live.' He knocked back his drink and pushed his chair back. 'Let's go.'

Sullivan swirled the ice in his drink and took another gulp, wincing, then got up and followed him outside.

Jake was glad there was no sound coming from the boot as they got into his car and drove down towards the back roads into the outskirts of La Cala de Mijas a couple of miles away. He pulled the car into the spot Sullivan directed him to, just outside the back entrance to the chalet he was renting. The place was deathly quiet and a couple of hundred yards from other apartments, down a dirt track road. It had been more of an outhouse attached to villa than a house, but the owner must have fallen on hard times and was now renting it. It was ideal for what they needed right now. Once they were outside the back door, they got out and went around to the back of the car. Jake put his fingers under the lid and popped open the boot. Immediately the hands came up pleading, the eyes of the Colombian wide and terrified.

'Please, please, *señor*. No kill me.'

Jake put a forefinger to his lips and made no reply. He and Sullivan leaned in and yanked the Colombian out and he stood on shaky legs, blood on his knee and a hole in his jeans. He groaned in pain. Sullivan glanced at Jake.

'Christ! Did you kneecap him?'

'Not quite. Just grazed him. He'll be fine when he gets cleaned up.'

They both looked around and then helped the Colombian to the back door and into the house. Jake pushed him onto a chair in the kitchen, as Sullivan went to the fridge and brought out a bottle of water. He unscrewed the top and handed it to the Colombian, who nodded in thanks. They watched as he glugged the water down, dribbling it out of his mouth and down his chin. Sullivan switched on the kettle and took out three mugs and placed them on the worktop. He put spoons of black coffee in the mugs and took the milk out of the fridge. They stood in silence with only the sound of the kettle hissing away.

'We have to get him to talk more,' Jake said. 'And if he's going there, to Tarifa, then he needs to work with us.'

Sullivan nodded. 'Okay. Let's get some coffee into him and fix up his knee first.'

Sullivan went into a cupboard and took out some first aid bandages and iodine, then signalled to the Colombian to drop his jeans. He revealed caked blood and a wet wound on his knee, not quite a hole but damn near it. Hard blood had formed a trail down his legs. Sullivan poured iodine onto a rag and washed down the wound. The Colombian was shaking, his face contorted in pain. Sullivan finished cleaning it out and wrapped a bandage tightly around it. The Colombian looked up at him, the fear gone from his eyes. Then he looked at Jake, and his expression changed. Sullivan handed him the coffee and he sipped it.

Jake pulled up a chair opposite him.

'Now, you talk,' he said. 'Tell us about the English boy. Vinn . . .?'

The Colombian took a drink of his coffee and wiped his nose with the back of his hand. He pulled up his jeans.

'They will kill me,' he whimpered.

'Tell me,' Sullivan said. 'The English boy. He is my friend.'

'He is police. *Mi jefe* say he is police.'

'Who took him? Why did they take him?'

The Colombian shrugged. 'I not know. I only go there with two other people to guard him.'

'In Tarifa?' Jake said.

The Colombian nodded.

Jake pulled out his mobile and brought up a photo of the building where he had seen the men.

'In this place? He is in this place?'

The Colombian studied the picture. Then he pointed at the top floor. Jake glanced at Sullivan. They were in business.

'How long has he been there?'

The Colombian shrugged again. 'Maybe more than one,

two weeks. I go there two times to guard him. Two days I stay, each time.'

Jake looked at Sullivan who looked relieved that they were making a breakthrough.

'What happened to the English boy?' Jake said. 'You told me they cut off his finger. You see this? What happened?'

He shook his head. 'No. I not see. I come later – maybe two days after. By then is infected and English boy is maybe have fever. I was with one other guard, and I go to *farmacia* and get antibiotics and bandage.' He shook his head. 'But he is still sick. They cut his finger off because he won't tell them the information.'

'What information?'

The Colombian puffed. 'I not know for sure everything. But they said he is police and knows about the shipment. They are trying to find this from him, if the police know, in case they are waiting for them, but he won't talk.'

'What shipment?' Sullivan asked.

'The cocaine.' The Colombian looked surprised at Sullivan. 'Is the shipment coming in to Cadiz. Is from Colombia.'

For a long moment nobody spoke, and Jake could see the wheels in Sullivan's brain turning, processing what he could now do with this information. Jake touched his arm and gestured to the lounge.

'We're not here to get information for a drugs bust, Sullivan. I'm here to get Vinny out. That's all.'

Sullivan spread his hands. 'Of course, Jake. I know that. Christ! That's why I'm here; my bosses don't even know or they'd crucify me. All I want is to get Vinny out of there.'

Jake gave him a stern look, but wasn't all that convinced.

'Good. Well let's concentrate on that. This prick is either lying to keep me from shooting him, or he's so seriously scared that he knows he's fucked if the Colombians find him so he's spilling his guts to us. What do you think?'

Sullivan folded his arms. 'I think he's telling us what he knows. I believe him. He's only a foot soldier – fodder for the cartel. And he knows he's not getting out of here alive unless he cooperates.'

Jake nodded. 'Okay. Let's see if we can take him further.'

They went back into the room and the Colombian, who was sipping coffee, looked up at them.

'Okay. You said you have to go back to Tarifa. When is that?'

'Tomorrow afternoon.' He pointed at his knee. 'This is a problem. If they know I have been shot they will ask questions for sure.' He shook his head. 'Is not good that you did this.'

Jake glared at him but didn't answer. He wasn't about to apologise to the little prick. The Colombian looked down at his knee and said nothing. Jake turned to Sullivan and they both walked away from him.

'We need to keep him here tonight,' Jake said, his voice

low. 'Get him some sleep. Then we need to be telling him what's going to happen in Tarifa.'

Sullivan looked at him, a little confused.

'What's going to happen in Tarifa?'

Jake sighed. 'I don't know yet. But this will be our best chance, maybe our only chance, to get Vinny out of there.' He jerked his head towards the kitchen. 'So this little fucker is going to have to play along with whatever we want to do.'

'Christ, Jake! He's seriously shitting himself. I'm not sure he could carry something like that off. He might just buckle and blow the whistle as soon as he gets there, and then everyone will get done – Vinny first.'

Jake looked at him, eyebrows raised.

'You got a better plan?'

Sullivan shook his head. 'No.'

'Okay. Get him a place to sleep, and I'll organise some backup for tomorrow down in Tarifa.'

Sullivan said nothing and turned back into the kitchen.

CHAPTER EIGHTEEN

Lambie was roughly pushed onto a plastic chair alongside Thomson. Their eyes met and he saw a look of terror in his face that he had never seen before. Thomson was as hard and ruthless a bastard as you could get, and Lambie had witnessed him kicking the shit out of people until they were lying unconscious in a pool of blood. He'd seen him stab a guy in the chest and casually sip his drink while he bled out on the floor of the backroom in the White Horse. But now, as he caught a whiff of the fresh blood dripping from the gash on Thomson's eyebrow, he knew that things in this room were about to get a whole lot worse. He waited for someone to speak as he stared straight ahead. A suffocating silence filled the room. Lambie shifted in his seat, looking up to where Jack was still standing, his backside leaning on the table. Behind him was this big baldy fucker who was permanently wearing a weird smile like all his birthdays had come on one day.

Finally, Jack spoke.

'You know who I am, Lambie, don't you?'

'Aye.' Lambie looked at him, then glanced away.

'You know who I work for.'

It was a statement, not a question. Lambie nodded, but said nothing. He didn't want to say the name Casey. By saying it out loud, he was confirming that he knew why he was here.

'Who?' Jack persisted.

Lambie gave him a confused look.

'Who do I work for?'

Lambie knew he had to say it.

'Caseys.'

'That's right. Kerry Casey. You know her?'

Lambie shrugged. He had managed to calm himself a little so that his heart wasn't pounding in his chest the way it had been in the car. He had to find a level of self-control if there was any chance that he could talk, or buy, or deal his way out of this.

He heard Jack tut impatiently, and he looked up and saw him let out a bored sigh.

'Listen, Lambie. You're well fucked. So there's no point in trying to act the fucking wide boy. You'd better start talking if you want to have any chance of getting out of here alive.' Jack jerked his head in the direction of the henchman behind him. 'Right now, the big man here is choking to have a bit of fun with you. So, let's hear it.'

Lambie tried to moisten his lips, but his tongue was bone dry. He ran a trembling hand over his face.

'Jack. Look. I don't know why I'm here, and that's the truth.'

Nobody spoke for a few seconds and the sound of the big man cracking his knuckles echoed through the Portakabin.

'Kerry Casey is in jail,' Jack said. 'Along with Danny. You want to talk to me about that?'

'I . . . I don't know what to say, Jack,' he muttered. 'I saw it on the news.' He looked up and saw the irascible look on Jack's face. He was running out of patience.

Jack took a step towards him, and before he could brace himself, Lambie felt the shock and pain sear through him as Jack backhanded him so hard it nearly knocked him off the chair. He felt light-headed. He tasted blood.

'Listen, you fucking dirty UVF bastard. We know you put her there. We know it was you who set Kerry and Danny up, so don't even think about trying to fucking lie your way out of it. Don't waste any more of my time here. We know it was you and your mob. So the only reason you're still breathing is because I need names. I need the name of who gave you the job and why they gave you the job. You tell me that, and we can talk about the possibility of you having a future beyond the next fifteen minutes.'

Lambie swallowed the sick that had come into his mouth. Sweat broke out all over his body and he felt his arms grow heavy like lead. He glanced from the side of his eye to see Thomson doubled over, almost on the point of collapse. They knew. How the fuck did they know? It could only have been Gimpy. He knew that once Bo was out of the picture, there was not a single other person who would talk. Except Gimpy. Because Bo opened his trap, Gimpy knew. And now that he was missing, it had to be him. He would kill the fucker with his own hands if he could. Or maybe Thomson had broken and talked? Fuck knows. Right now none of that mattered. If Lambie spoke to this mob, and they acted on his information, the Belfast command would be on him like a ton of bricks. He'd be face down somewhere by the weekend. But if he didn't talk, these cunts would do him in the next ten minutes. He had to at least try to deny it.

'It wasn't me, Jack. You've got it wrong.' He managed to lift his head and look Jack in the eye. 'You've got this wrong. I don't know who's telling you this, but it's ... it's just wrong.'

Jack said nothing. The chat was over. He stood, arms folded, then turned to the big man behind him and nodded. Lambie and Thomson watched frozen as the knuckle-trailer clicked open a metal toolbox. The guy was built like a fridge and he had his back to them so they couldn't see what he was doing. But they could hear the sound of something clicking onto something else, and then the sudden terrifying whirr of a drill. Fuck! Lambie could feel his breathing quicken as the big man turned to face them, clicking and revving the drill like a demented lunatic, the noise deafening. Lambie thought he was going to pass out as he came towards them. But it was Thomson he approached. Thomson flinched and pushed back on the chair as though if he pushed hard enough he could break out of the building. But the two minders behind him held him by the shoulders and grabbed his arm. He whimpered. Oh, fuck no. They planted his hand on the wooden desk and held it tight. Thomson was struggling and crying.

'Please, no. Aw, man. Please no!'

Then he let out a blood-curdling scream as the drill bit was placed on the back of his hand and the gorilla pressed the trigger. Lambie nearly passed out. He had never heard anything as sickening as the whirr of the drill, and the screams of Thomson. He heard the sound of bone and gristle being bored into, then just before Thomson passed out, he screamed, 'Fuck, boss! Just tell him! We're going to die here anyway!'

Thomson slumped forward, his hand drilled to the desk, blood, skin and bone splattered over the place. The big men behind him held him so he didn't fall to the floor. There was silence and then the sound of dribbling water hitting the lino floor as Thomson wet himself.

Lambie looked up at Jack, who shrugged.

'So,' he said. 'Let's hear it. I won't ask again.'

Lambie nodded. For a fleeting, surreal moment, he saw a

picture of himself on the cruise ship, the sun on his face, a colourful cocktail in his hand. It didn't get more ridiculous than that. He opened his mouth and began talking.

'I wasn't there,' he began. 'I was just given the job by Belfast.' He looked at Jack. 'You know what it's like. You don't say no. You can't say no. They gave me the job and told me to get it done. So I did.' He paused. 'It's not as though I had a fucking option.'

Jack said nothing and kept staring him down. Lambie knew he would want names, and he knew the moment he gave them it was like committing suicide. But what the fuck was he supposed to do now? Thomson was out for the count, the blood seeping out of his hand and the colour gone from his face. Nobody was even making a move to help him, or take the drill out now that he was talking. He knew he would have to keep going, because if he didn't, the next person to have the drill treatment would be him.

'The job was given to Billy Dobson. I gave it to him. He's a UVF man from Belfast. It was the commander there who suggested him. I've worked with him before. He's done stuff for me. So I got him to do it.'

Jack nodded. 'Who in Belfast gave you the job?'

Lambie looked at him and puffed out a breath.

'Fuck's sake, Jack. I can't do that. I can't give you his name. You might as well shoot me now.'

'Don't tempt me, cunt,' Jack spat. He looked past him at the big man with the drill and the other two behind him.

Lambie sat for a long moment, recollecting the scene in Belfast when he'd been given the job, around a month ago. It had been the usual few drinks in the pub on the Shankill, the meets and greets with the boys, all of them UVF, most of them killers and torturers and robbers. Lambie was comfortable in their company. He'd carried out their orders many times, but these days he didn't get his own hands dirty. He was rich enough and powerful enough to give orders back across the water to his Glasgow mob. He remembered the big boss, Wattie Townsley, sitting in the bar in Shankill, his power base, surrounded by his closest associates. It was always good to swap stories and talk about the good days. Also, for Lambie, being there and being seen among these men gave him a status and kudos that a lot of others didn't have. Wattie trusted him. They worked well together. Even in times when he was pulled in by cops as he arrived back in Glasgow airport or off the ferry at Cairnryan and he'd been quizzed as a person of interest, Lambie knew they'd had nothing on him. In fact he quite enjoyed the big-shot untouchable feeling when they glared at him as he walked away after questioning. Being a person of interest to the cops was like a badge of honour. He'd talk to Wattie in their own code about it afterwards, knowing their phones were being tapped, and they'd laugh it out. When a big job was going down, he always went across and saw the troops in person, as it was safer. That way nothing could get out. But now here he was, spilling his guts to a big-time organisation run by fucking Catholics. What the actual fuck was happening here?

'Wattie Townsley.' When he said it, the name echoed in his head. 'He's the head of the UVF. He gave me the job. I mean, it's not as if I could have refused.' He looked at Jack as though he was expecting a bit of sympathy, even though he knew it wouldn't be forthcoming. It wasn't. Jack glared at him.

'You mean he ordered you to hit Kerry Casey. Frame her?'

Lambie nodded sheepishly, seeing the disgust on Jack's face.

'Why? Did Townsley say why? Or do you just do what you're told, no questions asked, no matter what you're told to do?'

Lambie took a moment. Truth was he didn't know why, and he knew better than to ask Townsley why he wanted to frame Kerry Casey. But he recalled a moment during their conversation in Belfast, when Townsley had told him not to fuck this job up, because it came from somebody well up the line. He didn't quite know what that meant. The UVF did hits, robberies and punishment beatings on request and for a fee. That was standard. If the money was good enough, the Belfast command would take on any job. That's how they worked.

'I don't make the decisions,' Lambie ventured. 'Townsley would never tell me who ordered a job or why it was being done. But I do remember him saying that this had to be done right, because the order came from up the line.'

'Up the line? What the fuck does that mean?'

'I don't know. Could be anyone. Any of the Caseys' enemies.'

Jack didn't answer and Lambie could see his brain ticking over. He would know that the Caseys had a few enemies, but going to the trouble of framing Kerry Casey was something bigger than an ordinary hit. There had to be more to this. He could see that if Jack had any answers, then he wasn't going to share them with him.

'Okay. Go on. Walk me through the night it happened. Every detail. Everyone who was there and took part. Where they are now. Every fucking detail.'

Lambie swallowed, his mouth dry.

'Can I get a drink or something? A glass of water?'

Jack went across to the sink and filled a chipped mug with water and handed it to him. Lambie put it to his lips, hands shaking, and drank from it. He felt faint and tired and defeated. He went on talking.

'I had to make a plan. I knew it wouldn't be easy to lure Kerry Casey into a meet or a trap or anything like that. So the plan was fucking basic.' He turned his head to Thomson who was still out, his body twitching from the shock of the drill still attaching his hand to the desk. 'Thomson gave me the bodies – the boys who would be involved – and I okayed them. I brought Billy Dobson in from Belfast to do it. We decided to have someone stop in the middle of the road as if they were in trouble. We had been following her car for a couple of days. We knew she was coming back to the house but on the backroads. So we were waiting for her.'

'Give me all the names,' Jack said.

Lambie swallowed. 'The main man was Billy Dobson. He was organising it for Thomson. They were both there. And Bo – Billy Bo Black. But Bo's dead now. He had to be dealt with because he was coked out afterwards and shooting his mouth off about what'd happened. We couldn't have that, so we got rid of him.'

'At the quarry?' Jack glared at him.

'Aye. The bodies we put in Casey's car were Thomas Lumsden and Peter Hawkins. The pair of them were stealing from me, so they had to be got rid of anyway, and we used their bodies that night. Dobson had shot them both, earlier, before the Casey car arrived. Then the boys were lying in wait in the bushes when they stopped.'

Lambie wasn't surprised, but it confirmed everything he suspected. The little prick Gimpy had run to the Caseys and spilled his guts. Fucker.

'Gimpy came to you,' he said, deadpan.

'Shut the fuck up and keep telling the story. Give me names,' Jack hit back.

'Thomson, Rab Downey, Davey McKay. They're all my boys. They were the guys who ambushed her. The boys dragged the bodies over and put them in the Casey car.'

'So you just executed two of your own boys for convenience?' Jack said. 'What kind of fucking snake in the grass are you, Lambie?'

'It's not as if they were just innocent bystanders. They were two pricks who'd been stealing from me. They'd stiffed me on collections from a batch of heroin recently. They were on the road out anyway. I just brought it forward because it suited me.'

Jack didn't answer but the contempt was all over his face.

'Give me addresses and phone numbers. Tell me where these guys are.'

Lambie sat for a long moment. He had just ratted on everyone who was close to him, from Wattie Townsley to the guys he kicked around with every day. How the fuck was he going to get out of this? He went into his mobile and reeled off the names and numbers and rough addresses of where they lived and where to find them. One of Jack's men wrote them down. Then Lambie sat, waiting.

'Right,' Jack finally said. 'Here's what you're going to do. You're going to set up a meeting in Belfast with Townsley. You're going to wear a wire and talk to him about what happened. Get him to talk about the hit, that it came from him, that it was an ordered job. Then you give that to me.'

Lambie looked at him in disbelief.

'How the fuck am I going to suddenly set up a meet with Townsley and get him talking about the job? He'll be suspicious.'

'Well if he is, he'll shoot you. It'll save me doing it.'

'Fuck's sake. You'd be as well shooting me now.'

'Don't tempt me, arsehole.'

This was do-or-die stuff. If Lambie could pull this off, he might be able to do a runner and disappear for the rest of his life. He would have to. He had enough money. But he would have to go to the other side of the world.

'And what happens if I can make this work? What happens to me then?'

'We'll see,' Jack said, stone-faced.

'What about him?' Lambie jerked his head towards Thomson who was beginning to come to, groaning and crying.

'We'll see.'

'So what happens now?' Lambie said.

He knew one thing for sure – he wasn't going home to pack for the cruise. But what the Christ was he going to say to his wife?

'The boys will take you somewhere. For the night. Then tomorrow morning, you'll make the call to Townsley.'

'And tell him what?'

'You're the fucking mastermind,' Jack said. 'You can work that out.'

Jack looked at the two big men standing behind him, and nodded. They pulled Lambie to his feet, and walked him to the door. As he looked back, he saw Thomson half conscious, reaching out with his free hand.

'Dick. Wait. Don't leave me,' Thomson groaned.

Those were the last words he spoke. Lambie watched as one of the men stepped towards Thomson. He took a gun out of the waistband of his trousers, shoved it into the nape of Thomson's neck, and fired.

CHAPTER NINETEEN

A pall of grief hung over the prison in the days that followed the Linda's suicide. The usual banter and joshing among the younger women had all but stopped, and it was as though their spirit had gone. Even though most of the girls hadn't known much about Linda, and in fact didn't even know each other that well, Kerry had noticed that there was a certain camaraderie that existed between the women. Being locked up in jail, losing your freedom, and for most of them, having not much of a future to look at when they got out, somehow made their time inside feel they were part of something. There was a level of protection in here, because many of the girls were from broken homes, already scarred by the system, most of them on the fringes of society. But in here, they found others in the same boat. Someone Kerry used to know said that everyone finds their own level in life. It had been a glib, snobbish, remark, she thought, made to her at the start of her law career, about some persistent reoffender in court again. Kerry always felt it was unfair to judge people immediately because you never knew what brought them to where they were. She was a bit of a bleeding heart that way. But in jail, she could see a completely different world rolled out in front of her. She was lucky because at least no matter what happened here, she'd already had something of a life; she'd travelled, seen places, had a successful career. But many of these girls had nothing. They'd come in here with nothing and they'd leave with nothing, and didn't have much to look forward to.

But Kerry noticed that after Linda's death, there was also anger brewing, and prisoners were unsettled and often aggressive, more often than not towards the prison officers. Some of the long-term offenders seemed to be high on drugs and there had been fury when the officers initiated cell searches after they'd discovered pills had been circulating. Free time in the evenings was beginning to take on an edginess that Kerry found disquieting, and more and more she wished she could be out of there. It came to a head one night over the drugs. Janice, a girl in her late twenties who had been in and out of jail for years, had arrived back two weeks ago, and rumour was that she was the one who had grassed about some diazepam that had been found. The night it happened, Kerry had been sitting in the communal area after dinner reading a book while others watched the TV.

'Don't look now,' Ash said to Kerry and the other two

girls who were on the sofa, 'but Aggie's spoiling for a fight. She's been bitching all day how she's going to batter Janice for grassing.'

'But does she know it was her?' Kerry felt naive as soon as she'd said it.

'No, but there's no courtroom in here, Kerry. It's the law of the jungle.'

The place went quiet as Aggie got to her feet and the others around her table glanced at each other as though they knew what was about to happen.

Janice sat by herself, reading a magazine. She looked up to see Aggie standing over her.

'Fuck!' Ash said. 'Look! Aggie's got a spanner! She must have stolen it from the bike shop.'

No sooner were the words out than Aggie lashed out with the spanner and hit Janice smack on the shoulder then the side of her head. The girl looked dazed, as she turned around.

'What the fuck are you doing, you fat bastard!'

'You're a skinny bastard grass!' Aggie said. 'And you're getting it.' She struck out again, this time hitting her above the eye where blood spurted out.

'Hey!' Kerry suddenly heard herself saying. 'Stop it. You're going to kill her.'

Everyone turned to Kerry, and Aggie swivelled around to face her as Janice slumped to the floor. Then Aggie ran the few steps across and lunged at Kerry, screaming, 'You and all the fucking Caseys are grasses! Your brother Mickey was a grass!'

For a second, despite her terror, the words stung Kerry. Mickey a grass? That was something she'd never heard before. But even as the thought streaked across her consciousness, Aggie had lifted the spanner and was about to strike her, when suddenly Ash jumped up and tackled Aggie from the waist, bringing her to the floor and knocking the spanner out of her hand. Two wardens came racing from the canteen area and one of them grabbed Aggie, sitting astride her. But she wriggled and elbowed the warden, trying to get to the spanner that was a couple of feet away from where they were struggling. Most of the girls were now in a circle surrounding the action, and Kerry then saw one of Aggie's lifer mates kick the spanner across to her so she was able to grasp it. And before the other warden could wade in, Aggie brought the spanner down heavily onto the officer's head. Then again.

Blood pumped out from the side of her head. As the siren wailed, the other officers came rushing as the prison officer lay in a pool of blood. None of the inmates came to help. Two officers forced Aggie onto her stomach, handcuffed her behind her back, then dragged her to her feet. Everyone watched as she was led away.

'Right! Show's over! Everyone into their cells!' one of the officers shouted.

Ash leaned in to Kerry. 'Aggie'll get another four years

for that. Look. The warden is unconscious. She's no' even moving. Maybe she's dead.'

Kerry stood looking around as the prisoners filed away, and the officer lay motionless on the floor, the trickle of blood oozing from her temple now flowing onto the tiled floor.

Back in the cells there was a deathly quiet outside in the communal area. Earlier, there had been some activity that Kerry assumed was paramedics arriving and stretchering the prison officer away. She could hear the crackling of police radios, so this was obviously going to be a major incident. Ash and she hadn't said much as they got undressed and into their beds. It was only in the silence and the blackness after lights out that Kerry finally broke down. She'd been holding back the tears and the tension of earlier, and everything over the last few days, and suddenly the floodgates opened.

'You all right, Kerry?'

'Yes,' she sniffed. 'I . . . I'm just a bit overwhelmed by all that stuff going on out there. It was terrible. I feel I'm trapped and I can't escape. I don't know if I can take much more of this, Ash. I really don't.'

Kerry heard Ash sit up on the bed and then climb down the ladder. She sat on the edge of her bed and took Kerry's hand.

'Listen, mate. We all get like that sometimes, when we can't see the end of the road. Especially when it's your first time locked up. But you'll be fine in time. You're a good woman, Kerry. And you're strong.'

'But I can't stand it. I can't bear the thought that if I don't get out of here and it goes to trial, I might have my baby in here.' Kerry sobbed.

'Sssh.' Ash wiped Kerry's tears with the sleeve of her pyjamas. 'Listen. You've got top people trying to get you out of here. Just hang on. It's just that shit tonight that pushed you over the edge. But hey. You stood up to Aggie. You told her to stop when she was beating the crap out of Janice. That was well brave.' Ash grinned. 'Good job she's away in handcuffs.'

Kerry stopped crying, and could see that Ash was trying to lighten the mood. She forced a smile.

'Jesus. I can't believe I did that. I hope to hell she doesn't appear back here in the morning.'

'Nah,' Ash said. 'She'll be locked up in isolation for a bit. They might even move her to another jail. She's a trouble-maker.'

'I hope I don't see her again. But what about her mates?'

'Don't worry. We'll keep out of their way. I've got your back anyway.'

'Thanks, Ash. You were brilliant, jumping in like that.'

'Aye. I'm a good fighter. Wiry.' She beamed.

With each passing week, the way things were going for Kerry, she didn't know if she would get out of there, but she had to keep hoping and believing. Marty kept telling her to keep her spirits up and that something would give. He said that they'd realise it was all too easy for the cops to find someone caught red-handed like this, with bodies in their car. That it was a process she had to go through, bear with, and that once they started looking hard, they would find – through forensics or DNA, that she and Danny had nothing to do with this. It was only a matter of time. Kerry hoped so. Because she was now almost six months pregnant, her bump showing, the life inside her kicking away. The idea that she might give birth behind bars was unthinkable. In her darker moments, and there had been many in recent days, she thought of Vinny. Not a trace or a sign that he was anywhere. She knew he would never do that. If he wanted to take himself out of the picture with Kerry, she knew him well enough to know that he would sit her down and tell her. He was too much of a man to do a runner. And even if he didn't want to be with her – and she understood that, given who she was – he would have told her. *One day at a time*, she told herself. And today, she had a visitor in the afternoon – Jack. She'd only seen him a few times since she was in, so she was looking forward to hearing what was going on outside.

Kerry was glad to see big Jack as she arrived along with other women into the prison visiting area. He'd got her a coffee and sat at the table waiting for her. He stood up when she approached.

'Hey, Kerry. Good to see you.' He opened his arms.

Kerry walked into his embrace and it was good to feel his strong arms around her. They stayed that way for a few seconds, and for a moment Kerry felt a little choked. When they parted, Jack searched her face, and she knew he could see it.

'You all right?'

'Yeah,' Kerry lied. 'I'm fine. It's just good to see you, Jack. Makes me homesick for everything when I see you.'

'I know.'

They sat down and Jack slid the coffee over to her.

'They don't do lattes in here apparently.' He smiled, lightening the moment.

'I know. But it's not that bad. I've got used to it.'

'So how are you coping?' Jack said. 'I saw on the news about the suicide of that young girl. That must have been awful.'

'It was,' Kerry said. She lifted the cup to her lips and sipped. 'She was only nineteen. All the women were really shattered by it. There's a few tough cookies in here, but something like that – the mood seemed to go from sorrow to anger. It's been a hard few days. There's been a bit of trouble among the prisoners and a warden got attacked by a lifer. She's a real hard case, and she's been having a go at me. She tried to hit me as well, and shouted at me that our Mickey was a grass – that all the Caseys were grasses. I mean, where the hell did that come from, Jack? I've never even heard anything about grassing, or our Mickey.'

Jack shrugged.

'I wouldn't worry about it, Kerry. Accusing someone of being a grass is just about the worst thing you can say to anyone. So she must have been mad or maybe just threatened because the head of the Caseys is in jail. I was worried that something like this would happen. But listen. Just keep your chin up. We'll get you out of here soon. I promise.'

They sat for a moment in silence. Kerry didn't really want to pour her heart out to Jack about everything she'd been feeling in recent days.

'So how are things going?' Kerry asked.

Jack nodded slowly and leaned forward a little.

'Good,' he said softly. 'There's been a bit of a development. A breakthrough.'

'Seriously?' Kerry wondered why it was Jack who was telling her this and not Marty.

'Yeah. We know who framed you. Who set it up. Who carried out the hit and planted the drugs, the guns. We have names.'

Kerry's stomach did a little jolt of delight. But if this was Jack giving her this information, then she knew it had to have been acquired by force. From where she was sitting, right now that didn't matter a damn. She was innocent, and she didn't care how her people went about proving it.

'Really? Tell me.'

Jack's voice dropped to a whisper. 'Wee guy came to us. His name is Steven. He worked in the White Horse for Dick Lambie's mob.' He paused. 'You'll not know them, Kerry, as you've been away. But they're UVF, violent loyalists. They carry out hits, robberies and stuff for big money. It all comes from Belfast. It was Lambie and his mob who set you up.'

'So this guy broke away from them and came to us? Why?'

'He's not one of them. Just worked for them in the bar. They've been bullying and using him for years. He's just a wee guy with a limp and not a lot going for him. But he's up to his eyes in debt with them – they're loan sharks as well – and they were extorting fortunes from him. He'd never have paid them off. It was all about bullying and abuse. They got him involved in a murder, and made a veiled threat that if he opened his trap then they'd kill his sick old mother. That was the last straw. But before he ran out on them, he overheard information that it was their mob who did the set-up on you and Danny.'

'Jesus! Is it definitely true?'

'Oh, it's true all right. We've already established that a hundred per cent.'

Kerry didn't reply. She was processing all this in her head.

'So where is the guy, this Steven and his mother? We've got them somewhere safe?'

Jack nodded and blinked in agreement.

'Of course. We've got them in one of our flats out of the way. The mother's a right old character – coughing her lungs up with emphysema. Steven is a good man, and he's been invaluable to us.' He paused. 'The information we've got will get you out of here, Kerry. I haven't spoken to Marty or Danny yet. But I'm sure this will make the cops and the prosecution think again.'

Kerry reached across and touched his hand. This was a game changer. It was all about how they approached the information now.

'So what about Lambie? What'll happen with him now?'

Jack sat back and folded his arms. He tried not to give anything away, but Kerry could see a glint in his eye that meant he knew he was winning.

'We've got him with us. He's helping the Caseys with their enquiries, so to speak.'

For the first time in a few days Kerry smiled. She didn't need to ask – at least not right now. She knew that no matter how much information they got from Lambie and his mob, that even if it did get her out of jail, the retribution for putting her there in the first place would be swift and deadly. Of course it was wrong. Of course it was something she would have run a mile from a year ago, even eight months ago. But right now, it all sat fine with her.

*

Steven watched his ma dunking her digestive biscuit into the mug of tea he'd put down on the table next to the arm-chair. She sat toasting her feet in front of the flame effect gas fire. Outside, the early evening gloom of a winter's night had settled over the street, and Steven gazed out, watching the well-heeled people getting out of their upmarket cars and heading to the front doors of their homes. The view was a world away from High Street. He'd lived three floors up from the day he was born and when you looked outside all human life was there, from the homeless guys sleeping in doorways to the sharp-suited lawyers heading down to the High Court on the Glasgow Green. Or just the typical Glas-gow punters, heading to and from the station or into the city centre in search of shops, pubs or a day out. It was always interesting, an evolving picture every day. This place was different. Jack and Cal had taken him and his ma to some place on the edge of the West End of Glasgow, out towards the outskirts of the city. He knew the road well enough. He remembered going on it for bus runs with his ma as a kid, and eventually they'd get to the seaside town of Helens-burgh. He remembered getting his picture taken with a wee monkey dressed in dungarees and a yellow polo-neck sweater. Looking back, the poor monkey was probably tran-quillised, but back then as a wee guy, having a monkey on your shoulder for a photo, you were well made up.

In this street of large, smart, detached and semi-detached houses, people came and went to work early in the morning and returned at night. There were no shops nearby, no buses coming through, and it felt a bit isolated. But that was the only downside of it. The upside was how lovely it was. How Jack had looked after them, and how much his ma was loving every minute of their new surroundings, their new life. Everything had happened so fast, he'd scarcely had time to consider if this would indeed be a new life. He wondered what would happen once this all died down, but he was afraid to ask. He'd been assured at their first meeting with Jack and Marty that he would be looked after, and that they'd keep looking after him. He hoped so, because he knew if he put his head above the parapet anywhere in Glasgow city, someone would find him. He thought for a moment of how he'd gone to the addresses of Rab Downey and Davey McKay, and pointed them out as he sat in the back of the blacked-out car. That was all he'd had to do. Just show them the right guys and the Caseys' boys would do the rest. He could only imagine what would be happening to them right now. And he knew that Thomson would have been picked up by now and so would Lambie. He didn't care what happened to them. All of them deserved what they got. He was just grateful for the break, and he'd never slept so well as he had in the last few nights in the comfort of a warm cosy house after a meal with his ma. It gladdened his heart to see how happy she was. She even seemed to be breathing and moving around a little easier. Deep down he chastised himself for not making a bigger effort to make her life better. But he didn't have the means to do that – he'd had no real education, no trade and no finances. So he was never going to get out of the mire. Still he blamed himself. If he could have got his ma to a place like this years ago, she might not have got so ill. And maybe if he'd been living in a place like this, with a good job, he might even have found a girl to settle down with. All now water under the bridge, he told himself, but the thoughts were still there.

'You look miles away, Steven.' His ma sipped her tea. 'You all right?'

'Aye, Ma,' Steven replied. 'I'm fine. Just kind of trying to take things in. It's all happened that fast.'

'I know, son,' she said, her voice consoling. 'You're not regretting what you did though, are you?'

He looked at her, shook his head. 'No. There was no way out for me, Ma – for us. When I walked in to our house and saw that scumbag Thomson in your bedroom, my blood ran cold. If I'd have stayed, Christ knows what they would have lined up for me next. They thought they had me right where they wanted me.'

'But you showed them, son, did you not?'

Steven wished he shared his ma's triumphalism. He still felt that Lambie and his mob would hunt him down. But as long as the Caseys protected him he'd be safe.

'Aye,' he said. 'More like you showed them, Ma. The way you just made your mind up that night was enough. I don't know if I'd have had the courage to do what I did without you, and that's the truth.'

'Ach, nonsense. You're a good man, Steven. And you're a better man to come. When this settles down a bit and if that Kerry Casey gets out of jail, maybe you should see about working for them.'

Steven gave her a surprised look.

'The Caseys? But they're gangsters too. That might be like going out of the frying pan into the fire. I'm not even thinking that far ahead, Ma. We'll just wait and see what happens.'

'Aye,' she said. 'I suppose the Caseys are gangsters like all the rest of them. But I remember back in the old days, that Tim Casey fella – he'd be Kerry's old man, I suppose.'

'You knew them? You knew the father? You never mentioned it before.' Steven said, surprised.

'I knew of them,' she said, wistfully. 'Everyone did. I remember him, and he was a robber all right. But I remember he and his boys got involved in a big rumpus one time when a teenage girl was battered and they sorted it all out, and the boys who did it were beaten within an inch of their lives. The Caseys didn't need to get into that – it wasn't their affair, and not even in their area. Police were involved but they didn't even charge them. You got your own justice back then, and sometimes it was better than it is now. So maybe there's a bit of good in them somewhere, that's what I'm saying. I mean, they could have just given you a few quid after you helped them and sent us on our way without any protection.' She gestured with her hand. 'But look what they've done for us. They've got us well set up here and they're making sure we're fed and stuff. I don't know that they had to do that. But they have, and I've a bit of respect for them.'

Steven found himself smiling at his ma's logic.

'Jeez, Ma, you're beginning to sound like a gangster yourself.'

'Aye, well, if it comes to that . . .' She gave a hearty laugh that turned into a bout of coughing, but she was still smiling at the end of it.

CHAPTER TWENTY

Sharon sat on the chair next to where Kerry normally would have sat during meetings with her closest aides. In Kerry's absence, and with Danny gone too, she was overseeing everything that was going on in the organisation, but she didn't want to sit in Kerry's seat. She had too much respect for her to do that. Jack had already been to see Kerry in Cornton Vale, and Danny in Barlinnie, to let them know of the latest developments. Vic had been working closely with Jack and the boys to prepare the next step.

'So how are they bearing up, Jack?' Sharon asked.

In her own visit to Kerry, Sharon had sensed that she was feeling emotional but putting on a brave face for her.

'Danny is okay,' he said, nodding. 'It's a long time since he's seen the inside of a jail, but he's dealing with it fine. We've got a couple of people on the inside looking out for him. Danny's not as young as he was – or as he thinks he is – if any of the young blades try to take him on. So I talked to some people to make sure he's looked after.' Jack paused, sat back. 'But he's well buoyed up with the developments. And he's angry all right. Raging that he's not out here dealing with these bastards who brought all this on us. He said whatever it takes, just do it. Kerry is fuming too that they've been totally framed and she's banged up in jail, pregnant, and not knowing when the hell she'll get out.'

Sharon wasn't surprised to hear Danny's reaction, and she knew how upset Kerry was. The out-of-the-blue news that this little Glasgow guy Steven had come to them with information had changed everything. She knew that the retribution had already begun, but she hadn't asked Jack or Vic what they'd done with Thomson's body. As far as she was concerned, it wasn't relevant. He got what he deserved. Sharon didn't suffer from the crisis of conscience that she knew Kerry did when it came to the heavy-duty retribution, especially when it was carried out in cold blood. If someone had crossed the Caseys and placed them in a situation where they could lose everything and the head of their organisation was facing life in jail – there was only one way to deal with them. But she knew the show wasn't over yet. They had Lambie, and they were working on a plan.

'So, Jack,' Sharon said. 'Let's see how we can work this, so that when it comes down to the big questions, we actually have evidence that Marty can take to the prosecution.'

Jack glanced at Vic. 'We're on it, Sharon. I think we should hit this Wattie Townsley in Belfast. Go right to the heart of it. Apart from sending a message to these bastards, if it works out, we can get him talking about ordering the set-up.'

Sharon liked the idea, but how could they make that work?

'Townsley's UVF. Is there a snowball in hell's chance of him grassing anyone up?'

'Depends on how it's put to him,' Jack said, seriously. 'If he's no option but to squeal, then he will.'

Sharon clasped her hands on the table in front of her. She had to admit that stuff like this, organising how to extract information from thugs like Townsley, wasn't really her forte. Back in Spain, she'd been running the Casey businesses, getting the hotel ready for opening in a few months' time. Sure, she hadn't been shy when it came to putting a bullet in the Colombian after his thugs had kidnapped her and were going to murder her. Nor had she flinched when she'd shot the two bastards her late husband Knuckles Boyle had sent to execute her. But that was about survival, a spur-of-the-moment, white-heat reaction. Planning it in cold blood was a different matter.

'But going into Belfast, Jack,' she said. 'Townsley will be surrounded by guys who would take a bullet for him.'

Jack nodded, glanced at Vic. 'True. But we've thought of an alternative to that. Vic and me have talked a lot about this in the last couple of days, and we've come up with something. You need to hear it first, see what you think.'

Sharon waited, wondering what Vic had talked secretly with Jack about and not told her. They'd been living in Kerry's guest house together, since they'd both came back from Spain to help run things while Kerry and Danny were gone. Vic had always played his cards close to his chest in all the time she'd known him, but when they'd got together after he'd come out of jail, and now that they were both entrenched with the Caseys, Vic was more open. He knew she was running the show in Spain. But here in Glasgow, though she was overseeing things, Vic was more in his comfort zone with Jack. He'd been there when they picked up Thomson and Lambie, and he'd told her about Thomson's fate. And he'd been on the crew who rounded up the rest of Lambie's guys who'd set up Kerry. This kind of hardman stuff was meat and drink to him. And Sharon knew Vic felt he owed Kerry a huge debt. If it hadn't been for her blackmailing the Attorney General with compromising pictures and videos, he'd probably still be languishing in Belmarsh prison awaiting trial. He would do whatever was required to get her and Danny out of jail.

'I'm all ears,' Sharon said.

'Well, as you know, we have Lambie holed up, and he's being very cooperative.'

Sharon nodded. 'What kind of nick is he in? Did you not tell me he was supposed to be going on a cruise or something when you picked him up? Has he talked to his wife?'

'He has,' Jack said. 'He phoned her that night to say that something had come up, that they had to cancel, and that he'd been summoned to Belfast for a special job. He said his wife knew better than to ask questions. But he'll do whatever we tell him, because he thinks if he does, then he's going to get away with it if we get Kerry out.' Jack paused. 'Of course he's wrong about that, but we'll let Danny take care of that when, all going well, he gets out of jail.'

'And is he up for going to Belfast? I'd be worried about that.'

Jack nodded. 'He doesn't think it's a good idea. He said it would be too dangerous and that him suddenly pitching up in Belfast might get Townsley's hackles up and could get us all killed if it went tits up. So he says it's better if we can get Townsley over here.'

'How are we going to do that? Would Townsley not be more suspicious if an invite to Glasgow suddenly comes across his table?'

'Aye,' Jack said. 'He would. But he comes over quite a lot for the Old Firm matches. Next week is a quarter final of the Scottish Cup. It's midweek, so he might fly in and back the following day. Lambie can find out. If he does, then Lambie can talk to him about an offer on the table that looks like it will make him a huge amount of money. He says he might buy it, that he's greedy. He says Townsley is stashing away a lot of money for his future, and when the time comes, he wants to leave Belfast and go and live abroad. He said he has plans to buy a couple of bars in Spain. Set himself up there. Apparently he's well connected.'

Sharon puffed, a little indignant.

'Yeah. Well the bastard might find out when he gets there that other people are much better connected. So what kind of money-making deal are we talking about?'

'Lambie said he might be lured over by the promise of a big coke deal. One that would make him more money than ever.'

Sharon thought about it for a long moment. The Caseys didn't have a lot of cocaine around their organisation these days. Kerry had seen to that in recent months. Sure, they'd stolen the shipment of coke from the Colombians, but it was long gone, sold and profited from, and the money invested in legit businesses, helping them to grow both in Spain and the UK.

'Can we get our hands on a load of cocaine like that? I mean, would he not want to see it?' As she said it, Sharon felt she sounded a little naive.

Jack shrugged. 'He wouldn't need to see it if the offer is coming from Lambie. He trusts him completely. It was Townsley who pushed Lambie all the way to where he is now. They were a couple of scallies when they were younger and did work for Loyalists in the early days, earned their spurs. They trust each other. Totally.'

'So Lambie sets him up? Brings him over here? Then what?'

'Well, some of it will have to be played by ear. But if he comes here, ideally we'd get him to talk to Lambie about the hit. And after we've got that, we take it from there. Take him on a night out.'

Sharon glanced at Vic who raised his eyebrows.

'Fair enough. Sounds good. I'll leave you guys to it.'

Lambie hadn't slept much in the flat the Caseys had dumped him in yesterday. It was like being in jail. He'd been told he wouldn't be going anywhere until this was finished. They'd locked the bedroom door last night, and he knew that one of their henchmen was in the bedroom next to him or in the living room watching television late into the night. There was no chance he could get out, or alert anyone that he was here. They'd taken his mobile off him, and later in the evening someone came in and dropped off a couple of shopping bags with clothes for the next few days. They didn't speak to him or discuss anything, other than to tell him the takeaway food had arrived. He'd sat at the dining table in the living room while the Casey man ate on an armchair, one eye on the television, one eye on him. It occurred to him that he could grab a knife and have a go, but looking at the big burly bastard with the scar down one side of his face, it wouldn't be a good idea. There was nothing he could do but wait it out until they told him what was next. Lying in bed the previous night, he'd felt a twinge of guilt for Nora, who had built up to go on the cruise. But that was the least of his worries right now. She really didn't have a clue about anything, and never had. As long as he threw enough money at her all his life she pretty much let him do what he wanted. There was no point in dwelling on it, he decided. The next few days would be difficult and crucial. When he'd spoken to Jack last night, he'd convinced him that going to Belfast was not a good idea. He knew that even if he could find a way to warn Townsley once he got there, he would still get bumped off in due course for even bringing the Caseys to his turf. So it had to be Glasgow. Townsley had said a few weeks ago that he was coming over for the match on Wednesday and they'd planned to meet up for a drink and a bite to eat, as they usually did. This would be the trap he would lay for Townsley, the man he'd been loyal to most of his life. He knew the Caseys would execute Townsley as easily and coldly as they'd done with Thomson. But if that meant *he* could get out of this shitstorm alive, then so be it. It was all about *his* survival now. As soon as this was over, he would disappear, he told himself. Of course there was always the chance, the distinct possibility, that the Caseys would put a bullet in him too, but he didn't want to think about that. He heard the buzzer on the door and the voice of guy in the living room buzzing someone in. Then he heard Jack's voice. There was a knock on the door and the minder shouted, 'Lambie! Out here!'

'Right,' Lambie said, suppressing the rage that he was kowtowing to this fucker.

He took a deep breath, stood up and caught a glimpse of his ashen face in the mirror, sniffed and braced himself as he opened the door.

In the living room Jack stood with his hands in his jacket pockets, glaring at him. Beside him was another Casey man, a big stern-looking bastard called Vic, who'd driven them to this flat on the waterfront across from Kinning Park.

'You ready to make the call?' Jack said, his face like flint.

'Aye. I've no phone though. His number is on my mobile.'

Jack reached into the inside pocket of his jacket and took out Lambie's phone and switched it on. He stood for a moment as the phone pinged to life and registered messages and missed calls. He held the phone out to Lambie.

'Don't be doing anything stupid now, like making a panic call to someone. Because if you do, it'll be the last word you speak. Got that?'

Lambie nodded and said nothing. Before Jack handed it to him he took it back again.

'Have you got an app on there that lets people know where you are?'

'No,' Lambie said, wishing to fuck he had.

'Okay. Make the call. The usual kind of call you'd make

when Townsley's coming over for the match. And suggest a curry or something – whatever you normally do. But tell him you might have a wee business proposition to put to him.'

'You think I should say that now? This early?'

Jack seemed to think for a moment.

'Aye. Just tell him there's a chance to make a whole lot of money but that you can't talk on the phone.'

Lambie shrugged. He knew money and the possibility of making loads of it would give Townsley a hard-on.

'Okay.'

He knew Jack and the others were watching him as he scrolled down the phone for Townsley's mobile. Jack nodded to the minder who took out his gun, cocked it, and kept it on him. Lambie's mind was racing with thoughts of just blurting out to Townsley quickly what was going on, but he knew if he did, he'd be dead on the floor by the time he finished the first sentence, if he got that far. He held up the phone to show Townsley's number to Jack, who nodded but said nothing. Then he pushed the call key, and put the mobile on loudspeaker. A voice answered after four rings. Jack took a breath and composed himself.

'Wattie. How's it going?'

'Not too bad. What about you, brother?' The chirpy, sturdy Belfast accent filled the room.

'Aye, good. Just working away and stuff. Been a busy week.'

'You on loudspeaker, mate? You sound a bit distant.'

'Aye. Sorry. I'm getting ready to go out, running around like a blue-arsed fly.' He glanced at Jack with an expression that asked is it okay. 'Hold on till I switch the speaker off.' He switched the speaker off. 'That better?'

'Aye. Don't like them fucking speakers. Every fucker can listen in.'

'Aye. I won't keep you, man. But you still coming for the match?'

'Planning to. Got the flight booked and a hotel. Staying at the Radisson again.'

'Great stuff. You fancy going for a curry after? I've a couple of things I wanted to chat to you about.'

Silence. Then Wattie spoke. 'What like? Problems? With the recent job?'

'No, no, man. Far from it. Listen. I don't want to talk on the phone. You know what it's like. But something I think you might fancy. A wee proposition.'

'Aye? Throw in a couple of birds then as well, man. That'll get my interest up.'

Lambie heard Townsley's chuckling and was relieved that he wasn't at all suspicious.

'I'm sure that can be arranged, mate. What time you over?'

'I'm on the three o'clock flight. So I'll be in my hotel getting organised by back of four. Give me a shout and we'll meet for a pint before the match.'

'Perfect. See you Wednesday, mate.'

The line went dead, and Lambie stood for a long moment with the phone still at his ear. He was already in deep shit even before he made that phone call. Now there was no going back. He glanced at Jack who had his hand out-stretched for the phone. He handed it to him, but Jack didn't speak. He just blinked in a kind of acknowledge-ment that he'd done what he'd been asked to do. Then he nodded to the guy next to him, and turned towards the door. As he opened it, he looked over his shoulder to where Lambie was standing.

'Talk later. I'll be back.'

He left and Lambie stood for a moment feeling isolated, lonely and fucking terrified.

CHAPTER TWENTY-ONE

Jake knew that Tarifa could turn into a battle if Mateo was right. So he was preparing for every eventuality, packing several guns and weapons into the hard-shell case he took with him on jobs. He always looked as though he travelled light, but inside the case was enough lethal weaponry to wipe out any mob. He packed a lightweight Kevlar bulletproof jacket and a spare one for Sullivan. It was important to be prepared. He sipped from a mug of coffee on his balcony, and gazed out over the sun twinkling on the sea. The village was beginning to get busy with people going about their business. He looked at his watch. If he picked up Sullivan and Mateo shortly, they could be in Tarifa by lunchtime. Then his mobile shuddered on the table and he could see Pam's name on the screen. He picked up the phone, curious as to why she was phoning him this early.

'Pam.'

The silence was brief, but Jake got a sense that something was wrong.

'Pam. You all right, sweetheart?'

Then he heard the sniffing.

'Oh, Jake. I'm sorry. I . . . I didn't have anyone else to phone.'

'What's up?'

Again the sniffing. Then she spoke. 'They came here. To the bar. Just now. They . . . they hit me, Jake.'

Cold rage flooded through him.

'Wait there. I'll be right over.'

He ended the call, shoved his phone into his pocket and went back into the apartment. From his case, he took a Glock pistol and pulled on a shoulder holster. Then he put his jacket on and went out the door, downstairs and into his car. As he drove the two miles through traffic to Fuengirola, Jake cursed out loud, blaming himself for bringing this shit to Pam's door. She didn't deserve this. In all the time he'd known her, Pam was a decent, hard-working, sometimes hard case of a woman. But she had the biggest heart, and would always go out of her way to do someone a good turn, give them a lift if they were down. Over the years, they'd become more than friends, and even when her husband had been alive, she'd shared Jake's bed from time to time. But it was more than that. Jake had never quite figured out what it was, because the way he lived his life meant he always ran a mile from any commitment, but Pam had filled the emptiness in his life – not just because of the sex, but because of her attitude, her charm, and her determination to see the good in a pile of crap. That's why she'd gone on for so long with the bar after the gangsters had steamed in and more or less taken it from her. The last thing she needed was to be dragged into his fight with the Colombians. He pulled his car off the main street and parked at the rear of the bar. The shutters were down and she wasn't quite open yet. So he punched in her number.

'I'm outside, Pam.'

'Okay.'

The shutters slowly went up, the noise filling the back alley, and then he saw her. Fuck! Her face was puffed up, one eye was red and swollen and her lip had been cut. He ducked under the shutter before it was fully up and dived inside. She buckled into his arms.

'Christ, Pam. I'm so sorry. They'll pay for this.'

He hugged her close and felt her sniffing on his shoulder. He held her tight, comforting her and stroking her hair as she sobbed.

'It's okay, sweetheart, you're safe now. Don't worry. I'll get these fucking Colombian bastards.'

She pulled away and looked up at him, her face tear-stained and puffy. It tore at his heart.

'It wasn't the Colombians, Jake.'

'What?'

'It wasn't them. It was the Spanish, the thugs who more or less took over the place, extorting money; the arseholes who made me change my bar into what it is. They came last night and said they needed me to move out of my apartment, that they were bringing girls in over the next few weeks, and that the place would also be a brothel upstairs. I told them to fuck off.'

'Why didn't you call me last night?'

'I . . . I didn't think they'd react like this. I thought maybe they'd send the boss and we'd come to an agreement. They've never been like this before, this heavy-handed. Something has changed now. It's all about money and women and all that shit.'

'So they told you the place was going to be a brothel.'

She bit her lip. 'I can't have that, Jake. I won't work here. My name is still on the deeds so I own the place on paper and they can't legally make me do it. But they can beat me into it.' She shook her head. 'I don't know what I can do now.'

Jake sat her down on a bar stool and sat opposite her, holding both her hands. In the darkness of the bar, her face was lit only by the neon of the bar taps and the gantry lights. She looked broken and bruised. Jake felt a dig of guilt that he was glad it hadn't been him who'd done this to her by dragging her into the Colombian shit. He hated himself for feeling that way, but he could never have forgiven himself if this had happened because she'd helped him last night.

'I'm going to fix this for you. I promise you that. I'll get these people, and I'll make sure they don't come near you again.'

She looked at him, her eyes pleading but hopeless.

'But, Jake, I don't know how you can. They run everything along this strip – all the protection for the shops and bars and restaurants.'

'I'll get them,' Jake said. 'But I need to go to Tarifa now. After last night. With the guy. Me and Sullivan are going down there now. But I'll be back in the next day or so. I promise you. Just lie low. Tell them you'll do what they ask, but that you need a bit of time to get organised and pack up your things. You got that?'

She nodded. Jake got off the stool and glanced at his watch.

'I have to move now. But I'll deal with this when I get back. Maybe you should take the day off and stay in the flat. Call them and tell them you'll agree to everything they ask. But say that you need time to get the legal stuff done. Can you do that?'

'Yes. I think so.'

He stepped towards her and pulled her close to him, kissing her cheek, and she buried her face in his neck. They stayed that way for a long moment, then he pulled away.

'I have to go, sweetheart. I'll call you. Don't worry.'

He turned and left, guilty at leaving her like this. But he

couldn't do much more right now. He considered taking her with him, but he didn't know what kind of shit was going to blow up in Tarifa, so she was probably safer here.

The Colombian had been silent for the entire journey down to Tarifa, and it crossed Jake's mind that he was either beginning to fall apart, or he was planning to double-cross them. Sullivan had said he wasn't sure they could trust him, but they both knew that right now they didn't have a lot of options. The Colombian had confirmed that Vinny was being held there, and he'd promised he would help them. But that would come at a cost.

As he drove, Jake reflected on the previous night when Mateo had opened up to them. Either he was a great bullshitter, or just a desperate man. Jake had decided he was desperate. Mateo had told them he'd been living on the Costa del Sol for three years with his wife and two-year-old son. He worked as a barman for the Colombian owner of the café in La Cala de Mijas, and though he knew it was a front for the cartel to wash their money, he didn't ask questions. When he'd got the job, he was told that if he kept his mouth shut he could have a good life here. But that if he talked to anyone about what he saw, he'd be a dead man. Mateo had said he'd tried to leave the job once to go and work on a building site, but he'd been told that leaving wasn't an option. You don't leave the cartel. They'd threatened to kill his wife and child. That was the moment Mateo had burst into tears, taking

Jake and Sullivan by surprise. They'd exchanged perplexed looks. They were stuck with this guy who was out of his depth with a bunch of hoodlums and he had nowhere to go. And now they were relying on him to help them. Anything could happen. Once Mateo had calmed down, Jake had told him that they would look after him. He'd said he would send someone to get his wife and child, and put them somewhere safe, and when this was all over, he would get them back together. To Sullivan's wide-eyed surprise, Jake had even promised they would be given a wedge of money to go and settle somewhere else, probably in the north of Spain. Mateo had agreed, and once he'd collapsed into a deep sleep, Jake had told Sullivan that he would keep his word. If they got Vinny out of this alive, with the help of this guy, then he would make sure he was looked after. By the time they were leaving Sullivan's apartment, Jake had got Mateo to ring his wife and tell her someone was going to come and pick them up, not to worry, just to go along with them, and that they would be safe. Jake had arranged for someone to do that. He didn't call Sharon or Jack to sanction any arrangement. He knew that if he'd phoned them they would tell him to do whatever it took to get Vinny. But he didn't want to tell them any of this anyway, or even that he knew where Vinny was, because it would only get their hopes up, and right now, he didn't know if he was going to be able to get Vinny out of this alive, or dead.

*

Jake pulled into the car park in the main area of the town so that they could let Mateo out. The arrangement was that once he was settled into the apartment and taking over his guard duty, he would come back out at some stage to go to the shop or bar, and he would phone Jake with whatever information he had picked up. As he was about to open the back door, Jake and Sullivan turned around to face him. He was pale and nervous, and hung-over, with dark bags under frightened eyes.

'Okay, Mateo,' Jake said. 'You are clear with everything we talked about, yes?'

Mateo nodded and looked at both of them, expression pleading.

'Please. You will make my wife and my son safe like you promised?'

'Like I promised,' Jake said. 'And when this is over, we will take you to them.'

'You are sure?'

'Mateo,' Jake said. 'I'm sure. Now it is up to you. You must be strong. You understand? You can do this. Just tell me once you know any information, and we will do the rest.' He paused. 'I told you. We will look after you. Today, this is over for you. Understand? For you, and your family.'

Mateo nodded again, opened the door and eased himself out of the car. They watched as he limped across the car park.

'Christ!' Sullivan said. 'He looks pathetic. I hope to fuck he doesn't go in there and completely burst.'

Jake kept his eye on Mateo until he disappeared out of sight in the direction of the apartment.

'I don't think he will,' he said. 'He's desperate. You know what the cartel is like. Once they have no further use for him, either in the bar or whatever drug-running shit they've involved him in, they'll just put a gun to his head. He knows that.'

Sullivan sighed, nodding.

'Yeah. That's about the size of it. Poor bastard.' He turned to Jake. 'What are you going to do with his wife and family?'

'One of my friends will pick them up this morning and take them to their home. It's up in the hills near Marbella. They'll be safe there. With Irish friends of mine.'

'Good. So is anyone else around here at the moment? I mean, your friends who you called last night?'

Jake nodded. He didn't want to go into a lot of detail about who was doing what. That's not how he worked. Sullivan would be told on a need-to-know basis, and he didn't need to know every move.

'Yes. Two of them are. They know where the apartment is, so they'll be on hand. These guys know what they're doing.' He narrowed his eyes, looking out towards the harbour. 'And I've got someone coming down on his boat this afternoon. I get the feeling that if anything is going to happen with Vinny – I mean if the Colombians are planning to get him out of there – then they'll do it under cover of darkness. Mateo said they told him they were taking Vinny for a swim. So we'll be here for a while.'

Jake and Sullivan sat in the café on a side street off the harbour in Tarifa. It had been two hours since Mateo had left them at the harbour, and it crossed Jake's mind that the Colombian had done a runner. The quayside was heaving with tourists coming off the boat from Tangier, laden with trinkets and heading for their tour buses. Other buses were arriving to catch the next ferry, and it would be easy for anyone just to disappear in the crowd. But his instinct told him that Mateo would stick with the plan, especially now that he'd told his wife to go with Jake's men. He was sure he wouldn't squeal to the Colombians, but his worry was if he got rumbled in any way and was asked awkward questions, he wouldn't be able to handle the pressure. Jake had already had a call from one of his own men saying he had a surprising development. They were waiting for him to come to the bar. Jake looked up as he could see him walking towards where they sat outside at one of the little wrought-iron tables.

'Here he comes,' Jake said to Sullivan.

A big man with dark cropped hair walked over to them with a swagger. As he approached, he pushed his aviator sunglasses onto his head, his piercing blue eyes scanning the harbour.

'Howsit going, Tommy boy?' Jake shook the big man's outstretched hand.

'All good so far, Jake.' A smile spread across his face. 'Even better than I hoped.' He shot a glance at Sullivan as he pulled a chair out and sat down.

'This is Sullivan, Tommy. He was undercover with Vinny,' Jake said.

Sullivan reached across the table and Tommy shook his hand, and gave him a kind of cold stare that Jake knew was about Tommy's basic distrust of cops. His brother had been shot dead by a British undercover cop in Belfast during the Troubles, and it was Jake who had talked Tommy into getting out of Northern Ireland rather than staying and seeking vengeance. He knew he would have ended up in jail. Jake could see that Sullivan wasn't fazed by Tommy as they shook hands.

'So what's the craic?' Jake said. 'Where's Bonzo?'

Bonzo was Tommy's best mate and the two of them worked together if they were ever required on anything Jake wanted them to do. Tommy pulled his chair close to the table and leaned in.

'We had a bit of a result this morning,' he said. 'We got on the road and came down here early, to have a decent recce and see if there was any movement in any of the other apartments. Believe it or not there was a time when the front door was left wide open by someone who was coming out, so the pair of us just went right in there.' He glanced from Jake to Sullivan, as though he was relishing telling his story.

'You walked right in?' Jake said. 'Is it not all locals in that place? Would you not be out of place?'

Tommy put his hand up. 'I don't think there is anyone in most of the flats. There are only about eight in total, and we'd watched for a while as people left looking like they were going to work. It was a chance we took. We'd seen some woman opening the shutters of her apartment and shaking out a rug, you know, like doing her housework. So we thought we would give her a knock.'

Jake put his hand to his eyes and massaged his brows. He really wasn't sure any of this was good news. But Tommy was no idiot, even if he did take flyers sometimes. He'd told him how crucial this operation was and how carefully they had to tread. So he had to trust the big man's judgement.

'You knocked on her door?'

'Yep,' Tommy said. 'She came out. Spanish woman. So I talked to her in Spanish and told her we were part of a film crew working on a documentary about Tarifa and the harbour and the tourist trade and stuff. And I asked her if it was possible to film and watch from her apartment over a day. That her window and balcony was a good vantage point.'

Jake was aware that Sullivan's mouth had dropped open. They exchanged glances and said nothing, but inside Jake was saying, 'Oh fuck!'

'So,' Tommy went on, 'she was a bit iffy in the beginning,

asking how long for, and for ID, and I gave her this old pass I had from a TV production company in London. Seemed to work. Then she said that she was going to work and wouldn't be back until later in the night and didn't know if she could trust us. All that shit.' Tommy looked from Jake to Sullivan. 'Then I offered her three hundred euros cash if we could work out of the apartment all day and into the evening.' He paused for effect. 'And she took it.'

'Fucking hell!' Jake said. He sucked in a breath through his teeth. 'Jesus, Tommy! Are you sure we can trust this woman? That she's not already in the police station telling them about the dodgy men in her apartment?'

Tommy spread his hands in a pleading gesture and shrugged, as though he did this sort of thing every day. 'Well,' he said. 'Truth is, you never really know. But she seemed sound enough. My instinct tells me she's hard-up and was glad of a wedge of money. Her eyes lit up when she saw the cash.'

'What about a man? Has she no husband or kids or anyone who's likely to wander in later?' Sullivan asked.

'No,' Tommy said curtly. 'She has one kid. There was a picture on the wall. Little boy about four, I'd say. She said he was with his gran up the coast a bit for the holiday weekend. That's where she was going to spend the day.' He paused. 'So she took the money, and off she went. Said she won't be back until around eleven this evening.'

Jake sat back and folded his arms. It was a good ploy – he

had to give Tommy ten out of ten for improvisation. He remembered the big Belfast man had been used by a TV investigation show years ago, to do undercover jobs when the programme was trying to expose villains. Who better to use for the job than a villain himself. Tommy used to regale them with stories of working with the production team, so his idea here might just work. In any case, it was already too late.

'So where's Bonzo?' Jake asked.

'He's already in the apartment, keeping a watchful eye on any comings and goings. The flat where you think Vinny is being held is the floor above, to the right. We've been in there two hours, and only heard the door being opened once. Two guys came out and down the stairs – we saw them in the street. They looked Colombian. And Bonzo saw one guy coming in. He looked Colombian too. He had a limp. But that's all the activity so far.'

Jake looked at Sullivan, then at Tommy, and half smiled.

'Okay. We'll see what the day brings.'

CHAPTER TWENTY-TWO

'The Billy Boys' anthem was being belted out in the packed White Horse pub as the Rangers fans crowded four deep at the bar. A quarter-final cup match between Celtic and Rangers was not just a big crowd puller, it was a chance for Lambie's boys to bang the drums around London Road that they were the team to beat. The song, as well as all of the vile chants from both Celtic and Rangers fans, had been banned from the football grounds a long time ago, so the only place the fans could vent their bigotry was in the bars around the football stadiums. The White Horse was on the London Road, where Celtic fans would be flocking to the stadium nearby for the match. It was always the dream of Rangers fans to beat them on their own turf. On any other Old Firm night, Lambie would have been counting the takings in his head as the tills rattled behind the bar and reckoning how many goals his team could put away to beat this Fenian scum. But not tonight. Because tonight, he felt like a condemned man. He tried to put that thought out of his mind, tried to convince himself that if he played the game the way the Caseys asked him, then they'd cut him loose as they'd promised. Of course, he couldn't come back here, or anywhere else in the UK, so he would be far away in the next few days. So he hoped. Jack had set him up with this tiny USB recording device which was inside his jacket pocket. It was completely undetectable, but every now and again, Lambie would put his hand in his pocket and just touch it. He wished he could just take it out of his pocket, bin it and keep on running. But he knew that was unlikely. Every now and then he glanced over his shoulder, and saw the two big brick shithouses – the Casey minders who were keeping an eye on him. One of them had been the guy who'd put a bullet in the back of Thomson's head in the Portakabin the other day, so he wasn't going to take any chances of upsetting him. He sipped from his pint and tried to look interested in the conversation between two of his old cohorts as they discussed the match and their team's chances. He looked at his watch. Townsley was due in any minute and they'd have a drink together before going to their season ticket holder seats for the match. There wouldn't be much chance to talk about this bogus coke deal in here, as it was noisy and he knew he wouldn't get much on the tape, but if it all went well, they'd meet up later for food and a night on the town. The swing door opened as far as it could in the throng, and in walked

Townsley, followed by two of his sidekicks. Lambie felt his gut flip a little as he strained his neck to look through the crowd. His eyes met Townsley's, and his friend's face cracked a smile; well, as much of a smile as Townsley was capable of. He had a jowly piggish face, ginger hair and thin lips. His cheeks were mottled from years of alcohol abuse. His minders pushed their way through the crowd, and anyone who was nudged out of the way looked around furiously, then their expressions changed when they saw the size of them. Many of the men in here would recognise the Belfast boys from Orange marches over there on the twelfth of July, or from Loyalist jobs over the years. But to anyone who was a visiting Gers fans, everyone was just a fan on their way to the match.

'Howsit going, mate?' Lambie managed a blustery smile and he stretched a hand out to Townsley who pumped it hard then held it a few seconds longer in a Masonic handshake.

'Good enough, mate. Good enough.' Townsley's beady eyes took in the packed room. 'You must be fucking coining it in here, you cunt,' he grinned. 'Fucking jam-packed.'

'Aye,' Lambie said, trying to give the smug look that was expected of him. 'These are the good days, mate. Makes up for all the fucking empty Tuesday nights in the winter, when it's pissing down and nobody's leaving the house.' He laughed. 'I'll take this any day of the week. What can I get you boys?' Lambie gestured to his minder at his side who seemed to know he was there to get the drinks in as well as take care of any trouble from hyped-up fans.

'Lager for me. Dying of fucking thirst.' Townsley turned to the others who mumbled lager too. 'Four pints of your finest, mate,' Townsley said to the squat skinhead with a sleeve tattoo of King Billy on his white horse in 1690.

'So how are things, Dick?' Townsley stood, legs apart, with his hands in his pockets. 'That was a right good job you and the boys did, by the way. Right good job.' He sniffed and drew the back of his hand across his nose. 'I've been watching the news and reading the papers. Looks like that bird and her uncle will be away for a long time. Fuck them! Taig cunts!'

'Aye,' Lambie said. 'It worked well. My boys did good.'

'Any repercussions? I mean from that Irish mob, the Caseys?'

Lambie shook his head. 'Nothing. Not a peep. They seem to have gone to ground, mate. Normally I hear on the grapevine a wee bit, but there's been nothing. I think this has hit them hard.'

Townsley nodded slowly. 'Aye. Good enough for them. But it might just look like they're lying low. Just be careful. I'd be surprised if they take this lying down.'

'They haven't a clue how it happened. I made sure of that. Left no edges anywhere, nothing for them to look at. It was a good job.'

The two minders came across with drinks and handed

them out. Townsley took a long thirsty drink and licked his lips.

'Fucking needed that.' He flicked a glance around the room. 'Where's your sidekick? Thomson? We usually have a bit of a side bet on who scores first in the matches. I'm fed up of taking fortunes off the cunt. Was going to dig him up.'

Lambie managed not to blink at the words 'dig him up', because right now if he wanted to speak to Thomson he would probably *have* to dig him up.

'Fucker's away on holiday. I gave him a good wedge for doing the job, so him and a couple of the boys are over in Benidorm. Getting pissed and laid, no doubt.'

Townsley sniggered. 'Quite right too.'

There was a moment of quiet, just the din of the crowd in the pub, then the banging of a Lambeg drum and the sound of flutes. In a few seconds the entire pub was singing 'The Sash'. Townsley and Lambie in full tilt, joining in.

'I fucking love this place,' Townsley said, taking a swig of his pint. 'Salt of the earth, these boys.'

'Aye,' Lambie said as enthusiastically as he could. 'We'll hump the Celts tonight, big time.'

'Hope so,' Townsley said. 'I've got a grand on at the bookies in the Shankill that Rangers will win two nil. They fucking better!'

'That's ambitious at Celtic Park, but I'd fucking love to see that. Wipe the floor with them.'

They made small talk for a couple of minutes about life

in Belfast, and holidays for the summer, as the crowd began to slowly trickle out of the bar singing and chanting. Once they'd finished their pints, they all buttoned up and did the same. On the way out, Townsley turned to Lambie.

'You fancy a curry after the match? Then we can go somewhere. I really need a ride.'

Lambie chuckled. 'Don't worry about that, mate. That's all sorted.'

CHAPTER TWENTY-THREE

Lambie had bought into the lap-dancing club three years ago. At the time it had been the haunt of stag-night lads on the lash as well saddos looking for a bit of no-strings titillation where nobody could see them. But as soon as he'd invested in it, along with an old mate who lived in Spain most of the time, they both saw the potential for it to make more money. Above the dancing bar there was enough floor space to make private rooms where clients who paid good money were able to have sex with any of the scantily clad women who paraded their wares around the bar. The girls were mostly East European and a few Vietnamese – women who had been bought by Lambie from the traffickers who'd imported them. Prostitution hadn't been something Lambie had really aspired to as a business venture, but the kind of money they were making was too easy to knock back. The girls were clean and drug free, and punters had to pay a hundred and fifty quid for a shag, which kept the lowlife riff-raff out. The clientele in the upstairs area were mostly business and wealthier men with money to burn. They bought the best champagne in the cocktail bar and used the rooms, and nobody got hurt. As far as Lambie was concerned, it was a licence to print money. The girls weren't housed in some shithole with no food. He made sure they were looked after. In fact, he was quite proud of what he'd achieved here. It wasn't the first time he'd entertained Townsley at his place, and he knew he'd be gagging to come back.

They were sitting in a shadowy corner of the cocktail bar with a couple of tumblers of large whiskies on ice in front of them. Townsley's minders were downstairs with Lambie's boys enjoying a few drinks to celebrate the Rangers humping Celtic two-nil. Townsley was six grand up, and already well-oiled from the beers before and after the match. Lambie had to make sure he was keeping up with Townsley in the drink stakes in case he aroused suspicion. He was somewhere between sober and getting drunk, but the nerves and the not knowing how the night would pan out somehow kept him from letting the alcohol take over his faculties. Jack hadn't told him what would happen tonight, or even if anything would happen. He'd just been told to get to a point where he could ask some questions and get Townsley talking about the set-up of Kerry and Danny. But he had no idea if Jack was going to phone him and tell him when it was over. He just had to wait and see.

'So what's with the deal you were talking about, man?' Townsley stretched back, scratching his belly hanging over his jeans. 'What are we looking at? Coke? Where did it come from?'

Lambie looked at him. He'd been expecting this, and had a vague script in his head.

'Stolen.'

'You stole some cunt's fucking coke?'

Lambie drew his lips back in a smug expression.

'You might say stolen,' he said. 'But it had been stolen in the first place, so I figured that if we stole it, then it wouldn't really be stealing.'

Townsley sniggered. 'Fuck me, you chancing Arab!'

'It's all about timing, mate,' Lambie elaborated.

'So who did you steal it off? I hope to fuck they're dead, that's all I can say.'

'As good as dead,' Lambie said, picking up his glass and swirling the whisky. The alcohol was making him more confident, but he had to be careful not to make an arse of this.

'What do you mean?'

'It was the Caseys' coke.'

'Kerry Casey? The Casey mob?'

'Yep,' Lambie said. 'I got word that they stole a right load of coke from the Colombians a few months ago. The story was doing the rounds, and the Caseys got away with millions of pounds' worth of the shit. And it's true. They did.

Then they moved it on.' He paused, seeing Townsley engrossed. 'But not all of it. Before they got a chance to move it, our boys got in and took a few kilos. The fuckers probably didn't even miss it.'

Townsley shook his head in admiration.

'Belter. So where is it? How good is it?'

'I can get you some tomorrow morning, before you go. But it's pure class. High end. Four kilos will get you enough to run the show for a while once you cut it.'

'So what do I need to pay?'

'We'll talk about that tomorrow, once you see it.'

'How do I know the Caseys aren't going to come after it?'

'They're fucked after what we did.'

'Aye,' Townsley said, elbows on the table. 'It was some fucking job. They'll get twelve years for that.'

There was a pause, then Lambie leaned forward.

'Where did this come from, Towns? I mean the hit. The order. It seemed to come from nowhere.' He hoped he hadn't gone too far. Townsley gave him a look, narrowing his eyes.

'You know the score, mate. We don't ask questions. We just do the job if the money is right. And it was.'

'But it was strange to want to hit Kerry Casey like that. I mean, she's kind of getting their mob out of the game and going legit, at least that's what they're saying, even if it is with coke they stole. I was just wondering why her, why hit her?'

They were quiet for a long moment. Then Townsley leaned across the table.

'Look,' he said. 'The job came from London. I was told that someone at the top of the tree wanted Kerry Casey and her mob destroyed.'

'What, another mob down there?'

'No. Not a mob.'

Lambie looked at him, bewildered.

'Not a mob? Not one of the London gangs?'

'No.' He sniffed and swallowed a drink of his whisky. 'Not a mob. I mean from high up,' he whispered. 'The government.'

Lambie looked at him, incredulous.

'The fucking government? You mean the fucking actual government?'

Townsley shrugged. 'Well, not officially. But then it never is when they want someone to do their dirty work. But it was someone high up on the government who wanted her hit. That's how it came to me.'

They sat for a long moment as Lambie tried to process the information. Someone high up in the government wanted to ruin Kerry Casey and her family? That was beyond him. The people Lambie and his mobsters moved among were the thugs and killers and hitmen, a world away from White-hall and the corridors of power. He wondered if Townsley was drunk or if he was just dining out, trying to convince him that he was someone respected at every level.

'So you didn't ask any more questions.'

'Nope,' Townsley said. 'I was told what I would be paid, and told to organise the hit on Kerry Casey. The rest was down to you. It was your organisation of it that was fucking class, man. You did brilliant.' Townsley raised his glass and clinked it against Lambie's.

He half smiled but didn't answer. He didn't know what to say, but he hoped the tape he had under his shirt was working. Because this information might just save his neck.

Both of them looked up as the heavy dark-blue velvet curtain that separated the bar from the short corridor leading to the private rooms parted a little – enough for a tall, slim, semi-naked girl to slip out and into the bar. She stood for a moment and looked across at Lambie and Townsley. They both watched as her eyes settled on Townsley, giving him a sultry look. She raised a hand to her mouth and ran the tip of her forefinger across her lip, her tongue slowly pushing out a little to lick it. Townsley looked at Lambie and they both grinned.

'I think she likes you, mate,' Lambie said to Townsley.

Townsley didn't take his eyes off her. 'Where the fuck did you get this beauty?'

'She's new,' Lambie said, glad he approved. 'Ukrainian. Them birds know their way around.'

'I'll bet they do.'

Lambie raised a hand and beckoned her over to their

table. Townsley licked his lips as she stood close, her thigh touching his shoulder as she looked down at him, her lips parting, eyes full of longing.

'This is Ursula. Isn't she lovely?' Lambie enthused.

Townsley was entranced, shifting in his seat as the girl reached out and touched the back of his neck, his head. He closed his eyes for a second in ecstasy. He reached up and quickly pulled her onto his knee, glancing across to Lambie as he grinned.

'Fuck me, man,' he said, a hand running up the girl's thigh. 'You've excelled yourself this time, coming up with a stunner like this.'

Lambie watched as Ursula wriggled her backside so that she was over Townsley's crotch, and his eyes opened wide with delight.

'Fuck!' he croaked, his expression contorting a little in ecstasy. 'I think we should take this to a room, darlin'.'

Lambie feigned a smile and nodded.

'You know the way, Towns.' He jerked his head towards the curtain as Ursula looked at him. 'On you go, sweetheart.'

As he stood up, Lambie could see that Townsley was already aroused and he didn't even glance in his direction as Ursula led him by the hand through the velvet curtain.

Lambie sighed. He didn't know if he felt relief or fear because he didn't know what was going to happen next.

All he'd been told by Jack was that he had to bring him to the club and set him up with a girl. He swallowed a gulp of whisky and looked at his watch. He didn't have long to wait. Within a minute, he heard footsteps on the stairs leading to the bar, and muffled voices. As the door opened, one of Townsley's sidekicks was shoved in, his arms in the air, a gun in his back. Behind him was one of the minders he'd seen earlier in the pub, one of the guys who'd been watching him in the apartment. Then another of his henchmen was pushed in the same way, another Casey man had a gun in his back. Behind them, Jack came in, along with that Vic guy. Both were packing guns. Townsley's men were chalk white. Jack came forward.

'Where is he?'

Lambie stood up, a little light-headed. He pointed to the curtain. Last room on the left.

'Show me,' Jack said.

'B-But . . .' Lambie hadn't expected this.

He thought once he'd set Townsley up, they would do the rest. The last thing he wanted to do was look Townsley in the eye when he was ambushed.

'Move.' Jack pointed the gun at him.

Lambie moved towards the curtain, pulled it back and stepped into the dimly lit corridor. He looked over his shoulder and could see that Jack and Vic were behind him. He walked softly down the corridor and stopped at the door. He could hear the panting and groaning of Townsley inside. They all waited and for a few seconds the only sounds were of Townsley's ecstatic moans. Jack motioned at him to stand back from the door, then he reached down and turned the handle softly. Jack stepped quietly into the room, lit by an orange lamp on a bedside table. He was followed by Lambie who was pushed in with Vic's gun in his back. In the dimness they saw the naked backside of Townsley, trousers at his ankles, at the edge of the bed, lost in the throes of orgasm, as he thrust himself into Ursula on all fours on the bed. By the time he glanced over his shoulder Jack had already fired a bullet into his back. His face twisted in disbelief as he gasped, pulling himself back from Ursula. He turned, naked, his limp manhood hanging dead. As his eyes met Lambie's, he mouthed, 'What the fu—' Before he could finish, he was on the floor still conscious but gasping, as Jack stood over him.

'This is a wee message from Kerry Casey, you cunt.' Jack fired into his chest.

Lambie's legs buckled as Jack turned to him. He gripped the wall to steady himself. He knew there was no point in pleading for his life. His bottom lip trembled and he bit it to fight back tears. He closed his eyes tight and waited for the shot. But there was none. Only the dead silence in the room and the faint smell of the gunshot that had been pumped into Townsley, who was now lying in a pool of blood. Ursula was next to the bed, hurriedly pulling on her panties like some bizarre scene from a low-grade porn flick. Then she too stood silently, waiting. Eventually, Jack turned to Lambie.

'Open your eyes, you prick,' he commanded.

Lambie opened his eyes as Jack came towards him.

'You're not getting shot. Not today.'

Jack reached out and ripped open his shirt and yanked the device from him. Then he jerked his head towards the curtain.

'Move.'

Lambie's legs faltered as he walked along the corridor. Then, pulling back the curtain, he saw his two minders standing with guns at their backs, a look of sheer terror on their faces. As he stepped into the cocktail bar, Jack came in behind him. From the corner of his eye, he saw Jack nod to the men. And in perfect timing, both of them raised their guns to the back of the men's heads. Before they could protest, they'd hit the floor.

CHAPTER TWENTY-FOUR

Sharon watched out of the upstairs window as the steel automatic gates opened and Jack's car came in. She saw Jack climb out of the passenger seat and approach Vic who was standing in the yard, talking to one of the guards. Whatever was being said, Jack was nodding as though he was being briefed on something. He was carrying a small zipped bag and he and Vic disappeared into the back door of the house that led to the kitchen. Sharon guessed that inside the bag was the tape that he'd ripped off Lambie last night. She reflected on the moment Vic had come home after midnight. As he'd slipped into bed beside her, she'd woken up. She'd known where they'd been, she'd been told of the plan. Part of her had been afraid to ask. Vic had said nothing as he'd lain on his back in bed, and she'd kept quiet for a moment, wondering if he was actually going to say anything. It was only when she slid herself across to him, that he responded.

'How did it go?'

'Well. We got the tape from Lambie,' he said softly, then he turned to her, stroking her hair. 'But it didn't go well for Townsley.'

She hadn't answered, and for a moment they'd said nothing, and she'd turned to watch Vic's eyes wide open in the dark. His face showed nothing. Whatever had happened, whatever bloodbath he had just left, he didn't look fazed or disturbed, and there was something a little chilling about that. She'd decided not to ask any more for the moment.

She was sitting at the long table when Jack and Vic came into the room, both of them quiet, just nodding in greeting. She motioned at them to sit. She'd called the meeting early so that they could listen to the tape before calling Marty Kane.

'Have you listened to the recording yet, Jack?' Sharon asked.

He shook his head as he placed the bag on the table and unzipped it.

'No. I thought it best to hear it together. Not my place.' He unzipped the bag brought out his laptop and inserted the USB device.

Sharon said nothing. She was surprised that Jack would feel he had a 'place' where he didn't want to overstep his mark. But that was Jack. Respectful. Decent. But deadly when required. She couldn't think of a better right-hand man to be at Kerry's side.

'Okay. Let's have a listen then.'

Jack switched on the laptop and turned up the volume. At first it was just noise and the sound of singing and flutes and drums. Sharon screwed up her eyes and looked to Jack.

'What's this? In a pub or something?'

'Yep.' Jack nodded. 'It was in his pocket while he was in the White Horse – maybe when Townsley arrived. Our boys were there all the time in the background. They saw him come in.'

After a few seconds the singing and chants lessened and it was the din of chatter in the pub. Everyone strained their ears and leaned closer to the tape as though it would help. Eventually, they could hear a voice – Lambie talking, and someone, presumably Townsley, answering. From what they could hear it was football banter, nothing more. Then the recording stopped abruptly. Everyone looked at each other.

'Give it a minute or two. The way that sounded, they might have been leaving the pub for the match. Hopefully once it goes on a bit later in the night, it will get more interesting.'

They all sat waiting, listening, and the tape started again. This time the background noises were of crockery and glasses, and by the sound of it they were in a restaurant. They listened closely. They could hear Lambie asking how things were over there, which they took to mean in Belfast. Then Townsley was talking about a couple of problems with lads in east Belfast who'd got a bit out of hand and had had to be dealt with. Then they were discussing plans for the cup final, and families and holidays and all sorts of mundane nonsense. Sharon looked around the table and she could see they were all thinking the same thing.

'Christ, I hope it doesn't run out before they say anything interesting,' she said.

'It won't,' Jack said. 'The tape can last up to three hours. So far there's hardly any used up, though it seems a lot because we're sitting here waiting for something good.'

Vic nodded, and they kept listening. The next part was music and the sounds of a busy bar.

'I'm guessing that's them in the lap-dancing bar. We were already in there by that point. The boys were there waiting for them to come in.'

The recording went on, and the music and noise seemed to fade away.

'That'll be them up in the private area,' Jack said. 'There's no music there. It's a kind of VIP bar, and it's where they get the women.'

Sharon noticed that he shot her a glance in case he'd offended her. Then they could hear clear conversation. Lambie candidly talked about the Caseys' cocaine that his boys had stolen, and was offering it for sale to Townsley, who was chatting back. Everyone waited. And then, bingo! They started talking about the hit, about the Caseys, about

Kerry Casey, and even where the order had come from. Everyone's eyes widened when they heard that the job had come all the way from Whitehall.

'Fucking dancer!' Jack said. 'Smoking gun.'

'That's brilliant, Jack,' Sharon said. 'Wind it back so we can hear that again.'

Again, they heard the conversation. It was unequivocal. They'd done it, they'd set up Kerry Casey and it was a hit that had been ordered from someone high up. Eventually the tape moved on and the conversation turned to a girl, introduced by Lambie as Ursula. Then it went dead.

'I suppose that's when Townsley took the girl to the room. Lambie remained in the bar when he went into the room with the girl, so you won't hear any more.'

Sharon nodded.

'This is explosive stuff, guys. Great work. So what about Townsley?'

Stony silence then Jack looked at her.

'The tape is his evidence, Sharon,' Jack said. 'He's gone.'

Sharon took a breath. She was a little out of her depth here, especially in the legalities. But she had had to ask the question.

'I'm not up on all the legal stuff, but would he have been any good as a witness? I mean, to actually admit to the cops that he set Kerry up?'

Jack glanced at Vic and they both shook their heads.

'Not a chance,' Vic said. 'Firstly, as soon as you brought

cops in he would say he'd been kidnapped. Forced into saying things. And even if he did sign a confession, which he wouldn't, you can guarantee that he would never make it to any court, or trial. The lads he'd betrayed in the UVF would have him done in while he was in custody. That's how these things work. He would be a grass, and he'd be dead.'

'That's exactly it,' Jack said.

'What about Lambie?' Sharon asked.

'We've still got him,' Jack said. 'It might be a bit different if we can go to the cops with Lambie. He might be more cooperative if there is a chance he can get a deal from the cops and disappear. We're not sure. But we thought we'd keep him for the moment, and let you talk to Marty first, see what he thinks. But if it's decided that Lambie is of no further use, and this tape itself actually gets Kerry and Danny out, then we would leave Danny to deal with him. I think it's only fair.'

Sharon glanced from Jack to Vic, whose face showed nothing. They sounded like they were divvying up the spoils, and while part of her might be a little squeamish about that, she believed that Lambie should get his day after what he'd put Kerry through.

'Okay,' she said. 'I think I'll give Marty a ring and get him over for a listen to this tape. Why don't you guys go downstairs and have some breakfast and I'll see if Marty can come over this morning.'

They got up and left the room. Sharon sat back and took a long deep sigh.

An hour later, Marty Kane sat listening to the tape, then he went back to the beginning and listened again, taking notes, stopping at different parts, rewinding and listening again. When it came to an end he sat back and stretched out his legs, tapping the pen on the table.

'What do you think, Marty?' Sharon asked.

He put down the pen and folded his arms, adjusting his rimless glasses even though they didn't need adjusting. Then he took a breath and pushed it out slowly through his pursed lips.

'Well,' he said. 'On the face of it, when you hear Lambie and Townsley talking casually about what they did, then it does seem explosive. But the problem is – and it's a big problem – that this audio evidence alone is not proof of anything.' He paused, looked at each one of them. 'Because a defence lawyer could argue that this is just a couple of hoods making up a story. It could be anyone really, and it proves nothing as it is.' He glanced at Jack. 'Where is Townsley?'

In the long silence, Marty raised his eyebrows a little and glanced at Sharon. He knew the answer before Jack said it.

'He's dead.'

Marty put his hand up to stop him before he elaborated. 'What about Lambie?' he asked.

'He's still here,' Jack said. 'He's in a flat in the town.'

Marty nodded slowly. 'Okay. We're going to need him to talk. He'll have to go on the record to the police, make a full confession to his part in the job, hit, or whatever he wants to call it.'

Nobody answered for a long moment. Then Jack spoke.

'That might be signing his own death warrant – you know, with the UVF boys.'

Marty looked at him, then at Sharon.

'Well,' he said. 'I don't imagine he's got a great future anyway.'

Sharon watched as Marty took off his glasses and polished the lenses with his tie, as though he was looking for something to break the moment, something to do, as though he was uncomfortable with the truth that he knew was in front of him.

'Would he talk? To the police? The only way to make this evidence valid is if he can confirm being there, confirm that it is his voice, and that the other person is Townsley. In effect, he would be turning Queen's evidence. If he does that, and I can find a way to present it to the police and the Crown, then they will know that the case against Kerry and Danny is at the very least tainted. He would have to completely confess, though. If he does, then they may consider putting him on witness protection, getting him a new life and a new ID somewhere. But to do that, and to get that, he would have to confess to a lot more than this.'

'You mean like other things in his life as a crook? As a UVF man? As a drug dealer?'

'Yes,' Marty said. 'He would have to be able to drop some big names to the police that would help them pick up people for other crimes and put them away. That's how these things work. He should be behind bars anyway, it's not as though he's an innocent man. He took on this job to frame Kerry Casey. He has to admit that and provide information and evidence, but I know they'll want him to provide other scalps.' He paused, glanced at Jack and Vic. 'Do you think he will do it?'

Jack sat for a long moment, then he spoke.

'I don't think he has a lot of choices left, Marty.'

Marty closed his notebook and put the pen back in his pocket.

'Can I have the device? I'll put it in my safe in the office.' He stood up. 'Okay, you need to act swiftly though. You need to talk to Lambie and lay it on the line for him. Then if you get him to agree, let me know and I'll take it from there.'

Sharon stood up.

'Do you think it will work, Marty, if Lambie talks?'

Marty pursed his lips. 'I'd be hopeful,' he said. 'But let's see what you can get from him first.' He put the device inside his briefcase and snapped it shut.'Keep in touch, and the quicker we can do this, the better, as the Crown Office will be considering the evidence against Kerry and Danny by now to prepare a case.'

'What do you think of the line where Townsley says the job was ordered by figures in Whitehall?'

Marty almost smiled as he snorted.

'Well, I do think it's entirely possible, but we'll never prove that. Let's stick to what we can achieve and take it from there.' He walked towards the door. 'Keep me posted.'

CHAPTER TWENTY-FIVE

Deep down, Steven knew he was never really going to get off scot-free. He'd known that from the moment he'd spoken to the Caseys and told them everything. They had promised they would look after him and his mother, and they had. Still were. They couldn't have done enough for them. The flat they'd set them up in was perfect, from the decor to the internet and satellite television which his ma was loving. He couldn't remember when he'd last seen her this content. Steven hid his fears well from her and on the face of it he seemed to be enjoying the way they were living; he wasn't even that bothered that he couldn't go for a walk in the city or anywhere else in case he was spotted. But there was another added attraction to his new life – a woman called Maria, who worked for the Caseys, had been assigned to bring them food, and cook them the odd meal. Steven enjoyed her company, and visits from Maria and spending time in the house with her were the highlight of his day. She was really kind to his ma, and told them that she'd lost her mum when she was in her twenties, and how tough it had been. There was no hardness about her, and even though she worked for the Caseys, she never spoke of anything, other than to say she worked sometimes in the bookies, and that she had a son, Cal, and a daughter Jennifer. Cal, he knew, as he had been with them that day on the moneylending when he'd fingered Lambie for Jack. Jennifer, she said, was working in a hotel in the Highlands. Steven admired the way she'd dealt with being on her own and how she coped with family problems. And apart from that, she was attractive – though he didn't think for a moment the feeling was mutual. He'd gotten used to women not being attracted to him, or if they were, it was the half-drunk loonies in the bar who made a fuss of him when they were three sheets to the wind. He'd never really had a proper girlfriend, not since since he was seventeen, and he wasn't going to entertain the idea that that would change now. But it was good to have someone around who could be a friend. She didn't ask him why they had been moved there or anything about his life, though Steven got the impression she knew that if the Caseys were looking after him like this he must have done something for them.

Maria had just delivered some home-cooked lasagne to him and his ma, and was sitting at the kitchen table with Steven, drinking coffee before heading home. His ma was in the living room watching afternoon television.

'Your mum is a real character,' Maria said, smiling. 'Her patter is brilliant.'

Steven smiled back. 'Aye, she's funny. She's old-school. Born and bred in the Gallowgate, so she came up the hard way. Some of the stories she told me about growing up there – unbelievable how people lived. You couldn't make them up.'

'Does she miss not being there, Steven?' Maria said, then quickly added, 'Not that I'm prying or anything.'

Steven put a hand up to dismiss her worry.

'No problem. I know you don't ask questions. But I think she might miss some of her old pals. They used to meet up at the café and stuff, but it's been a while since she's been able to get out with her chest being bad. I think just being holed up in the flat was not good for her, but I couldn't do anything about it. Here, she's really happy. The best I've seen her in a while.' He shrugged. 'But I don't know how long we'll be here.'

He felt his face burn, suddenly aware that he'd said too much. He shouldn't have mentioned not knowing how long he'd be here. That could raise suspicions in Maria's mind. But if it did, she didn't show it, and just moved on.

'I didn't always live in a nice area either,' she said. 'I was up in the high flats, miserable as sin, skint and up to my neck in debt.'

Steven raised his eyebrows in surprise. He had just assumed she was part of the Casey clan and had never even questioned that she'd known anything else.

'Really?'

'Yeah. It was a real hard time. But it was Kerry who rescued me. No doubt about that. If it hadn't been for her ... To be honest, I was struggling to know how I could go on.' She sipped her coffee, holding the mug with both hands. 'She got me out of it. Helped my daughter, who was hopeless and on heroin. Kerry paid for her to go into rehab. And she gave my son a job – and me. Kerry and me go back a lifetime when we were kids playing in the streets of Maryhill. She did all that for me, but she didn't have to. She's a great friend and I'll never forget her.'

Steven wondered what she'd done for Kerry for her to save her like that, and it crossed his mind that she may have been involved in something as illegal as he was. He knew Cal wasn't doing a simple job for the Caseys and he knew that he was some kind of foot soldier, along with the Iraqi boy, Tahir. He'd seen the two of them working for Jack, and they always seemed to be busy, whatever they were doing. He wondered if she knew what her son did, and thought she probably didn't. He decided to change the subject.

'Did you ever get many holidays abroad, Maria? Like when you were younger?'

'As a teenager I did. Benidorm. Majorca. Places like that. But once I got married and had the kids, that was all gone.'

Steven looked at her and he thought he could see the hurt in her eyes.

'What about your husband? If you don't mind me asking.'

She sighed. 'Long gone. He was a soldier. Served in Iraq. Not sure what he did, but he had a lot of mental problems when he came back. Would never talk about it. The mood swings just got worse and worse, and he was in a deep depression. I felt for him, but I just couldn't reach him. None of us could.'

Steven watched as she swallowed hard, the memory obviously painful.

'That's a shame. A lot of guys who came back from those places suffered and it wasn't really recognised. Not fair.'

Maria nodded. 'I felt it most for our Cal. He adored his dad, and the fact that he was a soldier really appealed to a wee six-year-old boy in need of a hero. Cal was totally obsessed by him, and when he used to come home on leave, Cal dressed up as a soldier marching up and down the living room.' She shook her head at the memory. 'Then one day, amid all the depression, he just got up and went out. He never came back.' Her voice tailed off.

They sat for a long moment, and Steven didn't know what to say. He waited for her to go on.

'I don't know where he is, or even if he's still alive. The last communication I had from him was a letter from France saying that he was trying to sort himself out, but that he couldn't come back because he'd ruin our lives. That was five years ago. So I don't know if he's dead or alive.

To be honest, I'm angry at him for that. He just left us. I can live with it for me, and to a certain extent for Jen. But it really did Cal in. I'll always be angry at him for leaving his boy like that.'

'Cal is a good lad,' Steven said, because he couldn't think of anything else to say.

'Aye, he is,' Maria said. 'Despite his father, he's a good boy. He turned out good.'

Steven nodded in agreement, even though he knew Cal was a boy loyal to the Caseys and both his feet were firmly planted be in the criminal world. Steven and Maria's eyes met for a fleeting second, and there and then he was about to summon the courage to ask her if she would consider going for a coffee or a walk to the park with him some time, once things died down a little. From the look in her face Steven thought she might know what he was thinking.

But then the doorbell rang, crashing in on the moment's silence. Steven wasn't expecting anyone.

'I'll get it,' he said.

He got up and left the kitchen and went down the hallway. He looked through the spyhole and could see Jack and Vic on the doorstep. He slid the chain across and opened the door. They stepped inside.

'All right, Steven?' Jack said. 'I meant to phone you first, but I need a wee word with you.'

Steven's stomach dropped. This was it. They were going to tell him the game was up. He was on his own now.

'Everything's all right.' Jack seemed to sense his unease. 'You're all right here. Don't worry. Just need to run some things past you.'

'Aye,' Steven said as he led them down the hall. 'That's fine. Maria's in the kitchen. She dropped off some lasagne for us, and we were just having a coffee. She's going now anyway.'

Maria was on her feet by the time they came into the kitchen.

'How's it going, Maria?' Jack said. 'All right?'

'Yeah. Fine, Jack. I'm just heading,' she said. 'Are you needing me to close up at the bookies later?'

'No, you're all right. I'll be going back in myself and I'll sort it out. I know you're back in the morning, so I'll leave some of the paperwork for you.'

She nodded, pulled on her coat, and said her goodbyes, smiling briefly at Steven, and left the room.

'Can I get you a coffee, guys? Tea?' Steven asked.

'Aye,' Jack said. 'Tea for me.'

'That'll do me too,' Vic said.

Steven shoved the kettle under the tap and filled it, then put it back and switched it on. He could hear the telly blaring in the living room and he closed the door. Despite what Jack had said, he could feel his hands were sweaty, and he rubbed them on his jeans and sat down.

Jack sat opposite him and took a breath.

'Okay, Steven,' he began. 'You know where we were the other day, and that we got Lambie and stuff.'

Steven nodded but said nothing, waiting.

'Well,' Jack went on, 'we're on our way to getting evidence to prove that Kerry and Danny were framed by Lambie and by his UVF boss Townsley. You were bang on with your information from the very start.'

Steven clasped his hands on the table then unclasped them, not knowing what to do with them.

'It all went very well,' Jack said. 'We've got Townsley actually admitting the set-up. Admitting everything on tape. And Lambie backing it up.'

Steven was wondering if they were both dead by now, and assumed they were.

'But here's the difficult bit, Steven, and this involves you.'

Christ, Steven thought. He knew a bombshell was coming. He listened, trying to keep his face straight.

'Townsley,' Jack said, pausing. 'Well, Townsley is no longer with us.' He glanced at Vic, whose face was like granite. 'But he left a full confession on tape – to everything.'

Steven's eyes darted from one to the other, but he didn't speak. He was trying to process it. 'Townsley is no longer with us' meant he was dead, bumped off. He was glad when the kettle pinged and he jumped to his feet like a boxer when the bell for the next round rang.

'I'll make the tea,' he said, realising how stupid that sounded. He went into the cupboard and brought out mugs, poured tea into a teapot and brought it to the table.

'So,' Jack said. 'Lambie is backing this up. He is going to talk to the police and confess everything.'

The word 'grass' was on the tip of Steven's tongue, but he knew he couldn't say if it out loud. At the end of the day he was a grass himself, even it was only to the Caseys. What he'd told them had certainly signed Townsley's death warrant – maybe even Lambie's. He nodded and said nothing.

'Lambie will be dealt with by the police. You know, like a protected witness. You'll never see him again. But his evidence will be used to back up our case. Our lawyer Marty Kane is already on it. Lambie has agreed to talk to the cops in return for a new life.'

Steven was imagining Lambie on the run, hiding in shadows, always looking over his shoulder.

'Will he have to go to court? Testify in the witness box?' Steven couldn't help asking.

Jack shrugged. 'Hopefully it won't come to that. But if it does he will. Marty is hoping that he'll present enough to the cops and the prosecutors and they'll see that they've got the wrong people in jail.'

Steven could see the logic in all of that, and he began to see where he would fit in. He dreaded it, but he knew it was coming.

'So what we want to do, you know, to build up the case, make it more solid, is to back up what Lambie has already told police, about the quarry, about the fact that you were forced into doing what you did. He's already admitted to us that he involved you in it without your knowledge, and he will admit it to the police.'

Steven felt a tension headache begin to throb around his temples. He was going to have to go and sit with police and tell them he was an accomplice to murder. What if this didn't work out? What if he ended up being thrown in jail?

'You mean you want me to tell the police I was a part of this? Of the murder of Bo?' he asked. 'But what if all they do is charge me as well?'

Jack glanced at Vic.

'We don't think that's going to happen. This will be done at a different level, Steven. It's not like you're going to the police station or anything. At this stage, you'll give a statement to Marty, and he will be the guy who will press on with this.'

'And then, will I have to go to cops, and go to court?'

Jack shook his head. 'No. As with Lambie, we don't think it will come to that. Lambie is going to throw some big fish to the cops involving other matters, other criminals, guys they've been trying to nail for years. And we are going to try to negotiate some kind of deal for him. At the end of the day, the police will know that Kerry and Danny are innocent, and that will be important to them. But it will be important to them to get some big names in pokey – drug dealers, Loyalist big shots. That kind of stuff.'

Steven nodded. He could see how that might work. But

he could also envisage how it might not. As he looked from Jack to Vic, he saw how easy they were in this life, sipping their tea, sitting back relaxed as they delivered the next chapter of his life. And his ma's. But he knew as he looked at them that they were waiting for answers and that he didn't have a lot of choice. They sat that way in the quietness, with the muffled blare of afternoon television coming from the living room. Then Steven looked at both of them and shrugged.

'Okay,' he said. 'Whatever it takes. But I worry about my ma. I mean, if something happens to me . . . you know?'

'Nothing's going to happen to you, Steven,' Jack reassured him. 'Don't worry.'

CHAPTER TWENTY-SIX

At breakfast, Kerry sat listening to Ash tell her about her news. She'd been called to the governor's office that morning to be told she was getting out. Her lawyer had managed to talk to social work and with the procurator fiscal's office, and they'd made the decision that the charges would be dropped. She was not deemed to be a danger to the public or herself – though they apparently had conceded that she might reoffend. That was a stick-on, Kerry thought, as Ash relayed all the information to her. But she was surprised to see that Ash was far from excited about the prospect of getting out of jail. She looked more depressed than elated, and Kerry watched her fidget as she listened.

'You don't seem all that happy about it though, Ash,' Kerry ventured.

Ash shoved her hands into her jeans pocket and leaned back. Kerry could see her hip bones sticking out of her skinny frame in her low-waist jeans.

'You know what, Kerry? The honest truth is I'm not looking forward to it. I mean, don't get me wrong, I shouldn't have been locked up here in the first place for that trumped up charge. But this time in here, I've felt something like family and I've never felt like that before in here, or on the outside.' She stopped and swallowed as she caught Kerry's eyes. 'I feel like you've been like a sister or a cousin or something to me, and you haven't judged me or anything and have just taken me as I am, warts and all.'

Kerry half smiled. If her time in this place had shown her anything it was that she was in no position to judge anyone. Many of the girls were here because of their circumstances, products of a broken family and a fractured system. Though from what she'd seen and experienced in the last couple of weeks there were some bad ones too. The drug addicts who had robbed and beaten an old woman or battered a man at the cashline, you could hardly call them victims, and Kerry could never reconcile herself to what they had done when she heard their crimes. Perhaps some of them had become addicts on the heroin that her brother Mickey had pushed in Glasgow before he'd got shot, before Kerry had come on the scene and started to change things. But his legacy was still there, and some of the people in here might be part of that legacy. And if she was the head of the family then it was her legacy. She'd tormented herself with thoughts like that through long sleepless nights in her cell. With too much time on her hands and riddled with guilt she'd promised herself she would make amends when and if she ever got out of here.

'I know what you mean, Ash.' Kerry eventually spoke. 'And I've felt the same kind of spirit in here because of people like you. To be honest, I don't know what I'd have done without you. You've been a real friend. And maybe everything that has happened – especially the death of Linda – made me feel it even deeper. I'll never forget that as long as I live, and the grief and sadness that hung over here.'

'Aye,' Ash said. 'I think that's why I'm not happy to be leaving. I've got support here, people to talk to who understand me, but outside I'm on my own. Just the usual pimps, dealers and robbers.'

'But did you not say you've got an auntie or something?'

'Yeah,' she said. 'But she's quite old now, and it's not as if I can go there, not to stay, anyway. I'm going to be getting methadone. But that's just to keep me going, stop me from stealing to get heroin. It'll never be enough. I need to get off the shit altogether.'

They sat for a long moment listening to the bustle of girls coming in and out and the cleaners with mops and buckets. Another day in jail was about to begin, Kerry thought. Not for Ash though. Her probation officer would come this morning to have a meeting with her and then she'd be gone. Dropped off in the city with a few pounds to get somewhere to stay for the night and some food. Tomorrow, she would meet the probation officer again. But she would feel abandoned. In another life, raised in different circumstances, it could have been her.

'Listen, Ash,' Kerry said. 'If you are serious about wanting to get off drugs and make your life different, I can help you.'

'Aye,' she said. 'I'm serious. I am.'

Kerry leaned across the table.

'Okay. I want to help you.' She looked around. 'God knows when I'll get out of here – hopefully soon. But I can give you a name and a phone number to talk to someone and they will sort you out.'

'What do you mean – sort me out how?'

'Well the first thing you need is rehab. I know there are no beds in the system, but if you are really serious, and I mean really serious, then I can get you in somewhere. Private.'

Ash's eyes lit up. 'Private? Christ! Like them celebrities? Like the Priory or something?'

Kerry nodded. 'Yes. Exactly.'

Suddenly Ash's eyes filled with tears and she tightened her lips.

'You'd do that for me? A wee bird from Easterhouse.'

'It's a chance. You deserve a chance,' Kerry said. 'I can give you that. The rest is up to you.'

Ash covered her face with her hands and started to cry.

'Sorry,' she sniffed. 'I'm a real shitebag, but I ... I'm just ... I mean, I can't believe you would do that. I'll never be able to pay you back.'

'You will,' Kerry said, feeling a lump to her throat. 'In fact you already did, being my friend in here, helping me when big Aggie was going to slap me around.' She manged a smile. 'And, if you get clean, I'll give you a job. You can come and work for me, for the Caseys. A job where you get paid and do ordinary things like get up, get showered and go to work, and bring home food and stuff. Like everyone else.'

Ash was sobbing now, and people were beginning to look at her.

Kerry leaned across and squeezed her wrist.

'Come on now,' she said. 'Dry your eyes and make your mind up. This is up to you now. I can make this happen for you – even from in here. But I need a complete, solid commitment from you.'

'I'll not let you down. I promise.'

Kerry looked her in the eye.

'If you do, that's up to you. I'm giving you one chance and one chance only. Things will change for you.'

Kerry went to the breakfast hatch and picked up a pen and piece of paper. She wrote down Jack's mobile phone number.

'Listen. My lawyer is coming in here this afternoon, so I'll get him to tell Jack to expect a call tonight from you. Jack will organise a place for you in rehab straight away, or as soon as it's possible.'

'Right away? Really? You can do that?'

'It's an unfortunate truth, Ash, but if you've got money you can do it.'

'But what will I tell my probation officer?'

'Tell her that you've got a relative who has just come on the scene and is going to help you get better. She'll understand. She'll be glad to get you off her hands, one less file in her workload.'

Ash shook her head. 'I can't believe this. I don't know what to say. I'm so grateful, Kerry.'

Kerry smiled; she could see one of the officers coming towards the table. It was time for Ash to go.

'Here's the woman with the keys to freedom coming,' Kerry joked. 'You're out of here, you lucky bugger.'

They both stood up, Ash blinded by tears, Kerry trying very hard to hold hers back. Ash stepped forward and put her arms around her, and they hugged each other tight. They stayed that way for a long moment, and Kerry could feel Ash sobbing onto her shoulder. She looked at the prison officer standing with her arms folded at a respectful distance. She'd probably seen so many girls go through the system, in and out like yo-yos every month.

'Come on, Ash,' the officer finally said. 'Before we change our minds.'

Kerry pulled away and Ash stood before her, flushed and tear-stained.

'On you go, girl,' Kerry said, biting her lip. 'It's all up to you now. Keep that number handy and call him as soon as you're out. Okay?'

'I will. I promise.' Then she whispered, 'And I'll never let you down. Ever, Kerry.'

Kerry smiled. She watched as Ash turned away and followed the prison officer towards the big door as it clicked open. Kerry stood there, suddenly feeling alone and isolated, and she swallowed hard. She had to pull herself together. Marty was coming to see her after lunch to give her an update. All she could do was hope it was something uplifting.

Kerry was glad to see Marty coming into the visiting room, and she stood up as he approached the table. A smile spread across his face and he opened his arms and they hugged.

'How are we doing, Kerry?'

He hugged her tight and she relished the warmth of his embrace. Then he eased himself away and flicked a glance up and down her body, resting for a second on the growing bump on her tummy. He smiled.

'Looking good, Kerry.'

She returned his smile as they sat down, knowing he was trying to keep her upbeat, but also knowing that it would be killing him to see her like this, pregnant and far from her family and friends.

'I feel okay, Marty,' she said, and she meant it. 'Just struggling some days to keep my spirits up.' She paused. 'Oh, before I forget, you know that girl Ash who has been in here with me from the start? Remember, the drug addict who was with me on the first morning I appeared in court?'

Marty nodded.

'Well she got out today. Charges dropped. But here's the thing, Marty. I got quite close to her while she was here, and my heart goes out to her. I know she's a bit of a hard case, and drugs and stuff, but I want to do something to help her.'

Marty smiled. 'You'll never change, Kerry. Ever since you were a little kid – I remember the day you brought all the stray dogs home and fed them everything that was in the house.'

Kerry smiled at the memory.

'I remember that too, Marty. My mum went nuts.' She stopped and sipped from her mug. 'But you know something, a lot of these people in here, they're a bit like strays themselves, and people like me and you, we never really see them, get to know them. Ash is one of them, and she deserves a chance. She helped me a lot in here, and to be honest I don't know what I'd have done without her. Do you know what I mean?'

He nodded gently. 'Of course I do. '

'Great. So I've given Ash Jack's phone number. I want you to tell him when you get back that he'll be getting a call from her. I want him to sort a place for her in the Priory – same as we did for Maria's daughter. As soon as possible.

Sooner if we can. Because give her a day or two or more, and she'll be back on the same road she was on before. I spoke to her this morning, and told her, and the poor girl was in tears. She's promised me if she's given the chance she'll be different. Can you tell Jack to expect a call from her tonight, please, Marty?'

'Of course. I'll call him as soon as I leave.' He reached across and touched Kerry's hand. 'You're a good person, Kerry. You probably don't realise that enough.'

She didn't answer, then he leaned across.

'Okay,' he said. 'I've got some good news.'

'You have? Jesus, Marty, I wish.'

'Well. I think it's good, and we're a bit away from it, but we are definitely on the road to getting you out of here.'

'But how? With all the evidence stacked against us.'

'The evidence was a lie, as you and Danny know. And if things go the way I'm hoping they do, then we can get these charges dropped. It's all behind the scenes stuff at the moment though.'

'What do you mean?'

He sat back and glanced over his shoulder in case anyone was listening, even though the other girls with visitors were several yards away at tables, and the officers were at the back wall, just watching.

'Well. I'll keep it simple rather than talk too much about the details in here. But let me put it this way: we have recorded evidence from the men behind the set-up, that it was them who did it – them who framed you. We have names, everything about the organisation, how it happened and why it happened.'

Kerry's eyes widened as she listened. A surge of excitement rushed through her and she felt a little light-headed.

'Jesus, Marty! You serious? You actually have that? Evidence recorded? Names? Who the hell was it? I mean, why?' She paused. 'How did you get that?'

Marty was silent for a moment, and Kerry guessed he wouldn't answer the last part of her question.

'I'm deadly serious, Kerry.' He leaned across, lowered his voice to barely a whisper. 'It was a UVF hit. By a Glasgow mob – you won't know him, but he's called Lambie. Owns the White Horse in the East End. He's admitted everything. It was a hit organised by the UVF by his boss in Belfast – Wattie Townsley.'

Kerry couldn't speak as she tried to process all of this. A UVF hit? But why? She knew the Caseys had always been Irish by descent and loyalty, and that there had been whispers of involvement with the IRA over the years – especially around Jake Cahill – though she didn't know for sure. But why hit them now? They weren't trampling on each other's turf.

'But why?' she asked again. 'Why would the UVF hit us? I just don't get it.'

Marty nodded slowly and looked at her.

'I don't have any real facts on that and maybe never will,

Kerry. But from what Lambie could tell us, and from what
Townsley has said on tape, he got the order from London.'

'London?'

'Yes. From Whitehall. All he said was that it was high up.'

Kerry actually felt her blood run cold. It could only be
one man. But she didn't even want to utter his name, not
even to Marty, because she knew he wouldn't be able to
confirm it. But she vowed to herself that if she got out of
this place then she would destroy Quentin Fairhurst once
and for all.

CHAPTER TWENTY-SEVEN

In a shadowy alcove at the far end of La Lanterna restaurant, Marty Kane sat back, swirling the remains of his full-bodied red. He looked across at his old friend who had knocked back the dregs of his glass, then he summoned a waiter with a wave of his hand.

'You fancy a brandy, Joe?' Marty said. 'For the road?'

Joe made a could-do-worse face.

'Sure, you're a long while dead, Marty. Might as well.'

Marty ordered two cognacs and sat back, his hands clasped across his stomach. So far so good. This was the first step in the push to see if he could get the police to be amenable to listening to new evidence on Kerry's case. His dinner partner and long-time friend since secondary school was Joe Cassidy, the head of the Serious Crime Squad in Glasgow, and due for retirement in the next two years. Cassidy may have been old school, in a world where police officers now came with university degrees instead of size ten boots, but he could play the game better than any of them. He was respected by everyone from uniformed cops to the top of the tree. He'd risen through the ranks by putting away serial killers, terrorists on both side of the divide, and drugs barons. Much of his success was down to the way he managed things and people, and as Marty Kane knew, the fact that he didn't always play by the rules. That was why Marty had asked him here tonight. Because if he was going to get Kerry Casey out of jail then it wouldn't be by playing by the rules. In his leather-bound case, Marty had the recorded evidence and a full statement from Lambie that told the real story behind the frame-up. And on top of that, he had told Joe that Lambie was also prepared to spill the beans on a host of unsolved murders, robberies and terrorist attacks. He would give them the locations of various UVF arms dumps. He knew Joe would be keen, and if anyone could make this work then it would be him. But Marty knew there would be a stumbling block.

'So,' Joe said. 'To cut to the chase, Marty, we both know that this is big information your man has imparted. But what happens when it gets to the part where Townsley has disappeared off the face of the earth? How is that going to be answered?'

Joe gave Marty a long look. They both knew that Townsley hadn't just 'disappeared', well he had, but he wasn't coming back. Joe knew the Caseys and everything about them, and he knew that Marty was their closest associate and defence lawyer. Marty knew that Townsley had been bumped off, but he'd never discussed it openly with Jack who'd been about as vague as he'd have expected him to be. He knew that it was morally wrong, but that was not what Marty was here to discuss, and at the end of the day he knew that Joe wouldn't give a damn if Townsley had been swinging from a bridge – as far as he was concerned it was one more piece of scum off the face of the earth. But there was a little matter of getting it past the Crown Office and the prosecutors. Either they accepted what they had and went for everyone named in the dossier, or they nit-picked piddling little things like the fact that Townsley had been got rid of. Marty was counting on them taking the dossier and running with it.

'I can't answer that for you, Joe. You know that,' Marty said. 'I didn't ask, and if I had asked I know I would have been told some unbelievable story, so that's where we are. But I'm hoping the Crown will be glad to get what we have.' He sipped his brandy. 'It wouldn't be the first time they turned a blind eye to something that was staring them in the face, so that they could justify the ends they wanted to achieve. Don't you agree?'

Joe looked at his friend and his face softened to a smile.

'I do, Marty. I very much agree. If it was down to me, I wouldn't give a stuff about the big hole that Townsley may have fallen into. There's a lot more to be achieved by going with this dossier. That's my view.'

'And of course,' Marty said, 'there is some justice in the fact that an innocent woman, Kerry Casey, and her uncle Danny, are not going to be jailed for something they had no part in. That is something that shouldn't be lost here in all of this. They are innocent, and this evidence on the tape completely proves that.'

Joe nodded. 'You're right. I'm with you on that.' He sighed. 'Getting these guys at the Crown Office to agree with that and take what they've got is another matter. But I think I know who I can approach.' He paused. 'And by the way, Marty, is there any indication or hint as to why anyone would frame Kerry Casey? Why would anyone want to do that in such an elaborate way?'

Marty thought he knew the answer to that, from what Lambie had said. But he would leave it to Lambie to repeat it to the police when and if the time was right. And even then, the police would probably not be able to make the connections as to why someone high up in Whitehall would want to frame a Glasgow crime boss. He would leave it to them to puzzle out.

In the back of the big Land Rover Discovery, Lambie gazed out of the window, the outskirts of the city a blur as the car sped down the M8 motorway. It was as though he was in some kind of parallel world where he'd been watching himself unravel over the last few days. Now he was being driven down south and it had been made clear to him that the life he'd had before this no longer existed. Dick Lambie was dead. Officially he would only have been recorded as disappeared, perhaps a missing person. But he would not, could not, ever turn up again. He knew that, and he didn't need the Special Branch to tell him that he couldn't pitch up to his old life again. There would be a contract out on him in every corner of the world where there were Loyalist connections, and that pretty much meant every corner. He was told that once his new identity had been sorted, he would probably be sent to live somewhere in Europe – possibly Germany, Belgium or France. He would be anonymous, low-key, and that was how he would have to live out his life. There was no alternative. His wife would not be contacted by police to tell her of the arrangement. And he was forbidden to ever contact her. That hurt more than anything because Nora was an innocent woman in all of this and always had been. She knew what he was, or some of it, but she'd never questioned him. She liked the money, all right, and the lifestyle, but she loved and cared for him and if she'd known what was happening to him now, she would drop everything and join him. But he knew it didn't work that way. The fewer people who knew about this, the better.

Yesterday, in a basement office in Stewart Street police station, Lambie had sat across a table from two Special Branch officers. He had been told that Townsley's body had turned up. He had then reeled off the names of the men at the top of the UVF and all through the ranks, and he'd told them about weapons' stashes, where they were held and the types of ammo and stuff they routinely stored. He passed on the names of haulage companies who had complied with bringing money, drugs and weapons over, to and from Belfast, and gave them the names of the drivers he knew had done it. He'd admitted to being part of robberies, beatings and killings over the years and named the men who'd been there with him, or who'd carried them out on his behalf at the behest of the UVF. By the time he'd finished talking, he'd felt exhausted by the knowledge that there would be a whirlwind across Belfast and Glasgow as the police moved in, rounding people up. As the car raced down the motorway and they headed past Carlisle, he imagined the doors that would be kicked in over the coming days and weeks, and once it had all settled down and they were licking their wounds, the boys would notice that one man was missing in all of this – him. Then they would know. They would know he had grassed them all up, and his name would be spat on for generations as the traitor who brought the house down. But right now, even as the full force of his treachery and the consequences of that were beginning to sink in, none of that mattered to Lambie. He was alive, and he would survive.

CHAPTER TWENTY-EIGHT

Kerry stood in her cell taking one last look around it as she waited for the prison officer to arrive. She looked at the bunk beds, the blue duvet, the thin pillow, then at the table and chair where books and magazines sat. The towel she'd used that morning hung on the hook behind the cell door. It would be collected and replaced for the next occupant. It was grim and spartan, but it had been her home, and she had buckled down and accepted it, once she'd got over the initial shock of being banged up. But she was counting down the minutes until she could walk out of the door and reclaim her life, and she sure as hell would never set foot in a place like this again. It had been a strange feeling since Ash had left, and Kerry was surprised at how lonely she'd felt since her cellmate had gone. She'd been worried that the hard cases who she'd been giving a wide berth would gang up on her. But none of that had happened. Kerry had gone to work in the gift card workshop every day, and found that a few other girls were now talking to her and sitting with her at meal times. She had no idea why, but was just glad things hadn't turned hostile after the unrest of a few weeks ago. But now she was going home. So why was she feeling so nervous inside? She knew it was silly, but in here she was limited to very few activities, she never had to make any decisions. Everything, from meals to work, was ordered and organised and she barely had to think for herself except to keep her mood up. Going home, she had to take charge again, run the show, smile and be happy, look forward to the birth of her baby, feel protected and glad. She wondered how she would cope when they handed her a little baby that she had to make the world safe for. It was a daunting thought, especially without Vinny. She knew her apprehension would pass, and once she got home she would adapt, just as she had in here. She thought of Vinny, how constant he had been in her mind each night and first thing every morning. No news had come of him, and it seemed that Jake Cahill hadn't been in touch with Jack other than to say that he was working on it and would let them know if he had something to say. It was Jake's way of saying don't call me, I'll call you, and it was accepted. Kerry heard the footsteps in the hallway and the prison officer appeared in the open doorway.

'You all right, Kerry? It's time.'

Kerry turned to her. 'I'm ready.'

'Follow me,' the guard said. 'You can pick up your belongings on the way to the exit. Someone collecting you?'

Kerry nodded.

She was looking forward to seeing Jack, and just the luxury of stepping into the car and being driven out of this area, and towards the outskirts of Glasgow where she could see the comforting church steeples and tower blocks of her city begin to emerge on the skyline on the rise of the M8 that took her home.

As she went out of the room, she saw a few of the girls hanging around. She remembered them by name and by offence – one of them was Tanya, one of the girls who smuggled drugs in from abroad, the mule whose life would now be in ruins for the foreseeable future. Everyone milled around, Aggie arms folded, and her girlfriend by her side, and Kerry wondered if there was some kind of protocol among prisoners that they should shake hands or something. She saw Natalie milling around, her mouth tight and downturned, a haunted look in her eyes. Kerry raised her hand a little to acknowledge her, to try to convey that she understood her pain, but in truth she would never understand it.

'Take care, Kerry,' one of the girls said.

'Aye, go for it, Kerry. And you mind that wee baby when it comes.'

Kerry walked past them, their faces displaying the pale look of people who spend most of their lives indoors, the sadness, and the hardness in their eyes. She felt choked as she nodded to them.

'Thanks, girls,' she said, stopping in her tracks. 'And you take care of yourselves.' There was nothing else to say that wouldn't sound trite. So she walked on without looking back.

She collected her handbag and jacket from the counter at the storage area before being led down a corridor towards the main exit. It felt strange to have her bag slung over her shoulder. A loud buzz signalled as the door slid across, and she stepped out. She stood for a moment, the damp drizzle on her face, and then she saw the car flash its lights from the car park. It eased its way out, drove along and then parked close to her. Jack got out and a smile spread across his face. Then Sharon got out of the back seat, a vision in her leather jacket and high boots.

'Well come on then, girl,' Sharon called out. 'Don't hang about! They might shout you back in.'

Kerry grinned and walked briskly towards them and into Jack's arms, feeling the warmth of his embrace. Her throat tightened with emotion.

'C'mere, you,' Sharon said, opening her arms to her.

'Oh, Sharon,' Kerry said as they hugged. 'Thanks for being here. I was beginning to think this day would never come.'

On the way back to Glasgow as the chatter slowed down, Kerry reflected on the last couple of days and how Marty had told her the good news about her release. Charges had been dropped. Marty hadn't told her any details of how it had come about as the news had only arrived via a phone call late yesterday afternoon, and there was no time to lose. He'd said Jack would fill her in.

'So tell me about it, Jack,' Kerry said. 'Marty just said the charges were dropped, but he did say when he visited a couple of days ago that there were things going on in the background.'

'Well that's one way of putting it.' Sharon gave Kerry a look of mischief as they sat in the rear seat.

From the front passenger seat, Jack turned around to face her.

'You want the full story, or the shortened version?' he asked.

'Well, as we've got half an hour's journey, let's have the full version. I know you told me while I was inside, but I want to hear it all again.'

'Okay,' Jack said. 'It all started with a phone call from some guy called Steven, who worked for Lambie – Marty will have told you who he is, yes?'

'Yeah,' she said. 'He mentioned. The White Horse, UVF.'

'Yep,' Jack said. 'The wee guy tipped us off that Lambie and his cohorts had been involved in a set-up to frame you.'

'He came to you with that? Out of the blue?'

'Pretty much, yes,' Jack said. 'To be honest, at that point we really didn't have a lot of intelligence on how the fuck it had come about. Nobody seemed to know anything, so before this guy got in touch, we were just clutching at straws, and that's the truth.'

'So did you meet him?'

'Yes,' Jack said. 'I went with Marty and we talked to him in a pub, and he spilled everything out. And a whole lot more.'

'Jesus. Does he have a death wish or something?'

'Well, you would think that, I suppose. But the fact is the wee guy had an axe to grind and Lambie and his mob had been bullying and extorting money from him for years. Anyway, he's safe now. We've got him in one of the flats. He's with his old mammy.'

'His mammy?' Kerry turned to Sharon, incredulous.

'Yes.' Sharon smiled. 'She's a real character. She's not well with some chest complaint. But Steven is devoted to her, so they came as a package.'

Kerry couldn't help but smile.

'Not that I'm complaining,' she said. 'I'll be glad to shake Steven's hand. So what then, Jack? What happened next?'

During the rest of the journey, Jack filled Kerry in on the turn of events, from the moment they'd identified and picked up Lambie and his sidekick Thomson, to the night at the lap-dancing brothel where Townsley had met his demise. Kerry listened intently, fascinated, finding herself excited at the power and decisiveness of Jack once he saw the end game. He hadn't hesitated, not once, in disposing of people like Thomson and Townsley once they'd no longer had use for them. She didn't like herself for feeling euphoric that people lost their lives the way they did, but told herself they were scum anyway. The truth was that if this hadn't been orchestrated by Jack the way it had been, then she'd still be in jail. And in any case, she was only in jail because the UVF took on the job, so they'd got what was coming to them. But her legal brain was trying to figure out why the police and the Crown Office had dropped the charges, but hadn't pursued the Caseys on whatever had happened to Townsley.

'So did the powers that be just take the evidence about Townsley not being around, and not ask what had happened to him?' Kerry asked.

Jack shrugged.

'Well, according to Marty they didn't make a big deal of asking about Townsley. Fact is, they'll be glad he's gone, because it's one less vicious bastard they have to worry about, track, follow, all that shit. They'll be shedding no tears. They were more interested in Lambie who spilled his guts on a raft of robberies and murders and drug deals. He threw in some big names and also pinpointed arms dumps in Scotland and in Belfast. All that shit is great publicity for them, and you'll probably see it in a few weeks' time when they decide to release pictures of the cops raiding some places and coming across a pile of sub-machine guns and ammo. Lambie dropped in a few big drug names too.'

'Jesus,' Kerry said. 'Talk about singing like the proverbial canary. So where is he now? I take it the cops are hiding him somewhere.'

'Yep. That was the deal. He would get his freedom for turning supergrass, but he would have to disappear. I don't know where they took him.' He paused. 'I'm guessing when Danny comes out, he'll be wanting to find out where he is. You know what he's like. Unfinished business.'

Kerry nodded and glanced at Sharon.

'Yeah. I suppose so, but I'm not interested so much in Lambie. He was just a vicious pawn in all of this. The guy who ordered the frame-up has to be Quentin Fairhurst. From what Lambie says it was someone high up in Whitehall. Who else could it be but Fairhurst?'

Nobody answered for a long moment. Then Sharon spoke. 'I'm sure it was him, Kerry. But proving it is another matter.'

'We don't need to prove it. It had to be him. There is nobody else in Whitehall who would go to that length to discredit me. He actually had me framed for murder. And Danny. I could have spent the next fifteen years in jail, my life and my baby's life ruined. That's the kind of guy Fairhurst is. So he'll get his comeuppance.'

Nobody answered, and Sharon and Jack glanced at each other. Kerry knew they would have expected nothing less from her. And they weren't offering any argument. For the remainder of the journey, Kerry listened as Sharon and Jack told her about the day-to-day stuff in the business.

Despite Sharon being in Glasgow, she'd still kept a tight rein on Spain and the Spanish hotel complex which was now almost finished. She filled Kerry in on what had to be done there, and how close they were to planning the big opening. Kerry listened, nodding in all the right places, but the elephant in the room that had not been mentioned was Vinny. Eventually she had to ask.

'Nothing from Jake yet?'

Sharon shook her head. 'No, pet. Nothing,' she said. 'Actually I haven't spoken to him in the last week or so, as I thought it was best to leave it to him.'

'It's taking such a long time,' Kerry said, gazing out of the window, thinking the worst. 'I thought something would have turned up by now, some information or some kind of trail.'

'Maybe it has, Kerry. But Jake isn't the kind of guy who has daily briefings, so to me no news is good news.'

Kerry automatically touched her swelling tummy.

'We have to believe that,' she said softly.

Kerry felt a wave of emotion as the gates of the Casey complex slid across and the Mercedes eased its way into the courtyard. The guards' familiar faces were all there, some working in the grounds, others by the gate, all vigilant. They smiled as the car pulled up. Then the kitchen door opened and Elsa came out, her apron on, beaming as Kerry got out of the car. For a moment she thought of her mother and father and how much this place had meant to them, how they had felt they had really arrived in life when they were able to afford to live here, away from the hardship of the council house scheme where she was brought up. She wondered what they would have made of all this. She wished they could be here. But what she saw around her now *was* her family. She was home.

CHAPTER TWENTY-NINE

Jake waited in the bar for Mateo to come out of the apartment. The Colombian had sent him a brief text – *'har en cinco'*. So he'd taken it that he would meet him in the bar with information. Ten minutes he'd been here, in a seat at the window, his eyes trained on the apartment, but no show. Jake had left Sullivan to cruise around the town in his car. So he was on foot like a tourist, but watching closely for any sign of anything resembling a Colombian mob arriving. But so far, nothing. Jake's mobile rang and he could see it was Tommy.

'Someone just came out of the apartment,' he said.

'Good,' Jake replied. Then he saw the apartment main door open and Mateo leave. 'I see him now.' He hung up.

Jake watched as Mateo limped across the street. The Colombian stood at the bar, then turned around and raised his chin in greeting to him. Jake nodded back as the old barman came shuffling out from somewhere behind glass string curtains. Once he'd filled the beer from the tap and pushed it across to Mateo, the old guy shuffled back and disappeared behind the curtains. After a moment, Mateo turned around to face Jake. There was nobody there to witness anything that the pair of them would say to each other, or even to see them talking, but Jake was very cautious. He folded the newspaper he was reading and went up to the bar, barely looking at Mateo. He went into his pocket and took out a five euro bill and left it on the counter, then he quietly turned to Mateo.

'*Que pasa?*'

Mateo glanced over his shoulder, put the glass of beer to his lips and took a long drink.

'They called my friend.' He jerked his head in the direction of the apartment. 'They are on their way. In next hour they say they will be there.'

Jake nodded. 'How is Vinny?'

Mateo puffed and shook his head.

'He is not good. He has fever, I think. Very hot, and he has been sick. Vomiting. The hand is swollen, red. Much more now.' Mateo indicated a swelling from the wrist towards the elbow. 'Is not good.'

'Is he conscious? Awake?'

Mateo made a face.

'Sometimes, but he is sleeping much. His body shaking.'

Jake shook his head slowly. This was not good at all. The infection from his severed finger was obviously spreading. If they didn't get him out of there and to a doctor soon, sepsis would set in, if it hadn't already. Time was running out. He looked at his watch, then out of the window where darkness was beginning to fall.

'What are they going to do with Vinny? Any more on that?'

Mateo nodded. 'There is a boat. Is coming soon to harbour. They are taking him to the boat. And then.' He drew a hand across his throat.

Jake spread his hands. 'Why are they doing this?'

Mateo shrugged. 'Because he won't tell them if police are watching the shipment coming to Cadiz. Is coming in a few days, but the cartel, they still not know if the police will be waiting.'

'Maybe Vinny doesn't know either?' Jake said.

Mateo shrugged. 'I not know. I only the guard.'

They stood in silence for a few moments. Jake took a long breath and let it out slowly.

'Okay,' he said. 'Then we will move soon.'

He handed him a twenty euro note. 'Go to the *farmacia* and get some more bandages and stuff to clean Vinny's wound, then give him some painkillers. Bandage it up as best you can.' He leaned closer to Mateo and lowered his voice to a whisper. 'Now I want you to do this: when you are fixing Vinny up, whisper this message to him. Tell him: "Jake is coming!" Okay? He will know what this means. Just say to him to hold on. Jake is coming.' He paused. 'Does the other guard speak English?'

Mateo shook his head. 'No. No English.'

'Good. Then you must make sure you pass the message to Vinny. Then just stay put, and we'll do the rest.'

Mateo's eyes dropped to the bar, then he looked at Jake.

'But what about me? You promised you get me out. My wife. My son?'

'Don't worry. You just keep your mouth shut and your head down whatever happens. Understand?'

The Colombian blinked in acknowledgment, finished his beer and wiped his mouth with the back of his hand. Then he turned and limped out of the bar towards the *farmacia*. Jake took out his mobile and punched in Sullivan's number.

'Head back to the bar. Bring the car. We need to move soon.'

Darkness had fallen in Tarifa and the stragglers from the last ferry from Tangier were leaving the town and heading for the motorway. The town itself would soon be busy with early evening tourists and locals going out for pre-dinner drinks or strolling in the harbour. But in half an hour, the harbour itself would be quiet, especially where Jake's mate had berthed the boat that would hopefully get them and Vinny away. It was risky going by sea, and Jake knew it, but making a fast getaway by road might be even riskier. At sea there was at best only one other boat to contend with if the Colombians had, as Mateo had told them, brought a boat to take Vinny out to sea and dump him. Jake decided that they could take the Colombians on if there was a battle at sea, and make their getaway fast up towards Malaga. By road, they'd run the risk of the Colombians ambushing them on the motorway, because they had no idea if they were coming down here mob-handed. Jake didn't think so, but didn't want to risk it.

The car was parked on a side street next to the apartment. Inside it Jake and Sullivan tooled up with Glocks and holsters, and Jake pulled his safari waistcoat over his eyes Kevlar vest, filling the pockets with ammunition. He shoved another pistol in the waistband of his trousers, just in case. When they were ready, he turned to Sullivan, also pulling on his Kevlar jacket.

'You all right? You ready?' he said. 'This could be a shit show.'

Sullivan nodded, mouth tight.

'I know. I'm good.' He glanced up at the apartment. 'I just want to get Vinny out.'

Jake pulled out his mobile and pushed the speed dial for Tommy.

'We're outside. Will be at the door in ten seconds.'

'Good.'

Jake put the phone back in his jacket pocket and opened the car door.

'Let's go.'

They walked briskly to the front door of the apartment,

and on their approach, they heard the security latch buzz, and they pushed open the door. Then they crept upstairs to the apartment as Tommy quietly opened the door. Inside the small apartment, Bonzo was standing with a sawn-off shotgun in his hand. Jake glanced at Tommy.

'Only one thing we can do, Jake. Blast our way in and keep firing. We don't have a lot of time.'

'I know,' Jake said. 'Let's go.'

They stepped downstairs to the landing outside the apartment where Vinny was being held. Everyone automatically stood back as Bonzo put the shotgun to the door. The blast echoed in the hallway and shattered the door into splinters as Bonzo kicked down what was left of it and climbed in. The others followed. Bonzo led, creeping along the hallway and past the kitchen which was filled with piled up dishes and rotting food. They went towards the closed door that presumably led to the lounge.

Jake stepped forward.

'*Guardia Civil!*' he shouted. '*Abierto! Ahora!*'

Silence. Everyone looked at each other but the door stayed shut.

'*Abierto!*' Jake shouted once more.

When there was no response he turned to the others. Then Bonzo stepped forward and booted the door in. It almost came off its hinges. It was wide open and as they stepped forward a shot rang out and everyone pushed themselves against the hallway wall. Another shot. Tommy dived to the floor and crawled his way in, and behind him Bonzo, who was firing shots, dived to the floor. The Colombians, at least one of them, was shooting back. Jake crept forward and saw Mateo. He indicated to him to dive down, which he did, and Bonzo fired again as the other Colombian stuck his head up from behind a chair. His head exploded across the wall. They were in. They glanced around quickly. Then they saw Vinny. He was barely recognisable. His bearded, bloodied face was bruised and thinner. He lay chained to the radiator. Vinny seemed to shake himself to consciousness and looked up at them. But his eyes were glazed. Sullivan stepped forward and knelt down.

'Vinny! Vinny! It's me! Sullivan!' he said. 'We're getting you out of here, mate.'

But Vinny stared at him and then collapsed.

'Stay with us, Vinny! We're getting you back home, mate.'

Jake looked around and went behind the chair where the dead Colombian was slumped, and pulled the keys to the padlock off him, then tossed it to Sullivan. Mateo lay down, hands covering his head.

'Get up, Mateo! Come on! Let's get out of here.'

He went across to Vinny and knelt beside him as Sullivan freed him from the chain.

'Vinny! It's me, Jake! Listen! You need to stand up, son. We need you walking so we can get you into the car and out of here.'

Vinny looked at him and tears came to his eyes.

'Jake.' Then at Sullivan. 'Sullivan. You came!' He shook his head and tried to lean on his arm, but his legs buckled.

Tommy and Bonzo came across the room and pulled him to his feet, arms over their shoulders.

'We've got you, mate. Come on. Let's go.'

A mobile rang on the dead Colombian, and everyone froze. Jake turned to Mateo.

'Answer it.'

Mateo pulled the phone from the dead Colombian's pocket and pushed it to his ear. He looked at Jake, his eyes filled with panic. They could hear him in Spanish telling them that the Colombian had gone to the supermarket but would be back in five minutes. Then he hung up.

'They be here in ten minutes. They are coming into Tarifa now.'

'Right,' Jake said. 'Let's get the fuck out of here.'

Tommy and Bonzo more or less carried Vinny out of the apartment and down the stairs to the main entrance. Outside, the street was quiet. They helped Vinny into the back seat of the car and Mateo got in beside them, Sullivan in the front. Behind them, Bonzo piled into Tommy's car.

'The harbour,' Jake said. 'Follow me.'

In the car, Jake keyed a number into his phone.

'Jimsy. On our way. Be there in three. There might be people after us, so be ready.' He hung up, and sped through the town and down towards the harbour and the quayside.

Once they were as close as possible to where the boat was moored, they screeched to a halt. They jumped out and as gently as they could, pulled Vinny from the back seat. Jimsy was on the quayside and helped them across to the boat and onto the narrow gangplank. Suddenly there was the squeal of car tyres. Everyone stopped in their tracks and looked around to see a car racing towards them.

'Get him in, Jimsy. Hurry.'

Vinny was being dragged, his legs trailing behind him, onto the gangplank onto the deck of the boat, where some-one was waiting. They lifted him by his shoulders and lay him down on the deck. A shot was fired from the car that had just pulled up.

'You go, Jake,' Tommy said from the open driver's win-dow. 'We'll take care of this.'

As Tommy and Bonzo got out of the car, Jake urged Mateo and Sullivan to get on the boat. Bonzo fired back towards the other car. Three Colombians were coming towards them, ducking and diving as bullets plinked off the headlights and body of the car. Then one of the Colom-bians fell down. More shots. There was the wail of sirens in the distance. Then the sound of the boat engine roaring. Jake jumped on just before they pulled up the gangplank. As shots were fired in the background, the boat sped out of the harbour and into the night, a frothy white trail in its wake. Jake went across and knelt down beside Vinny, whose whole body was twitching and drenched in sweat. Jake touched his forehead and pushed his hair back. He looked as though he was dying.

'You're going home, son. You'll be all right. Just hang in there.'

Vinny shook his head, his eyes rolling.

'I'm not.' Tears came to his eyes. He grabbed hold of Jake's wrist, and pulled him close. 'Tell Kerry. I . . . I love . . .' Then his eyes rolled back and his head dropped to the side.

Jake turned to the doctor who was crouched beside him.

'Is he . . .?' Jake asked.

The doc didn't answer. He knelt over Vinny and put his fingers to his neck and held it there for a moment. Then he looked at Jake.

'Pulse is there. But it's very weak.'

'Will he make it to the hospital in Marbella?'

The doc sighed and grimaced.

'I don't know. He is very bad.'

CHAPTER THIRTY

It had been so long since Kerry had enjoyed the simple things she'd taken for granted, that she wanted to take her time and enjoy every glorious moment. She'd decided to have a quiet dinner alone in her living room so that she could simply gaze around her and feel that her life was going back to some kind of normality – or whatever had passed for normality since the day she had come back to Glasgow to take over the family business all those months ago. That seemed like a lifetime ago. She could barely remember who she'd been before then, how she'd spent her days, what thoughts she would have had of an evening in her London apartment. Her life then had been full of work, and in her downtime she'd usually been exhausted and glad to have a night in. She sometimes felt that the past few months had been like watching someone else's life spiral out of control, the way events had unfolded. It had seemed as though just as they'd put out a fire in one place, another one would burst into life and that they were fighting a losing battle. She knew deep down that the time would come when this wouldn't be her life, but with every new step, her dream was being put on hold until they extinguished the latest fire. Even in jail, she'd had to step up to the plate and live the life that was in front of her, just do it day by day, one foot in front of the other. But now she was home, where she was protected and safe, she could start to sit back and enjoy what she had. She glanced down at the bulge in her white towelling bath robe as she lay back on the bed, fresh from the long, luxurious shower. She had already made an appointment tomorrow to see her obstetrician for another scan. The last one she'd had a couple of days before she'd been arrested, and although the doctors on the hospital wing of the prison had monitored her, there hadn't been a scan. She'd felt plenty of movement and that was what had kept her going, but she'd longed to see a screen image of her baby. Now that she was nearly seven months pregnant, tomorrow was the three-dimensional scan. She would be able to find out the sex of the baby, but she'd already decided she would wait. It was a decision she would have made with Vinny, but he wasn't here, so if he couldn't know the sex of their baby, then she didn't want to know either. She had to believe that she would hear some good news from Jake Cahill soon. She'd tried ringing his mobile when she'd got back to the house in the afternoon, and had left messages, but nothing.

She lay idly watching the television news, and knew that by tomorrow or the day after, the news would break that Kerry Casey had been released from jail and that all charges had been dropped. The newspapers would attempt to pull that apart and find out why. But nobody would get to the bottom of it. The only person who could give them answers was her, and she wasn't going to be giving any interviews. But what she could do was cause an explosion.

Over coffee when she'd come home late in the afternoon, she and Jack and Sharon had discussed doing something with the information she had about Fairhurst – the CDs and the tapes and photos they'd used to blackmail him. They both knew how much it meant to her, and that it was ninety-nine per cent certain he was behind it. She had later listened to copies of the tape from Lambie and Townsley and was even more convinced. There was no way it could have been anyone other than Fairhurst. He had been made to look a fool after Vic's release. And she thought it was plausible that people high up the chain of government used IRA and UVF people to do their dirty work. She'd heard stories about it before in the legal profession, but nothing provable and only anecdotal. Now she had a gut feeling, and she was going with it. She'd told Marty that she was going to drop the information to a journalist. She didn't know anyone by name, but she picked up the *Post* and saw the name Harry Foster on the front page. He'd written a story about allegations of corruption in the

Scottish government. She sat up and took a sip from a glass of iced water. Then she keyed in the newspaper number and asked for him. It was seven in the evening, so he probably wouldn't still be at work. She was surprised when he answered.

'Harry Foster.' His voice had a crisp urgency.

'Harry. My name is Kerry Casey.'

By the silence on the end of the phone, she knew that he recognised her name, and he would be as stunned as he would be excited to hear from her. An interview with Kerry Casey in the middle of her release from jail would be a scoop.

'Oh, Kerry Casey? The Kerry Casey who was just released from prison today?'

'You knew about this already?'

'We did. Within a couple of hours.'

'I'm surprised you didn't have a posse on my doorstep.'

'That wouldn't be the kind of thing we would do at this moment.'

Kerry almost smiled at the thought of it. Damn right you wouldn't send a bunch of hacks to her doorstep and expect to go back with anything other than a threatening look or worse.

Silence on the phone.

'I'm not phoning for a chat, Harry. I don't know you, but I saw your name on the front page of today's paper, and I decided to call you.'

'I'm glad you did, Kerry. Is it okay if I call you Kerry, by the way?'

'Yes.' She paused, knowing he was waiting for her next sentence. 'Look, Harry. I know there will be a lot of speculation in the papers as to why the charges against me were dropped. I won't be giving any interviews, but in essence, the charges have been dropped because they were never valid. I was innocent of those charges, as was my uncle Danny. We were framed. Simple as that. It was a set-up. And this is not an interview. Do you understand?'

'Yes, I do. But I could attribute your comments to an insider in your family or organisation if you would be prepared to do that?'

'We'll see. But the reason I'm phoning is that I have information that your paper might want to pursue. It's about the background of my arrest. Well, some of the background. And the reason I was framed.'

There was a moment's pause, then the reporter asked, 'Would you be in a position to say who framed you, Kerry? I mean off the record, if you want?'

'I can say that,' she said. 'But not on the phone.'

'And do you have any proof of this claim?' Then he added quickly, 'Not that I'm doubting you, but I know that when I go to my editor with this information the first thing he'll ask is whether I have proof.'

'I have. But I can only give you some parts of the proof. I don't want it all to come out because this information has already been passed to the police. Hence the reason I am out of jail.'

'So your information was believed. By police?'

'It was believed because it's true.'

'I'm not doubting your word.' Pause. 'Could we meet face to face if you are prepared to do that? I know you're just home and might be getting used to being free, but if you felt you were able to, I could meet you anywhere, anytime.'

'Okay. We can arrange that. I have information, documentation and photographs that will expose a top-level government official.'

Silence.

'What – in this framing allegation?'

'No. Not directly. But once you see what I have, and have the background – which you must keep to yourself, by the way – then you will see why I believe I was framed.'

There was a brief silence, and Kerry wondered if she was coming across as a nutcase, and whether she'd said too much.

'Okay. I understand. I'd be delighted to talk to you, as I said, anytime, whenever you can make it.'

Kerry thought for a moment. Was she being too hasty? She'd never dealt with the press before, and didn't want to suddenly find herself splashed all over the newspapers. This wasn't about her. She could be in the background. This was about Fairhurst. About exposing him. About ruining him. The first thing Danny had suggested when they'd got out of jail was that they should just get someone to bump Fairhurst off. It could be done, he said, and no comebacks. But that wasn't enough for Kerry. She wanted him alive, publicly shamed, his career ruined.

'Okay,' she said. 'I will meet you tomorrow. But remember. This story is not about me. I will give you information that you can look at and decide what to do with. But I don't want to find myself photographed or suddenly being all over your paper talking, because that is not what this is about. This is about exposing someone at top level who deserves to be exposed.'

Silence. Then:

'That's one of the reasons I get out of bed and go to work every day, Kerry. Where do you want to meet?'

'Name a place.' Then she paused. 'No. I'll tell you where. The Blythswood Hotel. You'll know where it is. It's quiet. Two o'clock tomorrow okay for you?'

'Absolutely. I'll be there.'

'Don't even think about bringing a photographer or taking my picture from behind some tree.'

She could hear him almost chuckle.

'Absolutely not, Kerry. You have my word. Just you and me.'

She hung up. Then she pushed the key for Jake Cahill again. Still nothing.

CHAPTER THIRTY-ONE

Kerry was wakened by the sounds that she'd almost forgotten about when she was in jail. She could hear the gate to the courtyard opening and closing and the quiet buzz of activity outside. That and the smell of food being cooked. At first when she'd come out of the deep sleep she was in, there was a second or two where she wondered where she was. In prison, there would have been the hum of conversation, the opening and clicking of doors and the sense that prisoners were making their way down to the dining room to start their day. She lay back and relished the feeling of being free and safe in her own home. But the relaxed feeling didn't last long as reality began to dawn on her. She picked up her mobile and checked it in case there had been anything from Jake, but nothing. She knew that to start her day by brooding over Vinny would plunge her into depression, because whatever was going on, whatever had happened to him was out of her control.

She had to find a way to push it to a manageable place in her mind and concentrate on the things around that she could manage. Her priority was to be healthy and to focus on her baby. In a couple of months' time she would give birth and she didn't even want to consider the prospect of doing that without Vinny. But right now, there was nothing she could do about that, so she had to put thoughts of Vinny to the side. She pushed back the duvet and got out of bed, padding across to the full-length mirror where she checked out her bulging tummy. She could feel the hardness of it. Just doing that, the simple touch, gave her a feeling as close to joy as she could achieve, and she tried to imagine what it would be like to have her own baby in her arms, to feed and clothe and care for another human being. She'd read that some mothers-to-be were filled with dread at the thought of their baby's arrival, but for Kerry this would be the best and most important thing she would ever do in her life. Nothing was going to get in the way of that, and worrying herself sick about Vinny was not going to stop the joy she felt. She knew that wherever he was, he would be telling her to do exactly that, to enjoy these moments, and that he would be with her some time. If only she could talk to him. If only she could hear a single word from him to say he was okay. She pushed the thought away.

Today was an important day in so many ways. She was going to the hospital for a scan, and afterwards she was meeting this reporter from the *Post* to drop the bomb on Fairhurst. This was payback time. What he had done had endangered her life and the life of her baby. She could leave it, and learn to live with it. But she didn't want him to get away with it, to live the way he did, high up in government, untouchable. He deserved everything that was coming to him. She went to the bathroom and turned on the shower, standing for a few seconds to relish the luxury she lived in. She would never again take anything in her life for granted.

Kerry was glad Maria had accompanied her to the hospital as she'd been with her at the first scan, and having her old friend with her was now part of the journey. Maria had become a feature of the Casey family, and if she was wary or didn't like what they did for a living, she never mentioned it. She'd been taken in by Kerry who'd looked after her when she'd most needed it. She was as loyal as any member of the organisation. Maria had been working mostly at the bookies and organising accounts, but had also been helping with this guy Steven and his mother, who Kerry was looking forward to meeting some time in the next couple of days. They sat in the ante-natal suite, Kerry on the bed as the sonographer put the gel on her stomach and placed the cold probe on her skin. She lay back, recalling the first time she'd been there and the nerve-racking wait to hear the heartbeat. Once again, there was an anxious moment, until the sonographer exchanged glances with her, then Maria.

'And here we are,' the sonographer said. 'If you don't want to know the sex of the baby, then look away while I do this bit.'

'I want it to be a surprise.' Kerry smiled. She closed her eyes.

'Okay. You can look now. Everything is looking great. We can see the baby moving and everything is ticking along nicely. Good size too. Looks like you're on course to have a big baby.'

Kerry glanced at her, a little worried.

'But not too big for this stage though?'

'No.' The sonographer smiled. 'Some babies thrive quicker than others, and yours is one. But everything is looking great.'

'Thanks. Are you sure?'

'Yes. Don't worry, Kerry. It's fine. A big healthy baby is not a problem. You might just give birth a little bit earlier than you were planning.'

'You mean like premature?'

'No, not necessarily.'

'Okay. As long as everything is fine.'

'It is.'

She pushed a button and printed out an image of the baby. She handed it to Kerry, who held it up to Maria.

'What do you think, Maria? Boy or girl?' Kerry asked.

'Just a beautiful wee baby, Kerry. Whatever it is, this baby will be lucky to have you as a mum.'

Kerry felt choked. 'I'm so excited.'

'I know. It's such a magical time. I can't wait either.'

An hour later, after Maria had gone back to work in the bookies, Kerry arrived at the Blythswood Hotel for her meeting with Harry Foster. She stood at the doorway wondering if she should wait outside or go in and wait for him. She turned when she heard the entrance door of the hotel open and saw a young man come from inside. He walked towards where she stood.

'Kerry?' he asked.

'Yes. Harry?'

He reached out a hand. 'Good to meet you. Thanks for seeing me.'

He was tall and handsome, but looked very young. Kerry wondered if she'd done the right thing by agreeing to meet the first name she could find. He held the door open and glanced inside.

'Looks nice and quiet here.'

'Yes,' Kerry said. 'It's one of my favourite hotels. Discreet.'

'Of course,' he said.

They sat down and both ordered tea. Kerry wondered if he would start the conversation or whether he was expecting her to do it. She watched and waited, then he spoke.

'Kerry, I want you to be absolutely clear that anything we talk about here is completely off the record. Unless you say otherwise, anything you give me or talk about is not attributable to you. Okay?'

Despite his boyish looks, he seemed mature and in command of his role here, and Kerry warmed to him. He couldn't have been any older than twenty-five, and she wondered what kind of frontline experience he would have had. But there was a look about him, something a little dark around his eyes, which she couldn't quite get.

'Yes. Absolutely. I don't want to be directly involved in anything I give you today. But you won't need anyone's involvement. Once you see the photos and hear what I have on tape, that will be enough.' She paused, knowing he was scanning her face. 'You look young, Harry, if you don't mind me saying. You been at the *Post* long?'

He smiled. 'Yeah. I've been there four years now, moving up the ranks It's a great job. You get right in at the deep end of life.' He paused. 'Mind you, I grew up in Easterhouse, so I was born at the deep end of life.'

Kerry smiled back at him, and warmed to him even more. She wondered what life would have been like in Easterhouse when he was being raised, probably a good ten years after she grew up in Maryhill.

'Not the easiest place to grow up in,' she said. 'And I should know. I grew up in Maryhill.'

'Yeah. Well you'll know what I mean.'

'So, what made you go into newspapers?'

She saw his face darken a little and he glanced away from her.

'Well, I always wanted to write. That and a natural curiosity. But to be honest, I lost my sister to drugs when I was only about ten years old and she was seventeen. Heroin. It shaped everything about me. Still does. Made me want to go out there, get big stories, expose the bad guys.' He looked her straight in the eye, then turned away.

There was a long pause, and Kerry felt a flush of shame. This was a young man who'd lost his sister to drugs, and here he was talking to the head of a criminal gang who had made a fortune from dealing. She knew that the Caseys had only shifted heroin for a short time when her brother Mickey was in charge, and that he'd quickly switched their market to cocaine. But at the end of the day, a drug dealer was a drug dealer. It struck her that perhaps this guy was here to get inside information. Perhaps his goal was to expose her and her organisation. She waited for him to say something and when he didn't she knew she would have to address the issue.

'Harry,' she said. 'I don't know if you're aware of this, or you've read anything about it, but from the moment I took over the Casey organisation my goal has been to change things. I'm in the process of doing that. I . . . I—'

He put his hand up to stop her.

'Kerry, look. Please don't take this the wrong way,' he said. 'But what your organisation does to make money is something I can put to one side. Honestly. I'm not here to talk about that. In my line of business I work with all sorts of people and I get stories and lines to pursue from everyone from police, to drug dealers, to some homeless guy in the street who talks to me. I'm not here to expose you or look into your life. I just want to make that clear. Okay?' He paused. 'I might despise how some organisations make their money, but hey, I'm not here to judge. I'm here to listen to a story you have to tell.'

He was matter of-fact and emphatic for one so young, and Kerry liked his honesty. But if he had an ulterior motive, then there was no point in being here. She would have to trust her gut. She was here now.

'Thanks for your honesty, Harry.' She spread her hands in a kind of surrender gesture. 'Okay. We're clear about that. So let me tell you, or show you, what I have here that you may be interested in.'

'Okay,' he said. His dark eyes shot a glance at the leather briefcase she had by her side. He watched in silence as she opened it and took out the buff envelope.

She took the photographs out and slid them across the table.

'I'm sure you'll know who these people are.'

He picked up each picture and studied them without

speaking, his expression flat. He looked at them again, then lay them on the table. To her surprise, his face almost broke into something between a smile and shock.

'Christ almighty, Kerry!' he whispered. 'Quentin Fairhurst? Henry Callaghan? Jesus! What the hell is this?'

'Photos that were brought to me some time ago. In case I ever wanted to use them.' She pulled out the DVD. There's film too!' She felt her face smile even though she tried not to. She could see how hooked he was.

'Christ!' he said. 'Who would bring this stuff to you?' He put a hand up. 'Obviously I don't expect you to tell me. But . . .' He shook his head. 'Why? I mean . . . how did they come to you?'

Kerry folded her arms. 'Would you believe it was more or less by accident?'

'Right now I don't know what to believe.'

'Well they came to me, kind of by accident, and it was only when I studied the photos that it meant something to me. I acted for a family years ago, when I was a rookie lawyer, who were suing a pharmaceutical company that had left their daughter paralysed. Fairhurst, long before he was who he is now, was a hotshot lawyer and he acted for the pharmaceutical company. To cut a long story short, we lost. But I always believed it had been fixed, you know. Witnesses had suddenly not been available or had changed their stories. It stank.'

He looked a little confused.

'So you thought this was a way to get back at him?'

Kerry blinked but didn't reply.

'But why now? I mean, how long have you had this for?'

'A few months. That's all.'

'Does he know you have it? Have you contacted him?'

She shrugged. 'He knows.'

Harry paused as though trying to process and work out his next question.

'Well,' he sighed. 'I'm totally stunned here, Kerry, and flying by the arse of my pants, so I'm just going to ask this. You don't have to tell me. But have you used it against him before – I mean recently?'

Kerry didn't answer, but she looked him in the eye and for a long moment she held his gaze. She could almost see him begin to figure it out in his head, until the penny dropped.

'So,' he said, puffing out his cheeks. 'So this frame-up of you and your uncle. You're saying Fairhurst did this?'

Kerry nodded slowly, but said nothing.

'But why? I mean why now? If he knew that this material was in existence, why didn't he do some deal with you so that you wouldn't use it?'

Kerry said nothing. She knew he would figure it out. Eventually he shook his head.

'Ah,' he said, 'and, completely off the record of course. But you *did* a deal with him before, using this as a threat to expose him, and now, months on, he decided to come after you. Am I on the right track?'

Kerry kept silent. Harry took a breath.

'You must have really fucked him over big time in whatever deal you did for him to get involved in a frame-up.' He shook his head. 'But how? I mean, he's the Attorney General. He's not a gangster. Are you saying he actually got someone to do this? Like a hit style job?'

'He did,' Kerry said.

'He did? Who did he get?'

'The UVF. A crew from Glasgow and Belfast. They did the frame-up.'

His eyes widened.

'You have evidence of this?'

'I do. Recorded evidence. Not of the Attorney General's involvement, but of UVF involvement.'

'Fuck! On tape? Of the actual story of what happened?'

'On a USB stick.. With the men behind it talking about doing it.'

'Jesus Christ! My editor will blow a gasket. Did these guys mention Fairhurst?'

'Sadly not by name. But they said it was someone high up in Whitehall who ordered the set-up. You can hear it yourself.'

He sat back, lifted the cup to his lips and took a gulp. Then he rubbed a hand across his forehead and through his mop of black hair.

'He's not named though. And even if he was, proving it is another matter. He's the Attorney General. You don't just go accusing him of hiring a team to carry out a hit on a Glasgow crime boss.' He didn't look embarrassed at using the words 'crime boss' to her face.

Kerry liked that. She gave him an understanding nod.

'You don't have to choose your words, Harry. I know what the organisation has been. But as I said, it is different now. I have moved us on.'

For a while they sat in silence, and Kerry wondered when the question was coming. It didn't take too long.

'So,' he said. 'These guys on the tape, talking about you being framed. Are they around? I mean now?'

Kerry looked at him, her face straight.

'One of them is,' she said. 'The other is not.'

He said nothing and just watched for a moment. He knew what she meant.

'So the one that is around. Is he anywhere I could get in touch with him?'

'No.' She took a breath. 'He's with the police. He turned Queen's evidence, informer. Told them everything, so as you can imagine, he's now well out of the way.'

'Witness protection?'

'Yeah.'

'Was he UVF?'

'Yes.'

'Anything you can tell me about him? Name? Anything. You say you have these guys on tape talking about the set-up. Could I listen to it?'

Kerry was learning that you just didn't throw information like this to a newspaper and expect them just to publish it. This guy wanted more, he would dig and dig, but there was only so much she wanted to give. But she could see that even though he wanted to believe her, he would need more evidence than just her word.

'Yes,' she said, going into her bag. 'I have a copy of the recording here, which you can listen to.'

'You do?' His eyes widened. 'That would be brilliant.'

Kerry took out the USB stick and her laptop and pushed the stick into the port. She didn't want to explain too much about the location of the conversation, because to say it was the White Horse pub and later the lap-dancing bar would identify the places, and might open up all sorts of questions as to what had happened that night.

'Okay,' she said. 'All I am prepared to tell you is that the two men in this recording are the people who framed me. One is from Glasgow and the other, as you'll hear, is from Belfast.'

'Can you name them?'

'I can. But I won't. You're the reporter. You can do some digging yourself.'

He nodded. 'Fair enough.'

She waited until the couple who were in the bar put on their jackets and walked out. Then she played the recording with the volume low and watched as Harry listened, engrossed. When it was finished he sat back and let out a sigh.

'I suppose my editor could say that might be anyone talking there. Could be somebody at the wind-up.'

'But it's not.'

His eyes narrowed as he leaned across, his elbows on the table.

'Is there anything more you can give me? A name? Anywhere I can dig and find out who these guys are?'

Kerry was itching to tell him. She had to convince him.

'Okay,' she said eventually. 'All I'm going to say to you is go to the White Horse bar, and see if the owner is around.'

Harry waited a moment for her to reveal more. When she didn't, he spoke.

'The owner. You mean the owner isn't around?'

Kerry shook her head but didn't answer, and they sat that way for a moment.

'That's all I can tell you,' she said. 'It's really up to you now. But look, Harry. For the moment, all you have to do is go away and look at the photos and the DVD of Fairhurst. That is a major story in itself. Just having material like this, so that your newspaper can ask what these photographs mean, is a story. In the pictures he's with Russian oligarchs. You'll see, if you dig deep enough, one of them in the picture died in some mysterious house fire in millionaires' row in Kensington a few months ago. You could just look at that story. That might be enough. At the very least you can link him to the photograph and ask what the Attorney General is doing in his company.'

He bit the inside of his cheek.

'Yes. Of course. There's enough here to cause a major storm. Definitely the resignation of Fairhurst and Callaghan.' He paused. 'But I also want to get the story that he framed you. That's mega.'

'But you can't actually prove it. He's never going to admit it. Nobody will.'

He sat back.

'I have to speak to my editor. And our lawyers. There are ways to write stories like this. I need some time to look and think.' He glanced at the material. 'Are you okay with me taking this? I suppose they're not the originals.'

She nodded. 'You can take them. I have copies of everything.' She paused. 'But remember. I am nowhere in this story talking to you. Are we absolutely clear about that?'

He gave her a long look as though he could sense the veiled threat in her words.

'Absolutely clear. Nothing here came from you. Nothing. As I say, there are ways to write a story like this.' He collected the material and slipped it onto his bag. He stood up. 'I'm desperate to get back, go into a quiet office and listen to the recording again and watch the DVDs.'

'Of course.' Kerry stood up. She put her hand out, and

gave him a firm handshake. 'Good. It's over to you now, Harry. Here's my mobile number.'

She relayed it and watched as he keyed it into his phone. She could see that he was bursting to get away.

'Thanks, Kerry. I'll be in touch.'

He turned and walked briskly to the door. She hoped she had done the right thing. But it was too late now if she hadn't.

CHAPTER THIRTY-TWO

Kerry was having a breakfast of toast and poached eggs in the kitchen, when the back door opened and one of her guards came in with a copy of the *Post*. He held it up then went across and put it on the table.

'Thought you might want a look at this, Kerry.' Then he left.

She knew something was coming, because so far there had been nothing reported in any of the papers about her being released from jail. So she was sure someone would be first to reveal the news. The front page jumped out at her. In huge letters the headline screamed: 'FRAMED'. There was a picture of Kerry that must have been taken at her mother's funeral. This wasn't what she had expected. At least not so soon. The headline on the story read: 'GANG-LAND BOSS FREED AS MURDER CHARGES DROPPED'. And the article went on to tell the story of how Kerry Casey, head of the notorious Casey empire, walked free from jail after a string of charges against herself and Danny were dropped by the Crown Office. It also had a few talking heads – a lawyer and a former prosecutor – asking how this could happen. Police were making no comment, and the Crown Office remained tight-lipped. But it was only when Kerry got towards the end of the story that she saw the lines: *The Post has begun a major investigation into the case. We have an exclusive story on the circumstances that led to Casey's arrest. Read tomorrow's* Post *for the truth behind the frame-up.* Kerry was surprised that they looked to be going with that story and not with the Fairhurst pictures she'd given them. The framed story was hard to prove without using names, so she wondered how they would do it. Her mobile rang and she could see Marty Kane's name on the screen.

'Marty,' Kerry said. 'How you doing?'

'How are *you* doing, Kerry?' he replied. 'Have you seen the *Post*?'

'Just reading it now,' she said. 'I didn't quite know what to expect, if I'm honest.'

There was a pause, and Kerry's gut told her Marty wasn't happy. He'd advised her not to go to the press with any story, but just to be glad she was free. But she hadn't listened.

'That's the problem, Kerry. When you go to the newspaper with a story, you really have no guarantees how it will turn out. They don't give you any editorial approval, so once you hand it over, it's out of your control. That's why I wasn't keen on it.'

Kerry let his words hang there for a moment. She knew Marty was too much of a decent guy to give her anything resembling a row, and he cared for her too much to say anything that might upset her. But the point was taken. He didn't think she should have done it.

'I know, Marty. I hear what you're saying,' she said. 'I'm a bit surprised the paper is going straight in tomorrow with the frame-up story. I did tell the reporter what happened and gave him the tapes of Lambie and Townsley, but he said he didn't think that was provable, because the newspaper can't actually speak to either of them. I was more interested in just dropping the bombshell of the Fairhurst tapes. I mean, that's just sitting there, easy to do. All they have to do is use the pictures and the film and ask themselves what is going on.'

After a long silence, Marty spoke.

'Yes. I agree with that. But I just think it was a bad idea to get involved with the newspapers.'

'I know you do, Marty. But Fairhurst tried to ruin my life. I can't forgive that, and he should pay for what he did.'

She heard Marty sigh, then he said, 'I know how you feel. But I worry that it might put you in danger. That's all.'

'I'm fine, Marty. I'm safe here at home. Whenever I go out, I'm with someone. I'm okay.' She changed the subject as she knew she would never get Marty's blessing for what she'd done. 'I went for a scan yesterday, and everything is looking great. The baby is going to be big.'

'That's good news then. And really that's why you should just take it easy in the next few weeks and enjoy this time. Just be glad you're where you are, Kerry.'

'I am, Marty. I will,' she said, thinking of Vinny.

'Okay. I've had a few calls from reporters from other newspapers this morning asking about this story, and what is coming tomorrow. So I've just said I have no idea, and that my client hasn't spoken to any newspaper. So let's keep it that way. I take it this reporter has agreed that nothing will be attributed to you?'

'Of course. I told him I don't want to be anywhere near it.'

'Let's hope he keeps his word. We'll talk tomorrow once the paper drops and we'll see what we are dealing with.' He paused. 'And please, slow down, relax and take care of yourself.'

'I will,' she said, as the line went dead.

It was late afternoon and Kerry was in the kitchen watching as Elsa cooked the meal for tonight's dinner. Sharon and Vic, as well as Jack and Danny were joining her for a celebratory dinner at the house. She'd invited Steven and his mother to join them as well. It was the first time she'd been around the table with everyone since she and Danny had been arrested. She'd spent last night at Danny's house having a quiet dinner, and it was the first time she'd really had a chance to talk to him about his experience inside. Apart from losing a little weight, he hadn't seemed fazed at all by it, and was quite buoyed up that he'd met up with people who were friends and family of old connections he'd had years ago. Kerry had joked to him that his stint on remand was a bit like summer camp. She had told Danny and Pat of her experience inside, and the sadness when Linda died, and of the girl Ash, who was now in rehab courtesy of the Caseys. Now she was looking forward to meeting Steven, the guy who had started the ball rolling to get her out of jail. She owed him a huge debt. The food was cooking away nicely and Kerry was about to go and get dressed when her mobile rang. Harry Foster's name came up.

'Kerry, sorry to trouble you. It's Harry,' he said.

'Yes. I see your name, Harry.' She was a little short as she'd had no conversation with him since the first time they met. She wanted to distance herself from him.

'I'm really sorry, Kerry, but would you have a few minutes to meet me? There's something really important I don't want to talk about over the phone.' He sounded a little edgy.

Kerry said nothing. She wasn't sure what to say here. What the hell was so important that he had to see her in person urgently?

'Well, it's a bit difficult at the moment. I'm busy tonight.' Silence.

'I understand. But it would only be a quick chat.'

She wanted to ask precisely what this was about, but she didn't want to say it on the phone, just in case she was being recorded. But she was curious. She wondered if he'd already started looking at the Fairhurst story and was ready to roll with it and needed her to answer a couple of questions. Perhaps they had already approached Fairhurst for comment. She didn't know, but she was curious enough to want to find out more.

'I don't know,' she said, checking her watch.

'It wouldn't be long.'

'Where are you?'

'I'm up in Garnet Street, off Sauchiehall Street. On the side street at the top of the steep hill. I could wait there for you.'

Kerry thought about it and if there was anything she was sure of it was that she shouldn't be doing this at short notice. But something about Harry didn't sound right. What if he was in some kind of trouble? If he was, it would have been her fault, even though she knew that wouldn't be the way he would look at it. He had been desperate to do this story, and his name would be on every reporter's lips for a long time to come.

'Okay. I'll see you. But ten minutes. That's all I can spare,' Kerry heard herself saying. She hung up.

Kerry picked up her phone and keyed in Jack's number. He answered in two rings, and when she told him about the call, he wasn't keen.

'I don't think you should go, Kerry. What if it's some kind of trap? It's a strange thing to do, isn't it? To just get in touch like this. I don't like the sound of it.'

Neither did she. But something compelled her to go.

'He's a newspaper reporter, Jack. He's not going to shoot me. I thought as long as we went with you and the driver it would be okay. It's the city centre and I wouldn't be out of anyone's sight.'

'Okay. I'll be there in five minutes.'

On the way up Charing Cross it was growing dark and the area was busy with traffic. They inched along then turned up to the street that ran parallel to Sauchiehall Street. At the top of the hill, just at the edge of Garnet Street, she saw Harry standing on the street, next to a car as though he had just climbed out and was waiting for her.

'That's him,' Kerry said. 'The reporter guy.'

Jack nodded to the driver to pull over. He pulled the car into the kerb and Kerry opened the door slowly. Harry looked pale and as she walked towards him she thought he was shaking a little. He looked jittery.

'Kerry, I'm sorry,' he said, by way of apology for pulling her out of her home.

Then it happened so quickly. Before she could answer, a shot was fired from somewhere. All she could see was the blood on the side of Harry's head and the stunned look as he fell to the ground. In a flash, Jack and the driver were out of the car and Jack rushed up and dived on Kerry, pinning her to the ground against the kerb. He looked around, the driver crouching at the side of his car, looking for a shooter. It seemed to have come from somewhere in the flats overlooking the street. Then another shot. It sounded like an engine backfiring, and then a figure came out from behind a hedgerow in the ground-floor garden. He fired a shot, and Kerry's driver fell over. Jack eased off Kerry and fired back. She lay, her face grazing the ground, her hands over her head, praying and terrified. From the corner of her eye she could see Harry lying there, a pool of blood trickling down the hill towards her. He was still moving though, his eyes wide open, and his lips seemed to be moving. He must have been forced to lure her up here where the gunmen were waiting. But how in the hell had they got to him so quickly? There was another shot, and as Jack keeled over beside her, she suddenly felt someone drag her by the ankles. Then a huge figure pulled her to her knees as a car screeched to a halt beside them. Before she could see who it was, she was punched hard on the side of the head and was losing consciousness as she was bundled into the back seat. The last thing she saw before she was slapped into oblivion, was someone going into her pocket and grabbing her mobile, smashing it against the window and throwing it out as the car sped away.

When she came to, the car was still moving, but this time slower, as though it was weaving its way through country lanes. Her head was thumping and she could taste blood in her mouth. Her first thought was of her baby and she reached down to feel the swell of her tummy. She opened one eye. It was pitch black outside, and somewhere a dog was barking. Then the car stopped. She could hear voices. Someone else was out there. Then she heard the Belfast accent.

'Bring her out.'

Her blood ran cold. The rear door of the car was pulled open and big hands reached in and roughly dragged her out.

'Please, I'm pregnant,' she pleaded.

They stood her up, propped her at the car as her legs buckled. In the darkness she saw someone in a black balaclava step forward. He was so close she could smell his rancid sweat, and the alcohol on his breath. He put a gun to the side of her head. This was it. There was no way out of it. She was miles away from anywhere. Jack and the driver, even if they were alive, wouldn't have had a chance to phone anyone. She was going to die here, with her unborn baby in her stomach who never even had a chance to know how much she loved it. She thought of Vinny.

'This is what happens when you fuck with the big boys.'

The Belfast voice came from behind her, but she didn't dare move her head.

Then she heard the sudden blast of gunshot. But Kerry hadn't fallen down. Or had she? Was she already dead and in a place where a gun battle was raging? But there were lights somewhere in the distance. And again a sudden blast – more like a shotgun.

'Fuck!' The Belfast voice behind her. 'Let's get the fuck out of here. Shoot her.'

She closed her eyes tight, waiting. But another blast and the masked man fell at her knees. With every fibre of her strength she threw herself onto the ground and into a ditch, face down in the mud. She heard muffled voices and a car roar off. Then suddenly more lights in the distance and what sounded like a tractor. She was dizzy, but she felt herself being picked up and placed on something. She was on a bumpy road in the back of a tractor in a daze. Strong arms carried her into a house, and she saw a woman rushing towards her. Before she passed out, Kerry was conscious that water was running down her legs.

'Oh Jesus, Peter. The girl's in labour. Phone an ambulance.'

When Kerry awoke she felt sweat running down her back and the bed was soaked. For a moment she had no idea where she was. She could see daylight through vertical blinds. What had happened? Then it came to her. The baby. She suddenly realised she was in a hospital. Her head and neck ached as she turned to the side and saw she was hooked up to a machine making beeping noises. Her hand automatically went to her stomach, but it felt different, fleshy and no hardness. Empty. She turned her head to the other side. But there was no baby. *Where's my baby?* The sob came from somewhere deep in her soul, up through her gut and into her throat, but when she opened her mouth nothing came out. She couldn't catch her breath. Then she wailed, a primal scream, like a wild animal, lost and separated from its young.

CHAPTER THIRTY-THREE

Jake Cahill sat in the hospital café alone. He'd been there through the night and much of the morning, him and Sullivan taking turns to sit by Vinny's bedside. Jake had switched off his mobile after they'd been picked up from Malaga harbour by armed guards in a private ambulance, and once he'd made sure Mateo had been taken safely to his family, the concern that someone had caught up with them and was waiting to take potshots had faded the closer they got to Malaga, when he knew his boys would be lined up ready to take anyone on. His big worry had been that Vinny didn't look as though he was going to make it. He'd agonised as Vinny had drifted in and out of consciousness, his body going into spasms, the medic telling him that if they didn't get him into hospital soon he would be dead in a couple of hours. Jake had prayed for the first time in a very long time, because he didn't know how he was going to tell Kerry. He knew he had done everything he could, but Vinny had been weak and fading fast. As they'd got to the harbour and into the ambulance his heart had failed and they'd put the defibrillator paddles on him to bring him back. Sullivan had almost been in tears, holding his mate's hand, the expression in his eyes showing that he was thinking about his own stupid indiscretion with the bent Spanish female cop, and how that might have cost Vinny his life. By the time they got into hospital, Vinny had come back from the dead and was rushed to the operating theatre, but sepsis had set in and his system was beginning to shut down. It was now a case of waiting and hoping.

Sitting in the hospital café, Jake switched on his mobile and listened to a message from Kerry asking him to please call her. Then a message from Danny. He couldn't keep this up. Sooner or later he was going to have to tell them. He sipped his black coffee, wincing at the taste but at least it was keeping him up. Then he looked across the room as Sullivan came rushing in. Christ! He looked ashen. Jake stood up.

'He's come round,' Sullivan said, almost in tears. 'He's conscious.'

'Fuck!' Jake said. 'I thought the way you came running in that it was all over.' He shook head. 'Jesus! Let's go.'

As they walked briskly along the hospital corridor, Sullivan turned to him.

'He's going to be okay, Jake. He's asking for Kerry. That was the first thing he said after he recognised me. He's all right!' His eyes were filling with tears.

'What a fucking relief,' Jake said, surprised at how emotional he felt. 'I didn't know how I was going to tell her. It would have broken my heart. I've known Kerry since she was a kid.'

They walked along and into the room as a nurse was fussing round, checking his monitor and paraphernalia. Jake went across to the bed.

'Hey, hard man! You made it! You are one sight for sore eyes.' He squeezed Vinny's shoulder as he looked up, his eyes drowsy.

There was a bandage like a boxing glove on his hand.

'I need to talk to Kerry.' Vinny's voice was thick from drugs, barely audible.

Jake looked at him and nodded. He turned to Sullivan.

'I'll go outside and make a call. See if I can get hold of her.'

Jake knew that Kerry had been arrested and was in jail on remand along with Danny. But he purposely hadn't called anyone in the past couple of weeks. Christ! Vinny wouldn't know about Kerry's arrest, and this certainly was not the time to tell him. He walked out of the automatic doors exiting the hospital and took his phone out of his jacket pocket. He scrolled down until he saw Danny's name, then pushed the key. Danny answered after three rings.

'Jake! Christ, man! Been trying to get you for a few days.'

'I had to be off the grid,' he said. 'But mission accomplished, I've got Vinny.'

'Fuck! Jesus, man! Thank fuck for that. Is he okay?'

'He's alive. But not in great shape. Cunts cut his finger off and left it to fester. He's got sepsis. Just got to him in time.'

'Bastards. Is he going to be all right?'

'I think so. He's just regained consciousness. Wants to talk to Kerry. But I haven't even told him about her being in jail. Thought it might not be the best time.'

Jake listened, waiting for Danny to speak, and his hackles were up when the silence went on more than a few seconds.

'Jack! What's up?'

Again the silence.

'Christ, Jake. It's Kerry. She got out of jail a few days ago. All charges dropped. Will explain later. But there was a fucking ambush in the city centre. Jack got shot in the shoulder, but he's all right. Driver took a bullet too, but they're both all right. It was a set-up. But some fuckers kidnapped Kerry. She's in hospital.'

'Oh fuck! Is she okay? The baby?'

Silence.

'Oh no, Danny. Don't tell us that. Please tell me her baby is okay.'

Jake listened as Danny spoke, the croak in his voice.

'The baby might not make it. It's not looking good. She went into labour a bit early – in some fucking farmland outside Glasgow where these cunts took her to execute her. Belfast mob.'

Jake felt a surge of emotion that almost brought tears to his eyes. 'Bastards! I'll cut their fucking throats. Every one of them.'

'We're looking for them. But the baby – it's a wee boy – is in an incubator, all hooked up to a breathing machine and stuff. They're fighting to save him. I'm outside the hospital now. Pat's inside with Kerry. You can imagine the fucking state of the girl.'

'Jesus! But they can do all sorts of things these days with wee babies that are born too soon.'

After a long moment, Danny said, 'Aye. I know. We're all praying, mate. But I don't know if any fucker's listening.'

'What am I going to tell Vinny? He just woke up from being out since we got here last night, and the first thing he said is he needs to speak to Kerry. What the fuck am I going to tell him, Danny?'

He heard Danny push out a sigh.

'Christ knows. But we'll have to tell him something. He won't even know she was in the jail, so maybe you can tell him that part, and that she's in jail on remand, but that we're trying to get her out.' He paused. 'Is Vinny able to travel? I mean, when will he be able to get out of there and get home?'

'I don't know. He just came around. They'll be blasting him with intravenous antibiotics to kill the infection, but if that's the extent of it, then he might be able to leave in a day or so. I don't know. I'll have to ask the docs.'

'We need to get him home as soon as possible. We can't risk telling Kerry he's been found and he's alive. She'll want to talk to him, and she'll have to tell him about the baby. I don't think it's a good idea at the moment for him to be told. I mean the wee thing might not even make it through the day. The surgeon says if he gets through the next forty-eight hours there's a good chance he might make it.'

'So I'll just tell him that she's in jail, but hopefully she might get released in a few days?'

'Yeah. You're going to have to do that.'

Jake sighed, his heart sinking, as he thought of Kerry, of the little girl he had known since she was a kid, how she adored her father and was smart as a whip.

'He'll make it, Jack. He's a Casey.'

'I hope so. Let me know how you get on with Vinny and when you talk to the docs. But tell them he needs to get home.'

Jake stood gazing at the people coming in and leaving the hospital. He had to bring Vinny home safely to Kerry. Then there would be a reckoning for the fuckers who did this.

Jake went back into the hospital and along the corridor to where Vinny was being held in a private room. As he approached, the door opened and a tall middle-aged doctor in a white coat came out. He'd seen him when they'd arrived at the accident and emergency area, and he'd told Jake and

Sullivan that Vinny would be taken straight to surgery. The doctor pulled back his lips in a sympathetic smile to Jake.

'How is Vinny?' Jake asked. 'Is he going to be okay?'

For a moment the doctor didn't speak, but put his hand behind his back and pulled the door closed. He ushered Jake a few feet along the corridor.

'He was very sick when he came here, Mr er . . .'

'Jake,' he said. 'Jake Cahill.'

'Jake,' the doctor said. 'We almost lost him by the time we got him into theatre. The sepsis, you know? The poison of the blood?' Jake was glad the doctor's English was good. 'He went into cardiac arrest and we had to bring him back with the paddles, even before we operated.'

Jake nodded, grim faced, but said nothing. The doctor demonstrated with his hand.

'The operation on the hand. It was tricky. Because although only half the index finger was cut off, the poison had set in, and we had to remove all of the finger almost to the knuckle. We saved the knuckle as that is an important part, even without the finger.'

Jake didn't really know what to say.

'He had lost a lot of blood and was in septic shock, as I'm sure you saw.' The doctor paused. 'But the operation went well and the good news is that he is come back now and is conscious. He is talking and he is good, but obviously he is under a lot of heavy morphine painkilling drugs. He will be in pain for a long time.'

Jake shuffled his feet.

'When do you think I will be able to take him home, doctor? To Scotland? His family need to see him.'

The doctor took a deep breath and puffed his cheeks.

'If he is a quick healer, if he improves a lot, then he can go home. Right now he is sedated and just been operated on, so it is very early.'

Jake was already thinking ahead.

'But if the infection is going, then perhaps we can get him home and he can be in a hospital in the UK?'

The doctor gave him a long look.

'Can his family not come here to see him in Spain?'

Jake shook his head. 'No. I'm afraid his girlfriend has been in an accident, and is also in hospital. So she can't travel. I can't tell Vinny that. But I want to get him home.'

The doctor stood for a moment and Jake could see him studying his face.

'Who does such a thing to a man like this? I mean, who cuts a finger off?' The doc raised his hands a little in gesture of frustration. 'Is like a Mafia or something.'

Jake grimaced. 'Vinny is an undercover policeman. Bad people are after him.'

'I know he is a British policeman. I saw in his records.' He shook his head. 'Very dangerous people out there.'

'Yes. That's why I want him out of Spain and home to his family as soon as we can.'

The doctor nodded slowly.

'I understand. I will do my best for him. But you have to give him at least twenty-four hours to see if there is any reaction or lapse in his condition. These are crucial hours after surgery. If things are starting to get back to a little normal, then we will see.'

'Thank you, doctor.'

As he turned to walk away, the doctor said, 'You must be careful out there. Many bad people.'

'Of course,' Jake said, then he muttered under his breath, 'They'll get their day.'

He watched as the doctor walked briskly down the corridor then turned left out of sight.

CHAPTER THIRTY-FOUR

The nurse gently eased Kerry forward on the bed and put the pillow behind her to keep her upright. Just the smallest physical movement like that made her feel as though she'd walked a mile. She had never known exhaustion like she had felt over the last twenty-four hours. In fact she wasn't sure how many hours it had been, twenty-four, thirty-six . . . All she knew was that her baby was not by her side in a little perspex cot the way all the other babies were in the neonatal ward at the Glasgow maternity hospital. When she'd come to, whenever it was, she had gone into some kind of meltdown and passed out as she heard herself scream. She had vague recollections of the nurses around her, calming her and stroking her head, and a young doctor looking at her as they checked her vitals. Then she must have slept again for she dreamed she was in a park somewhere on a summer's day on a bench with her mother by her side. In front of her was a pram where her little baby lay snuggled and fast asleep. There was a stiff breeze sending petals from the cherry blossom trees behind them cascading down and making a soft pink path at their feet. She had never felt warmth like this in all her life as she sat with her mother holding her hand and telling her not to worry, that everything would be fine. But in her dream Kerry wondered why her mother was saying not to worry, because she had nothing to worry about. She was here with her mother, and her sleeping baby, safe in her pram. Then she sat forward and looked in the pram, but there was nothing there. No baby. Just an empty pram with blue fluffy covers and a small teddy bear with ink-black eyes staring up at her. She must have writhed and screamed in her sleep, because when she woke up, the nurses were round her bed again, soothing her, telling her everything would be fine. But once she was fully awake, she looked at their soft expressions and she knew everything would not be fine. The middle-aged paediatrician who had come in to see her yesterday gently took her hand and told her what had happened. Her little baby was struggling to survive, but they were doing everything they could. He had just come too early, she told her, with the trauma she understood that Kerry had suffered. In the end, the baby had had to be born by caesarean section, as it had got into difficulty and they couldn't detect a heartbeat during the panic rush of labour. She had been unconscious when her baby was born. When the paediatrician had come in to tell her that she had a little boy, who was fighting like a champ, Kerry had listened to the soft tones of her voice, tears streaming down her face, dripping off her chin. All this time she had waited. All these years of hoping and thinking she would never have a child, and now this. And no Vinny. She felt lost and helpless and completely abandoned. For hours afterwards she lay in the room, unable to make sense of it all, but slowly she began to gain strength and she had no idea where it came from. The midwives had told her she could visit her baby just to see how he was doing, but it was very early and too soon to say how things would progress. But so far, he was still fighting.

Now, as she sat up on the bed, the nurses eased her onto her feet, then they helped her into the wheelchair. She felt like an old, frail woman as they wheeled her out of her single room and past the other rooms where she couldn't help but notice that the new mums had their babies by their side and that some were breastfeeding. Kerry bit her lip and swallowed hard. She was going to see her baby boy. All was not lost, and it would not be lost until his last breath had been taken. She sniffed back tears as they entered the closed doors of the neonatal intensive care unit. It was warm and stuffy and the silence was broken only by the buzz and ping of alarms going off on the six or seven cots dotted around the room. It looked like some kind of weird scientific experiment, and she had to peer into the cots to see if there were any babies in them at all, because all she could see was equipment and oxygen masks and tubes and wires. She was wheeled along past two cots until she got to the one at the window.

'There's your little guy,' the midwife said, pushing her up close to the cot. 'There's the wee man.'

Kerry's eyes homed in on the tiny pink figure in the cot, his little tummy puffing in and out in time to the beeps of the machine, and in that single moment she was overwhelmed by a love she could never have believed would have been possible for another person. She sniffed back tears.

'He's tiny,' she croaked. 'Look at him. He's just a wee soul. Look at his fingers! And his feet! Oh God, please don't take him from me! Please, God!'

'Here.' The nurse pointed to two holes in the cot. 'You can put your hand into the gloves and touch him. Just for a moment.'

Kerry slipped her hand inside the socket and touched the warm little body of her baby boy. Her son. She could barely see his face for the tubes and the tapes and the wires and the helmet that was breathing for him. But this was her son. Again, the tears came as she thought of her mother, of her father, and how they would have loved this moment. And Vinny. Where was Vinny? He had to come back to her to see what he had here. She swallowed her tears and eased her hand back out. Then she sat for a few moments just gazing at him, engrossed in his skin and the silky, downy hair covering his body. She looked up at the nurses.

'Is he doing okay?'

The nurse smiled down.

'He's doing the best he can. Every hour of every day is crucial. And this wee fella looks like he's up for the fight.' She pointed to the monitors. 'His blood oxygen is getting better and the tests we've done are still being looked at. He was very early, as you know, but you got to the hospital in the nick of time.'

'Will he make it?' Kerry knew they wouldn't answer, but she wanted someone to give her more hope. 'I mean, other babies born early survive, don't they?'

'Of course. And younger too.' She paused. 'As I said, every hour is a bonus. He's got a bit to go before he's out of the woods. Next two days are crucial. So we'll just wait and watch.' She took hold of the back of the wheelchair. 'Let's get you back to your room. You need to rest, Kerry. You've been through a lot.'

'Thank you,' Kerry said, sniffing. 'Thank you for bringing me here. And for everything.'

They wheeled her back along the corridor towards her room as she wiped tears from her cheeks with the back of her hands. Then they helped her get back into bed and puffed up her pillows. She was exhausted. She closed her eyes, and the image she could see behind them was her little son, all pink and soft and breathing in and out. It was a picture she would carry in her head for ever. She drifted off to sleep.

CHAPTER THIRTY-FIVE

Jake knew Vinny would be anxiously waiting for his return to ask him about Kerry. He braced himself as he walked back towards his room, and hoped to Christ his face didn't give the truth away. He had to make sure it didn't. When he opened the door he was glad to see Vinny propped up and sipping some kind of juice through a straw in a plastic tumbler. Sullivan sat by his bedside.

'You're looking well, Vinny,' Jake said, as chipper as he could. 'Great to see you sitting up like that. Honest to God, man, it was hard going yesterday, so you're a hundred per cent better from then.'

'I'm feeling okay. Just desperate to get out of here.' He glanced at his bandaged hand. 'Did you manage to get hold of Kerry?'

Vinny took a slow breath and pulled up a plastic chair on the other side of the bed from where Sullivan sat.

'Well. No. Not exactly.'

Vinny's eyes screwed up, confused.

'What does that mean?' Then he looked worried. 'Is something wrong?'

'Look, Vinny. While me and Sullivan were looking all over for you, we . . . well I . . . have been out of contact with anyone back in Glasgow. That's how I work, and my only priority was to find you and bring you home. That was my instruction from Kerry.' He paused to see how Vinny was taking this.

'Yeah. I see that. And I'll never be able to thank you – and Sully – enough for saving my life. But have you been able to tell Kerry I'm okay?'

'That's what I was coming to,' Jake said. 'You see, while I've been out of touch, there's been a big development over there. Kerry and Danny are in jail.'

'What?' Vinny interrupted. 'Jail? What for? Is she all right? The baby?'

'Kerry's on remand,' Jake said. 'They were set up by someone – framed – for a murder and drugs and weapons haul. Total set-up. But the way it was done it looked open and shut. But Marty Kane is working on it, and we're hoping she will be out very soon.'

'Fuck me! Who the hell set them up? What are the cops saying?' He turned to Sullivan. 'You can make a few calls, mate – see what's going on.'

Sullivan nodded. 'I will.' He stood up and took his phone out of his pocket.

At that moment a nurse came into the room and glanced at the monitor Vinny was hooked up to. She peered at the readings, then at Jake and Sullivan.

'You can leave please for a moment. I need to check the patient.'

'Is he all right?' Sullivan asked.

'*Si*. But the blood pressure and heartbeat is up.' She pointed to the door. 'Please. Let me check things.'

Her timing was perfect as far as Jake was concerned, and he ushered Sullivan out of the door. As they walked down the corridor he turned to him.

'That nurse couldn't have timed that any better. Fuck!'

'What? What do you mean? Were you lying your arse off in there?'

'I was. Did it show?'

'I was suspicious, but Vinny doesn't know you so he probably wasn't. So what's up?'

Jake stopped and shook his head.

'It's all pretty much fucked up back in Glasgow. The bit about Kerry and Danny being banged up is true – well it was until three days ago. They were framed, as you know. But they've been out for a few days – all charges dropped – and then Kerry goes to meet someone and gets fucking kidnapped. Beaten up. Dumped in the countryside. Remember, she's well on in her pregnancy. So she goes into labour and the fucking baby is born and is now fighting for its wee life.'

'Oh, fuck!'

'Exactly. So I was just talking to Danny when I was outside and he told me not to tell Vinny what had happened – just to say that she was in jail. That would be easier for him to take rather than being told his baby might not make it.'

'Christ, man, this is terrible. You were right though. It's not a good time to tell Vinny that kind of news. Did you see his blood pressure and heart rate shot up just telling him that Kerry was in jail? We've got to keep that news from him.'

'We need to get him home, pronto.'

'I know. But we need to make sure for the moment he doesn't see any British newspapers. I imagine there will have been something in them about Kerry getting out of jail and charged dropped. If he sees that he'll know we've been lying.'

'I know. That's why we need to move fast. I spoke to the surgeon a little while ago and he said he was doing well but it might be a couple of days before he can look at getting out. But it needs to be sooner than that. I want us out of here tomorrow.' He paused, looked around. 'Even if we have to fucking smuggle him out.'

'Christ, Jake. That could be well dodgy, and dangerous.'

Jake looked at him. 'Like nothing we've done in the last twenty-four hours has been dodgy or dangerous?'

'Yeah. But we need to make sure he's strong enough to be out and to travel.'

'We'll see by the end of the day,' Jake said. 'But I'm book-ing flights for tomorrow afternoon. We have to get him home. Kerry needs him.'

The door opened and the nurse came back out.

'You can go in now. He is okay.'

They both nodded in thanks and went back into the room.

'Did you talk to anybody, Sully?' Vinny asked as soon as they came in.

'Can't get a hold of anyone at the moment, mate. But I'll keep trying. Anyway. Thing is to get you better and get out of here. You'll see Kerry soon enough.'

'I want out of here tomorrow or the next day at the lat-est,' Vinny said, shifting in the bed. 'I'm fine now. The painkillers will keep me going till I get home.' He turned to Jake. 'What do you think, Jake? Did you talk to the doc-tor or anything?'

'I bumped into him a little while ago and we talked. He said you were doing well, and that the antibiotics were killing the infection. But he said you've been very ill. Nearly lost you.'

'Yeah yeah,' Vinny said, impatient. 'I know it was bad. But I'm getting better. And I don't want to be stuck in here. Did he say when I can get out?'

'He said maybe a couple of days.'

'No.' Vinny shook his head. 'That's too long. Listen, guys. Check out what medication I'm on here and go to the *farmacia*. You can buy just about anything over the counter in Spain. Get me enough painkillers and antibiotics to do me till I get to Glasgow. I want out of here tomorrow.' He turned to Jake. 'Can you organise that, Jake? Please? I need to see Kerry.'

Jake nodded slowly. 'Don't worry, son. We'll get you home.'

Jake was glad when his mobile shuddered in his jeans pocket and he was able to get away from this. He pulled it out and could see Tommy's name on the screen. He glanced at Sullivan.

'I need to go and take this call,' he said, as he turned and left the room.

Outside in the foreground of the hospital, Jake listened as Tommy spoke.

'Howsit goin', Jake? How's the boy Vinny? Did he make it? He looked well fucked.'

'He did. It was touch and go. And by all accounts they nearly lost him in the emergency room at the hospital. But he's pulled through. Lost a finger and had sepsis, but he's alive. I'm at the hospital now, and was just with him.' He paused, looked out across the pale grey sky. 'To be honest I've never been as glad to see someone wake up as I was when he came to.'

'Great stuff, Jake. Thank fuck for that.' There was a moment's pause, then Tommy went on. 'Anyway, reason

I'm phoning you. You know these fuckers who were shooting at us back at the harbour?'

'Yeah?' Jake said hoping to Christ he wasn't about to say they were coming after them.

'Well, we downed two of them on the spot, and took another two with us. We slapped them around a bit and we've still got them. What do you want me to do with them?'

Jake was delighted to hear that.

'Did you get anything out of it? Any reason why they would kidnap Vinny? Or who was behind it?'

'A bit,' Tommy said. 'It was the Colombians for sure. And one of the fuckers said something about a Spanish cop. Not sure what that means, but sounds like someone was working for them – like a cop or something. Fuck me!'

'Yeah. That sounds about right,' Jake said. 'You got any name or anything like that? I mean of the Colombian they're working for?'

'Yep. They told us a name, Diego Lopez – whether it's true or not I don't know – but they said where we could find him. It's out past Estepona. Near Puerta de la Duquessa – down that way.'

'What – a house or what?'

'Aye. A villa. But there's a party tonight. In San Pedro, nearby. It's an anniversary party for him and his wife or something. That's as much as they said. But they told us where.'

'Christ! Some fucking foot soldiers they are. So much for any *omertà*!' he joked. 'He actually told you where the party is?'

'Yeah. Couldn't believe it myself. Unless he's bullshitting.'

Jake looked at his watch.

'Only one way to find out.'

CHAPTER THIRTY-SIX

Jake sat in the pavement café in San Pedro, sipping a glass of cold beer and watching the people arrive at La Bodega restaurant across the street. From what he could see, it looked like the information given to Tommy was bang on the money, because the people going into the restaurant looked as though they were there for a celebration. Some carried gift bags and floral arrangements. The women were dressed up and the men in suits or smart casual. Jake clocked that some of the men just had a look about them. You could dress them up in the best of clothes, but underneath they were thugs. He noted that some of the arrivals had a bulge in the back of their jackets, which meant they must be carrying.

'So what are you thinking, Jake? How we going to do this?'

Tommy sat opposite him next to Bonzo. The guys they'd ambushed at the harbour had given Tommy a picture of the Colombian he'd named, so they knew who they were looking for.

'We'll wait to see if our man comes and how many are covering him,' Jake said. 'But you'll have noticed that plenty of these bastards are carrying.'

Tommy nodded. He'd nipped into the restaurant a couple of hours ago on a recce, so they both knew where the top table was situated, where the band was, and he'd sneaked a photo on his mobile he could show to Jake. He'd also noted there was a back door entrance next to the gents' toilet, so they could make some kind of plan to get all of them inside.

'Look.' Jake pointed to the big black Merc with the blacked-out windows gliding along the street. 'This could be them.'

The three of them watched as the car pulled into the kerb outside the restaurant, and the driver, a huge mountain of a guy, got out and opened the door. They saw a man get out of the back seat and stand for a moment while a woman followed him. As the man stood, he glanced around as another car pulled up and the doors opened simultaneously and four thickset men got out. Jake thought they looked like Colombians. He watched the way the main man preened himself, his slicked back hair, his blue shiny suit and white open-neck shirt. He was short and swarthy-looking.

'That's our man. That'll be Diego,' Jake said.

The others nodded but said nothing.

By the time darkness was falling, the music from La Bodega was getting louder, and there was the sound of clapping and cheering. Perhaps the Colombian was making his anniversary speech. They could see two men posted outside. Earlier they had been standing either side of the door, but now that everyone was inside, they seemed more relaxed, and were sitting at a table sipping beer. The music came to a stop, and then struck up again and everyone was cheering and clapping. *The anniversary waltz*, Jake was thinking. *Little prick.*

'Okay, lads,' he said, finishing his beer. 'Let's move. Just the way we discussed it earlier. You all right?'

'Sound,' Tommy said, and Bonzo nodded.

Jake waited until Tommy and Bonzo crossed the street and went in the opposite direction of the bar for a couple of hundred yards, then saw them coming back into sight. But from where the minders were sat, his boys were shaded by the trees on the pavement, so he hoped they might not be able to see them. Then they disappeared. Jake got to his feet, and squared his shoulders. He put his hand inside his jacket and could feel the Glock in his holster. He walked across the street towards the restaurant, just as a couple of guests had come out to smoke a cigarette in the covered patio area. One of the minders started chatting to an attractive dark-haired woman in a figure-hugging dress split to her thigh. Jake took the opportunity of the distraction to slip past them and inside the restaurant. He knew he wouldn't have long so he had to quickly make sure that he'd clocked the boss as his eyes roved the busy room. He found him, going from table to table, chatting and glad-handing guests who exchanged hugs and handshakes.

Moments later it happened. Boom! The explosion had been timed to go off right at that moment in the old Ford Fiesta that Tommy had parked twenty yards away on a patch of waste ground. It was far enough away from the restaurant and bars not to kill anyone but close enough to make a big enough noise and create panic that would bring everyone running. And it did. Inside, guests dived under tables and ran for cover to the back of the room. The minders came in, guns raised, and scanned the place. But Diego Lopez was nowhere to be seen. Then Jake spotted him below a table near where the band was. He dived to the floor himself and crawled close to him. He knew he wouldn't know who he was and would presume he was the husband of a friend. As Jake crawled close, they came face to face, and he met the Colombian's eyes.

'My friend Vinny,' he said.

The Colombian's eyes widened in terror as he recognised that this man wasn't a guest. Jake pushed the Glock to the side of his neck and fired. In the noise and confusion nobody even noticed him as he got to his feet, went out of the back door and walked briskly up the street. Two minders were on the ground outside the back door, blood pumping out where Tommy and Bonzo had shot them. Job done.

On the way back to the meeting point, he took out his phone and pushed the key for Party Pam.

'Jake. You okay? I've been worried about you.'

Jake was cool and calm as only he could be after killing someone.

'I'm good, Pam,' he said. 'Listen. I'm probably going to the UK tomorrow, so how about you call up these bastards who are extorting you and get them to come to your bar and tell them you're signing over the whole shooting match to them?'

'Jesus, Jake,' she said. 'You mean . . . Sign it over? My bar?'

'No, Pam. I mean just *tell* them you're going to sign it over. Leave the rest to me.'

Silence. And Jake knew she was processing the info and hoped she could go through with it.

'Can you do that, Pam?'

'Yes. I'll do it.'

'Okay. Make the meet in the morning – about eleven. I've got things to do after that.'

He hung up. Then he called Tommy.

'Tommy. You free tomorrow morning?'

'Sure, Jake. What's the craic?'

'Bit of business.'

He told them where and when to meet him.

'What about these two fuckers from the harbour shoot-out though?'

'Dump them somewhere tonight.'

'Will do.'

Before he'd gone to bed last night, Jake had booked flights for himself, Vinny and Sullivan from Malaga airport for the following afternoon. He'd phoned Sullivan and told him, and asked him to speak to the consultant and plead with him to let Vinny out. He knew Vinny would be echoing that when he spoke to his doctor himself, so given that he seemed to be improving as the day went on, Jake was hoping he wouldn't have to smuggle him out of hospital. Because right now, he had enough stress on his plate, as he sat in Pam's apartment above the bar. He'd got there early in the morning, so he could lay out the plan with Pam before she went downstairs to open up and met the Spanish thugs who were thinking they were coming to push her out of the place she'd built up for fifteen years. Pam had been understandably nervous, but over breakfast and coffee, Jake had explained to her that all she had to do was stick to the script. She already had the official papers they'd hand delivered to her weeks ago telling her that she had to sign. All you have to do, Jake had told her, is look worried and heartbroken, and tell them you'll sign on the dotted line, that you just want to start a new life. We will do the rest when the time is right. He told her to ring his mobile twice, for the signal that it was about to happen. Then he and the boys and would pounce. He watched from the kitchen window that backed onto the alley behind the bar, and he could see Tommy and Bonzo arrive, as arranged. They entered through the door Pam had left ajar, and came upstairs. Jake was waiting for them at the top of the landing.

'All right, lads?'

'Aye,' Tommy said. 'All good here.'

'Did you get rid of these fuckers from the harbour last night?'

Tommy glanced at Bonzo who nodded.

'Yep. Fish food by now. Down off the coast a bit. I know the spot. It'll be months before what's left of them ever washes up.'

'Perfect,' Jake said. 'In you come, guys. Coffee's ready.'

They sat in the kitchen drinking coffee and keeping a watchful eye on any unusual cars or arrivals outside the bar.

'So these fuckwits, Jake,' Tommy said. 'Are they no marks? Spanish thugs? Not connected?'

'As far as I can gather they are local gangsters who own this area and operate a protection racket. A couple of the bar owners and the shops nearby told me they have to pay a few hundred to them every week if they want to stay in business. Fucking hooligans.'

Tommy nodded and they sat listening to the noise from the open windows of the cafés and traffic below. Then from the edge of the window looking onto the main street, Jake could see the big four-by-four pull into the kerb. A squat driver got out and another tall, skinny guy got out from the passenger seat. The driver opened the rear door, and the man in the back stepped out. He wore khaki trousers, moccasin leather shoes and a pale blue open-neck shirt. He stood for a moment, hands in the pocket of his suede bomber jacket as he glanced around the area. Then they made their way to the door of the bar.

'That's our men gone in,' Jake said. 'Three of them. They'll all be carrying. So be careful.'

'Will there be anyone else in the bar?' Tommy asked.

'No,' Jake said. 'Not at this time. Pam just left the shutters half open so they could come in, but it doesn't open to customers for another hour. So we've got time.'

The minutes ticked past and Jake checked his watch again. They'd been inside now for nearly five minutes. He hoped Pam was okay and was beginning to feel a bit edgy. Then his phone rang on the table. Two rings. Both Tommy and Bonzo looked at Jake. He picked up his phone as it rang off.

'Right, lads. Game on.'

Carefully, silently, the three of them crept down the stairs that led from the flat to the back alley. At the foot of the stairs, Jake jerked his head towards the gap in the fire exit door. He was glad it was still open, as that meant that the thick bastards inside were so cocky that they didn't even think they had to check the place out. Perfect. That gave him the element of surprise. Jake pointed his finger to his chest, indicating he would go first, then made a gesture with both hands, which he knew they would understand, meaning they should immediately follow him. Tommy and Bonzo stood, guns in their hands. Jake took out his weapon and held it casually in his hand, dropped behind his back. He peered through the gap in the door and could see the two minders sitting on bar stools a few feet away from where Pam was behind the bar, leaning and pointing to the document that was placed on the bar. The main man appeared to be reading it. He could see Pam was sniffing back tears. So far so good. Then Jake slipped inside the bar, and the minders turned around.

'Oh, sorry. Bar not open yet?' he asked, feigning surprise.

Before Pam had a chance to answer, Jake raised his gun and strode across the room.

'The first fucker to move gets this.'

The minders were so startled they didn't even have time to get off their bar stools before Tommy and Bonzo piled in and the three of them spread out, making a semicircle that nobody was going to escape from. The main man glared at Pam. He shook his head and waved a finger.

'This not clever, Pam.' He tutted.

In a few strides, Jake was on him, the gun pushed into the side of his head.

'No,' Jake said. 'You not clever, you fucking prick.'

The man put his hands up in submission.

'Please. I promise. We only want to do business here with Miss Pam.'

That brought a swift pistol whip on the side of his cheek from Jake and he tottered on his stool as though he was dizzy. Blood oozed from the cut above his eyebrow.

'The kind of business that involves beating Pam up?' Jake grabbed his chin and turned his face towards Pam.

Again the man put his hands up.

'Please. Is no my fault. I tell them no hurt anyone. My boys. They made a mistake.'

He shot a pleading glance at Pam, as if he was hoping she would help him. She glared right through him.

'Get down!' Jake said, gesturing for him to get off the stool. Then he turned to the others. 'All of you.'

Tommy and Bonzo kept their guns on the other two as they went into their jackets, pulled out their weapons and slid them along the bar, far enough away. Jake did the same with the main man.

'Please, don't kill me, man,' the main guy pleaded. 'I have children. Please. I do anything. I pay you.'

'Nobody wants your fucking money,' Jake said. 'Your money is no good here, and you were told that months ago. But you kept coming back. You do it all along the streets here.' He leant closer to his face. 'You are filth. A parasite on these people who only want to earn a living. Who do you work for?' he rasped.

'Nobody,' he said. 'I the boss. We only work together. But please. I sorry. No more. Not here. Not anywhere.'

There was silence, the air crackling with tension.

'Aye. You'll move somewhere else. Make other people's lives a misery.'

'No, no. Please. Is finish, I promise.'

Jake glanced at Tommy and Bonzo and could see the colour had drained from the faces of both minders. They knew how these things worked. When the talking stopped they knew they were waiting for a bullet. Jake looked at Tommy. Then he turned to the main man. He lowered his gun, held it at close range to his knee and fired. The man let out a high-pitched squeal as he buckled to the ground. He lay bleeding in agony. Then Tommy and Bonzo knee-capped the minders, and they buckled, their agonising screams filling the stillness of the empty bar. Then Jake went forward and aimed the gun at the main man's chest. He writhed on the ground, his hands up for protection as though that would save him.

'Please. Please. My children.'

Jake looked at Pam, whose hand was at her mouth, shocked by what she was seeing. Then he saw her slowly shake her head. Enough. Jake turned to the main man.

'You listen to me, you *coño*,' he spat. 'Today you live. But you come back here one time, or any of your fucking thugs, and you are dead. From now on. Every time you take a step, you will limp and you will remember this moment. You understand?'

'Yes, yes . . . please. I understand.' He was sobbing now, blood from his knee on his hands where he was pressing on the injury as though trying to hold it together. 'I remember. I'm sorry. *Los siento*, Pam. *Los siento*.'

Jake moved away from them and beckoned Pam to the other end of the bar. She had tears in her eyes and her hands were shaking uncontrollably.

'Christ, Jake!' she said. 'I don't know what to say.'

Jake took a breath and reached across and touched her hand.

'Don't say anything. The boys will clean this up. They'll dump them somewhere, and drive their car out of the way.' He paused, half smiled. 'You did good, Pam.'

She stood, biting her lip. 'I was so scared.'

'Not any more,' he said.

They stood that way for a long moment, and Jake felt anger that she'd been made to feel vulnerable and that she'd had to put up with so much. A decent good woman.

'Listen, Pam, I've got to go back to the UK tonight. But I'll be back soon. This is all behind you now.' He looked around him. 'Maybe best to close the bar for another day and take a breather.'

He could see the look in her eye, the sarcastic twinkle that always attracted him to the tough-talking sassy woman. That was more like it.

'A breather?' She shook her head.

Jake turned to his men.

'Guys. Can you sort this pronto and give me a shout when it's done? I'm on a flight out later, so I need to square up with you before I go.'

'No worries, Jake.'

He went over to them, shook their hands and walked out of the bar into the bright sunlight.

CHAPTER THIRTY-SEVEN

Kerry listened and tried to concentrate on the words the paediatric consultant was telling her. But she only wanted to hear hope, not the string of complications and difficulties that her baby son might suffer. Just tell me if he's still alive, she wanted to ask. Will he still be alive tomorrow? Can I hold him? But in the pit of her stomach was the agonising feeling that he was preparing the ground to tell her that her baby might not make it. Of course she'd known that the moment she went into labour far too early, and she'd known it before she was put to sleep for the emergency section to deliver her baby. But she'd seen him now with her own eyes. She'd seen his little tummy swell in and out and out, felt his tiny fingers move in hers and grasp her pinky tight. Nothing this doctor was saying to her now would make her give up hope. He looked at her with tired eyes that said no matter how many times he broke this news to parents, it never got any easier. But Kerry was refusing to believe any bad news. She lay back on the pillow after he left, and the tears came again. Her eyes were tight from crying, her throat continually tight with emotion. Even when she'd been visited by Danny and Pat, and later by Sharon and Maria, she went through the motions, but she could see on their faces that they felt this was not going to end well. She didn't want to hear that. She didn't want to talk about it. Her son was along the corridor in a little glass cot, and as long as there was a beat in his heart she would never give up hope. Additionally, she'd sensed Danny had been a little vague when she'd asked if there was any news from Jake Cahill about Vinny. He'd simply said he couldn't get hold of him but was hoping to talk to him before the day was out. She'd studied Danny's face when he said that and was wondering if he was telling the truth, that perhaps he was hiding some terrible news from her so as not to make things worse. But she didn't have the energy to quiz him, and part of her was afraid if she probed too much she might hear something she couldn't handle right now. For the moment it was just her and her baby son. She had this time with him, and no matter what happened, nobody could take this away from her. She eased herself off the bed and pulled on her robe and pushed her feet into her slippers. She was able to visit the neonatal unit several times a day and just sit with her baby. The midwives encouraged it, as it helped with bonding for new mums who weren't able to hold their babies in the normal way. In the past couple of days, Kerry had watched the other mums in the critical care unit as they sat watching and hoping. They would look up when she went into the room, a nod or as close to a smile as they could muster, an acknowledgement that they were all the same, just waiting and hoping. She left her hospital room and walked along the corridor; the silence, the heat, the beeping of monitors in what had now become her world. Inside the room, she could see two nurses at either side of her baby's cot and her heart sank.

'He's okay, Kerry.' One of them gave her an understanding look. 'We're just checking his cannula.'

As she approached she could see his tummy rising and falling. He was still here. She swallowed hard and sat down close to the cot. She studied every inch of him from the fuzzy blond hair on his head and the nape of his neck, to his eyebrows, the shape of his ears, his wrists, his legs and his little toes. He was just perfect.

Jake was glad when the plane touched down at Glasgow airport, and he breathed a sigh of relief that he didn't have to keep up the pretence any more. Danny would be waiting for them at arrivals, and he was the one who was going to break the news to Vinny about Kerry and the baby. Jake hoped Vinny would understand why he'd had to lie to him. At least he had managed to get him out of hospital without having to smuggle him out. Sullivan had met with the doctor and pleaded with him to let Vinny go home, and he had confided in him that there was an urgency about his newborn baby, but made him promise not to tell Vinny about it. That appeared to be the clincher, and the doctor had allowed him to travel, loading them up with enough medication for the next couple of days. Jake had watched Vinny drift in and out of restless sleep as he'd sat next to him on the plane, and he guessed he'd have that twitching, stressful sleep for some time to come.

At arrivals, close to the automatic door, Jake spotted Danny, and waved to him as all three of them walked towards him.

'Jake!' Danny said, giving him a handshake and a short but hard bear hug. 'Good to see you, big yin.'

Without asking Jake any more, Danny turned to Vinny.

'Vinny! Jesus, man! Are you a sight or what!' He stepped forward and gave Vinny a hug. Vinny returned it, his heavily bandaged hand over Danny's shoulder in the embrace.

'Thanks, Danny,' Vinny said. 'For everything. For my life.'

'No sweat, son. I'm just glad you're okay. It was Jake here who did all the work.'

Danny glanced at Jake, then at Sullivan, unsure of who he was, until Vinny spoke.

'Danny, this is John Sullivan. We were working together undercover when I got snatched. As you know it was him who went to Kerry for help.' He paused. 'How is she, Danny? What about the baby? She's nearly due. Have you told her

I'm home? Did you talk to her? I heard about the jail, the frame-up! Christ!'

Danny glanced at Jake, and then took Vinny by the arm. Jake and Sullivan waited as they moved a few feet away.

'Vinny,' Danny said, 'come with me a minute, son. I want to talk to you.'

Jake could see Vinny hesitate for a moment. He glanced back at him, then walked with Danny. He couldn't hear what Danny was saying, but he could see by the way Vinny's head went into his hands that he'd told him about the baby. Vinny was looking around him frantically for a way to get out of this situation and to hospital. They came back as the car pulled up beside them.

In the back of the car, Vinny turned to Jake.

'I can see why you didn't level with me.'

'I couldn't,' Jake said. 'It would have been too much for you, being so far away and all.'

Vinny nodded. 'Can you take me straight there, Danny?'

'That's the plan. Don't worry.'

'Have you spoken to Kerry today? Does she know I'm coming?'

'No.'

Kerry was watching again as the nurses and the paediatric consultant came in and were hovering over the baby's cot, glancing at the monitors. She could feel her heart pounding in her chest, terrified they were going to tell her something awful. The monitors were going up and down but she had no idea what that meant, but at least there was no alarm going off. Then the consultant turned to her, his pale tired expression suddenly changing to a bright smile.

'Well, Kerry,' he said. 'Your wee boy is looking good. He's passing all the tests here, and now that we're two days down the line, his oxygen levels are going up and we're going to be able to take this helmet off him and just put the oxy tube in his nose.'

'Really?' Kerry felt a sob somewhere in her chest. 'Is he going to be all right?'

'Early doors. He's not out of the wood yet, and a bit to go, but this is the first step.' He gestured to the nurses and they began to gingerly loosen the helmet, then their expert fingers very gently eased a tube up into his nostril. The consultant studied the monitor, his eyebrows knitted in concentration as they did it. Then the helmet was removed, and no alarms had gone off. He nodded slowly.

'You can have a hold of him now.'

'I can?' Tears spilled out of Kerry's eyes. 'Oh God!'

Very slowly and carefully, the nurses lifted the baby out, so tiny and pink with his little blue wool hat on. They placed him in her arms on her bare chest. She felt the warmth of his soft body on hers. As long as she lived nothing would ever come close to this moment. She touched his back, skin so soft, so fragile, his calves, his legs, and the tears spilled out of her eyes so much that the nurse leaned over and dabbed her cheeks with a tissue. Then the door opened, and she looked up, blinking.

It was Vinny. It was. It really was.

'Oh, Vinny! Oh, Vinny! Look at our baby!'

Vinny stood, rooted for a moment, his face a mask of disbelief and joy at the same time. Then he was across in two strides and dropped to his knees beside her, his arm around her as he broke down.

'Oh, Kerry! It's our baby. Is . . . Is he all right? Jake told me what happened to you. I'm so sorry I wasn't here.'

Kerry sniffed. 'You're here now.'

'Did you . . . Has he got a name?'

She shook her head. 'I was waiting for you.'

'You choose, Kerry. Whatever you want.'

'I-I thought we could call him Tim, after my father.'

Kerry looked down at the little pink face and vowed that this Tim Casey's life was going to be so very different.

Four months later ...

Kerry walked at the water's edge, watching her footprints with every step. The baby was in a harness around her. Little Tim was sound asleep, his face beneath his sunhat and snuggled into her chest. The warmth of his skin on hers gave her a surge of joy she never would have believed possible. She stood for a moment, gazing out at the sun twinkling on the ocean, and closed her eyes, grateful for everything she had. But even now, as the days and weeks had flown past, there was still the niggle of worry at how quickly this could all be taken away. She folded her arms across the harness, subconsciously trying to protect her baby, even though she knew that this sun-kissed lagoon was the safest place she could be.

Kerry had moved to Spain as soon as it was deemed safe for Tim to travel abroad. She had left Glasgow and set up home in Nerja on the Costa del Sol, with Vinny and their son. It had been a huge step and commitment for both of them, and they were still finding their way together, determined to make it work. Vinny was exploring the possibility of working as a private eye for Brits abroad who ended up in trouble or in jail, and his job would be to hook them up with lawyers and the help that they needed. It was a world away from being an undercover cop rattling the cages of drugs barons from Glasgow to Colombia. But so far he was happy. The Casey empire was flourishing across the south of Spain, and the flagship hotel would be open by the autumn in a blaze of publicity. The Caseys were legit, and they could sit at the top table with any company bosses in UK and abroad. She had done everything she had dreamed of, and she'd walked away, leaving it to Sharon and her growing staff to run the show. This afternoon, their baby would be christened in the little chapel in the town, and Kerry couldn't wait to see Danny and Pat, Jack, and Maria, who'd made the trip across. Cal and Tahir were coming too – they were now based on the Costa del Sol learning the Caseys' real-estate business, and by all accounts doing well, and it made Kerry happy that she'd given them a new start. It was up to them now. Even Steven and his mother would be there. They'd relocated to Spain, where Steven worked as a bar manager for the Caseys three bars along the coast, and his mother was thriving in the warm climate. Ash, who was now working for the Caseys in the kitchen of a restaurant they'd bought over in Glasgow's West End, had been thrilled to be flown to Spain for the baptism. She was drug free and relishing her new job, and was planning to go to college to train as a chef. Kerry stood with her back to the sea, as she saw Vinny coming down to the beachside café and waving to her as he sat down and opened the newspaper he was carrying. She walked back to the café, picking her feet through the warm sand. As she was about to sit down she was struck by the front page of the newspaper Vinny was holding up for her.

'ATTORNEY GENERAL RESIGNS'. Beneath the headline was a picture of Quentin Fairhurst skulking out of Whitehall, ashen faced. Below it a picture of him with a Russian, and another with money changing hands and two women. She sat down and picked up the newspaper. There was now a police probe into allegations of corruption and backhanded payments. The article said he could face years in jail if found guilty. Staring at the lurid headlines was the sweetest revenge for Kerry. Had he not cheated and humiliated her as a young lawyer, her entire life may have been a different story. She may still have been a lawyer, a champion of people who had been abandoned, let down. By framing her, he was determined to completely destroy her, but it was Fairhurst who now stood to lose everything. She saw the byline that read Harry Foster and smiled. She hadn't heard from Harry since the day she'd seen him shot and bleeding in the street as she was being kidnapped. But she'd never ever believed he'd betrayed her. Perhaps one day he would tell her exactly what happened, but right now that didn't matter. As she scanned the story, her eye caught a paragraph at the foot of the page, urging the reader to turn to page five:

*The body fished out of the river in Utrecht in Holland has been
confirmed as missing Glasgow bar owner Dick Lambie. He was
identified by dental records, as the name on the driving licence
found in his possession was a pseudonym.*

Job done, Kerry thought. She was looking forward hearing all about it later from Uncle Danny.

ACKNOWLEDGEMENTS

Where to start, in a year like this, a year overshadowed by grief and a global pandemic.

But we are still here, still working, still hoping. I have so many people to thank for their love and support.

But first of all my nephew Christopher Costello and his wife Laura, who have shown such courage after the recent loss of their newborn baby girl. They put one foot in front of the other every day, and keep going for their wee boy Ruairi. And they still find time to support me.

To my sister Sadie, who has had to live through the tragedy of that day, and remains my rock and greatest supporter, as well as her husband Matt.

For her family, Katrina and Iain, Matthew and Katie, who have all pulled together in these hard times. And the kids Jude, Max and Cillian who make us laugh even in the dark days. Also brother Des who has always been one of my biggest supporters.

Life is going on, though not as we knew it. During lockdown the only upside was I finished *Trapped* ahead of schedule.

I also want to thank the friends I seldom see these days but hope we will soon be able to share a drink and a laugh.

To Mags, Annie, Eileen, Mary, Phil, Liz, Helen, Donna, Louise, Barbara, Jan and cousins Annmarie, Anne, and Alice and Debbie in London.

My old journalist pals – I hope we get together soon – Simon and Lynn, Mark, Annie, Keith and Maureen. And the cherished veteran hacks, Brian, Gordon, Ian, David, Jimmy and Brian. And to Tom Brown and Marie let's hope next year is better.

Special thanks to Bruce McKain for his legal expertise, and Tom Fox for his insight into life in HM Prison Cornton Vale.

Thanks also to my cousins the Motherwell Smiths who missed their trip to Dingle for the first time in nearly twenty years.

And my good friends back west, Mary and Paud, Sioban and Martin, Sean Brendain.

I'm grateful and blessed to have such good people around me. My lovely friends in La Cala de Mijas – Lisa, Yvonne, Mara, Wendy, Jean, Maggie, Fran, Sally, Sarah, Donna, Lillias and Natalie.

My agent Euan Thorneycroft for his help driving my ideas and ambitions forward.

At Quercus, my editor Jane Wood, for her encouragement and great advice over the years, and Florence Hare for her great edit on *Trapped*. And all the team at Quercus who push and promote my books.

And last, but not least, the growing gang of readers I have out there who have followed my novels and enjoyed them. Thank you. Without you, I wouldn't be writing this.